KALEIDOSCOPE OF Stars

Shari Cylinder

other books by Shari Cylinder

Making Waves
Red, White, and You
Sands of Time
Watercolors

BACK COVER PHOTO OF AUTHOR
BY KRISTEN KIDD PHOTOGRAPHY

Published by
GTI Press
Huntingdon Valley, Pennsylvania

Paperback ISBN 978-1-7369568-2-3
Library of Congress Control Number: 2021923257

Book format by Annette Murray

For Mom, Dad, and Marissa –

thank you for showing me that the sky is indeed limitless.

Acknowledgements

*T*o my family, for, well, everything. With my writing and every other part of my life, you are there without fail. You are my cheerleaders, my counselors, my champions. I love you so much. Cita, I can always count on you! You have been my most understanding and fervent supporter in everything I do, and I so appreciate you reading an early draft of **Kaleidoscope of Stars** and being an editor extraordinaire. Dad, you remind me to look on the bright side, and you are proof that anything is possible with strength and drive – and a goofy joke (or two!). Marissa, from our shore days, to our Words With Friends tournaments, to our early morning and late night text conversations, you are more than my sister, you are also my friend, and for that I am so thankful.

To Jasper Jellybean, for being the best friend a Ma could ever hope for. You fill my days with bunshine and my heart with hoppiness. The way you ask to play "Follow the Leader," nudge me with your twitchy little nose to ask for pets, and flop down on my feet for a snooze ... you are proof that home is where the hop is. And when it comes to pondering plotlines? You are "all ears" when I run ideas by you. Your adoption fee is the best money I've ever spent, and I adore you very much.

To Stacy, for helping me to change my life in so many ways. The person I was when I first walked into your office would never have had the courage to take a leap of faith and publish one novel, let alone two. Thank you for showing me that I can be stronger than my anxiety, and that when I turn down the volume on my brain and listen to my own voice, it makes all the difference. Although the journey is challenging, how lucky I am to have your guidance and dedication as I chart out a different path. I am deeply grateful.

To Annette, for working your magic in turning another of my manuscripts into a beautiful book. All your efforts are most appreciated, and so is your kindness in sharing your wealth of knowledge about the publishing process. I am so thankful for your help and generosity (and your patience in indulging every different cover and formatting possibility I sent your way)!

To Joanie, for your willingness to answer any and every question I had about the ins and outs of being a restaurant manager in an oceanfront hotel. The Port-O-Call and Ocean City are my happiest of places, the true definition of seaside serenity for the soul, and you will always remain a special part of my memories there.

To my Luv-N-Bunns family, for your constant support and friendship. What an honor it is to work with you at the rescue, and what a joy it is to be part of such an exceptional group. You all inspire me more than words can say, and I am "hoppy" every day that adopting Jasper also brought all of you into my life. You are truly sunshine for the soul.

To my wonderful family and friends, for your enthusiasm and excitement about this publishing journey, and so many others I've gone on. You have touched my heart in countless ways. Thank you for being the best, thank you for being steadfast, and, quite simply, thank you for being you.

To all my incredible teachers, for your wisdom and insight. You taught me about sentence structure, literary analysis, and creative writing – and also about the importance of dreaming big and working hard. Thank you for your encouragement not only when I sat at a desk in your classroom, but in all the years since. You are an omnipresent reminder that we are granted twenty-four hours every day, and it's up to us to decide how we use them.

And to anyone who reads *Kaleidoscope of Stars* and goes on an adventure alongside Hillary, Noelle, and all the characters – I hope you will enjoy reading about their journey as much as I enjoyed writing it. May their story inspire you to create your own happiness, and may you always remember that sometimes in life, it's not about wishing on stars, but rather about reaching up to grab them.

Table of Contents

1

Hillary

January 13, 1987

The day my daughter was born was also the day she nearly died.

I had spent so many months daydreaming about how my life would change in the breath of time when I first felt the featherweight of my baby nestled into my arms. I'd paged my way through the pile of parenting books on my nightstand, taken a birthing class at the hospital, and logged countless hours decorating the nursery. Tiny infant clothes filled the dresser drawers, the shelves were lined with picture frames, and marshmallow-soft stuffed animals sat on the gilder, along with the afghan I'd knitted. Everything was in its place, ready to welcome the little love who would add a new piece to our family's puzzle.

My husband Carter and I couldn't wait.

We'd been over-the-moon about the baby since the day I found out I was expecting. Watching as a curve began to smile out from my stomach, feeling those delicate flutters strengthen into swift kicks, talking about our hopes and dreams for our child as we painted a mural on the nursery wall . . . it all made my heart feel like it might burst. It hadn't been the easiest pregnancy for me – I'd quickly come to realize that morning sickness did not simply disappear once the clock struck noon – but still, I felt lucky to carry such a precious life inside me. Each day was its own miracle.

Now there were only five more weeks to go. Sometimes it seemed as though they'd stretch on forever, but on the cold January evening when Carter walked in the door from his job at the law firm and declared that he was taking me out to dinner "just because," I was happy for the chance to soak up our time together while it was still the two of us. It had been a bit over three years at that point, since the day we fell for each other – literally, at one of the local ski lodges when Carter lost control and slammed into me – and as excited as I was for us to turn the page on the newest chapter in our lives, I couldn't help wanting to linger in the current one, too.

"It reminds me of when I was working as a library aide," I told Carter, as we sat down in a corner booth of our favorite restaurant in town. It was a quaint little place, with blue and white checkered tablecloths and candles that glowed in stained glass jars, and it was relatively empty that night, now that the holiday season had come and gone. Tourists still flocked to the Poconos on the weekends, but during the week they left it to those of us who lived there year-round. Invigorating as the hustle and bustle was, it was nice when everything settled back down, too. There was such a peacefulness to it.

Carter typically preferred the thrum of adrenaline, but that night even he seemed to appreciate the chance to have a quiet conversation. "The library," he said, as he met my gaze across the table. "How so?"

"Well, there was a girl who came in every Saturday," I explained. "She must've been thirteen or so. She would stay for hours, but she never checked out more than one book at a time. I asked her about it once, and she said it was because she wanted time to live inside each story before jumping into another one. That's how I feel now. I'm counting down the days until we meet our baby, but at the same time . . . " I gestured between us. "I'm not ready to let go of this yet."

Carter's dimple curled a crescent into his right cheek. "I know," he said. "I get it."

He always did.

He always had.

Carter and I were different in just about every way imaginable. I had grown up on a farm in the Pocono Mountains, and he'd spent his childhood going to museums and Central Park in Manhattan. He had moved out to California for college and law school, while I'd stayed close to home to get my degree in English. Our experiences were so completely divergent. The first time I tried to convince Carter to go horseback riding with me, he'd looked at the horse as though it might throw him off for the fun of it, and the first time he'd taken me to visit New York City, I had been so overwhelmed by the crowds of people, the blaring horns, and the skyscrapers that shot up like glass pick-up-sticks, I'd simply stood there with my eyes wide as saucers. Carter and I were not two halves of a whole. We were each our own whole, and that meant we often challenged one another's perspective. For all of our differences, though, we shared what was most important – a deep love and the knowledge that our lives were better with the other one in it.

Sitting across the table from Carter that evening, talking about the baby shower my best friend Meredith had organized the weekend before, seeing the smile on my husband's face and feeling the gentle graze of his hand each time he purposely brushed his fingers against mine, I felt closer to him than ever. "Thank you for this," I said, leaning over to kiss him as we walked outside after dinner. "I love you. You will always be my very favorite surprise."

His laughter filled the chilly night air. "That's not what you said originally," he teased.

That made me laugh, too, because he was right.

As I had picked myself up from that collision on the mountainside, I hadn't exactly been feeling forgiving. Everything hurt. Blood was seeping from my fingers into the fabric of my gloves, making them stick to my skin like blankets of tiny, sharp needles, and my ankle was throbbing so painfully it might as well have been on fire. My hair was damp from the snow, making the caramel locks look a shade darker than normal, and a spasm shot through my neck as I turned to address the skier still on the ground next to me. I was prepared to chide him for being so reckless . . . until I got a good look at him. His cheeks and nose were a wind-burned cherry red, his dark hair speckled with a sprinkling of snow. It was like powdered sugar atop his curls. His gray eyes seemed unfocused as he squinted at me, and I noticed the pair of tortoiseshell glasses laying in the snow, snapped in half right down the middle.

"I . . . I'm so sorry," he breathed, as he eased into a sitting position.

In that moment, my anger faded.

He just looked so vulnerable, sitting there in a navy coat that wasn't remotely suited for winter in the mountains. I was wearing a puffy bright green parka, and I could still feel the icy air creeping into my bones, so I knew he had to be freezing. "Are you okay?" I asked.

"No." A tremor shook his voice. "I never should have agreed to this trip," he said. "My brother is getting married next month, and this is his bachelor weekend. I told him I didn't know how to ski, but he swore it'd be fine, that I'd pick it up quickly. I should have known better." He shook his head in frustration and immediately flinched. "Aren't beginner trails supposed to be easy?"

"What?" I asked, shivering against the wind. "This isn't a beginner trail. It's one of the toughest, actually."

"Oh." He looked like he was on the verge of either laughing or crying, maybe both. Instead, he offered a rueful half-smile. "So not only am I a pathetic excuse for a skier, but evidently I also can't follow directions. I wanted to . . . " He stopped for a second, funneling some air into his lungs, and I held up my hand, trying to get him to stop talking, to conserve his energy, but he continued anyway. "I wanted to practice a little before hitting the slopes with everyone later," he said slowly. "I figured it might save me the embarrassment of not knowing what to do in front of the group. I thought this was the trail my brother said we'd be skiing, but I must've heard wrong." When he sighed, it made him wince and press a hand to his ribs. "I couldn't get enough balance or traction, and I went flying down far too fast." His eyes met mine and lingered for a beat too long. "I'm sorry for slamming into you," he apologized again. "I promise, I'll make it up to you."

The way he was staring at me blurred the edges of my nerve endings.

Suddenly, the burning pain from our collision didn't seem quite so bad anymore.

I raised an eyebrow. "Oh really?" I asked him. "How?"

He didn't get to answer, because at that moment a doctor hurried up behind us. Meredith had been skiing with me and took off for help after the crash. She'd brought a doctor from the ski lodge back with her, and she took one look at Carter and me and told us we had to go to the hospital. We were both loaded into ambulances, and as mine sped away, siren wailing, I actually felt disappointed at the thought of never seeing him again. Lucky for me, we were on the same floor at the hospital. He was asleep when I went to see him, but I left a note with my name and phone number.

Carter ended up with cracked ribs, a broken arm, and a concussion that day.

I had a fractured ankle that required months of physical therapy.

It wasn't especially a fairytale beginning, but it was our beginning. It was the story we'd tell our child one day when he or she asked how Mommy and Daddy had met. I couldn't wait for that. We had so many special times ahead of us, so many moments to share and memories to create. As we got back to our car after dinner, Carter opening the door for me the way he always did, I was struck by a feeling that we were right on the verge of everything I had always dreamed of.

The thing about dreams, though, was that sometimes they could be stolen away.

We were only a few miles from home when I first noticed the car approaching from the opposite direction. Even from a distance, I could tell something wasn't quite right. The blinding beams from its headlights were bouncing erratically, slicing through the darkness of the narrow, winding road in jagged spurts. "Maybe you should pull over," I told Carter, as the car picked up speed. "This is – " I never got to finish my sentence, because that was when the glare of the headlights trapped us in its crosshairs. The car swerved into our lane, heading right toward us. "Carter!" I shrieked, so loudly it ripped my throat raw, and he slammed the brakes hard, yanking the steering wheel to the right in a frantic attempt to avoid a crash. The screech that shattered the night made my blood run cold, and as our car hit a slick patch on the road, my hands instinctively reached to shield the baby. My heart pounded in panic with every beat, tears stinging my eyes as our car spun sharply to the side, out of control.

It was true, what people said about your life flashing before you in moments like that.

It wasn't the past twenty-seven years I saw, though.

It was the next twenty-seven.

It was everything I'd miss if I never made it out of the car that night. Rocking my baby to sleep, teaching him or her to ride horses and read books and tend to the farm, just as my own parents had taken such pride in teaching me . . . the images switched on and off in my mind, frenzied and dizzying as they whizzed by. I tried to hang onto them, to keep them sheltered firmly within my grasp, but it was all too fleeting. Terror sped up time, even as it also slowed it down.

"I love you," I said to Carter, my words barely audible. He knew that, of course, but I needed to tell him anyway.

"I love you, too," he said, right as our car careened into the guardrail along the side of the road. The sound of cracking glass reverberated in my ears, followed by a high-pitched squeal as the other driver revved his engine, thundering by us so quickly his tires left skid-marks. I couldn't catch my breath. It was stuck to the walls of my throat, suffocating me from the inside out. I heard Carter telling me it would be okay, felt his heart tap-tap-tapping against my back as he wrapped his arms around me, but I couldn't process any of it. How had we gotten here? How had our cozy evening turned into this nightmare?

It didn't seem real.

We were now facing the direction we'd been coming from, instead of the one where we'd been headed. The dashboard of the car was littered with shards of glass, and the choking smell of smoke drifted through the splintered windshield. Somewhere in the adjacent woods, I could hear the hoot of an owl coming from the inky silhouette of the evergreen trees. Normally I loved that sound, but it was haunting that night.

I forced myself to breathe in, then out. "Are you alright?" I asked Carter in a wobbling voice. He had a nasty gash on his cheek, the blood creeping down his ashen face. His glasses were nowhere in sight, he was coughing from the smoke, and as he reached for my hand, his knuckles were as white as the snow dusting the treetops.

"I . . . I think so," he sputtered. "Nothing some stitches won't fix. How about you and the baby?" His eyes were ringed with worry as he looked at me.

I sat quietly for a moment, trying to figure out the answer to his question. I could hear a siren in the distance, and the sight of the crushed guardrail danced unevenly in my line of vision. The world felt upside-down and my collarbone was pulsing in pain in the spot where the seatbelt had dug into it, but I was still in one piece. The baby, thank God, was moving around, poking me with a tiny foot here and a little hand there. "I think we're okay," I said.

"Talk about a miracle."

Carter exhaled slowly. "I've never been so terrified in my life," he admitted, and I squeezed his hand gently. I had no idea what we were going to do next, or whether it was even safe to extricate ourselves from the mess of metal and glass, but even so, even with a heartbeat that still insisted on racing ahead of itself, I was comforted by the feel of Carter's fingers intertwined with my own. We'd get through this, together.

Thankfully, we also had a little help.

The siren I'd heard must have belonged to a police car, because one pulled up in front of us not even five minutes later. Two officers climbed out, both of them holding flashlights, and hurried over to our car. "We got a report of an accident," one said. "Hang on, we'll get you out." He cut through Carter's seatbelt, which had jammed from the pressure and wouldn't unlock by itself, and the other policeman took me by the hand and guided me through the dented door. The moment Carter and I were free from the wreckage, my eyes flooded with tears again. We were safe. We'd survived.

"Thank you," I said to the officers. "Thank you so much."

"Just doing our job," the one who had helped me said. "Now, can you tell us what happened?" Right there by the side of the road, the red and blue lights from their car casting an eerie glow onto the asphalt, they took down our information and promised to do everything in their power to catch the other driver.

"Whoever it was didn't even slow down," Carter said. "I don't know if alcohol was involved, or if it was something else, but that person is dangerous."

"We'll launch an investigation," the officer promised. "But right now, we need to get you two to a hospital." He ushered Carter and me into the back of the squad car, and his partner stayed behind to start gathering evidence. Maybe it should have upset me, seeing him radio for backup before he began to take photographs of the mangled mess that had once been Carter's silver car, but it didn't. I felt nothing but the greatest, most overwhelming relief. Life could change in a flash. How lucky we were that ours hadn't shifted in irrevocable ways.

"This could have been so much worse," I said.

That was when my water broke.

"Oh, God." I turned to Carter. "I think . . . I might be . . . " I gestured at my skirt. It was dusty with the debris from the accident, but there was no mistaking the dampness soaking through the fabric. "My water just broke," I whispered, and his eyebrows went sky-high.

"What?" he yelped. "But it isn't time yet. Are you sure?"

"Quite."

The color had slowly been returning to his face, but now it drained back out again. "Aren't you supposed to have contractions first?" he asked me. "Isn't that what they told us during the birthing class?"

At that moment, the birthing class seemed like it had happened in some alternate reality. I had tried so hard to do everything right with this pregnancy. I'd taken my vitamin each day, avoided any heavy lifting at the country store I managed for my parents, and stopped riding Twinkle, my favorite horse on the family farm. I had devoted all that time to planning, and preparing, and making certain things would be perfect for our little one. It was not supposed to happen this way, five weeks early. It didn't feel right.

A pain twisted through my abdomen, squeezing around in a tight circle.

I supposed it didn't matter what felt right.

Obviously the accident had had even more of an impact than we'd realized.

Our baby was on the way.

KALEIDOSCOPE OF STARS

2

NOELLE

May 28, 2017

Amelia Watson is creating a volcano.

Again.

I can hear the little girl's delighted giggle as soon as I walk into the hotel restaurant where I work as the assistant manager. She and her family are seated by the floor-to-ceiling glass windows, and I see that she's already stacked the biscuits from her breakfast into a neat tower, the center hollowed out of the top one. As I watch from across the room, she picks up all the syrup containers from the bowl in the center of the table and starts emptying them onto the biscuits. "It's like lava!" she says excitedly, just as she did yesterday. The makeshift science experiment makes me smile. Once upon a time, I was like Amelia. Science mesmerized me as a child. Astronomy spoke to me the most, but I'd found geology to be fascinating, too.

And so I don't get angry when Amelia adds one syrup container too many, causing a waterfall of brown, sticky liquid to cascade over the biscuits and onto the table. Amelia and her brother seem to find it hilarious. Their mother? Not so much. I see her level a stare at them, the classic think-about-what-you're-doing expression that, after working at a hotel all these years, I've come to learn is just universal for parents. She grabs a napkin and leans over to clean up the mess, but it's too late. The syrup has already started dripping off the edge of the table. It hits the chair, the floor, and Amelia's pastel pink sandals. Just like that, her smile flips upside-down.

"Oh no!" she screeches. "My shoes! They're all messed up!"

People at the surrounding tables begin to glance over to see what the fuss is about.

Shoot.

The restaurant is practically two-thirds full this morning, and that's such a rare occurrence lately, I don't want anything to ruin it. Ever since a new hotel opened across the street last year, business at our hotel, the *Anchor Stop*, has been struggling. It doesn't seem to matter that it's been a seaside institution for the past three decades. Sure, we have our loyal guests who return every year, but the other vacationers here on Tybee Island appear more drawn to the state-of-the-art amenities at *Sea Glass* than to the chocolates we leave in each guestroom and the little ice cream stand by the pool. *Sea Glass* has double the number of floors as we do. There's a fitness center and business complex, a minibar in every room, and a hot tub alongside the Olympic-sized pool. I get why people would be attracted to that, I really do, but seeing our occupancy numbers drop has been painful. It's already affected the restaurant. We have had to reduce its hours this year, only serving dinner on weekends and closing the kitchen at two o'clock during the week instead of three. We were hoping Memorial Day weekend would be a chance to turn things around.

Which is why I need Amelia to stop pitching a fit.

Her arms are folded across her chest now, her cheeks flame-red as her brother says something I can't quite make out from where I'm standing. "Stop it!" she yells at him, sticking her tongue out as she stomps her foot.

Okay. That's my cue.

I stride across the restaurant to their table. I see the wary glances Amelia's parents cast at me, like they're just waiting for me to kick them out, but I simply smile instead. "Hi," I say, in my calmest and most pleasant voice. "I'm Noelle Martin, the assistant manager." I direct my gaze to Amelia. "I have been taking note of your volcano building skills," I tell her. "And I have to say, I think it's super cool that today's volcano erupted."

She tilts her head to the side, appraising me. "It *was* super cool," she agrees. "Until it dripped on my shoes. My Grammy gave me these. She'll be sad because they're ugly now."

"I don't think they're ugly at all," I say. "And hey, one of the best parts about science is that it's messy. Things are always growing and changing. That's how we learn about the world. When real volcanoes erupt, lava gets everywhere, so that must mean you were doing a fantastic job. The syrup was your lava, and it flowed right down the sides of your volcano just like it was supposed to. Now," I add, "I know not all scientists like to wear the results of their experiment, so how about I bring you a wet napkin so you can clean off those shoes?"

"Yes, please," she says.

"Great. I'll see what I can do about getting our cook to whip up a special treat for you and your brother, too. How do you guys feel about banana pudding?"

"We love it," she declares, all traces of distress now gone from her voice.

"Thank you for being so understanding," her father says to me. "We appreciate it."

"Happy to help," I say. "If there's anything else you need, please don't hesitate to ask." I smile again, before heading in the direction of the kitchen to get them an extra glass of water and a spare napkin. The other diners have turned back to their meals now, and I heave a sigh of relief. Problem solved, meltdown averted, customers satisfied. All before nine o'clock. My job always involves a lot of scheduling and overseeing, making sure things move along in a timely manner and that the dining room is both presentable and pleasant for our guests, but today has taken it to a new level.

Coffee. I could use a cup.

Once the breakfast rush has slowed, I slip out the glass door that leads to the hotel's lobby. My friend Owen is behind the front desk, and I wave hello as I pass by on my way back to the employee lounge. It's a decent-sized room, with a mini-kitchenette, a couch beneath the window, and a photo collage that shows the hotel's transformation over the decades. Even though I've only worked here for ten of its thirty years, I can tell what an important part of the coastal landscape it has been, and also what an important part of people's memories.

Hearing about those memories is one of my favorite things about my job. I love to listen to the stories from couples who got married on the sundeck, grandparents who treated their grandkids to a special week away, and families who have booked the same room every summer. There's almost a magical quality to it – maybe not the tales themselves, but in the eyes of all the guests who share them. This is their happy place. It's mine, too. The *Anchor Stop* is much more than a job to me. It's my solace, my safety, my security. When I stormed out of that church nearly twelve years ago, tears streaming down my face as I left my mother behind and ran home to pack a suitcase, never would I have imagined this is where I'd end up.

Now I can't imagine being anywhere else.

Tybee Island is soft sandy beaches and blue ocean waves, marinas filled with fishing boats and a horizon that never fails to inspire. It's also the polar opposite of the snowcapped Pocono Mountains I once called my home. And that's a good thing.

There is no betrayal here. No disappointment. No pain.

Except when I find myself watching the guests, a silent observer on the outskirts of their lives. It makes an ache tug at the corners of my heart sometimes, to see the fathers who carry their children on their shoulders and the mothers who kiss skinned knees and apply sunblock. Those kids have no idea how lucky they are. It's been a long time since my own family fell apart, and I'm used to it now, but that doesn't mean I don't still feel a twinge when I see families like the one I intervened with at breakfast this morning. As I sit down on the sofa in the employee room, a mug of coffee settled into my hands, I can't help thinking about the Watsons. I hope they enjoy their time with us. The typical childhood incidents aside, it's clear that they love and look out for each other.

That's a gift which is far too easy to take for granted. I should know.

"Penny for your thoughts."

The voice that startles me out of my reflections is deep, with the soft drawl of a Southern accent curling around its edges. Owen. He first spoke those words to me nearly ten years ago, on a warm June evening when he pulled his pick-up truck into the parking lot of the diner where I was working as a waitress at the time. I was twenty then, and still trying to find my way in the life I'd created for myself. It hadn't been going so well that day, and all I wanted was to be alone while on my break. I needed a breather. But Owen had gotten out of his truck, smiling at me as I sat on a bench outside the front door.

"Penny for your thoughts," he said.

To this day, I'm not certain what prompted him to stop, or what made me answer the way I did. Maybe it was the kindness in his sky-blue eyes. Maybe it was the fact that it sometimes feels easier to talk to a stranger than to a person who knows your intricacies. Or maybe I was just tired of being lonely. Whatever the case, I gave a little shrug. "It's been such a long day," I said. "Every last thing has gone wrong."

"I'm sorry to hear that." He sat down next to me. "My mom always says that if a day is getting away from you, then you've gotta make a conscious effort to reel it back in."

"Good advice," I said.

"She's full of tidbits like that. I don't think I really appreciated it until I moved away for college. It's been almost four years, and sometimes it still feels weird, being all the way across the state from the rest of my family. I'm from Atlanta," he said. "How about you?"

The air seemed to tighten around me. "Pennsylvania."

He waited for me to say something more, but the words eluded me, or maybe I eluded them. I was too busy thinking about *my* mother, the woman who'd once been my steadiest failsafe. I tried not to let myself miss her, but it was hard sometimes. So I sat in silence beside Owen. It should've felt awkward, and yet it didn't, really. I snuck a glance at the stranger beside me. I wanted to thank him for stopping, for his kindness.

But that's when I noticed it.

The tattoo on his wrist.

The navy ink was striking against his tanned skin, and as I looked at the design, a braided anchor with an arc of stars angled above it, I felt a spark of curiosity. The stars. Why had he chosen them? Could they possibly mean to him what they did to me? I knew it was unlikely, but I still couldn't stop staring. Slowly, I pushed aside the dark waves of my hair so Owen could see my neck. Because I had a tattoo, too.

The stars were also a part of me.

There were three of them, teal-colored and arranged in a small triangle. I had gotten the tattoo the same night I left the Poconos behind – not so I'd always remember, but so I could never forget. Perhaps that was foolish. It made things worse sometimes, to look into the mirror and see my past reflected back. But it also made things better. It gave me a chance to appreciate all the nights spent by the pond, or with my telescope, or out on the porch, watching as the stars turned on a light in the sky above.

There were three of us who did those things in the beginning.

My parents and me.

Like the three stars in Orion's belt.

Then there were only two. Then one.

But I didn't feel quite so alone when I was sitting there with Owen. "Great minds, right?" I said, as he looked at my tattoo. "I've had mine for two years. You?"

"Only a month, actually," he said. "I got it after my first week interning at one of the hotels here on the island. It's called the *Anchor Stop*, and I'm hoping they'll hire me once I graduate at the end of the summer semester. I'd love to work by the ocean. There's just something about it. I like how it makes me feel big and small at the same time." I nodded at that. I understood, because I felt the same way about the sky.

"So the anchor's for the ocean," I said. "Why the stars, too?"

"Because my favorite time of day is when they first appear above the water," he explained. "It's so peaceful, like no matter what's happened during the day, it's finished for the time being, and all is calm." He smiled. "What about you? Why the stars?"

I thought about it for a few moments.

"Because in another life," I said, "I thought they would lead me someplace amazing."

"But not anymore?"

I shook my head, and my hair fell back in a curtain around my shoulders. "No."

He was quiet for a long while, and so was I. I could have filled the silence by telling him why my day had been such a long one. The table of nine who hadn't bothered to leave a tip that afternoon, or the baby rattle I tripped over by one of the tables, causing me to drop an entire tray of drinks, or the phone call I'd just gotten from my dad to tell me about the charity fundraiser he'd been invited to at the Metropolitan Museum of Art. So many things had twisted together to make it a tough day. But instead of unknotting them, I simply sat there, enjoying the company of the guy who somehow put me at ease.

It was Owen who eventually broke the silence.

"You know," he said, "I just realized I never introduced myself. I'm Owen."

"Noelle."

"It's nice to officially meet you, Noelle." He glanced at the diner as the door swung open and a man walked out. "I should probably get going," he said. "I'm shadowing the night staff at the front desk tonight. I'd better grab dinner and head over so I'm there in time. But – " He motioned to the order pad and pen in my waitress's apron. When I passed them over, he jotted down his number. "I happen to be a good listener," he said, "in case you ever want to talk again."

He *was* a good listener. He had proven it.

And from that day forward, he also became a very good friend.

He's the reason I work at the *Anchor Stop*, too. He did indeed get a job here after he graduated with a degree in hospitality management, and his enthusiasm was contagious. It sounded like such a warm and welcoming place to work, so when the restaurant was hiring waitresses, I jumped on it when Owen told me. I've moved up the ranks over the years: from waitress, to hostess, to assistant manager. I was so excited last year when my boss offered me the latest promotion. It seemed like everything had fallen into place.

Well, almost everything.

Every now and then, on the days when my past won't quite let me forget it, I'll go into the closet in my bedroom and take out the box I have tucked into the farthest corner. Sitting cross-legged, I'll sort through the only things I have left from my time as a Pennsylvanian. When I get to the college acceptance letter and scholarship information, it always unleashes a spiral of emotions deep inside my chest. And it makes me wonder sometimes, what my path would've looked like had things been different – or, I suppose, had they stayed the same.

Mostly, though, I am happy here.

I have a job I genuinely enjoy, friends who have come to replace the family I've lost, and hey, it's always a good thing to spend every day looking out at the seemingly never-ending swath of blue on the coast. Georgia is home now. It was the safety net that caught me when I was falling. Settling in took awhile, but once I found my footing – or, maybe, once it found me – I no longer considered an alternate route.

I pride myself on looking forward.

The rearview mirror won't take me where I want to go.

But the Watson family, like so many others I've seen here through the years, is a reminder of all those things that are behind me now. All those people. And so when Owen drops down on the sofa next to me in the employee lounge, running his hand through his strawberry blonde hair and stifling a yawn after being on his feet behind the desk for so long, I do what he suggested. I start to tell him my thoughts.

I'm in the middle of relaying the volcano story when the hotel's general manager strides into the room. I take one look at his face, his normal smile flattened into a straight line, and forget all about Amelia. "Is everything okay?" I ask.

"No." He shakes his head as he levels his gaze on me. "I'm afraid not."

3

Hillary

January 14, 1987

It was after midnight by the time I finally got into my hospital room. The doctors had run many tests when we arrived, checking both of us to be certain we were okay after the accident. Carter did indeed need stitches, and a soft-spoken nurse told me I'd likely be in pain for awhile from the nasty bruises already forming in the spot where the seatbelt had dug into me, but thankfully we'd escaped any serious injury. Now we needed our baby to be fine, too.

Five weeks early . . . that made me nervous.

The nurse told me to try to relax as I settled myself into the hospital bed, but how exactly was I supposed to do that? I wasn't ready for this to be happening. The duffel bag I'd packed for my stay at the hospital was still at home, and we hadn't even decided on final name choices yet. None of it mattered, though, because the contractions that'd started on the way to the hospital were growing more uncomfortable with each tick of the clock.

"What can I do?" Carter asked. "Tell me how I can help."

I cringed as the pain pinched through me, taking a long breath and exhaling slowly. "Maybe give my parents an update?" I said, once the contraction faded away. He had already called both sets of parents after we'd gotten to the hospital. His were on their way from New York, and mine – despite Carter telling them there was plenty of time – were sitting in the waiting area. I thought about them after Carter left the room, how growing up in our old white farmhouse should have prepared me for a moment like this, when everything I'd planned got thrown into an upheaval. Time after time, that was exactly what had happened on the farm. My parents were meticulously careful with the crops they grew. I'd heard them discuss soil conditions, irrigation control, and optimal temperatures ever since I was a child. When it came down to it, though, they had no more control over the weather, or its impact on the farm, than I did over this.

"Sometimes we just have to go with the flow and make the best of it," my mom liked to say.

I tried to do that as the night crawled on.

I swore, it felt like time was actually moving backwards. I sipped the water a nurse brought me, walked up and down the hall with Carter, and tried to mentally transport myself to my favorite place – the summit of one of the mountains that surrounded our home, where I liked to sit and relax after hiking on the trails. The air felt crisper up there, more pure. It was pine needles and stream water, wildflowers and sunshine. Sitting on the ground, gazing at the valley below, a sea of blue and green speckled with red farmhouses and silver silos, always filled me with tranquility. I found that serenity in other places, too – the pond on my parents' farm, the garden my mom planted every springtime, the horse barn on the property – but there was something about the mountaintops that brought my soul such peace. I needed that tonight.

The contractions hurt.

Oh, how they hurt.

They grew longer and stronger, squeezing and pulling and leading me to grip onto Carter's hand so tightly my nails left tiny half-moons in his skin. Still, though, as the dark of night brightened into the pastel patchwork of dawn, there was no indication that this baby was coming anytime soon. "Is anything wrong?" I asked the doctor, when she returned to check on me again. My voice cracked on the last word, and Carter leaned over, resting his hand on my shoulder.

The doctor smiled kindly at us both. "Labor's a process," she said. "Sometimes it happens more quickly than others. Please don't worry. I know this isn't an ideal situation, but at thirty-five weeks, your baby is almost full-term. He or she may need extra attention, but we'll be on top of that." She looked at the clipboard the nurse handed her, then nodded. "Another half hour or so, and you'll be ready to start pushing. I'll be back then. In the meantime, try to rest, okay? Conserve that energy, Hillary."

I sank back against the pillows as she turned to leave. I was completely exhausted. My body felt as though I'd just run a marathon, and my brain was *still* racing from one thought to another: the car crash that had caused this, the baby who would soon fill my arms, the song Carter had played on his guitar the night I'd told him I was pregnant. Music was such an important part of who he was, and I couldn't wait for the day he'd play for our child, too.

"Can you believe we're almost there?" I asked him, as he sat back down beside my bed. "This is the day we get to meet our baby."

Out popped his dimple. "It's pretty remarkable," he said.

It was.

Today was the day I became a mother. It was thrilling, and scary, and awe-inspiring all at once. My life was about to change in the most beautiful way. Maybe it was silly, to already have so many dreams for the little one who'd grown below the curve of my heart, but maybe, also, that was what it meant, being a parent.

It was soon time to find out.

The doctor returned, and another nurse joined us, as well. As she went over the instructions on when I should push, I glanced at

Carter. Never had I loved him so much as right then. I was beyond excited to start this next part of our journey together.

"Are you ready?" the doctor asked.

"More ready than I've ever been for anything," I said.

Our baby, though? It turned out he or she wasn't quite on the same page. I pushed and pushed and pushed, until my hair was sticky with sweat, my skin clammy and tingling. The pain scorched its way into me, stealing the breath from my lungs, and I could hear Carter talking to me, but it was like he was at the end of a tunnel. There was a beeping sound, too, I realized, as I closed my eyes, trying to summon up enough energy to keep going.

"What is that?" I murmured, as it got louder, quicker, more insistent.

"It's the monitor that measures the baby's heartbeat," the doctor said.

The tone in her voice terrified me.

My eyes flew open. "Why is it increasing like that?" I asked. "What's going on?" All around me, the room turned into a watercolor of beige, gray and white, and I tried to stay calm, tried not to give in to the fear pumping through my veins, but it was no use. Something *was* wrong now, and I knew it.

"The baby's heart rate is dropping," the doctor said. "It's normal for it to decelerate during the contractions, but . . . " She trailed off as the beeping grew even more rapid and then shook her head sharply. "We're going to have to do a c-section." She turned to me, saying something about a lack of oxygen and baseline rates and acceleration, but the explanation evaded me, my brain not able to latch onto it. It was too busy zeroing in on one word that I heard the doctor say to the nurse next to her: emergency.

My heart flapped wildly in my chest as everyone jumped into action, preparing me for surgery. I felt like the walls were all closing in. "This isn't how it was supposed to be," I whispered, and it was bizarre, the way my voice didn't quite sound like my own.

"It's going to be okay," Carter promised.

"You don't know that," I said.

He reached for my hand, tracing the lines in my palm the way he always did when he wanted to calm me down. "Yes," he said. "I do."

I knew it was a bluff, but at that moment I didn't care. It was the shred of hope I needed to hold onto so badly. Even once I was in the operating room, my hair tucked into a surgical cap and a long curtain draped in front of me, I clung to his words as fervently as I did his hand. I considered myself to be an independent woman. My parents had trusted me with the responsibility of helping on the farm when I was still in middle school, and it had instilled a strength inside me that went beyond the physical. Growing up on a farm wasn't only about riding horses and planting vegetables. It had also been about getting back on that horse when I fell off, and figuring out how to salvage our crops after weeks of bad weather, and understanding when it was time to stop trying to save something and let it go instead. I'd moved down the road from our farm after Carter and I got married, but the lessons it had taught me still stood tall and proud. I didn't give in, and I didn't give up. On that day, though, I needed to lean on someone.

Carter was my rock.

I knew he was afraid, too. I could hear it in the constant tap of his foot against the floor and see it in the way he kept trying to sneak a steadying breath when he thought I wasn't looking, but even so, it helped, having him by my side. *Please*, I thought, as the doctor worked. *Please let our baby be okay.*

Please, please, please.

The word ran through my mind over and over again, a mama's mantra of faith and fear, a prayer stronger than any I'd ever spoken before. It seemed as though the c-section would never end. Life as I knew it was hanging in the balance, dangling close, so close, but just out of my reach, and it was all I could do not to let my emotions spill out everywhere – until I saw Carter's face break into a grin I could only describe as radiant. It was like he had the light of a thousand suns illuminating him from the inside out.

"She's here," he whispered.

"She?" I echoed.

When he turned to look at me, there was a glossy sheen in his eyes. "We have a daughter."

A daughter. Somewhere, in the deepest crevices of my heart, I'd had a feeling it would be a girl. I couldn't wait to see her, and hold her, and kiss her. Wait, though . . . why was she so quiet? "She's not crying," I said, as my pulse began to pound in panic. "Is she alright?" Perhaps it was instinct, or desperation, or simply the overwhelming magnitude of a mother's love that flooded me all at once, but without even thinking about it, I tried to sit up to see what was going on. I made it about three inches before Carter put his hand on my shoulder, gently keeping me in place.

"Don't," he said. "You'll hurt yourself."

"But our baby – "

"Don't worry," the doctor said. "I've got her."

Don't worry? How could I possibly not worry? A cacophony of sounds filled my head: the sirens from the police car the night before, and the first dance song from our wedding, Billy Joel's "Just the Way You Are," and the tense words being passed between the doctor and nurses, as they worked on the baby. It was killing me that I couldn't see, but then all the noise stopped. It stopped because of the one sound that overpowered the rest, the sound that was the most beautiful, wondrous thing I had ever heard. The cry was shaky, but it was there.

She was there.

She was staying with us.

I didn't even realize I was crying until the tears began to dampen my cheeks. Carter choked up, too, especially when the doctor brought our little girl to us. The moment I first laid eyes on her, my whole world froze in the very best way. So that was how it felt, to know magic was real.

"Oh, Carter," I breathed. "Look at her."

"She's beyond words," he said.

She was. There was simply no way to describe how dear she was, and maybe it was only fitting, because didn't the best, most precious things in life transcend words? They could only be felt in the heart. Gazing down at our daughter, with her dark hair, button nose, and soft, rosy cheeks, I felt an instant pull somewhere deep inside. I wanted to protect our girl, to love her, and teach her, and do everything in my power to make certain she was always as happy as she'd made me in that moment. My mom had told me it would be like this, that when I saw my baby for the first time it would fill my soul with a love I couldn't possibly have known before, and she was right. Now that this sweetheart was here, everything was different.

The axis of our lives had shifted, and we were forever changed.

I realized, then, how much it didn't matter that things hadn't gone according to plan. As long as our baby was healthy and safe, all the rest would somehow fall into place. Really, wasn't that what parenthood was? It was perfect in its imperfections. I understood that now in a way I couldn't have before.

"Welcome, honey," I whispered. "I'm your mommy."

"And I'm your daddy." Carter stroked her cheek so, so gently, and there was something about it that made me fall in love with him all over again. Seeing him with our daughter made my heart feel like it might overflow with joy. Life was warm, and fuzzy, and delightful. Even though I wasn't able to hold the baby just yet – I had to get stitched up and she was taken to the NICU for some tests – I already felt connected to her. When I *did* finally get to nestle her close, it deepened that connection further. I rocked her back and forth in the glider I was sitting in, the steady beeping of the machines punctuating the quiet of the neonatal intensive care unit where our girl needed to stay for awhile. It hurt my heart, seeing the oxygen tube in her tiny nose and the cord connected to the sticker on her chest, monitoring her breathing, but at the same time I was so grateful it hadn't been worse, that it was still possible for our parents and Meredith to peek in on her, and for us to hold her. I brushed a finger across the curves of her cheeks.

"What do you think of Noelle for her name?" I asked Carter. It'd been one of the options on our narrowed-down list, and now that I was looking at her beautiful little face, I thought it suited her oh-so-well.

"Noelle." He smiled. "Yes. That's who she is. I love it. It reminds me of Christmastime: peace, goodwill, all of those wonderful things. What about Joy for her middle name?" he suggested. "For the happiness she's already brought us."

Noelle Joy Martin.

That was it.

That was her name.

I couldn't wait to see what she did with it.

I couldn't wait to see who she'd become.

4

NOELLE

May 28, 2017

Paul, our general manager, is one of the friendliest people I've ever known. His laugh is jolly, he has two bunnies he rescued after they were found abandoned by the side of the road in the months following Easter, and he makes a point of treating the hotel's staff to breakfast every few weeks. As bosses go, he's a great one. But today he wears a pinched expression.

"Do you mind giving us a minute?" he asks Owen, and I feel my stomach do a nervous little flip. Whatever's wrong . . . does it have something to do with me? My mind skips ahead of itself. Joan, the restaurant manager and my supervisor, is away on vacation this week. That means it's been up to me to keep things running smoothly in the dining room, while also seeing to it that the checks are voided, the time cards and after meal paperwork all filled out, and the food and beverage contracts prepared. Have I made a mistake somewhere along the line?

"What's going on?" I ask tentatively, after Owen's popped back out to the lobby. Paul motions to the table in the center of the room, and once I join him there, he opens up the folder he's holding and slides a paper across to me. I recognize it immediately. It's a spreadsheet tally of the meals we served in the restaurant over

Memorial Day weekend last year. Then Paul passes me another paper. The meals we've served so far this time. It takes all of ten seconds to see that we've fallen woefully behind when it comes to breakfast. Even though the dining room was more crowded today than it's been in months, it still didn't come close to the numbers we should've been seeing on the weekend that's supposed to be the kickoff to summer for any seaside town.

A sigh escapes my mouth as I look up to meet Paul's gaze. "This isn't good," I say.

"No it isn't, and unfortunately we're seeing similar numbers across the board. So far, everything is down from last year and the previous ones: occupancy, restaurant sales, even the traffic at the gift shop. Even with two days left of the holiday weekend, it'll be impossible to hit our goal." He shakes his head. "I wanted to make you aware, and to ask you to brainstorm ideas about how we can turn things around specifically for the restaurant. I'm going to speak to the other management folks, as well, and set up a meeting for either late this week or early next week so we can figure out what to do." He leans back in his chair, turning to look at the collage of photos on the wall. It seems almost sad now, seeing the hotel in its glory days. I knew things would change when *Sea Glass* opened last year, but I never imagined quite how much.

"I'm on it," I tell Paul. "I'll try to come up with a long list."

"Thank you." He flips the cover of the folder shut and stands up. There's gratitude in his eyes as he gives a little nod in my direction, but something else, too. It takes me a couple minutes after he leaves to place it. Doubt. But about what? That we can fix this situation which seems to be getting worse by the day? Or that I'm the right person to help? After all, I'm in charge of the restaurant this weekend. And I know it isn't only on me, that it has just as much to do with the gourmet food being served at the hotel across the street, but I still can't help feeling responsible. Does Paul have a bit of skepticism in mind now, when it comes to me? The thought makes my skin crawl.

Because I've been there.

I've done that.

Or, rather, I've had it done to me.

I can feel my heart begin to beat quicker as the memories flood back. I remember that day like it just happened. The concern etched on my mother's face as she poked her head into my room and asked me to stop doing my physics homework so we could talk. The delicate touch of her hand, soft and sweet-smelling from the lilac-scented lotion she wore. The way she had averted her gaze from mine, looking instead at the telescope she and my dad had bought for my sixth birthday, and at the collection of stuffed animals on my hutch, and out the window that overlooked the backyard below. Anywhere but at me. She hadn't been able to meet my eyes.

I wonder if she realized that I noticed.

I wonder if she still thinks about it now.

I wonder if the memories haunt her.

More than once, when she was supposed to be on my side, she'd let me down.

How could she?

How could *he*?

Jesse.

A spring of anger uncoils inside me as I think of the man who turned my life into something that was unrecognizable. I've gotten pretty good at banishing him from my thoughts in the years since I made Georgia my home, but not now. That man stole my joy. My mother's love. My breath comes quicker as I shove aside the recollections of that horrible day at the church. It suddenly feels like the walls of the employee lounge are closing in on me, creeping ever nearer as they bring the memories along with them.

I have to get out of here.

I practically run for the lobby. There's a family waiting for the elevator, an elderly couple at the front desk, talking to Owen, and a toddler who's scampering away from her parents, holding a blue bucket that falls out of her hands and spills sand all over the walnut-colored floor. Normally I'd stop to help clean up. But today I hurry past everyone and head for the sliding glass door. The sun's rays are bright as I step outside onto the deck, warming my face almost instantly.

Sunshine for the soul.

That's the way I once described this place to my best friend Eliza.

She and I have known each other since we were eight, when her dad brought her into the store my mother managed for my grandparents. It was after school one day, so I was also there, helping to arrange the recently delivered fruit pies. I liked helping my mother. It made me feel special.

Eliza wandered over to me while her dad browsed the shelves. "Hi," she said.

"Hi," I answered.

She pointed to the *American Girl Doll* book I'd turned over on the shelf beside the pies, marking the spot where I'd paused reading. "I like those, too," she said. "Felicity is my favorite. How about you?"

"Me, too!" I exclaimed.

Just like that, we became friends. Family, even. Eliza is the sister I've always wanted and never had. I can still remember how upset I was on that icy January morning when I stood in her driveway, watching as her dad's SUV drove down the road for the last time. It was the middle of our freshman year of high school, and Eliza's father had been transferred to Georgia for work. Standing out in the snow, wearing my half of our best-friends necklace, I'd kept my gaze on their family's car until it was out of sight.

Never would I have imagined that less than four years later, I'd be following them down South.

Eliza is why I chose this state.

Nothing made sense that night I left. So I followed my heart.

I let it lead me to my best friend. I wasn't sure of anything for those first several months, but I did know that Tybee Island was right for me. "It's different here," I said to Eliza one day, about six months after I'd made the eight-hundred mile drive from Pennsylvania. "Everything feels better."

But not today.

Today, everything feels exactly the same.

I pause for a minute before walking onto the beach, taking in the scene in front of me. There is the pavilion, with its picnic benches, grill, and 'Georgia's Peach of a Beach' sign. There's the wooden swing, where I've sat and watched the waves more times than I can count. And there's the crowd of people here for the holiday weekend, their beach umbrellas big and their towels bright. I sweep my hair up into a ponytail before joining them, its long locks already damp against the back of my neck, thanks to the humidity which lays heavy like a blanket during a Southern summer. Then I slip off my shoes and head for the ocean. The water looks postcard-perfect today. It's a deep blue, the waves breaking all the way out beyond the pier. To my right, a group of kids charges forward, their boogie boards tracing lines into the wet sand, and to my left, a woman holds a toddler by the hand, helping her jump over the water as it washes onto the coast. Everybody here is happy. Relaxed. Carefree. That's one of the reasons I love Tybee Island. It's hard to be stressed when the peace of the ocean is right beside you, when the scent of the seashore makes you feel alive.

I let myself breathe it in.

The serenity, the sparkle, the salty sea air.

It helps to quiet the thoughts still ping-ponging off the walls of my brain. The memories that put up a fight as I try to settle them back where they belong. How could my mother have let Jesse make her doubt me? She saw what she was told to see, instead of trusting her own eyes. It's sad, really. I should feel bad for her. I don't, though. I can't.

Her words ring in my ears as I watch a red and purple sailboat glide along the horizon. "I'm just asking, Noelle. It's a question, not a statement. Is there any truth to what Jesse said?"

What Jesse said.

Jesse was always saying things.

Some of them were true. Others weren't.

An image of him pops into my mind, his back to me as he stood next to the French doors in the kitchen, counting the money in his hand before slipping it in his wallet. I can still see the look on his face as he turned around and realized I was there, the way his smile froze at the corners. Perhaps I should've picked up on something then, but I suppose sometimes it's hardest to see the things that are right in front of us.

But not anymore.

I bend down, scooping up a pebble that I arc into the ocean. I'm just about to send another one in the same direction when I sense someone walking up behind me.

"Hey," he says. "I saw you run out before. You okay?"

Owen.

I should've known he would follow me.

The sight of him makes a grin tug at my mouth. He looks completely out of place, standing here in his pinstriped shirt and tie, but then again, I suppose I do, too, in my white skirt and aqua *Anchor Stop* polo shirt. It's like we've been dropped into someone else's photograph. "I'm fine," I tell him, then relay my conversation with Paul. "He was perfectly nice," I say. "It was just the way he looked at me afterward, like he wasn't quite sure about something, even if he didn't realize what it was. It took me back . . . "

"To how your mom treated you," Owen says, when I trail off.

Hearing that out loud is an arrow to the heart.

"Yes," I say.

He takes a step closer and rests his hand on my shoulder, rubbing it reassuringly. It distracts me for a second, how soft his touch is, but then he continues talking and it snaps me back to reality. "I am really sorry she hurt you so badly," he says. "And I'm sure she's sorry, too."

She is. I know that.

But sometimes sorry isn't enough.

Sometimes a relationship is too broken to be pieced back together.

When my mother and I talk these days, our phone conversations are more reminiscent of those between acquaintances, rather than family. She asks about the weather in Georgia, and if I ever find myself picking up on the phrases people say down here. I ask about the farm and whether any new ski resorts have opened lately. It's stilted. Stifled. It never used to be that way. When my dad was around, the three of us were almost always laughing. And after he left . . . my mother and I so deeply missed him, and I think that made us even closer. We'd talk about anything. Everything. The books I read, the afghans she knitted, the stars that glimmered above. I confided in her about my first kiss, and she told me all about the day she and my dad met, their love story unfolding with a literal bang. I suppose I was a confidante for my mother, and she was mine.

I miss that.

The bond between a mother and her daughter is its own kind of special. The one I had with my mother was ripped apart at the seams, but before the pieces shredded, we were everything to one another. So many things she taught me. That I should stand up for myself and fight for all I believe in. That no mountain is too high or too hard to climb. That not only is it alright to cry, but also good sometimes. That my worth comes from what's inside, not out. That it's possible to power through anything if you refuse to give up. It still hurts, all this time later, to think of how we gave up on each other in different ways. Aside from Eliza, Owen is the only other person here who's heard the whole story behind that. And so, when my eyes fill with sadness at the memories, he immediately pulls me into a hug. His hand on my back is steady, and I let him hold it there for a moment.

It's comforting.

He's comforting.

Ever since the day we met, he has had that impact on me. Maybe it's the way he's so laidback, so go-with-the-flow and make-the-best-of-things. He's the kind of person it's just easy to be around. It makes me feel better, having him stand beside me now.

"Thanks for checking up on me," I say.

"You'd have done the same for me. In fact, you have, countless times."

"Well, of course."

We fall into silence for a minute, and I listen to the sounds filling the air around us. There's the radio on the lifeguard stand, the motorboat speeding by and creating waves where there once were none, and the seagulls who squawk loudly as they fly above. It is a picture-perfect day here. Maybe I should forget about my mother and focus on that instead, and also on the fact that I've got such a terrific friend in Owen. He doesn't have to spend his lunch break consoling me, and yet here he is. I appreciate that. I appreciate him. I may have moved here because of Eliza, but Owen is the person who's helped me really carve out this life among the sea grass and sand dunes. My path would have been completely different if I'd never met him. I open my mouth to tell him that, and to thank him again.

And that's when my phone rings.

5

Hillary

January 25, 1987

The house felt different when we entered it for the first time as a family of three. Everything in the living room was just as we'd left it – the yellow afghan was draped over the back of the blue and white gingham couch, the vase of flowers Carter's brother and sister-in-law had sent us to welcome Noelle sat atop the table, and the sun angled in around the curtains, reflecting in the picture frames hanging on the cornflower blue walls. On the surface, nothing had changed, but the truth was that everything had. The sweetest little girl was fast asleep against my chest now, her fingers resting on the fabric of my sweater. She was, quite literally, leaving a handprint on my heart.

"This is your home," I told her. "Daddy and I hope you'll love it here as much as we do. There's a cozy fireplace, a porch with a swing out back, and a window seat in the kitchen where you can tuck yourself away with a book, or a sketch pad, or whatever else you'd like. I wonder what that will be," I said, gazing at her, still a bit in awe that this baby was actually ours to love. "You have your entire life ahead of you, honey bunny. There are so many things for you to discover."

"She seems impressed," Carter teased, as he came over to

stand beside me. "I'm so glad we can finally have her home," he said, and I nodded. It'd been a week and a half since we'd welcomed her into the world, and somehow those eleven days had passed in the blink of an eye while also feeling like they would never end. That was simply how life unfolded, I had come to understand, when your baby needed to stay in the hospital even after you were released.

Leaving without Noelle was like walking away from a piece of myself, and it didn't get any easier over the week that followed. My head understood it was best for her to stay in the NICU, that it was important for her to get excellent care so she could grow stronger each day. Being born five weeks early meant her lungs weren't fully developed, and there had also been an issue with regulating her body temperature. The NICU kept her safe, and I was so deeply thankful for the doctors and nurses, but it'd still hurt my heart, not being able to bring her home. Not anymore, though. She was finally where she belonged.

Everything felt bright, and shiny, and right . . . and also confusing.

"What do you think?" I asked Carter, as Noelle stirred slightly against my chest. "Should we take her to the nursery? Put her in the bassinet? Keep holding her until she wakes up or it's time to feed her?" Suddenly all the possibilities seemed overwhelming. The nurses who had watched over her in the hospital always seemed to know what to do and when to do it. They'd made it seem simple, but as I cradled Noelle close, feeling the pitter-patter of her heartbeat against mine, it hit me, how many decisions there were to make. Suppose I did something wrong?

I looked at Carter and he looked back, tilting his head to the side the way he always did when he was deep in thought. "I think . . . maybe we just stay here awhile?" he said tentatively. Perhaps that should have made me more nervous, realizing Carter felt as uncertain as I did, yet it was actually the opposite. We were new to parenting, yes, but at least we were new to it together.

"Okay," I said, and eased myself down onto the sofa. Not even five minutes later, Noelle began to cry. Her cheeks turned crimson as her wails grew higher and higher pitched, her face scrunching up and her tiny hands curling into fists.

Nothing would quiet her down.

We tried changing her diaper, feeding her, and walking her around the room. Carter rubbed her back, and I checked her hands and feet, concerned about jaundice since she was out of the newborn warmer from the NICU. Everything looked fine, so why was she still screaming? It seemed to go on and on and on. I had no idea what to do, and Carter looked every bit as helpless as he peered at our daughter.

"I wish you could tell us what's bothering you," he said.

"We want to help you," I added. "We just don't know how."

That was when I remembered something from one of the books I had read after finding out that I was pregnant. There had been a section on positions which made a baby feel secure, and I figured it was worth a try to test them out. I stood up slowly, bringing Noelle close to my chest and keeping one arm underneath her, the other around her side. Gently, quietly, smoothly, I began to rock back and forth in an attempt to mimic the swaying motion of a boat on the water. According to the book, there was something about that movement which was supposed to make a baby feel safe.

It worked.

Holy cow, it actually worked.

"You did it." Admiration filled Carter's voice. "You're officially a hero."

I laughed. "It was only a bit of luck," I said.

"You're not giving yourself enough credit," he said. "You knew just what to do. Noelle's lucky to have a mom like you."

I was the lucky one. As the afternoon stretched into the evening, the hours passing by in a haze of that intoxicating newborn scent – this perfect blend of milk and baby powder and freshly washed clothes – I was so enchanted by this new life of ours. Sure, I was still intimidated by the magnitude of the responsibility that now rested with Carter and me. Having this innocent little love completely dependent on us felt like the most important job we'd ever have. It was daunting and humbling, but it was also enchanting.

How blessed was I to have something so precious in my life that it stirred up such a glass house of emotion? When Carter and I took Noelle into her nursery for the first time that night, it was as if all the apprehension swept away. I watched as Carter carried her around, showing her the books on the shelves, and the farmland mural we'd painted on the wall, and the plush pony we'd bought after my first prenatal appointment. It wasn't until he stopped in front of the window, though, that I felt my heart leap in my chest.

"There are hundreds of stars tonight," he said to Noelle. "Every one is unique. Each has its own light. Just like you."

I joined them at the window, following my husband's gaze up above. He was right. The sky was a dark velvet tapestry that night, spotted with tiny glittering diamonds as far as the eye could see. It was normal to see a lot of stars in the country – away from the city lights, the sky was free to sparkle on its own – but that night seemed different.

That night, it was like they were shining especially for us.

* * *

Sleep deprivation was no joke. I'd always been an early riser – as a child, I heard my parents get up with the sun to tend to the farm, and it stayed with me over the years. The world felt so special at that hour, with everything hushed and still, and I loved to sit with a mug of coffee, taking it in. As the outdoors awoke to a new day, it filled me with energy, and I, too, got going.

At least, that was what I'd done before.

Now my energy ran on love and adrenaline, rather than rest and relaxation.

Noelle was the piece of my heart I hadn't even known was missing until it was already filled, but she wasn't an easy baby. She refused to sleep anywhere except for someone's arms, and she made certain we knew it. Carter and I took turns consoling her when she cried, and that helped, but still, I was exhausted in a way I never would've comprehended before. One morning, two weeks after we had brought Noelle home from the hospital and the day Carter was returning to work, I even poured orange juice into my cereal instead of milk, and didn't realize it until I'd taken a spoonful.

"Oh!" I exclaimed, my eyes going wide with surprise, and I couldn't help it: I began to laugh a bit uncontrollably.

So did Carter, his shoulders shaking and the corners of his eyes crinkling up. "Shh," he managed to whisper, gesturing to the bassinet where, by some miracle, Noelle had actually fallen asleep. The last thing either of us wanted was to wake her, so I bit my lip and took a couple of deep breaths until my giggles subsided.

"You'd better tread carefully when you get home from work later," I said, as I walked over to the kitchen sink and emptied the bowl of juice-soaked corn flakes. "If I can't get a handle on breakfast, who knows what mistakes I'll make when left to my own devices for the day?" I said it lightly, airily, trying to make it sound like I was joking, but truthfully I was nervous. Carter and I were just starting to develop a rhythm when it came to parenthood. We were slowly figuring out what worked for us and what didn't. Teaming up with him had made the overwhelming seem doable, and now I would be missing my best partner.

"You'll be a superstar," Carter assured me. "Same as always."

Oh, but I didn't feel like a superstar, not at all.

Not even half an hour after Carter walked out the door, Noelle woke up screaming, her tiny feet kicking wildly. I fed her, burped her, and changed her into a little yellow outfit that was one of many gifts from Meredith. She was planning to stop by since she had the day off – as an instructor at one of the ski resorts she had to work weekends, so she was home on Mondays and Tuesdays instead – and I knew it'd make her happy to see Noelle wearing the outfit she'd bought. Noelle, however, had other ideas. I barely made it out of the nursery before she spit up all over herself … and all over me, too. I cringed as I felt it slide underneath the collar of my favorite Esprit sweatshirt. Gone were the days of spotless clothes and teased hair. Sweatshirts and ponytails tied up with scrunchies were the name of my game instead, and I didn't mind, truly, but this mess wasn't pleasant.

"It's okay," I said to Noelle, grazing my finger along the curve of her cheek as she started to wail again. "You're alright." Back to the nursery we went. Ten minutes later, Noelle was cleaned up and dressed in her third outfit of the day. "See?" I said. "It's all better now." I bounced her gently in my arms, and she rewarded me with one of her sweet gurgles.

Sugar and spice: this girl *definitely* had them both in spades.

"She's perfect," Meredith said that afternoon, as we sat in the kitchen. She had made me lunch and was holding Noelle so I could eat. The sight of my best friend with my baby brought a grin to my face.

Meredith and I had known each other since we were six years old, when her parents bought the farmhouse down the road from my family's, and I'd always admired her determined and outspoken personality. She was bold and daring, the kind of person who blasted through life the same way she skied down mountainsides and climbed up their trails. She was also happily single, married to travel and adventure and the art she created in her spare time – and so it seemed especially heartwarming to see her taking care of a baby.

"She likes you," I said, as Noelle gave a tiny contented sigh.

Meredith cocked her head at me. "Are you sure that wasn't just gas?" she asked.

I laughed. "Trust me," I said. "She's a fan of her honorary auntie." I paused to take a bite of my pasta, savoring the warmth of the sauce and the zest of the parsley Meredith had sprinkled on top. "This is delicious," I told her. "Thanks again for making it. I really appreciate the help."

"That's what friends are for," she said. "Tell me what else I can do."

"This is more than enough. Honestly, you're the best."

"I am, aren't I?" She grinned. Then, almost in slow-motion, the corners of her mouth flipped to their mirror image and she wrinkled her nose. "Umm . . . so much for Noelle liking me. Paging Mom. Cleanup's totally needed in the diaper aisle."

That was the end of my nice, hot lunch.

It was okay, though. I didn't mind.

How could I, when, after I had changed her diaper, Noelle reached out, latching onto my thumb and holding tight? That little darling, how I adored her so. She was worth all the cold meals and the circles under my eyes from lack of sleep – because, much as her daddy did, she turned the ordinary moments into the extraordinary. It was a better world simply because she was in it.

Carter, too.

When he walked in the door from work that evening, he held the prettiest flower bouquet. The blooms were red, pink, and purple, and as Carter came over to the sofa, where I was stretched out, half-asleep, with Noelle curled on my chest, I could smell their sweetness. "For you," he said, giving me the bouquet before picking up Noelle and kissing her cheek. "I missed you both. My day wasn't the same without my girls."

"We missed you, too," I said. "The flowers are gorgeous. Thank you."

"You're welcome. I know it isn't easy to do this on your own." He nodded at Noelle. "I wanted to bring you something as a reminder that I am always in your corner, even if I can't be at your side. Actually, I wanted to bring you two things."

That was my guy.

As he sat down beside me on the couch, he pulled a velvet

jewelry box from his pocket. Inside it was a bracelet, set with diamonds and garnet, January's birthstone. It was beautiful, but that wasn't what made it special. The meaning behind it was the real gem.

"Oh, Carter," I whispered, as he clasped it around my wrist. "It's perfect. Thank you."

"My pleasure." He brushed his lips to mine in a lingering kiss.

It was the best ending to what had been a long day.

If only every evening could have played out that way.

6

NOELLE

May 28, 2017

$\mathcal{D}$ad.

When I pull my phone out from the pocket of my skirt, I'm not surprised to see he's the one who is calling. After all, it's Saturday, and he hasn't missed one of our weekly phone chats in . . . honestly, I can't even remember how long. Steady and dependable, that's him. Like the way he always used to decorate our house for each holiday. There'd be red, white, and blue streamers for the Fourth of July, hand-carved jack-o-lanterns for Halloween, and so many twinkling lights for Christmas. I loved that. I loved that I could always count on it, that I could always count on him.

Until I couldn't.

Until everything changed.

Sometimes, when I catch a glimpse of the stars in the night sky, or when I take my old flute out from my closet and run my fingers over its keys, I let myself think about what life was like when my dad was around. I still miss it. It has been more than twenty-two years now since I went downstairs one morning, a couple months after my eighth birthday, to find my mother on the couch, a letter in her hand and a dazed look in her eyes. It was a cowardly way to leave. He hadn't even had enough courage to tell us face-to-face.

Maybe I should be angry with him for that.

Maybe I should resent it.

Maybe I should tell him how I kept asking my mother when he was coming back. How she, late at night when she thought I was asleep upstairs, would pour herself a glass of wine and let loose the tears she'd been holding back all day. He should know those things. And yet I've never been able to tell him. I've already lost out on so much with him. I don't want to jeopardize anything else.

So I answer the phone without hesitation.

"Dad, hi," I say, and nod as Owen catches my eye, tapping his watch and gesturing to the *Anchor Stop*. "It's okay," I whisper to him. "Go on. I'm fine. Thanks again for checking on me."

"Anytime," he says. Then he's off, navigating his way between the towels spread on the sand. I watch as he goes, feeling much calmer than when he arrived. He seems to have that effect on most people. It's one of the reasons he's so great at being the front desk manager. No matter who steps up to it, whether it's a businessperson who can't get the hotel's Wi-Fi to connect or a parent whose child lost a toy out on the sundeck, Owen's able to smooth things over like no one else. He's such a good guy.

As is my dad. Despite it all, I genuinely believe that.

"Do you have a few minutes to chat?" he asks me. "I know you're working, since this is a holiday weekend, so no worries if you can't."

I think of the restaurant, with its tables that were mostly empty when I passed by on my way out of the hotel. Even if this wasn't the time when I usually take my lunch break, it still would have been fine to talk to my dad. The wait staff is fantastic and I know they can handle things.

"Sure, I can talk," I say. The sea breeze rustles my hair, and I reach up, tucking it back behind my ears. "How are you?" I ask.

"I'm good," he says. "Enjoying the rare quiet of the city. You should see it. Most people are out of town for the long weekend. Manhattan's practically deserted."

I listen as he tells me he'd actually been able to get a seat on the subway that morning and that Bethesda Terrace – his favorite spot in Central Park – had been quiet enough for him to relax by the fountain with a newspaper. When he flips the conversation back to me, though, and asks what I've been up to, I pause. Talking to my dad is normally easy, but today . . . I don't know.

I could tell him what happened with Paul.

The memories it triggered.

The feelings it stirred up.

He knows about the downward spiral with my mother. In fact, after the first accusation flew, he was the one I turned to for reassurance. Sometimes it seems like a lifetime ago, that winter evening when I burst out of the house, but other times it feels like yesterday. If I close my eyes, I can still see the moon suspended in the sky, can still hear the crunch of frozen leaves beneath my boots and feel the scrapes that stung my palms after I tripped over a pinecone and attempted to steady myself by grabbing onto a branch from a nearby tree. I'd sunk down onto the ground, and for the first time in forever, I didn't even pay attention to the stars that had come out to play on the night sky's canvas. I just held onto my blue cell phone like a lifeline, tears spilling down my face as I confided in my dad about the conversation that was so insulting.

"Okay, that's it," he said, when I finished. "I'm on my way."

I hadn't argued. I knew it'd add to the tension, him showing up unannounced, all the way from New York, no less, but I didn't care. In that moment, I didn't feel like a senior in high school. It was like I was a little girl again, and I wanted my daddy – the daddy who *had* been there, who used to lift me up on his shoulders so I could pick apples from the tree, and who spent countless hours helping me learn to play the flute when I was tempted to quit my school lessons because they were so hard. That daddy had been a hero, and I needed one that night. He came through for me then, and I know he'd do the same now.

I just don't want to dredge up that time in my life again.

All it does is bring heartache, and I've worked too hard to move past that.

So I decide to keep the conversation with my dad upbeat. I tell him about Amelia's volcano, the new restaurant I went to with some coworkers, and the lobby decorations the hotel ordered for July Fourth. "It won't be as elaborate as what you did at the house," I say, "but it'll do."

He chuckles. "In retrospect, I may have gone a bit overboard."

"I loved it," I tell him, as I begin to make my way along the water's edge. I think I'll take a short walk before heading back to work. "Hey," I say, as a thought comes to mind. "Did you still decorate for the holidays after you moved back to Manhattan? I know you did when I visited, but what about otherwise?"

His voice dips down a little. "No," he says. "There didn't seem much point, since it was only me there."

I picture him sitting alone in his Upper East Side high-rise, with its sepia-toned artwork and boxy furniture and the view overlooking the river. I shouldn't feel sad about that. It was his choice to go back to that life. And yet I can't help myself. It's not like he left us for no reason. I understand that now. My parents tried. Truly, they probably tried longer than they should have. Besides, how can I fault my dad for putting the mountains in his rearview mirror when I've done it, too?

He and I are alike in that way.

People used to tell me I was a blend of both my parents. I have the same green eyes my mother does, the same dark hair as my dad. I inherited my mother's love of being outdoors, although unlike her, my favorite days are spent by the water, not on horseback, and my dad taught me the magic of living inside the melody created by our own music. Those things are still true, but when I look in the mirror now, I do not see my parents reflected back. The diamond stud in my nose, the tattoo inked forever into my skin, the fingernails covered with polish, instead of soil or grass stains . . . that's mine alone, and I'm happy for it. Down here, I don't have to stay within the confines of my parents' lives. It's easy to get stuck in somebody else's shadow, much harder to step outside.

But worth it.

When I jumped into my car that fateful June night twelve years ago, I wasn't thinking about how scary it'd feel, branching out on my own, away from the place where my roots had grown. My drive was fueled by anger, hurt, betrayal. In some weird, twisty way, though, it had somehow steered me where I needed to go. Back then, I didn't know where that was. I only knew it had to be far away. I think that's what made it so tough to call my dad later that night, after I'd stopped to rest at a little hotel not far from the tattoo shop where the stars had become a permanent part of me. Exactly as I had predicted, he'd offered to drive from Manhattan to get me.

"Come stay here for awhile," he suggested. "You have the whole summer before college starts. We'll go to Central Park, see some Broadway shows, tour all the museums." Excitement poured into his words. "You've always enjoyed visiting. Hey, do you remember the planetarium at the Museum of Natural History?"

I could tell how much he wanted me to say yes to his plan – not only for myself, but also for him. It had been so long since we'd spent a summer together. For the first couple years after the divorce, I had stayed with my dad in New York one weekend a month, for half of the holidays, and a week in both July and August. But as I got older, it became harder to schedule our visits. I had tests to study for, papers to write, science fairs to enter. My dad was busy, too, especially after he was named one of the partners in the law firm he'd returned to after moving back to the city. Staying with him for a summer would've been a chance to put all that aside.

I couldn't do it, though. I just had this sense that I needed to keep going.

I know I hurt him when I turned down his offer.

Even now, I still feel a little pinch whenever I think about it.

The same goes for my dad's next words. Instant sting.

"You remember my friend Finn, right?" he asks casually. Too casually. The trying-so-hard-to-be-nonchalant kind of casual.

"Yes," I say. "Why?"

"His wife was recently hired to teach physics at Columbia University," my dad explains. "He told me the school has an opening in their astronomy department, too. Now, I don't know any specifics, but . . ." He clears his throat, and I instinctively curl my fingers a bit tighter around my phone. I know what's coming next.

"Dad – " I begin.

"Maybe you can research it," he says. "See if it could be an opportunity for you."

I sigh. "We've been over this already," I tell him, as I step around a group of kids who are sitting in the wet sand with oversized buckets and shovels. "My home is here now. My place is here. That whole astronomy thing was nothing but a pipe dream. It stopped being a possibility a very long time ago."

Because of inaction.

Fear.

Disappointment.

"It's not too late," my dad says. "It's *never* too late to reclaim a dream."

He does this frequently when we talk, tries to convince me to take back all the goals I had before coming here to Georgia. I can never quite tell if it's driven by guilt, or compassion, or a blend of the two. But what I do know is that it's pointless. Each star has a lifespan. Every light dims. And for me now, some things are just better left in the dark.

* * *

The rest of the holiday weekend is busier than the first day. The restaurant still isn't as crowded as it has been in previous years, but we have enough people coming through the door that I actually need to help wait tables at one point. The restaurant staff is smaller this year – since we've lost out on guests to *Sea Glass*, we didn't have to hire as many summer employees – and so I'm glad to pitch in. It reminds me of when I first came to the hotel. Waitressing wasn't a job I had imagined myself having before moving to Tybee Island, but really, I never minded it at the *Anchor Stop*. It was nice to chat with our guests. I heard stories about why they'd chosen Tybee for their vacation, and with the families who returned every summer, I got to watch their kids grow up. Some guests felt more like friends. They still do.

That's one of my favorite things about the *Anchor Stop*.

Our pool might not be Olympic-sized, and we may not have mini-bars in all the rooms, but what we lack in state-of-the-art amenities, we make up for in charm. The seating area in the lobby is filled with oversized chairs, sofas covered in seashell-patterned fabric, and framed pictures of the beach. Guests often sit at one of the small tables to play cards or read a newspaper. Outside, the sundeck offers a quiet place to relax, and then there's the ice cream stand, where people can order vanilla or chocolate soft serve. The restaurant expands on the dessert choices, and though its menu is shorter than the one from *Sea Glass*, our chef is first-rate and the dining room is open and airy, with rattan furniture and green carpeting which reminds me of the maritime forest here on the island. But the best part of the hotel, at least in my opinion, is the guestrooms. Each one is decorated in shades of mint and peach, the furniture is wicker, and the lamps are seashell-themed. And the view from the balconies?

It can't be beat.

When I first applied for a position at the hotel, I figured it'd be another stop on the road whose destination was still hidden around the bend. I had no intention of staying for ten years. But then I was hired. The tips were good, my coworkers were warm and welcoming, and it was nice to spend time with Owen. Eliza was still in school then, studying to become a history teacher, and sometimes she was too busy with her classes and fieldwork to devote much energy to anything else. So I sort of latched on to Owen, and I let myself lean on his friendship. I don't regret that. I don't regret any of it. Despite what my dad may think, when he not-so-subtly brings up the way I've done a one-eighty from the Noelle he once knew so well, I'm sure I made the right choice by dropping my own anchor here. This weekend has proven it yet again. So many people have told us throughout the years that coming to the *Anchor Stop* is like going to visit their "summer family." And it's true for all of us who work here, too. This hotel is special.

I think of my coworkers who make it that way. There's Allison from the gift shop. Winston and Mike, who work as bellhops. Sierra and Diego, who watch over the pool. Owen, Isabel, Taylor, and Shannon at the front desk. Kerry, Andreas, and Dani, the wait staff who help Joan and me to keep the restaurant running smoothly. Each of us has such a different story. There are people who have worked here as long as I have, and others who come only for a summer or two before moving on.

We are all different.

But still, we are a team.

In good times.

And in bad ones.

When I walk into the hotel on the Friday after Memorial Day, I see a group of my coworkers are huddled together in the lobby. I had taken the morning off to watch Eliza's daughter in her nursery school's play, and the moment I see the serious look on everybody's face, it becomes clear I missed something major.

"What's going on?" I ask them. "What happened?"

7

Hillary

May 15, 1987

Carter loved to practice law. In fact, in the months after we met, one of the first places he took me to see in New York was the forty-story office building where he'd been working since graduating from Stanford Law School. "There's something about it," he'd said. "The rush of arguing a case, the satisfaction of representing clients and knowing you're making a difference for them . . . I really can't imagine doing anything else." Even after he left that law firm – after he moved to the Poconos to be with me and got a job at Smith and Sanders in town instead – the adrenaline of his attorney life was as strong as ever. I was so glad, and relieved, it'd worked out. The building that housed his new law firm might not have soared into the clouds like his former one did – there were no marble floors, no fancy bank of elevators, no wall of windows that looked out onto a street bustling with people – and yet, I still saw the excitement in Carter's eyes when he would tell me about his day.

Now, though, he thrived in a different way.

I loved that he was home by five-thirty, that he hadn't missed a single dinner together since we had welcomed Noelle. I was enjoying all of my maternity leave. I liked taking Noelle for long walks in her stroller, and visiting my parents' farm so they could spend lots of time with her, and curling up on the window seat at home with her in my arms. Still, my favorite thing was when Carter got back and the three of us were together.

One night in May, though, five-thirty came and went.

Six o'clock did, too.

By six-thirty, I was starting to get really worried. I called Carter at work, but the phone just rang and rang. "Where's your dad?" I asked Noelle, and she flashed me a heart-melting smile. That was my favorite of all her milestones in the four months since she'd turned our lives upside-down in the best possible way, but even her sweet face couldn't ease my concern.

The clock ticked on, the front door remained shut, and the lasagna I had made for dinner turned cold. Logically, I knew there had to be a reasonable explanation for why Carter was late, yet I simply couldn't shake the sense that something was off. I'd go look for him, I decided. I packed up Noelle's diaper bag, grabbed my keys, flung open the door . . . and nearly walked directly into him, as he stood on the front stoop with his own keys dangling from his hand.

"Oh!" I exclaimed, startled. "Carter! Where in the world – "

I broke off as I looked at him. His mouth was pinched into a line, the knot of his tie loose around his shirt collar and his fingers clenching the handle of his briefcase. His eyes, usually so bright when he greeted us, clouded over at the sight of me. "I'm sorry," he apologized. "I should've called." He brushed against me as he walked in and set his briefcase down. He stared at it like it was a nemesis for a few seconds, then swiveled around to face me as I stepped back inside and shut the front door behind me.

"What happened?" I asked quietly.

"Let's sit," Carter suggested, but instead of going into the living room or kitchen, he headed for the back porch. It was a cool night, the warmth of the spring day hidden behind the mountains now that the sun was setting, and he sat down on the porch swing, silent. It wasn't until I sat next to him and rested a hand on his arm that he said anything more.

It was the opening his floodgates needed.

"I was let go today," he said, and my heart dropped. What? "Steve called me into his office as I was getting ready to leave," Carter explained. "I thought it was weird, because our office meetings are in the morning. That should've been a clue." He turned to look at me. "I was in there with him for over an hour," he said. "He told me it wasn't about my work, that my clients spoke highly of me, but . . . " He sighed, dragging a hand through his curls. "The firm is downsizing. Business has slowed lately. Since it's just the three of us, and they founded the practice . . . you get the picture."

As fast as his explanation had poured out, it came to an end.

Silence rushed into the space between us.

It was my cue to say something, anything, to make him feel better, but I was lost for words. All I could think about was the day Carter had been hired at the firm. It was a month and a half after he had packed his life into boxes, leaving the glitz and glamour of Manhattan for the sleepy old country roads of the Poconos – or, more accurately, for me.

Our love story had been written quickly. I knew Carter was the one for me after just five months together. We'd gone hiking on my favorite trail one afternoon, and as we reached the end, he'd laid down flat on his back and proclaimed he was too exhausted to ever move again.

"City boy," I'd teased.

He intertwined his fingers with mine as I flopped beside him. "The streets and sidewalks of New York may be crowded," he said, "but at least they're flat." The sun lit up his face as he smiled at me. "On the bright side, at least this time we climbed a mountain instead of falling down one. Why you decided to give me a chance after I broke your ankle is beyond me."

"Because of this." I grazed my mouth over his. "Because you

make me happier than I have ever been. From the day we met, I knew you were special. It *did* take you way too long to call after I left my number in your hospital room, but I can forgive that since you were feeling guilty. I have to say, though, these last five months have been the best of my life."

"Mine, too. I love you. You know that, right?"

His words had flowed so easily, like they were simply a fact, an absolute in the world.

My heart had drifted up into the clouds. In that moment, I was weightless.

"I love you, too," I said. "Very much." That was the day I knew he was my forever. Four months later, he moved to Pennsylvania. My parents weren't all too pleased at first – they thought we were taking it too fast – but they came around eventually.

"Just be careful," my mother had cautioned. "Carter is great, but his world has always been very different from yours. You two will have to put in a lot of effort to make it work."

We had.

It'd been quite an adjustment for Carter, trading in the hustle and bustle of the city for a life that followed a calmer track. There were no Broadway shows, no restaurants that stayed open all night long, no billboards flashing or cars honking. "Sometimes it takes me forever to fall asleep at night," he told me once. "I'm so used to hearing the sounds of the city that the quiet is almost deafening." One thing that made a big difference for him as he learned to enjoy the country life was getting that job at the law practice so quickly. It meant he could blend part of his past into his present. Being an attorney was such an important piece of who he was.

Now that piece had been stolen.

How could I comfort him?

What could I possibly say to make things okay?

"I'm so sorry," I told him. "You deserve better."

"They offered to be references," he said. "Steve said I've done great work, and he'd hate for me to think they didn't still support me. I do understand," he added. "It doesn't make sense to pay my salary if the two of them can manage the workload on their own. It's just such bad timing. We have all these added expenses now." Concern filled his eyes as he looked at Noelle. I handed her to him, and he held her close, kissing the top of her head, but not even our sweet girl could ease the burden that had settled on his shoulders.

"Don't worry," I said. "We'll figure it out. We always do."

This time was different, though.

The very next day, Carter began to work on updating his resume and cover letter. I lost count of how many times I walked into the study and found him sitting at the desk, gnawing on his lower lip as he marked up his drafts with red pen or as his fingers flew across the typewriter's keys. He asked me to proofread everything, and he called his brother Richard and closest friend Finn, both of whom still lived in the city, to get their suggestions, as well.

"I want it to be as polished as possible," he said that night. It was late, and I'd just climbed into bed after getting Noelle back to sleep in the nursery. My eyes were already almost half-closed, but Carter was still sitting up against the headboard, that morning's newspaper in one hand and a pen in the other as he circled job openings. "I *need* it to be as polished as possible," he continued. "There are so many law practices in Manhattan. Here, though . . . "

I glanced at the paper as he set it down. There were only three circles.

"You are fantastic at what you do," I said firmly. "Anyone who interviews you will see that you'd be such an asset." I picked up the newspaper and moved it to the nightstand. "I think you deserve a break now. It's almost midnight."

He nodded, and smiled at me for a moment, all softness and affection and love, before reaching over to shut off the lamp. His breath was warm on my mouth as he kissed me goodnight, his touch feathery as I tucked myself against his side and he trailed his hand gently down my arm. I loved the way he still brought out the blanket of goosebumps on my skin. There was a comfort to being with Carter, but also an electricity.

He was my safe place in a storm, and yet at the same time, he was the bolt of lightning, too. We didn't get much alone time anymore – Noelle seemed to have a knack for crying the instant Carter and I started to lose ourselves in one another – but in a way, that made us appreciate it even more. We savored every minute, every touch, every kiss, and that night definitely was no exception. I fell asleep afterward cocooned in Carter's arms, his heart tapping a steady rhythm against my back, and when I woke to the sound of Noelle's cries drifting over the monitor a few hours later, I didn't even mind that I hadn't gotten enough rest. Sometimes it was better to dream with your eyes open.

As the weeks went by, though, those dreams had to fight to stand their ground.

For all of Carter's efforts, he was having the hardest time finding a job. He woke up with the sun each day, got dressed in a suit and tie, and spent hours in town, searching for places where he could drop off his resume. I was so sad to see the defeat on his face every time he came home.

"You'll find something soon," I told him. "I know it."

"You have to say that," he replied. "You're my wife."

"I also happen to know what an excellent attorney you are."

The doubt in his eyes broke my heart. I hated that he was questioning himself, that the jobs he did interview for were going to other people instead, and most of all, that there was nothing I could do to fix it for him. Hearing his voice lose its joy was horrible.

"There aren't enough positions available," he said wearily. "And when it comes down to hiring a thirty-year-old who's been practicing for six years or a forty-five-year-old who has more experience, they're going to go with the person who can earn a higher retainer." He took his glasses off, rubbing his temples with his thumb and forefinger as he sank onto the sofa. "I'm sorry," he said.

"You have nothing to apologize for."

"I do." His gaze shifted to Noelle and me. I was sitting on her play mat with her, playing peek-a-boo with her stuffed animals and listening to her laughter as I helped her uncover each one. Carter watched us for a moment. "I feel like I'm letting you both down," he confessed.

"Oh, Carter." I lifted Noelle up and went to sit next to him on the sofa. "You're not. You could never."

"Even though we have to watch our money now?" he asked. "Even though your maternity leave is finished next week and I'll be the one home with Noelle? Even though you left that rocking horse at the store the other day instead of buying it for her?"

Shoot.

It had been my idea for Carter to take a day off from the job search. His muscles were so tense from the weight he'd placed upon his own shoulders, and I thought it would do him a lot of good to take a breather. We had packed up Noelle's diaper bag, settled her in the stroller, and spent the day out and about. It did wonders for Carter's spirit. It was great to see him smile again. In fact, he was the one who'd suggested stopping into the toy store in town to buy a little something for Noelle as a special treat. I hadn't realized he had seen me sneak a glance at the price tag on that pastel rocking horse.

"She's too young for it anyway," I said. "It makes more sense to get it when she's older." I was careful to keep my tone light, hoping he'd shrug off the conversation as no big deal. He saw through it, though. He always could hear the words I didn't say.

"I really *am* sorry," he told me. "You deserve better."

"Nonsense. I already have the best."

"Do you? Or does my sister-in-law? Richard works at one of the top ad agencies in the city. Or what about Finn's wife? She's married to a doctor. I highly doubt she has to think about what she's buying when they go into a store."

"Maybe not," I allowed. "But she also isn't married to a man who makes pancakes from scratch every Saturday morning, or a man who takes on half the nighttime feedings so his wife can sleep, or a man who tried to milk a cow to impress her." This memory made Carter smile in spite of himself. I couldn't hide my grin, either, as I remembered the day I'd first shown him around my parents' farm. He'd only been joking when he asked if we had cows so he could learn how to milk them. We didn't – our family's animals were limited to horses and chickens – but down the road, Meredith's parents' farm was home to Polly and Clarabelle. Never would I forget the expression on Carter's face when I took him there to meet the dairy cows – or when he tried to make good on his teasing and the milk squirted everywhere *but* the bucket. "You could have backed down," I told him. "Instead, you went through with it and even made that comment about being glad all the animals were free to live out long, happy lives on our farms. *That* is why I married you, for those reasons and so many more. Not a single one had anything to do with money."

"But – "

"But nothing," I said. "Don't compare yourself to Richard or Finn. Their lives are theirs, and our lives are ours. We'll get through this."

"I know."

As he looked at me, though, I could tell he wasn't so certain.

8

NOELLE

June 2, 2017

The reason for everybody's solemn expressions?

"Someone almost drowned this morning," Owen tells me.

Allison gives a shudder. "I saw it from the gift shop window," she says. "There was a family with three children in the pool. The parents had the baby in a float in the shallow end, and the other kids were in the middle. The oldest was doing underwater flips, and I guess his younger brother wanted to copy him? I'm not sure what happened, exactly, but he went beneath the water and didn't come back up."

Her words send a chill careening down my spine. "Is he okay?" I ask.

"We think so," Allison says. "Sierra dove in to rescue him. By the time the ambulance got here, his color was already beginning to return a bit. Thank goodness." She shakes her head. "It was the most horrible scene. The parents were hysterical and the older brother was so freaked out he didn't move an inch the entire time Sierra was performing CPR. She was incredible. She knew just what to do."

"She and Diego are in Paul's office now," Owen says. "He wanted a full report." He looks at his watch. "They've been in there for a long time. We were waiting for them, but I guess we should get back to work . . . not that there's much to do."

It isn't until he says this that I realize how empty the lobby is. There's a couple sitting on one of the sofas and two teenage girls waiting for the elevator, but that's it. Gone is the uptick in business we saw over the holiday weekend, with the dripping towels and sandy flip-flops and excited chatter. "I take it our occupancy isn't so great today?" I venture.

Owen is the most optimistic person I know, but even he can't put a positive spin on this. "Down fifty percent from the weekend," he says.

Damn it.

"Maybe this is temporary," I say, trying to sound more convincing than I feel. "If everyone who stayed over the holiday weekend would just spread the word about enjoying it, I think we could ride that wave further."

Now, that I do genuinely believe. Even with today's social media explosion, the Facebook pages, Twitter accounts, and email newsletters, good old-fashioned word-of-mouth is still what we rely on most in attracting new guests. It's one thing to read reviews on the computer, another to hear them from people you trust. I think that's partly why *Sea Glass* has been so successful straight out of the gate. How could their vacationers not gush over the spa? The cocktail hour in the restaurant? The live bands who play poolside? Compared to all that, the *Anchor Stop* sometimes seems like it's been out to sea for a little too long.

Maybe it's time to reel it back in.

After Sierra and Diego emerge from their meeting with Paul and we get an update that the little boy is going to be fine, we all go our separate ways. The restaurant is quiet when I walk inside – no surprise there – which gives me time to do the brainstorming that Paul requested. I think it needs to be about more than just increasing business, though. The restaurant, and the hotel in general, must move forward. The *Anchor Stop* prides itself on tradition, which is good, but in an industry like this, staying still is basically the same as falling behind. We've got to find a balance.

I sit down with a notepad and pen, drumming my fingers against the tabletop as I stare out the window. The view is natural now. But when I first moved here, it was practically blinding. The sun's rays shone so intensely onto the water sometimes, making it look like it was comprised of sparkling diamonds. The glare was so strong, I had to blink a few times before it came into focus. I had been accustomed to the earth tones of the Poconos. Moving here allowed me to literally see everything in a new light.

Now it's time to return the favor.

I uncap my pen and start to write.

> *Serve refreshments in the lobby each afternoon – sweet tea and pastries prepared by our chef*
>
> *Give percentage off coupons for the restaurant*
>
> *Set up a brunch buffet on the weekends*
>
> *Offer poolside service during lunch*
>
> *Establish frequent visitor perks: free appetizer, dessert, etc.*
>
> *Advertise in local papers to attract people who aren't hotel guests*
>
> *Remodel the dining room to look more polished and chic*

Reading over the list I've made, I feel a twist of excitement. These things are doable. At least, I think so. I don't have the background in hospitality or management to support that hunch. A lot of people who work here at the *Anchor Stop* have a degree in those fields, and it makes me feel out of place sometimes, knowing I don't have a degree at all. But I try not to let that stop me. I've worked hard to get where I am. Besides, after having been here so long, I feel like I have learned more than I ever could've in school. There's no substitute for hands-on experience.

Hmm. Hands-on experience.

That's another thought, and this time it isn't just limited to the restaurant.

I flip to a new page in my notepad and begin jotting down a fresh list of ideas.

> *Partner with schools and camps to offer summer programs for kids*

> *Get involved in charity work – ocean conservation, maybe?*

> *Hold a scavenger hunt around the hotel, with a variety of prize levels for the winners*

A smile grabs a hold of my face as I write. I'm looking forward to our management meeting next week, so I can share these ideas with everyone and hear all the possibilities they have dreamed up, too. We can do this. We can help save the hotel.

The thought of it buoys me up with hope as I leave work later that day. Clouds have rolled over the island in the hours since I was last outside, and as I climb into my car, the first raindrops splatter on its windshield. By the time I pull into the parking lot of my condo complex, a gusty wind is kicking up. It reminds me of the summer storms we used to get in the Poconos. One of my favorite things was to sit on the porch and watch as the rain fell all around me. It was like I was in a bubble, dry and safe and protected. Really, that's what life in general was like up there. The cornfields. The winding roads that formed a maze through the mountains. The country store my mother managed, with its wooden floor, angled ceiling, and floral curtains on the windows. The animals, the pond, the canopy of trees. It was different from what I imagined life would be like elsewhere.

Different from what life is like here.

Tybee Island is its own kind of oasis, and maybe it's a bubble, too, for the people who come for vacation. But when island life is your everyday life? It's not entirely the same. I try not to take it for granted: the palm trees, and ocean air, and the grains of sand that speckle the floors of my condo no matter how vigilant I am about cleaning up. I know how lucky I am to call this place my home. The summer is my favorite, when the island comes alive with the energy of all the people who flock to its shores, but I enjoy the quiet of the off-season, too. And perhaps it is also a bubble for me, one that welcomed me inside when the security of my previous life popped.

I remember when Eliza and I first went to look at apartments here, two months after I'd shown up on her family's doorstep. They had let me stay with them for the summer, but that couldn't be a permanent arrangement. Eliza was going away to college. I needed someplace of my own. Most of the apartments in my budget were tiny and off the island. Even though I had found two jobs during the summer – one as a waitress and the other as a cashier at a souvenir store – I still wasn't making much money. The places I could afford . . . well, let's just say they wouldn't have been featured on an episode of *House Hunters*.

"This is seriously ridiculous," Eliza said, as we stood in the kitchen of the first one. "I can barely stretch both arms out without hitting the wall." She peered out into the main living area, which was essentially a glorified box with one window and wallpaper that looked like it was from the nineteen-seventies. Then she scrunched up her nose, making her freckles dance. "Honestly, I think my dorm room is bigger. There's gotta be a better place than this."

It took quite a few tries to find that place. The second apartment we saw was practically in the backyard of a fire station. As somebody who'd grown up surrounded by the sound of water flowing and crickets chirping, the idea of hearing that siren blast wasn't very appealing. Then there was the third apartment, with its barely-there water pressure. It wasn't until Eliza and I walked through the door of the fourth possibility that she flashed me a thumbs-up sign. The apartment wasn't big, but its galley kitchen had space at the counter for two stools and the living room windows let in a ton of light. I signed a lease that same day.

Now, twelve years later, I've moved on. This is the third place I've lived since coming to Georgia, and when I walk inside tonight, my shoes, wet from the rain, squeak on the blonde hardwood floor. I toss my keys and the mail onto the white wrought-iron shelf in the entryway, and then go straight to the living room, where I settle on the sofa and rest my head back against one of the green paisley throw pillows. The television I flip on isn't high-tech, but it's good enough. And then there are all of my plants. There may not be any place for a proper garden here, at least not like the one which my mother and I used to tend, but it still makes me happy to look at the wicker table below the window and see the leaves bursting from the clay pots. I used to live in a world which was very, very green, and this reminds me of all the best parts of that.

So does Eliza. "For you," she says, handing me a turquoise box when she comes over for dinner that night. Inside is a collection of fancy cupcakes from a bakery in Savannah. "I figured they'd pair perfectly with the pizza and wine." She grins. "What better combination, right?"

"Right," I agree.

The pizza and pinot noir are already set out on the table. Pizza night has been a tradition for us ever since Eliza and I were in middle school. Back then it was accompanied by apple juice. The rest, though? Sitting at the table with her now, watching as she pulls a string of cheese from her slice and drops it in her mouth, I'm struck by how much some things have stayed the same, even as so much else has changed.

We are no longer the girls who wore matching parachute pants and bedazzled jeans, partnered up for school projects, and went hiking in the woods so we could giggle about boys without anyone overhearing. Now Eliza's happily married to Nathan, whom she met in college, and along with being the mom of three wonderful kids, she is also the head of the history department at a high school in Savannah. We used to talk about our biggest dreams on those hikes, and Eliza's fulfilled all of hers. Me, not so much. But that's okay. Dreams can change over time. That doesn't make the new ones any less important. It simply makes them different.

I used to think I'd be married by the time I was thirty.

That I'd be working in an observatory, doing the kind of research that makes a real impact.

That maybe I'd even have a son or daughter of my own, one I could teach and inspire just as my mother had done for me. It was lonely sometimes, being an only child, but whenever I felt a pang of jealousy for the families my friends had, I reminded myself that they didn't have a mother like mine. "So you're Hillary's girl," people would say when she introduced me, and they'd tell me how she was always bragging about me, how her face would light up at the mention of my name. I loved it. She used to call me her sunshine, and it made me happy to know I brought a light to her life. Especially after my dad left, I felt like it was my duty to keep those rays shining.

But not now.

Not for a very long time.

When I turned thirty last January, it was Eliza and Owen who sat next to me at the restaurant as I blew out the candles on my cake. There was no job in astronomy, no child to show me how such a huge love could live inside such a tiny being, and no husband to hold my hand. There wasn't even a boyfriend. Eliza gets on me about that sometimes, how I will never find anyone if I don't put myself out there, but truly, it doesn't seem worth the trouble. What's the point, when relationships end up causing more pain than anything else? I don't need that.

My mother cried for months after my dad disappeared into the night. The smallest things would set her off – the daisies in our garden that he used to pick for her, the record collection he'd play so they could dance in the kitchen, and the newspapers that sat untouched, because Dad was the only one to page through them. She couldn't listen to Billy Joel anymore, and her favorite bracelet, with the diamonds and my birthstone, went into her jewelry box, never to be worn again. Why on earth would I put myself through that? Between the anguish of the divorce and the near-disaster that her relationship with Jesse disintegrated into . . . I don't have much to do with my mother these days, but I can still learn from her example.

Some roads are better left untraveled.

Some mistakes are better left unmade.

I'd rather focus on the good things in my life, like my best friend.

I fill her in on my day at work, the near-miss in the pool and all the ideas I brainstormed for the hotel. She listens attentively, her amber eyes intense beneath the fringe of her ginger bangs. "Can I do anything to help?" she asks. "You need me, I'm there."

This is who she is.

This is who we are to each other.

When Eliza's mother needed a kidney transplant and her father was the donor, I stayed with her at the hospital the entire day. When she lost her first teaching job because the school district had to downsize the number of classes in each grade, I brought over a pint of her favorite chocolate fudge ice cream and we spent an entire evening watching Hallmark movies on television. And when Jesse wormed his way into the fabric of my family, turning my mother into somebody I barely recognized, Eliza convinced her parents to let her fly to Pennsylvania so she could be there for me. She's never stopped being there for me. We've never stopped being there for one another.

Sometimes sisterhood has nothing to do with blood.

Sometimes, also, it's the answer to a question you didn't even know you had.

Because as I look across the table at her, an idea pops into my head.

"You know what?" I say. "I think there *is* something you can do."

9

Hillary

June 8, 1987

I was fifteen-years-old when my parents bought the barn. It was settled along a road about ten minutes from our house, and with its faded blue paint, dusty walls, and high-angled ceiling that was crisscrossed with cobwebs, it needed a lot of work before it could ever become the country store my parents envisioned. In fact, when I walked inside it for the first time, my immediate instinct was to curl up my nose. The barn smelled musty, as though rain had slipped through the cracked windows and into the woodwork.

"Do you really think this is the best idea?" I asked, as we stood in the doorway and surveyed the dimly-lit area.

"We do," my mother said.

"Just wait until we work our magic," my father declared. "You won't even recognize it."

He was right. Over the next six months, my parents transformed the barn into a space so warm and welcoming it was hard to believe it was the same place. Wooden boards created a new floor, all the foggy windows were swapped out and framed with floral curtains, and the entire exterior got a fresh coat of paint. Rows of shelving went up, my mom stenciled a sign to hang above the door, and my dad built a counter to put by the wall. They even planted cherry trees outside and added a pair of rocking chairs underneath them. The difference was remarkable. The store that'd once lived only in my parents' dreams was now a reality.

From day one, it was different from everything else.

My parents loved our family farm. It'd been passed down from generation to generation on my mother's side, and tending to it was a labor of love for them. The country store, though, which they named Home Grown, was their creation, and with that came another level of devotion. Sometimes it felt like that store was the fourth member of our family.

That was why I didn't hesitate when my parents asked one day if I could manage it, even though I already had a job I loved, working as an aide at the local library. I'd been hired there not long after graduating from college. For a moment in time, after I received my diploma and life was all promise and possibility, I'd considered what it might be like to move away from the only place I'd ever called home. If I went to a big city somewhere, would I be able to parlay my English degree into writing for a newspaper or magazine? Even as I imagined a life like that, I knew it wasn't for me. I had already found my place, and it was right here in my hometown, with its rolling pastures and impossibly blue skies. Working at the library had seemed like the perfect compromise. Reading had always been my way of exploring worlds outside of my own, of taking journeys and making discoveries that would've remained hidden otherwise. How lovely it was, being surrounded by people who felt the same hope between the pages.

I couldn't say no to my parents, though. It was a lot for them to maintain the farm and the store at the same time. Sad as I was to leave my job at the library, it was an honor to be trusted with such an important part of their lives, and for more than five years I'd enjoyed stocking the shelves, ringing up the purchases, and talking with the customers.

I didn't quite feel that way on the day I had to return to work after my maternity leave.

A steady rain greeted me when I woke up in the morning, and all I wanted was to put the pillow over my head and hide from the day a bit longer. I could hear Carter downstairs, clanging pots, and Noelle's soft breaths whispering through the monitor on my nightstand. I was going to miss my dear girl. It hurt my heart, thinking of the things I wouldn't be there to see. The way she kicked her legs when I went into the nursery to get her after a nap, the way she turned toward the song of the wind chimes hanging in our window, the way she lifted her arms when she wanted to be picked up . . . how could I have a day not filled with those treasures? I tried not to dwell on it, but as I walked into the kitchen to find Carter at the stove, spatula in hand, I couldn't help it.

I was normally the one who put breakfast on the table.

The role reversal made everything seem off-kilter.

Carter felt it, as well.

He tried to disguise it behind a smile, but I heard the truth in the inflection of his voice that was just a touch too upbeat. It would be a hard day for him, too. Glad as we both were that he'd be the one taking care of Noelle while I went back to the store, it didn't change the fact that he was still out of work. By that point, it felt like every lead had gone nowhere. There were only so many positions available, and he had applied for them all. Instead of spending his days drawing up legal briefs and meeting with clients, he was making scrambled eggs, home fries, and cinnamon rye toast.

"Thank you," I said, as he gave me a plate. "You didn't have to do this."

"I wanted to." He took a jar of my mother's homemade cherry jam from the refrigerator and set it on the table, pausing for a moment afterward to lean down and kiss me. I rested my hand on his cheek to keep him there. Some kisses were simply meant to last longer. This time, as Carter smiled, it didn't seem like he was overcompensating. Even as he joined me at the table and we discussed if he should start looking for jobs elsewhere, he seemed to free himself from the rain cloud which had been following him around lately. "Maybe I need to broaden my search," he said. "I don't know if I would be good at anything other than practicing law, but at this point it can't hurt to try."

"What about something with music?" I suggested.

"That's only a hobby."

"Right now it is," I said. "But maybe it could be more. You're so talented at playing instruments, and you read music better than anyone I know. Just think about it. I bet there are a lot of jobs you would excel at. In the meantime, enjoy being with Noelle."

"I'm looking forward to it," he said earnestly. "I know this isn't how we planned for things to go, but it'll be great to have the extra time with her." He reached for his fork, then promptly set it back down again as Noelle began to cry. "You eat," he said, as I instinctively started to stand. "You have to leave soon."

I did, and I hated that.

It took three tries for me to force myself into the car. The first time I realized I'd forgotten to tell Carter where the extra bottles were, and the second time I noticed Noelle's favorite blanket on the backseat and hurried it over to her. When I finally backed down the long gravel driveway, though, it was with the comfort of knowing she was in the best hands. That made the tug on my heartstrings a bit more manageable.

Once I was at work, it became more challenging. Nice as it was to be back at the store, I was still distracted. The customers who knew me all asked about Noelle, and I probably spent as much time showing them photos as I did ringing up their purchases.

"How many times have you called home today?" Mrs. Grigsby asked me as I emptied her basket full of items. She'd been shopping with us ever since the week my parents opened for business, and I was glad she happened to drop by on my first day back.

"Three so far," I told her, pushing buttons on the cash register as I rang up her jars of grape jam and orange marmalade. "In my defense, though, Carter didn't answer the second time. He told me later that he'd taken Noelle for a walk once the rain stopped. She loves the fresh air." I reached for the homemade soaps Mrs. Grigsby was buying and entered in their prices. "Sometimes, if she won't settle down for her nap," I said, "I'll bring her out to the porch until she falls asleep. Then we end up staying there forever because she wakes up again the instant I move."

Mrs. Grigsby chuckled. "My oldest son was like that, too," she said. "And boy, that child would cry until the cows came home. No pun intended." A twinkle danced through her eyes. "It's hard to believe he's married with a baby of his own now. This will sound cliché," she told me, "but savor the times when you're just sitting there with her. Be present in each moment and soak up those details: the big, the small, the happy, the sad, the easy, the difficult. Time passes too quickly. It's up to us to preserve it."

I thought of the late nights in the nursery, the room illuminated only by the nightlight's soft glow as I fed Noelle, and the early mornings when I'd open my eyes to the sound of Carter's voice drifting through the monitor as he sang to our girl. Sure, there were the milestone memories – Noelle's first smile, first laugh, first time rolling over and sitting up without help – but it was the flashes of quieter magic I cherished most.

"I'm trying my best," I told Mrs. Grigsby, as I pulled a bag from the shelf underneath the register and placed her purchases inside. "Carter and I have taken so many pictures."

"You know," she said, as she counted out her money and handed it over to me, "I think you will find it's the mental pictures which have the most clarity in the long run. Fifty years from now, you'll still remember how it felt to have her sleep on your chest, and hold your hand, and stop what she's doing to smile at you from across a room. That's the best thing about memories. Times will change, and so will we, but no matter what, nobody can erase what's in here." She tapped her head. "Or in here." She placed a hand over her heart.

Her words stuck with me long after she left the store.

As I straightened up the display of handcrafted wooden signs, met with a farmer who turned his homegrown fruit into some of the delicious pies we sold, and helped a man find a Poconos-themed vacation souvenir, Mrs. Grigsby's comment bounced through my mind. By that point, I'd lost count of how many times I had glanced at the clock since arriving at work. It was hard not to wish the day away so I could go home to my loves, but Mrs. Grigsby was correct: even if I wasn't with them, they were still with me.

Of course, that didn't make me balance the cash register receipts and lock the door to the store any less quickly when it was time to finally close up for the day. The drive home seemed to take an eternity, and I all but ran up the driveway once I got there, a grin overtaking my face as I opened the door and stepped inside. Except, wait . . . why was everything so quiet? All I heard was the tick of the antique clock in the living room.

"Carter?" I called out softly, not wanting to wake Noelle if she was asleep.

There was no answer.

"Carter?" I repeated, a bit louder.

There was still no answer.

I checked the kitchen, but all I found was a baseball game muted on the TV and the ingredients for homemade pizza on the counter. Why would Carter have left that sitting out? It made no sense. I walked onto the back porch, thinking maybe he had taken Noelle outside again, but there was only a blue jay there, enjoying the evening air as it ate from the bird feeder we'd hung up. Hmm. I went back into the house and climbed the steps, but when I peeked into the nursery all I saw was an array of Noelle's toys scattered across the yellow carpet. My heart began to pick up its pace. Where *were* they? My mind skipped ahead of itself, taunting me with fears of some awful emergency . . . until out of nowhere, I heard the very sweetest sound: Noelle's laughter. It was coming from the direction of our bedroom.

Oh, thank goodness.

I hurried down the hallway, and when I poked my head into the room, it was all I could do not to laugh, too, at the sight that greeted me. Carter was leaning back against the headboard of our bed, a burp cloth draped across his shoulder and his eyes closed. Noelle was still settled into the crook of his arm, but the bottle he must've been giving her had fallen onto the bed and was leaking milk onto the blanket.

"What did you do to Daddy?" I whispered to Noelle, lifting her into my arms and brushing a kiss onto each rosy cheek.

Carter stirred at the sound of my voice, and when his eyes popped open, that was it – I could no longer contain my laughter. The expression on his face when he saw me standing there was simply too comical. It reminded me of the time, a few months after we'd started dating, when we'd gotten a flat tire on the way back from seeing a show in Philadelphia. Carter had pulled the car over to the side of the road, rolled up his sleeves, and set about trying to replace the tire with the spare he kept in his trunk. A half dozen attempts later, he'd watched with raised eyebrows as I took over and had the new tire in place on my first try.

"How did you do that?" he asked.

"My father taught me when I was sixteen," I explained. "That was one of my parents' conditions for allowing me to get my license. I had to know how to change a tire, jump start the car, and check the oil."

His smile was sheepish. "Yeah . . . living in a city where I mostly walk or take the subway, I guess those things never seemed as important." He took the tools from me and stowed them in the trunk. "It's a good thing I have you to save the day."

My heart had melted as he tossed his dimples my way. The same was true now, too. As Carter blinked the sleep from his eyes and stood up, I felt that familiar rat-a-tat inside my chest. "Rise and shine," I teased.

Pink seeped into his cheeks. "I swear, I only dozed off for a minute. I was going to make dinner for you, but then she woke up from her nap and was all fussy. I changed her diaper, tried to give her a bottle, and we played with pretty much every toy in the entire house." He shrugged. "No luck, so I thought I'd try the music box."

The music box he was talking about had been a gift from my mother on my tenth birthday, and Noelle loved listening to the song it played. It made her light up. I was already planning to give it to her on her own tenth birthday. "Let me guess," I said. "It calmed her down right away."

Carter nodded. "I had her bottle with me, so I figured I would sit for a couple minutes to let her finish. That way she'd be content, and I could still manage to get dinner ready." He shook his head a little bemusedly. "Obviously, I never meant to fall asleep. I suppose she wore me out today more than I realized."

I leaned over and kissed him. "I know the feeling," I said. "Come on, let's make dinner together. You can tell me about your day, and I'll fill you in on mine."

"That sounds good," he said.

It was the evening I'd been looking forward to since I'd left the house that morning. We topped the pizza dough with sauce, cheese, and broccoli, let Noelle stay up past her bedtime so I could read her one more story and Carter could sing her one more song, and watched out the nursery window as the crescent of the silvery moon slipped into the night sky. I couldn't have been happier in those moments.

That made it easier to go to work the next morning, knowing I had all this to come home to, and the same held true for the days that followed. As the sun's rays grew stronger in the summer heat, Carter and I fell into a new kind of routine. I surprised myself by actually enjoying it. I'd been happy when my parents had asked their friends' daughter to fill in for me at Home Grown after Noelle was born, but honestly, it was good to be back. As much as I missed being at home with my daughter, it also felt good to recognize the role that had been carved out for me on my family's tree. Managing the store again reminded me of that.

All was well . . . until I came home one day to news I never expected.

10

NOELLE

June 6, 2017

*H*alf of the management team at the *Anchor Stop* is already in the conference room when I walk in for our meeting on Tuesday morning. Paul is seated at the cherry wood table, scrolling through a spreadsheet on his laptop. Owen is standing by the refreshments we provided from the restaurant, talking with Joan and Gail, the housekeeping supervisor. Next to them, the maintenance director Tim is pouring a glass of juice. As I head over to join them, Dennis and Bethany – our operations and finance managers – come into the room together. The expressions on their faces immediately give me pause. They look so serious.

I nudge Owen. "What do you think?" I ask under my breath. "Bad sign?"

His gaze travels to them as they sit down with Paul. "Maybe they just haven't had their morning coffee yet?" He smiles, but the concern clouding his eyes belies the levity in his voice. "Anyway," he says, "let's not jump to conclusions." He surveys the plate of muffins on the table and chooses one for me without even needing to ask my preference.

Cherry.

Always cherry, thanks to my grandparents' farm.

I actually lived there for quite some time. A few months after my parents' divorce was finalized, my mother and I moved into the farmhouse she'd grown up in. She needed somebody to watch me after school since she was at work – and, truly, I think she needed somebody to look after her, too – so it just made sense to stay with my grandparents. They were really happy to have us around, and it helped my mother a lot, being away from the house where memories of her marriage were tucked into every crevice and hiding around each corner. It did take some getting used to, though. I missed the old house: my bedroom, with its lavender walls, the kitchen, where I had practiced the flute, and especially the attic. The nights I'd spent there, looking out its triangular window with the telescope my parents surprised me with for my sixth birthday, were the best. My grandparents' house didn't have an attic. But it did have a lot of land, including many fruit trees. My mother and I would sometimes sneak off to pick the cherries, and my grandma would pretend to be mad when we came back in with a bucket of them.

"Those are for selling at Home Grown," she'd chastise, but her eyes sparkled just the same.

Sometimes the three of us would bake the berries into pies, or muffins, or scones.

Sometimes we'd eat them straight from the bucket.

Once my grandma even showed us how to make juice from them.

And so whenever I eat anything made with cherries now, it's not only about enjoying the taste. It's also about the sunshine warming my face as I picked the berries from the trees, the flour that'd get all over my hands as I stood on a stool and helped pinch the pie crust, and the glass of milk that my grandma would give me to drink as I sampled our piping hot creations. It's strange. So many of the memories from my childhood sting my heart now, but not these. These take me back to a time when things finally started to feel brighter again.

I told Owen about it once, probably five or six years ago. We were having lunch together on our break, and he commented about my eating the cherries from my fruit bowl first. It makes me smile that he still remembers, even after all this time. "Thanks," I say, as I take the muffin.

"Sure thing," he says.

I add a buttery biscuit to my plate before taking a seat at the table. Owen sits down to my right and Joan to my left.

"Fingers crossed this isn't too painful," she says.

But it is.

I don't know whose report is most discouraging.

Paul tells us that occupancy is down thirty-five percent compared to this time last year. Bethany says the finances are reflecting the downward shift, and she hands out a chart that proves it. Seeing the numbers right there in front of me is a slap in the face. I knew *Sea Glass* was outperforming us, but I didn't realize by just how much. By the time Dennis starts to talk about ways to reduce costs in order to "balance the scale," as he phrases it, I'm wondering if there's even a point in discussing the ideas I came up with last week. Most of them would require additional funding, which doesn't seem possible right now.

"What I need," Dennis tells us all, "is a list of areas where your department can downsize. I wish that didn't have to be the case, but in order to stay competitive, we're going to have to think wisely and creatively."

"Our goal is still to give our guests the best experience possible," Paul says. "They're always the priority. In order to do that, though, we must figure out a way to get the hotel back to what it used to be." He clasps his hands together atop the table. "You've all been understanding about trimming costs when we've come to you before, and I know it's asking a lot to do it again, but sadly that's our reality at this point."

"Maybe it doesn't have to be." The words are out of my mouth before I can stop them.

All around the table, heads turn in my direction.

"What do you mean?" Paul asks.

I look at the notepad sitting on the table in front of me. I could read my list of ideas. Share my thoughts on helping not only the restaurant, but also the entire hotel. After all, that's what Paul had requested, for us to come to this meeting ready to discuss our proposals. But I think this should be about showing, not telling. So I pull out a flash drive from the pocket of my linen pants, and motion to Paul's laptop.

"May I use that?" I ask.

He nods and slides it over. I turn it around so everyone can see the screen, then slip in the flash drive and pull up the slideshow I spent half the weekend working on. My heart beats a bit faster as I notice everyone looking at me expectantly. Public speaking has never been my favorite, even when it's in front of people I have known for years. But when I glance at Owen – my eyes always seem to instinctively seek him out when we're in the middle of a group situation together – and he smiles, it sets my nerves at ease. This is a good approach. I know it. Now I just need to get everybody else on board.

"The *Anchor Stop* is an institution," I say. "And that isn't only because of the ocean view and the prime location. It's also because of our staff. We address the guests by name, and we help with any request, no matter how big or small. This is about Joan," I continue, "who asked our chef to make a pancake in the shape of a teddy bear, because a little girl had lost hers on the beach and couldn't stop crying. It's about Sierra, who saved that boy in the pool, and about Owen, who came in on his day off just so he could congratulate Melina and Bradley when they got married out on the sundeck. True, they've been vacationing here for the last few years, but still . . . where else would that happen? This hotel is special, and it's because of you. Because of us. Sure, *Sea Glass* may be offering cheaper rates and fancier amenities. And perhaps we can find a way to do that, too. But I think we need to talk to people first. The guests who are still staying here. The ones who aren't. Even the ones who never have. Because this is not only about what the *Anchor Stop* used to be, but also about what it *could* be."

I click the mouse on the computer and advance to the next slide.

"My friend Eliza is a teacher and a camp counselor," I say. "Her husband is a dentist. They both interact with a lot of people, and they asked some of them last week what they look for in a hotel. It varies pretty widely, but there are definitely common denominators. Now, obviously these aren't all people who have stayed with us. I think this is a good starting point, though, and that we should ask the same question of the guests who have made the *Anchor Stop* what it is. We should be reaching out to them. Because just like it's not only about the views and location for them, we also can't let it only be about the bottom line for us. I get that saving money is crucial, but there are other things to focus on, too. Take a look at this." I flip slowly through the slides that show the results of Eliza and Nathan's informal survey.

Affordable room rate. Cleanliness. On-site parking and amenities.

These are the most popular answers, but there are a myriad of others, too. Complimentary Wi-Fi. Location. Pet policy. Star rating. Accessibility. Cancellation plan. Eco-friendliness. Proximity to public transportation. Charm and ambiance. The responses are plentiful.

"I know we can't check off all these boxes," I say. "There will always be people who are looking for something we don't offer. But we can send a survey to everyone in our database. See what they have to say and take that into consideration. I've drafted a list of ideas to help the restaurant, but I think this is where we should begin, with the guests. After all, without them, we're nothing."

"I think that's a great plan."

Owen is the first to chime in. Of course he is. He'd have had my back no matter what I said, but as he leans forward in his chair, his voice full of enthusiasm as he talks about how much he likes my idea, I can tell how sincerely he means it. "I've been brainstorming, too," he says. "I thought about things like offering an early check-in or late check-out for returning guests, and having some kind of free umbrella setup on the beach. We can do late night or early morning swim hours, and see about upgrading the internet to the highest-speed business package. Or maybe offer room rate specials? Noelle is right, though. We should start by asking people what *they* want."

I send a grateful smile his way as he finishes talking, and he nods slightly, almost imperceptibly. That's one of the things I love most about our friendship. We can have a conversation without even saying a word.

"Thanks, guys," Paul tells us, after everybody else has shared their thoughts, as well. "I can see how much work you put into this, and I appreciate it. I'm just not sure . . ." He glances at Dennis and Bethany, twirling his pen in his fingers. "I'm not sure we can afford all you're suggesting?" It comes out more like a question than a declaration. He drops the pen and it clatters onto the table. "I was reviewing our guest spreadsheet when you all came in," he says, "and we are holding steady on the repeat visitors who come each year. But the people who find us online, or in a guidebook, or simply by driving down the street, not so much." A frown tugs the corners of his mouth downward. "I like what you're proposing," he says. "The ideas are compelling. I just don't know if we have the money to make them happen. Even the survey – it would be expensive to send a mailing out to that many people."

I understand his reasoning, I really do.

Why spend money we don't have if there's no guarantee it'll even help?

I'm not giving up, though.

This hotel has been life-changing for me. It was my comfort and security when I needed it most, and the thought of it failing . . . of maybe having to close its doors . . . it's scary, and sad, and honestly soul-shaking. I can't let it happen. I won't.

"So we do the survey online instead," I say. "And we don't have to tell people why we're asking, if we don't want them to know the hotel's struggling. We'll just say we're always looking for ways to improve the guest experience."

"People like to feel involved in things," Owen points out. "I think they'll be glad to help."

"Plus, let's not forget that sometimes we have to spend money to make money," Joan chimes in.

"She's right," Bethany admits. She picks up the papers she passed around to us earlier, with all the hotel's financials printed out. "Also, the thing about cutting costs is that it's often evident. In a situation like ours, where we already have people comparing us to *Sea Glass* . . . " She peers intently at the paper in her hand. "Let me crunch some numbers and see what I can do."

"In the meantime," Paul says, "I agree that we should get the ball rolling with the survey. Online is fine."

I breathe a sigh of relief.

Next to me, Owen does, too.

"Thanks for backing me up today," I tell him that evening. We're outside on the patio of one of our favorite restaurants, this charming little place with overflowing flower boxes, tabletops printed with images of old-time Tybee Island postcards, and fruity drinks served with tiny pastel umbrellas. It's only a couple of blocks away from the hotel, and it's become an after-work tradition for a bunch of us. Today, Owen and I were the first to arrive, and as I settle back in my chair, the breeze rippling the waves of my hair, I let myself relax the way I always do when it's only the two of us. It's not that I'm uncomfortable around the other people we work with, nothing is further from the truth, but it's different with Owen. There's a peace to being around someone who knows all of your complexities and doesn't try to tie them up with a neat, tidy bow.

"Always," he says. "Not that you needed an assist. You were

terrific." He pauses as the waiter places our drinks in front of us. Peach beer for him, iced sweet tea with mint for me. "I saw the way everyone was looking at you as you spoke," he says, after taking a sip from his bottle. "They were all impressed. I am, too."

Warmth seeps into my cheeks.

That means a lot, coming from him.

"Thanks," I say. I smile, and he smiles back, and it's odd, the way it makes me suddenly feel kind of fuzzy inside. What is that? *Why* is that? It's unnerving, so I reach for my glass of tea, just to have something to do. The mint flavor-burst is strong, and I quickly take a second sip after the first, then another.

Owen raises his eyebrows. "Are you alright?" he asks.

"Fine," I say. I glance over my shoulder, searching for the others who are supposed to be joining us, but there's no sign of them. "It's been a long day, that's all," I add, as I turn back around to face him. He stares at me for a beat longer than necessary, and I stay perfectly still, feeling like I can't be the one to break the moment. I sort of want to, but also, I sort of don't. The way his eyes glitter in the light of the setting sun is almost spellbinding, holding me in place although I'm not even certain why.

Again . . . it's odd.

And even stranger? The ding from my phone that finally *does* get me to look away from him.

A text.

From my mother.

11

Hillary

August 25, 1987

It had been a long day at work. The repairman I'd called to fix the broken air conditioner arrived two hours late, a customer accidentally knocked over the display of postcards on the front counter, the cash register jammed right when there were six people in line, and I somehow managed to drop a whole peach pie as I was putting it into a shopping bag. By the time I got home that evening, I was ready to kick off my shoes and relax with an icy cold drink. I could feel it already: the grass beneath my toes and the taste of lemonade in my mouth. My mom had the best recipe, complete with lime and coconut, and I made a pitcher of it every single week.

Carter had something else in mind, though.

He was in the front yard with Noelle when I pulled up in the driveway, and a smile spread across my face as I watched him roll a ball to her. She grabbed it, squeezing tightly, then let go and scooted forward a bit. She hadn't quite mastered crawling yet, but I knew it was only a matter of time – and that made me hold her a little closer after I got out of my trusty blue Oldsmobile and walked over to join them. My baby girl was growing up too quickly.

"I missed you today, dear heart," I said, and kissed both of her cheeks. This made her erupt into giggles, which in turn brought a grin to Carter's face. My heart grew wings every time she made his dimple pop out like that. He loved her so much, and it made me love *him* in ways I never could have understood until we became parents. "I missed you, too," I told him, as he stood up from the lawn and brushed a few loose grass blades from his white-wash Levi's.

"That means I also get a kiss, right?" He winked.

I pretended to mull it over. "What do you have to offer in return?"

"Actually . . . " His smile deepened. "I have news. How do you feel about going out for dinner in town tonight? Meredith's agreed to watch Noelle. So what do you say? Let me take you out." His eyebrows rose a little as he looked at me beseechingly. I never could say no to that face. It'd gotten me to the top of the Empire State Building when I hadn't been sure how I felt about heights, and to a Mets game in Queens when I'd grown up cheering for the Phillies, and to the Metropolitan Opera House when I'd rather have been listening to a Madonna tape on the cassette player and wearing a t-shirt and cut-off denim shorts instead of heels and a gown. My idea of dressing up back then was teasing my hair with extra spray and adding a few more bangle bracelets to my wrists. Relationships were a give-and-take, though.

Maybe I didn't need that lemonade, after all.

"Okay," I said to Carter. "Sure."

He beamed at me. "Great," he said, and gave a playful bow. "Wherever you lead, my lady, I will follow. Choose whatever place you want."

That turned out to be an Italian restaurant down the street from the movie theater we went to shortly after we started dating. We'd strolled along the sidewalk after watching the film, looking for somewhere to eat dinner, and I could still remember the strong scent of garlic that wafted through the open door when a group of people walked out. We had stopped to check the menu in the front window, hoping to go in and try whatever smelled so good, but the prices were too steep.

"We'll come back someday," Carter promised.

I wasn't going to suggest it that evening. Truth be told, with Carter out of work and the not-so-impressive paychecks I earned from managing Home Grown, we still really couldn't afford to splurge like that. Carter saw me glance at it through the car window, though, and I tried to talk him out of it when he asked if I'd like to go there, but he saw right through it. He always had a way of being able to see right through me.

"Order anything you want," he said, as we studied the menu. When he looked at me, the flames in the candleholders on our table bathed his face in the warmest glow. "We're celebrating." There it was again, the smile that made his eyes crinkle at the corners. As he paused for dramatic effect, I found myself leaning forward in my chair, my thoughts buzzing with curiosity. This had to be about a job, right? It could've been family news – maybe his brother and sister-in-law were having a baby, or his parents had finally decided to sell their house on Long Island and move to California, like they had been talking about – but those things wouldn't require a special dinner.

"And *what* are we celebrating?" I asked.

I was right: it was a job.

What I never could have predicted, though, not in a million years, was what the job actually was.

A real estate agent?

What?

"I was at the market this morning with Noelle," Carter explained. "We needed some things, so I figured I'd get the shopping list taken care of for you. Well, there was an older man in front of us in the check-out line, and he took a shine to Noelle. He told me his grandkids live six hours away so he doesn't get to see them as often as he'd like, and I don't know, we just fell into a conversation from there. I found out he owns a real estate company, and he's hiring."

"Okay," I said, but I was still completely baffled.

"I know what you're thinking," Carter said. "I have no experience in real estate. The good news is that he's willing to let me start as an assistant in the office while I take a class to learn the ins and outs. I'll have to pass a test to earn my license, so there isn't a guarantee, but I'm hopeful about it." His words sped up, the way they always did if he was excited. "This is a crucial time for real estate in the Poconos," he said. "The old hotels and hotspots from the fifties and sixties are in decline. Shops are springing up, and golf courses, and those whitewater rafting centers. This could be the start of a revitalization, and if it is, there might be a jump in the number of people who want to own property here. I think this is a great chance to be part of a field that's up-and-coming. I've loved being home with Noelle, and I'll always treasure that time, but we need the extra money. I'm sure Noelle would love to spend her days at your parents' farm while we're at work."

Everything he said made sense.

It was just not what I'd been expecting.

"What about law?" I asked. "You love being an attorney."

"I did," he said. "I do. But Hill, we talked about me looking into a different field. The only way I can practice law right now is to work out of town. I could get a job in Manhattan again, or maybe in Philadelphia, but it'd be such a long commute. I'd hardly ever see you and Noelle, and I don't want that."

I didn't, either.

I'd have supported him no matter what, but I had to admit I wouldn't have been overjoyed with him working so far away. Perhaps this new direction was a good thing, then. He needed to get back to work, and he seemed genuinely enthused about it. In the end, that was what mattered. I wanted him to be happy, always, and if earning his realtor's license did that for him, then I was all for it. "In that case," I said, "it's time to toast." I raised my glass of wine. "To unexpected opportunities, and the doors they can open."

Carter didn't say anything for a moment, just looked at me with the softest smile.

"You're spectacular," he murmured. "Do you know that?"

I waved away the compliment, then added on to my toast. "To us," I said.

"To us," he echoed.

* * *

Carter's foray into real estate started off well. He enrolled in a course to learn all the nuances of the work, and borrowed books from his boss so he could study on his own time. Mortgages, loyalty contracts, and purchase agreements became topics of conversation at the dinner table, and I would often overhear him practicing out loud, talking to Noelle about market conditions and open houses while he pushed her in her baby swing.

"You better be careful," I teased. "Or her first words will be 'location, location, location' instead of 'Mommy' and 'Daddy.'"

He laughed. "I'm just trying to do a good job," he said.

"You're doing a great job," I assured him, and he was.

Carter passed his licensing exam on the first try, and as promised, he got promoted to a full-time real-estate agent at the company. The properties he showed were smaller at first – duplexes on the outskirts of town and cottages that polka-dotted the cornfields – but with each subsequent rental or sale, he took on bigger responsibilities. The duplexes and cottages became farmhouses and lakeside cabins, and then the farmhouses and cabins became buildings and other retail spots. Wally, Carter's boss, was a broker who worked in both residential and commercial real estate, and he really seemed to delight in training him to follow in his footsteps. It was hard work and made for some long days, especially when Carter had back-to-back showings, but when he walked in the door every night, he was content.

"Maybe it isn't my dream job," he said one evening, just over a year after he had begun working for Wally. "But most of the time I enjoy it."

We were sitting on the porch steps, watching as Noelle toddled around the backyard. She was a fiercely independent girl already. Sure, she loved to cuddle close as we rocked her in the glider, and her favorite game was to call out for us, then clap her hands together as we turned our attention to her, but we were finding that more and more, she wanted to explore the big, bright world all on her own. Just that night, she had let go of my hand within thirty seconds of touring the backyard to find fireflies.

"I do it," she insisted.

That was pretty much always how it went at that point. Whether it was getting dressed, feeding herself, or building a tower of blocks, her response was consistent. It made me sad sometimes, how fast she was growing up. It seemed like I had blinked my eyes and my tiny preemie had turned into an energetic toddler. She was always on the go, and she even picked out her own toys to play with – Rainbow Brite and her peach Care Bear were the current favorites. As much as I missed her being small enough to fit into the crook of my arm, though, I also adored watching her grow into her own beautiful person. It was the greatest joy and the biggest blessing.

"What do you think she'll want to do with her life when she's older?" I asked Carter.

"Everything," he answered, and I laughed, because it was probably true.

"Well, whatever she decides on, I hope it makes her as happy as those bunnies do." Noelle had given up on the fireflies and plunked herself onto the grass, watching as a pair of cottontails chased each other around a tree.

"Bun!" she exclaimed.

"Yes," I said, getting up from the steps and going over to join her. "They're super cute bunnies." I sat down next to her, and she climbed onto my lap. It made my heart leap with love, especially as her eyelids slowly fluttered closed, her head resting against my chest and her hand holding onto the bracelet Carter had given me after she was born. "You know I can't move now, right?" I said to him. "These moments are too fleeting. I'm going to enjoy them while I can."

"You should," he said. "We should." He came over to sit with us, and after Noelle woke up, he pointed out the stars to her as they began to twinkle in the sky.

I smiled as she looked up with wide eyes at the wonder of the galaxy above us. "Who knows?" I said. "Maybe she'll be an astronomer someday."

"Sto . . . mon . . . mer." Noelle attempted to repeat the word. She did that frequently, sometimes when we hadn't even realized she'd been listening. She would be playing with her stuffed animals, or shimmying through the oversized fabric tunnel my parents bought for her, or looking at the pages of a book, and all of a sudden we'd hear her mimicking something we had just said. She was always paying attention, and that night was no exception. "Sto . . . mon . . . mer!" she called out again, as she squirmed over so she was half on my lap, half on Carter's. "Mommy. Da-dee. Star." She lit up into a hundred-watt grin as she looked at us, and in that moment, I was no longer sad about leaving her baby days behind, not when there was so much to look forward to ahead.

Sometimes life just kept getting better.

Sometimes, though, it didn't.

Carter had been right when he predicted a resurgence in the Poconos as the honeymoon resorts of the past gave way to the tourist attractions of the present, but that didn't happen overnight. The retail spaces he was showing often did not sell, and it started to wear on him, putting in all of those hours and not seeing a return on the investment. The sparkle in his eyes dimmed. He switched back to residential sales, and that helped, but not enough. Instead of discussing his day over dinner, he'd gloss over the details and only ask questions about my day. Sometimes when I brought up a specific listing or client, he'd just shake his head and say it hadn't gone the way he'd hoped. His excitement that had shone so brightly in the beginning faded more and more, until he came home one day and told me he might start looking for another new career path.

"Real estate isn't as fulfilling as I imagined it'd be," he said. "For all the stories of people finding their dream house, there are so many others that don't work out. It's awful to see someone's hopes fall apart, and now that Wally is getting closer to retiring and delegating more of the work to me . . . " He took off his glasses and rubbed the bridge of his nose. "I'd have to be out on both weekends and evenings, because they're the most popular times for prospective buyers to see properties. I don't know," he said, and gave a half-hearted little shrug. "I don't want to leave Wally in a lurch after he's been so kind, but maybe this isn't for me, after all."

"Then you should find something that is," I said.

"You don't think it'd be foolish to throw away the opportunity that was supposed to be golden?"

"I think it'd be foolish to continue doing something that no longer makes you happy."

Just like that, it was settled.

Carter would move on to his next adventure, whatever that was.

12

NOELLE

June 7, 2017

*I*nsomnia is the worst.

Kicking the blanket off and dragging it on. Tossing to the left and turning to the right. Counting backward and counting forward. It's a routine that's unfortunately become familiar over the years. My first sleepless night happened when I was eight-years-old, shortly after my dad left. I remember lying in bed, holding my stuffed rabbit Floppity tightly in my arms and staring into the room that was illuminated only by the glow of a nightlight. Through the cracked-open door, I heard the murmur of my mother's voice as she spoke on the phone downstairs. I knew I was supposed to go to sleep. My bedtime had come and gone, and I had school the next day. But I didn't want to be up there alone. I wanted to be with my mother. As brave a face as she kept trying to put on for my sake, I could tell how upset she was. I saw the tears she wiped away when I walked into a room, and overheard the conversations with Meredith and my grandparents. Her heart was hurting just like mine. Of course. That was what happened when there was a hole inside it.

I gathered up Floppity, crept out into the hallway, and tiptoed down the steps. My mother was sitting cross-legged on the couch, the phone cradled against her ear and a photo album on her lap. I couldn't see what the pictures were from my perch on the stairs, but whatever memories they held, they must have been of my dad, because her shoulders were shaking with silent sobs as she looked at them. It scared me to see her that way. The yellow afghan that was usually draped over the back of the sofa was settled around her instead, and as I watched, she used it to dab at the tears slipping down her cheeks.

"How could he do this?" she said to whoever was on the phone. "How do I do this?"

My mother never knew I was there that night, huddled on the stairs just out of sight. Because I froze at her words. How did she do . . . what? Find my dad? Be without my dad? Take care of me by herself? She wouldn't leave, too, would she? I knew she loved me. She put little notes in my school lunchbox, French braided my hair whenever I asked, helped with my magnet making and Pom-Pom Pet kits, and always let me take the first turn when we played games. Even though she had been so sad since my dad left, she still made me breakfast each morning and helped me with my homework each evening. She had taken me out for ice cream just that night, and when she turned off my light, her goodnight message was the same as always: "Sweetest of dreams, my girl. Love you more than all the stars in the sky."

She'd done nothing differently.

But nothing had seemed different with my dad, either, the night before he left.

He'd played checkers with me. Asked about the *Boxcar Children* book I was reading. Reminded me that my flute was still in the kitchen, where I'd been practicing it with him earlier. "Don't forget to take it to school tomorrow," he said. "I'm proud of you for sticking with it when it'd be easier to quit. I hope you're always that determined."

In hindsight, that last sentence should've been a clue. But I didn't know then what I do now.

And so it scorched the ground beneath my feet when my dad wasn't there the next morning. It robbed me of that sense of sameness, the belief that life would keep rolling on just as it always had. I think that's why I grew so fearful about my mother disappearing, too. I was afraid to go to sleep in case I woke up to a world without her. When I finally confessed this to her, she burst into tears yet again.

"Oh, Noelle," she said. "I promise, I will never leave you. Ever."

She had, though, eventually, hadn't she?

Maybe not in the way my dad did, but that didn't make her abandonment hurt any less. Truly, it made it hurt more. I suppose that's why sleep is eluding me tonight. I can't stop thinking about the text she sent me. Between that and the puzzling moment with Owen at the restaurant, I can tell it's going to be another night of watching the numbers on the clock tick by.

It's been a long time since that happened.

My childhood insomnia came roaring back after I left Pennsylvania. Even though it was the right choice, it was difficult not to worry about what came next. Once I worked that out, the nights spent with my eyes wide open faded away. But tonight I'm reminded of the frustration.

3:30.

What made her decide to text me that?

3:55.

How am I supposed to answer her?

4:12.

I wonder what Owen thinks. We didn't get to finish discussing it, since our coworkers arrived.

4:20.

Also, why was he looking at me that way? What's up with that?

5:05.

Thank goodness I have the day off. I'd have needed three cups of coffee to get through work.

5:17.

Will Bethany be able to find the funds to put our plans into action at the hotel?

5:23.

Suppose it isn't enough? Suppose none of it is? Suppose the *Anchor Stop* has to close?

Too many questions.

Too few answers.

Somewhere around five-thirty, I decide to completely give up on the idea of sleep and get out of bed. I may as well go to the beach to watch the sunrise. It isn't like I'm getting any rest here. I pull on a pair of shorts and a shirt, slip my feet into flip-flops, and grab a hoodie in case it's still chilly, the way it sometimes is in the first hint of morning by the water. Then I head for the door.

Now, I've always been more of a night owl than an early bird. There's something so fascinating about the still of night, the way the whole world grows whispery-soft. The blanket of darkness feels protective somehow. Maybe that's a bizarre way of looking at it for a person who used to be afraid of losing everything to the shadows, but really, wasn't it the light of morning which spun my web of anxiety? I didn't know what I'd awake to anymore. It went beyond that, though, my love for sitting beneath the velvety sky and gazing up at its beauty. The stars are always there, even when we can't see them. Sometimes I let myself still think about that, let myself miss the nights when I would look at the stars for hours. These days I can't find the same reassurance in them. Maybe I can in the sun today. There's such a persistence to it. It rises, it sets, it rises, it sets, it rises. There's peace to be found in that, and as I walk onto the beach, I can feel something ease in my chest.

I try to put everything else out of my mind so I can live in this moment. A cluster of seagulls next to me draws my attention, and I smile at the way they're sitting, with their feet tucked beneath their feathers. As I watch, one of them stands, spreads its wings, and takes off toward the ocean, cawing loud and proud. That's one of my favorite sounds. It's such a quintessential beach thing, and I soak it in as I sit on the dry patch of shoreline just before the sea rolls in to meet the sand. It's quiet here today. There is a couple walking hand-in-hand along the water, their footprints washing away after they pass by, and a few people with cameras poised, ready to snap pictures of the sun and preserve this freeze-frame in time forever.

Then there's me.

I don't take any photos. I don't record video.

I simply sit, watching as the sun peeks its crescent face over the horizon. It's a bubblegum pink at first, but the higher it rises, the more vibrant the color becomes. It's like the sky is on fire, streaks of yellow and orange and even lilac painting their way across the pink and blue. And that's not even the most beautiful part. That honor belongs to the brilliant spotlight of sun beaming down onto the aqua water, making it look as though it's glowing below its surface. The sea is always calmest in the morning, I've noticed. Looking at it calms me down, too.

It also boosts me up.

I take out my phone and read my mother's message.

There was someone in the library today who reminded me of you. It gave me a pang. I miss you, my girl.

Her girl.

I'm really not anymore. I know it, and she does, too.

This text doesn't change that. But maybe it doesn't have to. Maybe it's alright to simply take it for what it is. Nothing more. Nothing less.

I let myself think back to life in the mountains. The sunrises were stunning there, too, with the rays peeking over the mountaintops, creating starbursts that seemed to emanate straight from the very heart of the land. One time, my mother took me camping, and I can still remember the sparkle in her eyes when she woke me up while it was still dark out. "Trust me," she said, when I rolled over in my sleeping bag and said I was tired. And I did trust her, unconditionally. So I got up, she poured us each a thermos of hot chocolate, and we sat on a log by our tent to watch as the Poconos greeted the new day.

That day, obviously, is long gone.

All of those days are.

But maybe it's okay to let their love in, just a little bit. Everything is so uncertain right now, with the future of the *Anchor Stop* hanging in the balance. For ten years, that's been the one place which has been free of the chance to get hurt. Free of upheaval, and surprises, and betrayal. If I lose that, I don't know what I'll do. It's exactly the same way I used to feel about my mother.

I pick up my phone and begin to type.

Thanks for thinking of me. Hope all is well.

No, too formal. I delete it and try again.

I miss you, too – and I miss us, the us we used to be.

No, too sentimental. I tap at the phone, erasing the letters until none are left, then stare at the blank screen, trying to figure out what to say. Navigating the rocky relationship with my mother has actually grown harder over the years. I was so angry at first, before I bolted out of the church on her wedding day, that the fiery words spat from my mouth without hesitation.

"How could you?" I screamed at her. Then I repeated it more quietly, more broken. "How could you?"

We were standing in the bridal suite, my mother all decked out in satin and lace, and I felt a vile nausea crash over me when I caught sight of my reflection in the mirror. Tea-length emerald dress. Curls cascading down my back. Makeup courtesy of Meredith, and the necklace my mother gave me on my sixteenth birthday, a diamond star that glittered like the ones in the sky. But what I zeroed in on was my bouquet. The flowers were pretty, a mix of pink, white, and green, but the way my hand clenched their stems felt ugly.

Fitting, since that's what my mother's marriage to Jesse felt like, too.

She didn't answer my question right away, just spun around and busied herself with putting on her pearl earrings. That took the crack in my heart and split it open even more. I wasn't going to let her ignore my concerns. Not this time. Maybe she wouldn't listen, but I was determined to at least make sure she heard. So I turned around, too, and reached out to grab the bracelet she was about to slip on her wrist. It had been a gift from Jesse at their engagement party. I'd long since accepted the divorce that tore our family picture in half, but it was tough not to draw a comparison between that bracelet and the one my dad had given her after I was born. I hated to see her wearing Jesse's instead, and I refused to stand by silently and watch her make the biggest mistake of her life.

"Noelle," she said softly. "Please, sweetheart, try to understand."

"I have tried. Over and over again. You know that."

"I'm sorry." Her eyes looked weary as she finally met my gaze. Weary, and agonized, and so, so sad. "This has been difficult on all of us, and you certainly have every right to be upset. But this isn't the time or place for that. Jesse and I are getting married today, just as planned, and I so want you to know how much I appreciate that you're here." She grazed my cheek with her hand. "I love you more than anyone in this world. You're the light of my life." She smiled at me. "Nothing could ever change that."

"But don't you see?" I asked. "Something already has."

My voice cracked on those last words, and I had to blink back my tears. My mother and I stared at each other for what seemed like an eternity. I didn't know what to say anymore, and apparently neither did she. I have no idea how long we'd have stood there, frozen in place, if not for the knock on the door. I expected it to be Meredith or my Grandma June, but it was someone else who strode inside.

Brendan. Jesse's son.

He was supposed to be the brother I'd never had. Not that day, though. That day, unwitting as it might have been, he was the one who chiseled the last piece of the crack between my mother and me. "Everyone is ready," he said, looking back and forth between us. "The organ player is here, the guests are seated, and Dad's raring to go."

I raised my eyebrows as I held my mother's gaze. "It's up to you," I said, my voice barely even a whisper.

My heart thumped wildly in my chest as I waited for her answer, protesting with every beat.

Don't do it.

Please don't do it.

But then she eased the bracelet from my hand and fastened it around her wrist. She picked up her bouquet. I dropped mine. I couldn't do it. I couldn't be her maid-of-honor, couldn't stand there in front of everyone, pretending I thought the marriage was a good idea when it so clearly wasn't. "I hope he's worth it," I said. Then I whirled around and hurried from the room, the tears I had tried to hold back springing out anyway. I caught another glimpse of my reflection in the mirror as I fled the bridal suite. The mascara Meredith had carefully applied was streaking down my face in black rivers, and my eye shadow was smudged. I looked distraught.

I *was* distraught.

Now, all these years later, the fury has quieted. When I think of my mother, there's more of an emptiness than anything else. And so maybe I'll never be able to find the right words to answer her text. That's simply not who we are anymore.

But I can find some words.

Every now and then, I see people at the hotel who remind me of you and Dad, too, I type. *Makes me wish we could go back in time, even if only for a day.*

I reread the second sentence, biting my lower lip as I contemplate erasing the confession. Then I do the opposite and send the message through. What's done is done, and it can't be changed, but if she took the time to reach out, I guess the least I can do is accept it. I put my phone away and rest my palms atop the sand. It is cool against my skin. Soft. I pick up a handful, then let it slip through my fingers. They are a sieve. Maybe I am, too, filtering out the bad in favor of the good. I watch as the sand falls down, scattering as it gets caught up in a breeze. It doesn't land in the place where it originated.

But that's okay.

It's fine just where it is. I'm fine just where I am.

Until my mother decides to call.

13

Hillary

May 1, 1991

One of the things I'd always admired about Carter was his decisiveness. Ever since our first date all those years ago, when he'd had to endure an inquisition from my overprotective parents, Carter had never hesitated to trust his own instincts. I'd been so impressed with the way he simply took a seat on my parents' floral-printed couch and answered their barrage of never-ending questions with ease.

"You were way cool," I told him, once we were finally out the door and settled in the front seat of his Pontiac Sunbird. Its navy paint was spotless and shiny, and I felt a quick burst of excitement as he retracted the convertible's roof. I was used to getting around town in my dad's station wagon, so this car was in a different league. Everything about Carter was. A guy like him wasn't the norm for a girl like me, and it made my heart run two beats ahead of itself. "You were totally calm," I said, and it made him chuckle.

"Was I?" he asked. "It didn't feel that way." He turned the dial for the radio and Kenny Loggins' "Footloose" pumped through the speakers. "I'm not so sure they like me," Carter confessed. "They seemed kind of . . . lukewarm, I guess."

"They're just accustomed to this." I motioned out the

window at the sprawling farmland. "This land is what they do and who they are. They're used to having dirt on their hands and baskets full of home-grown produce in the kitchen, so it might take awhile for them to understand somebody who thrives on the energy of a big city." A flush colored my cheeks as I snuck a glance at him. Perhaps I was getting ahead of myself. I couldn't help it, though. I had been on first dates before – there was Len, whose locker had been next to mine in high school, and Chester, who was the son of my mom's best friend, and Warren, who'd been in my English classes in college – but none of them had felt like this. Carter made butterflies dance in my chest. "You were great, truly," I said to him.

His smile was dazzling. "I was only being honest," he said, as he backed slowly down the narrow driveway. "Your parents just know me as the man who caused you to break your ankle. I wanted to show them there's more to me than that. I'm not simply a highfalutin city guy. That was what your dad called me, right?" He laughed again. "I was happy to answer their questions."

Oh, how many of them there had been.

What his family was like, why he had chosen a law school across the country, what appealed to him about being an attorney, whether he'd ever consider moving out of the city . . . the questions my parents fired at him had been too personal for somebody they'd just met. That was why I'd held off on telling them about Carter in the first place. When he had finally called me, nearly four and a half months after the skiing accident, I'd shared my excitement only with Meredith. I didn't want to say anything to my mom and dad until I was certain that Carter was going to ask me out, because I had anticipated a reaction exactly like the one I got. My parents were like an old-time Dolly Parton song, country through and through. They were proud of the traditions they carried on, and the thought of their daughter dating a New Yorker was difficult for them to wrap their heads around. I had known they'd insist on meeting him and learning more about who he was.

As it turned out, I had worried for nothing. Carter was gracious and understanding. It'd looked a bit comical, him sitting there in our living room with his neatly-pressed pants and polished loafers, especially because my dad was clad in his favorite blue and white checkered shirt and a pair of jeans that had flecks of soil ground into their fabric. It was as though someone had torn apart two photos and mismatched the halves. Still, it had gone better than I'd hoped. Carter had been warm, funny, and self-assured, not in an arrogant sense, but with the kind of confidence that came from knowing who you were and what you wanted.

That had never changed throughout the years.

At least, it had never changed until now.

Carter decided to stay at the real estate company for a bit longer, both to give Wally a chance to hire a replacement and also to give himself enough time to find another job. It was very important to him, after his last tangle with unemployment, not to close one door until he had opened another. That meant he was back to browsing the classified ads in the paper and to strolling up and down the sidewalks in town, trying to figure out where he'd land next. He didn't know what to expect, and so neither did I . . . but not even in the furthest reaches of my imagination would I have dreamed that he would come home one day with a job application from a local theater.

"Why not?" he said. "I always loved going to shows in New York. It would be nice to be in that type of environment again. I miss it. The theater is its own world, you know? When the lights dim and the curtain rises, you get this sense of being able to transport yourself somewhere else. It's an escape from reality for a couple hours."

Something about his words gave me pause.

I couldn't quite figure out why they were needling me, though, so I didn't make a big deal about it. I was not going to put a damper on his enthusiasm for a reason I couldn't even explain to myself, let alone him. Instead, I listened while he shared stories about the times when his mother took him and his brother to the theater as children.

"Richard hated it," he said. "He was never good at sitting still or being quiet. I really enjoyed it, though, especially the music, so when I walked by the theater here and noticed a sign advertising an open position, it piqued my interest." He came over to where I was sitting with Noelle, helping her with the shape sorting box that was her current favorite toy. In and out went the triangles, squares, and rectangles. I let Carter take over with her, and busied myself reading the application he handed me.

The description of the theater assistant position was long and detailed.

It was also about as different from Carter's previous jobs as could be.

So it went, over and over and over.

First it was the theater assistant, then a data supervisor, and eventually, nearly three years after he'd first expressed a desire to hang up his real estate agent's hat and find one that fit better, it was even a job helping out on my parents' farm. Carter bounced from place to place, never quite able to find something that grabbed him enough to make him want to stay. "Think of all I'm learning in the meantime," he'd say. "I guess sometimes we have to take the wrong paths so they'll lead us to the right one." I could tell it was getting to him, though. He started to wake me at night with his tossing and turning, and I'd sometimes catch him staring into the distance as he sat on our porch swing with his guitar. I didn't know how to make things better. Whenever I tried to bring it up in conversation, he'd tell me I worried too much. "Everything's fine," he'd say, so earnestly that I would've believed it if someone else had said it.

"No, everything isn't fine," I finally said one evening. It was the first of May, a day we normally celebrated because it was the anniversary of our first date, but rather than eat the lemon meringue pie I'd brought home from work, he reached for one of the markers Noelle had left scattered on the kitchen table and began doodling on a piece of construction paper instead.

"Sure it is," he said.

"Carter." I rested a hand on his. "Please talk to me. We've never shut each other out in all the years we've been together. That's seven, by the way. Today is seven years since you took me out to dinner and we ended up dancing in the middle of that field. Remember how we made wishes on the dandelions?"

He put the marker down and turned to me, nostalgia curling his mouth into a smile. "How could I forget?"

The same went for me. Every detail of our first date was forever etched in my mind. It'd been a wonderful night. I'd chosen a quaint little restaurant on the outskirts of town, and the hostess had seated us in the corner booth. I had been delighted when Carter glanced up from the menu to ask if I recommended anything. It made me feel good to know he already valued my opinion. That feeling grew as the evening went on. Carter and I talked about so much over dinner that our food got cold and our drinks warm. Even as he drove me home afterward, the conversation flowed as easily as it had two hours earlier. I pointed out some of the places that were special to me: the playground my parents had taken me to as a child, the ice cream shop where my friends and I went after our senior prom, and finally, when he turned onto my road, the wide, open field where I had found my furriest friend nearly fifteen years before.

"Meredith and I were riding our bikes after school one day," I explained. "We used to race each other sometimes, from my house to hers. She usually won, because that's Mer, talented at basically every single sport, but I remember I was actually ahead that day, until I saw a flash of orange among the green. We stopped riding and went to investigate, and it ended up being the tiniest kitten I had ever seen. I don't know if she'd been abandoned, or if she wandered off and got lost, but there was no chance we were leaving her there. I wrapped her up in my jacket and brought her home."

"You have a good heart," Carter said.

It felt like the greatest compliment. When I had first opened the front door to him that evening, he'd told me how pretty I looked, how the green of my shirt perfectly matched the color of my eyes. That had made me blush, but knowing he was impressed by what was inside, too . . . it filled me right up. "We tried to find out if she had an owner," I said. "My parents asked around, and I hung a flyer at school, but nobody claimed her. It was just as well, because I think she was meant to be mine. I named her Minnie, because she was so tiny when I found her."

"She sounds sweet," he said.

"She was. I so adored her. She lived to be fourteen, and used to follow me around everywhere. My dad joked that she was more like a dog than a cat, but I honestly think it was about gratitude. I swear, animals know when they've been rescued. It's like she always remembered the day I brought her home." An idea popped into my head then. "Hey, want to see something amazing?" I asked. "If you have time, that is. I know you have a long drive back to the city."

His smile reached all the way to his eyes. "I have time," he said.

I motioned to the side of the road and he pulled over, his tires stirring up the dirt. As I got out of the car, I could feel the cool of the night settle around me. That was the Poconos in the springtime: warm beneath the daylight's blanket of sun, still chilly below the glow of the moon. I shivered a bit, which made Carter reach into the back seat and grab a sweatshirt that had "Stanford" printed on it in gray letters. It was big on me, and I had to cuff up the sleeves around my wrists, but I didn't mind. It was like wearing the softest hug.

"Thanks," I said, and held out my hand. "Come with me. I have something to show you."

I saw the way he glanced warily at the field of green.

"Trust me," I promised. "It's worth it."

I'd felt a rush of joy when he slipped his fingers between mine, and when I led him to the middle of the field, right where the dandelions grew in whispery droves, I stopped still for a moment, trying to memorize everything about it. I had always loved how the moonlight made the dandelions look, so soft and almost whimsical. The first time I saw it was the night after I'd rescued Minnie, when my dad took me back to the field to make sure there weren't other stray kittens that needed help. "The moon!" I'd exclaimed. "Look, Daddy, it's like a big silver dollar in the sky!" I'd thought it was pretty back then. As I stood there with Carter, it seemed almost ethereal. Watching him take it all in made me feel warmer inside than his sweatshirt did.

It had been my idea to make a wish on the dandelion fluff.

"When I was young," I said, "my mom used to tell me the dandelion seeds would carry all of my wishes far and wide, until they found a perfect spot to land. Now, I'm still waiting for my unicorn to appear . . . " I grinned. "I did get the floor-to-ceiling bookshelves in my room, though, so perhaps we should give it a try."

"Perhaps we should," he agreed.

Seven years later, I still didn't know what he'd wished for that night.

"If I tell you, it won't come true," he'd said.

I'd kept my wish to myself, too, but even so, I just had this feeling that it'd settle exactly where it was meant to be. As we headed back to Carter's car, I felt emboldened by that – especially when he held up a finger, motioning for me to wait while he jogged over to his Pontiac, cranked the windows down, and turned on the radio. We danced beneath the light of the silvery moon that night, to the music drifting through the windows of Carter's car, and the sound of crickets and hoot-owls, and I'd wanted to kiss him, but I didn't. That was the beauty of a first date: there was still so much ahead of us.

Maybe I needed to remind Carter about that now.

Seven years into our forever, in some ways we had only just begun.

"You know," I said, as we sat at the table, "we never did tell each other what we wished for that night." As I looked at him, his own gaze fell away, his fingers finding Noelle's marker once again. He was more distracted than I'd ever seen him. How desperately I wanted to fix that – and so, just like seven years earlier, when I jumped out of his car and asked him to trust me, I extended my hand and hoped he would take it.

He had then.

He did now, too.

This time, though, we were a party of three. Noelle was already asleep upstairs, her long brown curls splayed over her pillow, and maybe we shouldn't have woken her, but we did. "Mommy?" she murmured in that sweet, groggy voice I loved so dearly. "Daddy? Are we going on vacation?"

"Not quite, honey," Carter said.

"Are we having a slumber party?"

"Not tonight."

She rubbed her eyes with her fists and yawned. "I'm confused," she declared. That was one of my favorite things about this age, how she spoke her mind so naturally. Being four-years-old meant just being herself . . . so beautifully, innocently, perfectly herself. How deeply I hoped that'd stay with her throughout the years. When I wrapped one of my afghans around her small shoulders that night and she reached over to grab her favorite Magic Nursery doll and My Little Pony to bring along, the world seemed to click back into place. Whatever was going on with Carter, whatever he hadn't felt secure enough to tell me before, I was confident this would change it. It was the reminder that he, and maybe *we*, needed.

We didn't have to go to the field that time.

There was a big patch of dandelions in our backyard, some still crowned with their golden petals and others already growing fluffy and white. I picked three of them, one for each of us. "Seven years ago," I told Noelle, "Daddy and I made wishes on dandelions just like these."

"Why?"

"Because Grandma June said it was a great way to make those wishes come true."

"Why?"

That was her favorite question now.

Carter knelt down next to her. "See this?" he asked, pointing to the soft tufts of white atop the dandelion. "These are seeds. Wherever they land, a new dandelion will grow. When your mommy was little, Grandma June told her that if she made a wish and blew on the seeds, the wish would go wherever the seeds did."

"What do you say we give it a try?" I asked her. "You can go first."

It was the sweetest sight, watching her bring the dandelion close to her face. She giggled when it brushed her nose, telling us it tickled, and then she sent that puffball up in the air and her wish out into the universe. Because four-year-olds were the worst at keeping secrets, it took no more than a heartbeat for her to tell us that she had wished for an ice cream cone, a new bottle of bubbles, and a "horsey to ride like you do with Twinkle, Mommy."

"Wow." I let out a low whistle. "Those are good wishes." As I met Carter's gaze over her head, I could tell he was already planning to make some of them a reality.

What about his own?

After we'd laid on the grass, our eyes to the sky as Noelle asked a hundred questions about the stars and proclaimed that her new wish was to hold one in her hand, after she'd dozed off between us, cuddled up under the afghan . . . that was when I finally let myself utter the words I had wanted to seven years before. "Know what I wished for that night in the field?" I asked.

Carter turned to look at me. "What?"

"More time," I said. "More days and nights just like that one, more days and nights with you." I saw the emotion rush into his eyes. "It's what I wished for tonight, too. Carter, please . . . whatever's bothering you, whatever you've been keeping from me, you don't have to. We've always been open and honest with each other. This isn't the time to stop."

He was quiet for so long that I thought my plea hadn't gotten through, but then he sighed. "You are right," he said. "We need to talk."

14

NOELLE

June 7, 2017

$\mathcal{M}$y phone has a jingly ringtone, and as I sit there on the sand, listening to it fill the quiet air, I'm reminded of the song from the music box my mother gave me on my ninth birthday. It was a tough day. My dad drove back from Manhattan to celebrate with me, but the thought of seeing him again had thrown my mother into a frenzy of nerves, so I'd had to spend time with them each separately. I remember sitting with my grandparents that night, my dad already on the road home to New York and my mother in the kitchen, icing the cake she'd baked while I was out to dinner and a movie with him. The tower of presents on the wooden coffee table was higher than usual. A banner was strung across the living room. Crepe paper streamers crisscrossed the ceiling, and there were balloons tied to the armchairs. And then there was the music box, which I'd always adored and which my mother said she gave to me "a year earlier than intended, because we could all use a little music in our lives right now." She and my grandparents tried really hard to make my day special, but as I sat between my Grandma June and Grandpa Travis, listening to their stories about the day I was born, I felt like I might cry. Why couldn't things just go back to the way they'd been before?

It was difficult to understand as a child.

As an adult, I get it, but as I stare at my phone, trying to decide whether or not to answer, I can't help thinking about the wish I made when blowing out the candles all those years ago: for the three of us to be a happy family again. Obviously that ship has long since sailed, but I can still do my part. I can have this conversation with my mother. Today, I can make an effort.

And so I do.

She sounds surprised when I answer. "Oh! Noelle!" Her voice goes up a little, the way it always has when something catches her off-guard. "I didn't expect to . . . I mean, you don't usually . . . " She gives a quick laugh, then tries again. "It's nice to hear your voice," she says.

The normal response would be "Same here," yet I can't quite bring myself to say that. *Is* it nice? Sort of. The last time we talked was on her birthday a few weeks ago. It went well – or well enough, at least – until the end, when she mentioned seeing Brendan and his three kids at the library where she works. Truly, I have no ill will toward Brendan. What his father did was no more his fault than it was mine. He deserves to have a good life, and I want that for him. Once upon a time, after all, we were as close as siblings. It's just that hearing about him brought back so many bad memories. Too many. And the thing is, that often happens when I talk to my mother. So no, I can't reciprocate her statement.

"I'm on the beach," I say instead. "I was having trouble sleeping, so I came to see the sunrise. It reminded me of all the times you and I did that in the mountains."

"Hence the early text?"

"I guess," I say, watching as a pair of men with bucket hats and fishing poles walk down the pier. "I didn't wake you, did I? You always used to get up even before the rooster began his never-ending routine."

My grandparents' farm was a produce one, but they had some animals, too. There were horses (Twinkle, Leo, and Posy) and chickens (Daisy and Fred). I loved being around them, and all the birds, squirrels, and cottontail rabbits, as well. The rooster, though . . . he wasn't my favorite, because each morning he was up crowing at an hour when I should've still been dreaming.

"Oh, Fred," my mother says, and this time her laugh is wistful. "I remember the day you opened your window and called down to him to be quiet. You said he was being rude. He crowed right back at you, like he was answering. Your grandma said Fred had met his match. You certainly had feisty moments."

So had she. There was the time she tossed a handful of flour at my dad when they were cooking breakfast together, for no other reason than she thought it'd be fun, and the time she jumped in the pond at my grandparents' farm, then grabbed my hand to pull me in beside her. What fun we'd had together. Then the divorce happened, and she retreated inside herself. For as much as she tried to keep a steady routine for me, to still do things like chaperone my class's field trips, teach me how to rollerblade, and go tobogganing with me when it snowed, there was a part of her that seemed like it was torn wide open. Like she had been exposed and left vulnerable to all of life's uncertainties.

With each year that passed after the divorce, I saw her stitch herself back up again.

But some wounds never fade completely.

Some bruises leave a mark.

Some scars stay with us for life.

I think that's what made it so easy for her to see only what Jesse wanted her to see. To see only what *she* wanted to see. I could remind her of that again now, but really, what would be the point? We've been over it before. So I don't bother. We're actually managing to have a conversation that doesn't revolve around something impersonal, like the weather. I'd rather stick to that than rehash the past yet again.

"So, you said someone came into the library who reminded you of me?" I ask.

"Yes," she says. "She had the same dark hair, and she was wearing a pretty purple sundress. Is that still your favorite color?"

"It is."

"Remember the time you tried to paint all the horses at the farm purple?" she asks. "I swear, I'll never forget the expression on your grandpa's face when we found you in the stable. I thought you were with him and Grandma, and they thought you were with your father and me. Instead, you had managed to sneak out the back door with the paint set Grandpa gave you."

I've heard this story before, but I pretend I haven't, because at least in the happy memories, we can find some common ground. I listen as she tells me about the tantrum I threw when she took the paintbrush away, and I even find myself smiling a little when she gets to the part about how I dipped my fingers directly into the paint instead.

"You were so strong-willed for a five-year-old," she says.

"Was that a good thing, or bad?"

"Definitely good," she says. "It's *always* good to stand up for yourself."

She fades into silence then.

So do I.

I can't tell if she was still talking about me with that last line, or if she was referring to herself. I could ask. I probably *should* ask. But then I think about her letter that's hidden away at the bottom of my box of Pennsylvania memories. It's beneath everything else, still in the same spot I put it after I read it, started to tear it in half, then pieced it back together with tape.

No, I'm not going to ask her that.

I'm not going to ask her anything.

In fact, I think it's time to end our conversation before it dissolves into something that neither of us wants. "Hey," I say, "I better get going. I promised my boss I'd work on a survey we're creating." That's completely true. I did tell Paul I would put together a draft. But it's the words I don't say that seem like the lie.

I don't think my mother realizes that, though.

She wouldn't. Not anymore.

"Okay," she says. "Well, good luck. Maybe we can talk again soon."

"Maybe," I say, and then I end the call.

* * *

Kids are exhausting. I realize this the following Sunday, when I join Eliza and her children at the beach. Nathan's at a dental conference out of town, so I offered to lend a hand. Now, don't get me wrong, I adore Eliza's kids – they even call me Aunt Noelle – but for a six, four, and two-year-old, the amount of energy they have is incredible. By the time Eliza opens the cooler she packed with lunch, we've already built a sandcastle, gone for a walk to find shells, jumped in the waves, and unfurled a kite that caught the breeze at exactly the right angle. And yet her children are still bouncing around with adrenaline.

"Let's pretend we're sailors!" exclaims Corey, picking up the pole from the spare beach umbrella and holding it to his eye like a telescope as he looks out at the ocean. He's the oldest, which means four-year-old Annabelle and two-year-old Grayson often follow his lead. Therefore, we've got three sailors today.

"Ahoy there," Eliza says, raising her hand in greeting.

All three children salute back, and it's so cute. Some days I'm not so certain anymore if a family is in the cards for me, but then I spend time with her kids and it reawakens the yearning I once had. Maybe I'm doing myself a disservice by keeping my heart under lock and key. Not every relationship gets lost in its own shadow, after all. Just because love broke my mother twice doesn't mean it'd do that to me. Sometimes I let myself think about what it might be like to open up my life, to share it in a way I never allowed before. Sure, I've gone out with guys over the years, but it's never progressed beyond four or five dates. Whenever it feels like someone is getting too close, I step back.

Distance is safe.

Reassuring.

Protective.

But distance won't make me a mom, and it won't give me the butterflies my mother used to say she got when my dad would walk into a room. Most of the time, I'm fine with that. Today, as I help Eliza unwrap sandwiches and put straws into juice boxes, I remember something I said to my mother back when I was in fourth grade. We'd had to write and illustrate an essay for Language Arts, about what we wanted to be when we grew up. My friends had chosen a variety of careers. Singer. Vet. Police officer. Teacher. Farmer. I'd drawn a picture of my mother, and wrote about how I hoped to be like her. When I brought home my paper, with a shiny gold star on top, she wrapped me in a hug and asked why I'd picked her.

"Because you work really hard," I said. "Because you taught me how to play chess, and you use my telescope with me, and you polish my nails even when I ask for crazy colors like green and blue. Because of what you promised me after Daddy left, about how everything would be okay. Grandma June says you are the strongest person she knows. I want to be that way, too. I also want to be an astronomer, so I can learn about every star in the sky . . . but I think I have to be strong like you to do that."

"Oh, my girl." She kissed the top of my head. "You are my greatest gift."

It stings, to think I might never share a moment like that with a child of my own.

But what about the other moments?

What about the raised eyebrows? The slammed doors? The shattered trust? All of it was every bit as real as the chess games and nail polish. As the French braids she'd twist, and the s'mores we would toast, and the puzzles we'd piece together. It's just not possible to think of one thing without the others. Even as I tell Eliza about the phone call I had with my mother a few days earlier, it seems difficult to disentangle the memories. "It was strange," I say. "I mostly didn't mind talking to her. It was almost kind of nice to reminisce."

"What did you talk about?" Eliza asks.

I fill her in on all of the details, watching carefully to see her reaction. When I first came here to Tybee Island, Eliza was fiercely protective of my pain. Not once did she suggest I talk to my mother or try to work things out. Ever since she became a mom herself, though, she has been vocal about it instead.

"See, this is what I don't get," she says. "Why are you so tough on your mom and not your dad? What makes it easier to forgive him than her?"

It's a good question.

A valid one.

My parents have both hurt me in ways I never could've imagined, ways I know *they* never could have imagined. If I can't forgive the betrayal from one, I shouldn't be able to with the other. Here's the thing, though: even after my dad left, he never fully went away. He may not have been there to teach me new notes on the flute, or read the newspaper's comics with me, or patch my bloody knee when I fell out of the tree I loved to climb, but he always answered the phone when I called. Even if it was seven in the morning or twelve at night, even after our lives diverged and became too busy to see each other often, he made certain to show me I was still a priority.

My mother stopped doing that.

Not through her words, but her actions said it all.

Like I told Owen, I know she's sorry. When she finally realized how wrong she'd been, she got in her car and drove straight through the night until she got to Georgia. I don't think I'll ever forget the look on her face when I opened my door. Her eyes were bloodshot and her face was splotchy from the tears I could tell she'd been drowning in.

"I'm so sorry," she whispered. "I am so, so, so sorry. Please, even if you never believe another word I say . . . know this . . . know that I'll spend the rest of my life regretting what a massive mistake I made."

I did know that.

I know it now, still.

I know it's not necessarily fair to harbor such bitterness toward her while never once telling my dad about all he's taken from me, too. But then I think, again, of the letter from my mother, the one camouflaged beneath everything else. And also the letter from my dad. That's inside the box, too. One on top of the other, so close and yet so very, very far. Perhaps they hold the answers to Eliza's question. I could remind her about them. But honestly, I would rather talk to her about Owen, and that little slice of time at dinner last week when he caught my attention in a way which felt different from everything else. I'd prefer to hear her thoughts on that, and then I'd like to treat her kids to ice cream, and help them jump over more waves.

Better to focus on those things.

Better to keep those letters where they belong.

Better, instead, to let the past stay behind me.

15

Hillary

May 1, 1991

"Do you ever feel like a piece of you is just missing?"

Carter couldn't seem to meet my eyes as he asked the question. Instead, he stared down at the grass, his fingers weaving between the blades of green as he plucked a few of them from their roots. I was glad he wasn't looking in my direction, because my face betrayed me in that moment. I wasn't surprised. I never had been able to control that sort of thing around him. He was a mirror, bringing out all my emotion that rested below the surface. Typically that was a good thing, but on that night, as I struggled to answer the question that somehow felt like it'd grabbed the breath from my lungs, I suddenly wasn't so certain.

"Missing?" I echoed. "Missing . . . how?"

"It's difficult to explain," he said. "I think it started back when I lost my job. Being a lawyer was such a big part of who I was, you know? Ever since I joined the debate club at school when I was in seventh grade . . . " He gave the smallest half-smile. "At first, I only did that because my friends did, but after a meeting or two, I was hooked. I loved everything about it: researching topics, working up an argument for or against them, and really fighting for my side. It gave me a rush, especially when my team won."

"And you miss that rush, now that you aren't practicing law anymore."

"I'm sorry – "

"Don't apologize," I told him. "You never have to apologize for how you feel, not with me. I just wish you'd have said something sooner."

"I should have. I know that. The thing is, though, I'm not sure if I even knew what the problem was until recently. Every time I got hired someplace, I was truly excited. Each job felt like it could be the one for me, until it wasn't. It was Noelle who made me figure it out, actually."

Almost in unison, we looked at her. She was still curled up in the afghan, her lips parted slightly as she dozed. She was growing up so quickly, learning how to pedal her tricycle, counting to fifteen, and even getting halfway through tying her shoes before the laces slipped out of her grasp and one of us had to take over. As I gazed at her that night, I found so much love even in watching her sleep. There was a pureness to it, and it reminded me of something that my mom had said when I started my senior year in high school and was considering what I wanted to study in college: that we all had a purpose in this life which was uniquely ours. Noelle was my purpose, and my reason. She taught me as much as I taught her, and it sounded like the same was true for Carter.

"The other day," he said, focusing his attention on me, "when you were working late, waiting for the delivery that got delayed . . . I was finished at the farm, so I thought I would take Noelle for a walk before we headed home. You know how much she loves to visit the horses and chickens. I figured she'd be happy, but instead she told me she wanted to learn how to do gymnastics first." He smiled. "Well, actually, she called it gymnasticals."

That made me smile, too. One of my favorite things was when Noelle invented her own version of words. There was such an innocence about it, this unfettered spirit that hadn't yet learned about the lines we were supposed to color inside of, and although I knew this phase couldn't stay forever, I sure hoped it would last as long as possible. As Carter told me about Noelle's sudden determination to do cartwheels and somersaults, I just felt an overwhelming desire to freeze time.

"You should have seen her," he said. "I explained that I don't know much about gymnastics, and that maybe we should ask Meredith, since she's good at anything having to do with sports, but you'll be shocked to hear that Noelle was too impatient to wait."

"Our daughter? No way."

His dimple creased his cheek. "She decided she'd teach herself if I couldn't do it," he said. "And I have to tell you, Hill . . . watching her, seeing the way she kept picking herself back up each time she tumbled onto the grass . . . it inspired me. Maybe that's backward – I know that as her parents, we're supposed to be the ones inspiring her – but there was something about how she kept going back to the same starting point and trying again," he said. "That's when I realized it: for me, being a lawyer is the starting point. These past few years without it . . . " He trailed off, and I moved over to sit next to him, curling my hand atop his, letting him know I was there, that I always would be. "Do you ever feel like you're . . . " Again, he paused, and my eyes searched his face, trying to read its secrets. That had never been a problem before, but that night I couldn't get myself on the same wavelength.

"Do I ever feel like I'm . . . what?" I prompted.

"Suffocating." The word dropped out of his mouth. "I know you love it here, and I can see why. The people are friendly, the pace is slower, and the air is the freshest I've ever breathed. It's just . . . " His hand grew tense beneath mine. "You've lived here all your life. Hasn't it ever felt like too much, or maybe not enough?"

Something dropped inside my stomach.

Where was this coming from?

Carter and I had talked extensively about all the differences between life in Manhattan and the Poconos before he had said goodbye to the skyscrapers, and the billboards, and the heartbeat of the city that pulsed through every street. He'd told me how much he would miss it, but he said a place was nothing without someone to share it with, and that he wanted *me* to be that someone. Moving away wasn't an option for me – the Poconos were simply who my family was and what I was meant to be – so he'd packed his apartment into boxes and let his faith lead the way.

I'd promised him we would visit New York as often as possible, and we'd held true to it over the years. How many times had we made the drive there, watching as the roads widened and the trees became fewer and farther between? When it'd just been the two of us, we would go out to dinner and a show, or to see a group of up-and-coming singers who were telling stories with their guitars in one of the lounges. Once Noelle was born, it turned into a family affair. We often stayed overnight at Carter's parents' house on Long Island, and – once they finally followed through with their dream of heading west and living on the California coast – with Richard and his wife Jennifer. Their son was a year and a half younger than Noelle, but oh, how those cousins adored playing together. Whether it was watching boats float down the Hudson River, cheering at the Macy's Thanksgiving parade, or seeing the animals at the Central Park Zoo, the kids were all sunshine. I'd thought that *was* enough, but perhaps it wasn't for Carter.

Perhaps none of it was. Had it ever been?

He'd certainly seemed happy here with me.

A movie film of scenes played in my mind: having picnics by the pond, complete with contests to see who could skip stones the farthest on the water; sitting on the porch as Carter played the guitar, saxophone, or flute, all three of which he'd learned as a child; walking in the door to the sound of a ballgame on television and the smell of garlic bread in the oven. There were so many memories that were part of the fabric of our life here, and never once, not during any of them, had Carter made me think he was anything other than at home. Could I have missed the cues somewhere along the line, or had he just hidden them impeccably?

I didn't know, but I had to find out.

"There was a time," I said to him, "in my senior year of college, when I briefly considered moving away. My professors talked a lot about all the paths that could open up with a degree in English, but it seemed like most of them led somewhere else, somewhere busier, I guess. I'd let myself imagine what it would be like to write for a big newspaper, or edit books for a publishing house, or work with a whole team at a magazine. The thing was, though – the thing *is* – those lives were never meant to be mine."

"How can you be so certain?" he asked quietly.

I motioned to the wide, open space around us – the towering oak tree, with its canopy of green and Noelle's swing hanging from one of its sturdy branches; the patch of dandelions that danced in the moonlight; the shed that had become a weekend project for Carter and me as we turned it into a playhouse fit for a princess. "I know because of this," I said. "Because this land gets under my skin and inside my soul. The feel of the grass beneath my feet, or the wind in my hair when I'm hiking, or the reins in my hand when I'm riding a horse . . . I wouldn't be me without that."

He nodded slowly. "I suppose that's how I feel about being a lawyer. It took losing that part of myself to make me realize how much I needed it." He sighed. "I love you and Noelle with all of my heart, and I wouldn't trade this family we've built for anything. It's just . . . working those other jobs, trying to squeeze myself into molds that didn't fit . . . I knew something was off, but I wasn't ready to admit it to myself. Until Noelle," he said. "I think it might be time to do what she did, to go back to my starting point."

"In more ways than one," I said.

He shot me a quizzical look. "What do you mean?"

I tried to summon up the courage to speak the words I was somehow unsure of and also entirely certain about at the same time. I knew they needed me to give them breath, but still, it didn't make it any easier. I sat quietly for a moment, listening to the chorus of frogs somewhere in the distance, and then I took a deep breath of my own. "If you can't find a job at a law firm here," I said to Carter, "or, honestly, even if you can . . . maybe you should look back in the city, too. I don't think legal briefs and courtroom hearings are the only things you're missing. If the Poconos are suffocating you, then you need to find something that will funnel the air in again."

"Hillary, that's not what I meant – "

"Yes," I said softly. "It is." I tilted my head back, staring at the clouds that were rolling in, hiding the stars. "I get it. You grew up with the soundtrack of the city. It's alright to miss that. If you want to look for a position there, I understand." Now it was my turn to sigh. "It wasn't fair to ask you to do what I couldn't. Staying here was a given for me, so how did I know you didn't feel the same way about New York?"

"You knew because I told you."

That much was true. He *had* told me that, on a chilly late November day when we were bundled up, walking through Central Park. We had stopped to take in the view of the lake from Bow Bridge, and as we gazed at the water, the tiniest flurries started to drift down from the sky. It'd seemed so romantic at the time, like the world had turned into a snow globe just for us. "I wish this didn't have to end," I'd said.

He'd stolen a glance at me. "What's ending?" he asked.

I flipped my hands palms-up, watching the pinpoints of snow gather on my gloves. "Today, this weekend, this chance to be together, only the two of us." It wasn't the first weekend we had spent with each other – there had been several in the city before, when the summer sun baked the streets below and when the colors of the changing leaves made the trees in Central Park look like they were straight out of a painting. There had even been the time Carter stayed with me in the Poconos. My parents had gone to a wedding in Maine, and I loved having Carter spend the night. It was a glimpse into what our future could look like. I savored every minute of that weekend, of every weekend we got to spend together, but that day in Central Park, something felt different. The thought of having to say goodbye to him that night, of going our separate ways until the next weekend rolled around, made something ache inside of me. Maybe that was what spurred me to take a chance on the idea that flitted through my mind, or maybe it was the way Carter reached over to brush the flurries from my cheek, or maybe it was simply standing there next to him.

Together was so much better than apart.

"Do you think I could convince you to move to Pennsylvania?" I asked.

Carter hadn't hesitated. He'd taken a step closer, rested his hands on my waist, and brushed his lips over mine. "I do," he said, his breath warm against my skin that had grown cold from the snowy air. "In fact, I think you already have." He'd picked me up and twirled me around, right there on the bridge, and I'd felt so over-the-moon, so invincible, like the whole world was nestled in the palm of my hand.

Now I couldn't help wondering if I'd stolen Carter's world from his own grasp.

I surely had never intended to, but what if I was to blame for his restlessness?

"Please don't think that," he said, after we'd tucked Noelle back into bed and were sitting in the kitchen. How many times had we done that before? How many times over the years had we looked at one another across the table? There were too many to count, and yet that night, it was like I was meeting the eyes of someone who maybe still held a little mystery. I knew he liked cream and sugar in his coffee, and that he'd been such a quick learner at playing the saxophone when he took lessons in fourth grade that his teacher had given him a solo in his very first school concert, and that he was the kind of man who'd play dress-up with his daughter just to make her happy. So how was it, then, I hadn't known about this piece of him that still held on to the life he'd had in New York?

Perhaps it was because he hadn't wanted me to know.

He'd sacrificed so much for me and our family, and now it was my chance to return the favor. "I want you to tell my parents that you're quitting," I said. "Being on a farm all day *so* isn't you, Carter, no matter how hard you try to convince yourself it is. I think we both knew that from the start. You would move heaven and earth for Noelle and me, and it's time you do the same for yourself."

"I don't know," he said.

"About which part of it?"

"Any of it." His chair screeched against the floor as he pushed it back and stood up. "Yes, I miss the city life, but I've learned to like it here, too. Even those narrow, winding roads don't bother me anymore. Plus, how do I purposely seek out a job that'll take me away from you and Noelle? We're talking a long commute. How selfish would that be of me?" He walked over to the window, folding his arms across his chest as he looked outside. The yard was covered in shadow, and as I moved to join Carter, my eyes were drawn to the blackened silhouette of Noelle's swing hanging from the oak tree.

It seemed so fragile in the dark.

For the first time ever, so did my marriage.

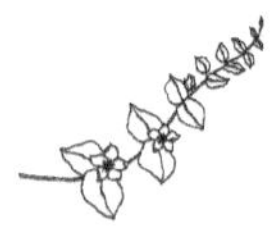

16

NOELLE

July 1, 2017

*F*or the past decade, July has been my favorite month of the year. It's usually such a happy time at the *Anchor Stop*, filled with vacationers who still have so much of the summer to enjoy. The days are long and the nights are short. Responsibilities fade into the sunset, and people come and go not according to the hands of a clock, but by the ebb and flow of the waves. Beach time is just different. It's horizons, high tides, and hope. One hour blends seamlessly into the next, and the next, and the next.

But not this year.

As we kick off the month that's typically one of our busiest, the change is painfully obvious. This July, we don't have to vacuum sand from the lobby quite so frequently. There is rarely a line at the gift shop's register, and Sierra and Diego often find themselves watching only a handful of people in the pool. Owen spends a lot of time behind the front desk with no reservations to take or guests to check in, and the housekeeping staff finishes early some days, because there aren't as many rooms to clean. We're feeling it in the restaurant, too. The clink of silverware is quieter, the chatter more muted.

And the worst part is, people are starting to comment on it. I overhear a group of teenagers as they get off the elevator, talking about how this place is "totally lame" and asking their parents why they can't stay at the hotel across the street, because that's where their friends went. There's also the man who comes in from the parking lot, marveling that he got the closest spot for the first time ever. I can't lie – it stings to hear these things. Even Betty and Irene, the eighty-year-old twin sisters who have stayed at the *Anchor Stop* each summer since it first opened, wave me over to their table one morning after breakfast and ask if we're going to be closing the restaurant.

"Definitely not," I assure them.

"That's good," Betty says. "I'd miss the banana walnut pancakes. I look forward to them every year."

"We look forward to all of it," Irene tells me. "The whole experience of being here. It's our girls' trip." This makes her chuckle. "We used to choose a different city each summer," she says. "Palm Springs, San Antonio, Chicago . . . we even did some traveling overseas, to Paris and Santorini. Once we came here, though, it turned into a tradition." She looks around, taking in the three other tables that are filled and the many more that sit empty, waiting for the guests who don't arrive. "This has always been a special place for us," she says. "Maybe we can bring everyone next year."

"We have six kids between the two of us," Betty says. "Thirteen grandchildren, and three great-grandchildren. We'd probably need an entire floor just for our family." Her eyes twinkle behind her glasses as she smiles at me. "Would that help, dear?"

I want to say yes.

I want to tell her how sweet she and her sister are, how much it means that they're looking out for us. I should ask them to fill out our survey, too, which is now up and running on our website. It's like my words get lost somewhere along the way, though. Because honestly, at this point who even knows if the hotel will still be around next year? The realization slaps me like a wave in a hurricane. Angry. Wild. Fierce. It isn't that the thought hasn't crossed my mind before, but it's always seemed hypothetical. Standing here in front of two of our most loyal and longtime guests, it becomes more concrete.

Thirty years of memories, these sisters have made here.

And they aren't the only ones. There's the Stuart family, who began vacationing on Tybee Island when their daughter was a baby and who recently spent a week with us to celebrate her high school graduation. There are Sofie and Brandon Jacobs, who got engaged under the pier thirteen years ago and whose family we've watched grow from two people to five. There's Robert, the television critic who wrote for his hometown newspaper when he first came to stay with us, and who now, a decade later, works for a national publication. Closing the doors of the hotel would mean closing the doors on all the future memories these people, and so many others, have yet to create.

How can we let them down like that?

We can't.

We won't.

Not if I have anything to say about it.

So I do thank Betty and Irene, and I do tell them that, yes, we'd love to host their families. Then, after they pay their check and gather up the cardigans they always bring in with them in case the air conditioning is too cool, I follow them out to the lobby. They turn left toward the sundeck, and I go right. Owen's behind the front desk. He glances up and smiles as I approach, and I immediately feel something settle inside me. Being near Owen is like exhaling after holding my breath for the longest time. I was worried things might feel strange after that evening out a few weeks ago, but either he didn't notice the brief moment when the electricity in the air seemed to change, or he hasn't gotten tripped up by that, because he's never once mentioned it.

I'm glad.

At least, I think I am.

Eliza's eyebrows went up when I relayed the story to her. "You know, Noelle," she said coyly, "I have always thought you two would make a great couple."

What?

Owen and me?

A couple?

No. I couldn't even wrap my head around that. The idea was completely bizarre.

"You can't be serious," I said.

"Why not?" she asked. "You clearly care about each other very much. He'd do anything for you, and I know you *have* done anything for him. Like when his parents got into that awful car wreck. He was too upset to drive back to Atlanta, so you took him without even thinking twice, and you stayed all night long, just so he'd have company until his parents were out of surgery."

"That's what friends are for."

"Yes," Eliza agreed. "But do friends also make you feel fuzzy inside? That's how you phrased it, right?"

I rolled my eyes. "Maybe that was the wrong description."

She smiled at me like she knew something I didn't. "Or maybe it was very much the right one."

I told her that she was being ridiculous.

That Owen and I are friends, nothing more.

That I had been tired that evening, on edge about the future of the hotel. Surely that was it.

Except . . . was it?

I don't know if it's simply because Eliza planted the idea in my head, or if maybe her words just awakened something that was already there, hidden deep below the surface, but sometimes when I see Owen now, it's like it takes me by surprise, even though we've known one another for ten years. I'll notice the way the sunlight streaming into the lobby makes his hair look a shade lighter than the dark blonde it really is. The way tiny laugh lines appear around his eyes when something strikes him funny, and the way he taps his pen against the desk as he talks to someone on the phone. All of the little details that passed me by before seem obvious now, and yet in no way do I actually think Eliza could be onto something. In fact, I wish she had never suggested it. I don't like having that thought lingering around the corners of my mind. It's inconvenient, flitting away only to return when I least expect it.

Like now, when I stop by the desk to chat with Owen.

It happens again a few days later. July seventh. The lobby is quiet as I enter it, the brief jump in business we saw thanks to the holiday fading as fast as the shimmery sea of sparkles that exploded over the pier in celebration. It makes my heart sink.

But then I see Owen.

"Hey," he says. "I've got something for you." He picks up an orange envelope from the counter behind the front desk and slides it over. "A little girl named Emme asked me to please give this note to the 'beautiful mermaid who works in the restaurant.'" Amusement dances in his eyes, and I feel a grin start to play on the corners of my mouth. Is it because of him? Or because of Emme, the six-year-old whose family checked out earlier today? They'd eaten in the restaurant every day, and she had taken a shine to me immediately.

"You look like the mermaid in the book my daddy and I are reading," she said, when I first visited their table to ask if the family was enjoying their meal. "She has long hair and green eyes. Same as you." She took a bite of her toast and flashed a big, jelly-covered smile my way.

The pang I felt was quick. Sneaky. Almost like it was trying to fool me.

But it couldn't.

Emme's family is nothing like mine was. She has a younger brother, Gabe, and the family lives in Nashville, I learned, where her father works as a weather producer for a television news station and her stepmom as a songwriter. There isn't a single quality about them that physically resembles the family I once cherished so much, but the book thing? Emme reading with her dad? And the way she looked at her stepmom as though she'd hung the moon?

That was me.

I wanted to tell Emme and her brother to be grateful for every moment. To tell their parents to never stop giving a hundred and ten percent for their family. It was none of my business, of course, so I stuck to talking about mermaids. But as I open the envelope Emme left, I feel secure in thinking that her parents have it covered. After working at the *Anchor Stop* all this time, I have gotten pretty good at reading people. The families who are happy. The ones who are stressed. The ones who are struggling, and the ones who love their life together. Emme's family certainly seems to fit into that last category.

"Listen to this," I tell Owen, then read her note aloud. "Dear Miss Noelle – thank you lots for the fun time at your hotel! I really liked the pancakes and swimming in the pool. The ocean was great, too. I hope Daddy, Mama, Gabe, and I can visit again very soon. The beach makes our hearts happy inside! Love, Emme."

"That's cute," Owen says, as I turn the paper around so he can see. Emme drew a picture of the hotel at the bottom, which he appears to find as endearing as I do. Not a surprise, since he's always had a knack for relating to kids. "The whole family is really nice," he says. "Hopefully they'll be back next year."

"Hopefully we'll still be here for them to come back to."

"We will." His voice is confident, but I can tell by the way his eyes don't quite meet my own that his worries match mine. What will happen to us if the hotel becomes nothing more than a memory? The thought of not working with Owen, of not hearing the gentle twang of his voice, or eating lunch together on the sundeck, or sitting beside him in meetings and seeing him hit homeruns during our employee softball games . . . I'd miss that. I'd miss him.

And there it is again.

Eliza's words creep out from their hiding place in my mind, and I look at Owen, trying to decide if there's any way I could ever see him in a different light. His friendship has been such a steady and comfortable presence in my life. Why would I mess with that? I shake my head, pushing the whole absurd notion away.

But not before Owen catches on to me.

"Is everything alright?" he asks. He narrows his eyes, appraising me.

"I'm fine," I say quickly. "Just thinking about our next management meeting, that's all." I make a show of glancing at my watch. "We'd better get going. It starts in a few minutes." I head toward the door that leads back to the conference room, careful not to make eye contact with Owen in case he's somehow able to read my thoughts. He's always been good at that. I usually am with him, too, but as he follows me into the room, it all feels like such a mystery.

Him.

Me.

The hotel.

The future.

Everything.

I make a conscious effort to refocus my attention on Bethany as she, Dennis, and Paul walk in to join the rest of us. Everyone falls silent as the three of them settle into chairs. There is no munching on muffins this time, no sipping of coffee. As we wait for them to say something – anything – it feels like our hopes are suspended in the air and dangling dangerously by a thread.

The clock on the wall taunts us. Tick. Tock. Tick. Tock. Tick. Tock.

Then Bethany takes a breath and her shoulders relax a bit. "Good news," she says. "I've spent a lot of time working on this the past few weeks, and I was able to switch some things around to free up extra funds. As you all know, we've been getting a decent amount of responses to the survey on the website, as well as the email version. We should be able to afford to implement a couple of the most popular suggestions." She pauses for a beat. "We could do more, but it'll mean a sacrifice on your part." She opens a folder and removes a stack of printouts from inside. "I need you all to look at this proposal. If you're okay with it, we can move ahead, but please read it thoroughly since you will all be impacted by it."

I have an idea what she's alluding to before I even lay a hand on the proposal.

When it comes to a hotel, there are simply costs that can't be avoided, corners that can't be cut, maintenance that can't be rescheduled. So the extra money we need to fund an adequate amount of the suggestions, both from the survey and our own brainstorming? It has to come from the place where the budget *can* be trimmed. Our salaries. If we want to give the hotel a fighting chance that doesn't involve scaling back, then we're going to have to make this personal. Honestly, the thought of it makes me nervous. My income isn't a battle anymore, not how it was when I first traded in the apple orchards of Pennsylvania for the peach trees of Georgia, but I do watch my money carefully to make sure I have enough for rent, utilities, and everything else. Siphoning cash from my paychecks is going to be tough.

I'm willing to do it, though.

But the question is: is everyone else?

17

Hillary

October 7, 1991

Apples, apples, apples . . . there were so many apples.

I looked from the crates on the floor to the display on the table, eyeballing the space as I tried to determine how to arrange everything without causing a big avalanche. Along with pumpkins, apples were one of the country store's biggest sellers each fall, and the last thing I needed was for them to come tumbling down everywhere. Autumn was our busiest time – people flocked to the mountains to see the color burst of trees – so it was important to always keep our stock full. With that in mind, I went off in search of another barrel to hold the apples. I'd separate them by type: Granny Smith in one wooden barrel, McIntosh in a second, Golden Delicious in the third. It wouldn't be as pretty as mixing them all together – sometimes I liked to think of the store as a photograph, and I was the one who got to frame the shot – but it'd work just the same.

How nice it was to actually have a simple solution for something.

Everything else felt like such a struggle now.

Carter had been back to work in Manhattan for nearly four weeks, and I was already longing for the mornings when the alarm didn't go off in the dark and the evenings when he didn't come home with a backache from the driving. So often, I was tempted to ask him if it was worth it, if all the city offered could truly compensate for everything it was also taking away. He'd had to listen to Noelle's excited chatter about her first day of nursery school over the phone, instead of in person, and when she had fallen off the slide at the playground, he could only comfort her from afar as she cried about her skinned knee and the broken jelly shoes she adored so much. I knew he was trying. He brought her treats from the city, a stuffed dog wearing an "I Love New York" hat and a lollipop so big it could have only come from a tourist destination, and he made sure he was almost always home in time to sing her a song before bed. It wasn't the same, though. It couldn't have been.

Still, I couldn't seem to bring myself to voice the concerns that swirled inside my head more and more with each passing day. After all, I was the one who had told him to go back to working in New York. How unfair would it be to just change my mind? He was so happy to be practicing law again. He'd debated about what to do for most of the summer, making endless lists of pros and cons, and finally, one day in mid-August, he had called his former boss at the firm and asked if there was still a place for him.

My stomach had dropped when he told me the answer was yes.

I hadn't been able to pinpoint why at the time, so I simply chalked it up to nerves about the one-eighty our lives were about to take. Now, though, I was beginning to wonder if it was less a case of apprehension and more one of intuition. Sometimes the heart could be a step in front of the head. There was just something about this situation that left me feeling uneasy . . . but not Carter. He was tired by the time he walked in the door each night, and his dinner often ended up forgotten because he preferred to see Noelle before she went to sleep. More frequently than not, he dozed off as we watched television together after she was in bed.

Those things bothered him, sure, but not the way they did me. He seemed torn between the fulfillment he had found in slipping back into his lawyer shoes and the tug he felt from the distance it put between him and his family.

"I miss you," he'd said the night before, as he climbed into bed and wound his arms around me. "I miss this."

"Me too," I said, as I turned to face him. His eyes were tired from a day that'd begun more than seventeen hours earlier, but there was a spark inside them, too, as he grazed his mouth over mine. I felt a flutter deep inside as I kissed him back. "I'm glad you're happy," I said. "I guess it's just taking me some time to get used to this."

"I'm sorry." He brushed his thumb over my cheek. "I never wanted to do something that would make it harder on you. I can quit. I don't have to keep doing this."

Quit.

I was ashamed by the little leap my heart gave at that word. Carter had never once asked me to give up on my parents, or the farm, or the country store. Sometimes, when he'd catch me curled up on the window seat, lost in the pages of a book, or when we would take Noelle to the library and I'd stand between the shelves for a couple of moments longer than necessary, he'd ask if I ever thought about going back to the career I once imagined. "You've always said that books take you outside of yourself," he said one time. "If you miss that, if you miss working at the library . . . you'd have my full support if you want to go back."

I couldn't lie: I *did* think about it every now and then. It wasn't that I didn't enjoy managing the store, because I did, truly. Sometimes I'd feel a twinge inside, though. I would be reading a book to Noelle, or listening as Meredith told me about a particularly exhilarating lesson she'd given at the ski lodge, or watching from my parents' kitchen window as they planted rows of seeds, and it would hit me. I missed getting to live out my own passion for sharing books and all the shiny new worlds they opened up. I knew that was in the past, that my parents were counting on me, but still, it was tough sometimes not to wonder how things might have been different if my own dreams had taken flight, too.

I loved that Carter cared enough to raise that subject, and also that he cared enough not to push it when I shook my head and said I was staying at the store. He'd always promised to back me up, so as I looked at him, the pang of guilt was palpable. No, I couldn't ask him to quit.

"You have to do what's right for you," I said. "If being back at your old job is filling up some part of you that feels empty here, that isn't something you – or we – should ignore. Yes, it has been a big change, but I'm committed to you so I'm committed to this."

The declaration sounded convincing even to my own ears – and the thing was, I really did mean it. It was just that I couldn't help wishing there was another way, that returning to his old life didn't also require Carter to step away from the one we'd built together. Maybe I should've told him that. The words danced on my lips, but I didn't let them slip out. Instead, when Carter kissed me again, I reached for his Mets t-shirt and pulled it off of him, sinking into his embrace as he wrapped his arms closer around me. For the time being, I was glad to let myself stay in that moment with him, rather than focusing on all the ones to come.

It was like we'd hit the pause button on life.

By this morning, though, it played on. Carter got up at five o'clock, whispered his goodbye, and crept out the door. It was nothing new, but after last night, it seemed to affect me even more than usual. What I really wanted to do at the moment was flip the "Come in and say hello!" sign my mom had painted for the store's door, and spend the rest of the day horseback riding instead. At twelve-years-old, Twinkle wasn't quite as full of boundless energy as she'd been when she was younger, but she still loved it when I took her out in the pastures and on the trails. What I would've given to feel her reins in my hand then, her silky gray mane tickling my face as I leaned forward to kiss her behind the ears. Riding horses had always made me feel so free. It was a chance to breathe in – or maybe to breathe out.

I craved that escape now.

The apples were waiting, though, and the merry chime of the bell on the door meant there was a customer waiting, too. I hoisted up the stack of empty display barrels and plastered a smile on my face as I walked back out into the main area of the store. I'd be cheerful and chatty, just like always. People didn't only stop by Home Grown to buy produce, postcards, or pies. It was also about more than stenciled wood signs, wicker furniture, and embroidered dish towels. It was about community. My parents had greeted everyone with a smile when they came through the doors, and I tried to do the same. Working a job like mine meant I had to keep parts of my life behind a curtain.

Not that day, though.

I felt a rush of relief when it was Meredith's face I saw. She was at the front counter, her blonde hair pulled back into a ponytail and a sweatshirt tied around her waist. I could tell from the flush in her cheeks that she had come by on her afternoon run, and I was so grateful, I nearly dropped all of the barrels as I hurried over. Oh, how I needed my best friend right then.

"Hi," she said, as I approached. "I was just looking at these lotions." She gestured to the display by the register. "Which do you recommend? Lilac, peony, or freesia?"

"Lilac, definitely," I said. "It's my favorite. I use it all the time myself. Carter's always telling me how pretty it is . . . or, well, he used to, anyway, when he was actually at home long enough to notice things like that." I tried to disguise the sudden quiver in my voice by clearing my throat, but she saw through it. Concern swept over her face as she set down the lotion bottle and focused her attention squarely on me.

"Hillary?" she asked. "What's wrong?"

Her words were the latch on the floodgate. I took one look

at her, this person who I had told all my secrets to for more than twenty-five years, and everything came spilling out. "I hate having him in New York," I confessed. "And I hate that I hate it, because it makes me feel like a terrible wife. It isn't like he's the first person to work in a different city from where he lives . . . it's just . . . " My fingers went to the bracelet I was wearing, the one he'd given me after Noelle was born, and I slid it slowly around my wrist. "I suppose it's more of a strain than I anticipated," I told Meredith. "I don't know how to handle it."

She was silent for what seemed like forever, which was completely out of the ordinary. Usually she was the type of person who spoke her mind without hesitation. Instead, she simply reached out and hugged me. "I'm sorry," she said. "I knew you weren't having an easy time with this transition, but I guess I didn't realize how big a toll it was taking."

Her comment laid heavy on my shoulders.

"That's because I haven't admitted it, not even to myself." I sighed. "The worst part is knowing how much Noelle misses him. She's too young to really understand why he isn't around as often. I try to explain in a way she'll be able to wrap her head around, but it's tough. How do you tell a child that her father is choosing a life that takes him away from her?" The biting sound of my own words made me wince. That wasn't who I was, and, truly, it also wasn't how I felt. Carter's happiness was vital to me. It had broken my heart to see him feeling so restless, stuck in a life that wasn't fulfilling him the way it should have. This hurt, too, though. There had to be some kind of compromise, but I didn't know what it was.

"You need to be honest with Carter," Meredith said. "Keeping these feelings bottled up is going to get you absolutely nowhere. Remember how frustrated you were when he wasn't letting you in? Don't do that to him now. It's better to be truthful than to make him think things are alright if they aren't. Otherwise, it's going to snowball."

That was one of the things I loved about Meredith.

She always told me what I needed to hear, even when it wasn't what I *wanted* to hear.

Everyone deserved a friend like that.

She was the kind of friend who stayed with me at work for the rest of the afternoon, helping to arrange displays and handwrite price tags, and the kind of friend who insisted on coming home with me for dinner, since Carter had called to say he was delayed with a client and wouldn't make it back until at least ten-thirty. She also happened to be the kind of friend who gave Noelle piggyback rides, and switched out my mug of coffee for a glass of wine, and waited patiently while I gave Noelle her bath and read her favorite book. It made me smile for the first time the entire day, seeing Noelle sit on Meredith's lap and listening as my girl chimed in with all her observations about the story. It was in moments like those that I believed everything could somehow be okay, if we put our whole hearts into it.

As the pages on the calendar flipped, though, the fiery colors of autumn fading into the gray and white of winter, I honestly wasn't so sure anymore. I tried to do what Meredith suggested and lay it all out there for Carter. When he took off of work for the week between Christmas and New Year's, I told him how wonderful it was to have him home with us. We strung lights around the house, took Noelle to see Santa, and built gingerbread houses. "This is the bestest ever," Noelle declared, as she added the final candies to her house, then licked the icing off her fingers.

"It certainly is," Carter agreed. A twinkle danced through his eyes as he reached for an open bag of confectioner's sugar and tossed a handful of it in our direction. This made Noelle squeal with the purest delight.

"It's snowing!" she exclaimed.

"I think it needs to snow on Daddy, too," I said, shaking the sugar from my hair as I reached for a handful of it myself. The kitchen was already a mess, so what did it even matter at that point? How much fun it was to let loose, to not think about schedules, or rules, or the fact that Carter and I were acting more like children than adults. Wasn't that what the holiday season was about? Making new memories was paramount.

I could tell Carter was savoring it, too, and it was like a weight lifted off of my shoulders, seeing him so relaxed again – which only made it all the harder when the holidays were over and life picked up right where it'd left off. I was open about my feelings then, too. When Carter came rushing into Noelle's school play just before intermission because there'd been a backup on the highway, I didn't hesitate to tell him she'd been looking for him in the crowd. When winter turned to spring and the trees found their canopies of green once more, I flat-out said it'd be nice if he'd be around more to enjoy the sight. Then there was the Sunday night in late April when he asked how I would feel about having another baby. I didn't even make an effort to hide my shock.

I stared at him across the table, where we were playing chess. "Are you serious?"

"Of course." He wrinkled his brow, like he couldn't fathom why I'd be unsure about it. "We've always talked about having more kids. Noelle's at the age now where I think she'd really love a little brother or sister." He moved his rook three spaces, knocking out one of my pawns. "Can't you just picture it?" he asked.

I could.

As an only child myself, I had known for a long time that I wanted to have at least two children, maybe more. Noelle would be starting kindergarten in the fall, and though she would always be my baby, it was also impossible not to tell how much she was growing up. I knew how happy it'd make her to become a big sister, and I wanted that for her. I wanted it for us.

Was the timing really right, though?

"I don't know," I said.

"What?" Carter's eyes went wide with surprise.

"I don't know," I repeated, and pushed my bishop diagonally

by two spaces, putting his queen in danger. "You work such long hours. I know you try your best to be here for Noelle and me as much as possible, but you have to admit, it's been stressful since you went back to the law firm. What will happen if we have another newborn who needs the NICU? Or if the baby has colic and spends every night crying, so you can't get enough sleep before your long drive to work the next day?" My words crashed over me, rough and tumble. Thinking about the reasons why this might not work made my chest pinch.

"I don't have all the answers," Carter said. "But what I do know is that our family will always be the most important thing to me. Everything else comes second. If that means I have to take a leave of absence after the baby's born, fine. I can do that."

"Really?"

The pinch stopped squeezing quite so painfully.

"Really." He leaned forward, stretching his arm across the table and brushing his fingertips over mine. It was the most delicate touch, gentle and whispery and barely even there, but I felt it all the way down to my toes. It reminded me of the way Carter had made me feel in the beginning: when I danced with him in the field that night, and when, two weeks later, his mouth had met mine for the first time. Everything had been so new then, so impossibly possible. It was like floating on a cloud. Marriage had grounded us in ways we couldn't have envisioned back then, but perhaps it was time to let ourselves be weightless again.

I could have thought about it more.

I could have suggested we take some time and talk it through, iron out all the wrinkles.

I *should* have done that. It would've been the logical choice.

Instead, I stood up from my chair and walked around to Carter, drawing him up next to me and weaving my fingers through his. I wanted to be close to him. I wanted to feel his mouth on my own, his hands beneath the fabric of my shirt. Mostly, I wanted to grab tight to the optimism while it was back within my grasp and to somehow make it so things would always stay that hopeful between us. That was what another baby could be, I thought: our hope, our love, and our bridge back to all that we held dear.

A baby could be the solution to the questions we didn't quite know how to ask or answer.

"Okay," I said, as a giddy smile swept across my face. "Let's do this."

I swore, his expression could've illuminated the darkest night sky.

It took us awhile longer than it did the first time, but four months later, on a humid summer day, we got our confirmation that the tiniest of new lives was growing inside me. I was ecstatic that day, playing with Noelle in the backyard, imagining how special it'd be to tell her about the baby. For the first time in a long time, all my worries faded away and I knew with certainty that things would truly be better from there on out. Checkmate.

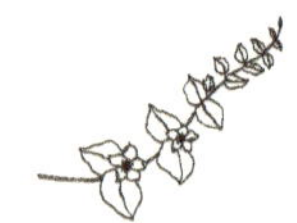

18

NOELLE

July 7, 2017

"I'm in," I say.

"Same here," Owen agrees, looking up from the proposal which outlines the salary cut for those of us on the management team. I knew he would be on board. The *Anchor Stop* is more than just a job for him, too. It always has been, ever since that evening we sat outside of the diner and he filled me in about his internship.

But the others?

I'm not so sure. The thing is, I know it'd be possible for most of the people sitting in this room to find a position elsewhere. The Georgia coastline is dotted with hotels. I have no idea what salaries they offer, nor if we could step into management roles that are on par with what we have here, but the option is there. Because honestly, not everybody may be able to accept this pay cut. Joan has four kids, one of whom is starting college this fall. Gail is supposed to be taking two months off from housekeeping to visit her family in Ireland later in the year, and Tim needed a leave of absence from his job in maintenance this past spring to care for his mother after she had surgery. Now he's paying for everything her health insurance doesn't cover. Perhaps having his salary slashed isn't a realistic possibility for him. For any of them.

"Obviously this isn't ideal," Bethany says, as she flips through the papers in front of her. "I think it's our best shot, though. If we funnel the extra funds from here, we can invest in upgrades, instead of having to cut back. The pay adjustment could be extended to the rest of the staff, also, although at that point they might leave to work elsewhere, which would cause even more issues." She looks around the table at us. "Scale down or build up, those are the two options we've got."

My heart beats a bit quicker as I wait to hear everyone's response. I so badly want this to work. Otherwise this could be the hotel's last summer. Each of us might have to hoist up our own anchor and find a new direction in which to sail. I kind of feel like that wouldn't be possible for me, though. I'd just be treading water without this place.

And so, when Joan says she's willing to give the plan a try, it's all I can do not to hug her. Gail, too. That leaves Tim, who takes out his phone and starts to tap away at the calculator. The look on his face makes me nervous. He's an easy-going guy, always ready to share a corny joke or two with our guests, but now his mouth is curved into a grimace. What'll happen if he says no? Can we move forward without everyone's approval? If not, and we're forced to go with the cutbacks instead, we might as well not even bother. People aren't going to return to a place that changes for the worse. The last thing we need is to give them a reason to choose our competition. I know that. As I glance at Owen, I can tell he knows it, too.

This is our best chance.

"Look, I agree with all of you," Tim says. "It's the way to go. But at the same time, I don't know if I can afford the pay cut right now. Much as I'd like to be on board . . ." He trails off.

"How about you take the weekend to consider it?" Paul suggests.

"That's fine," Bethany adds. "We can give it a few extra days."

So that's how we leave things. Still in limbo.

Uncertainty doesn't typically bother me – how could it, I guess, after the way I left the Poconos with no real plan in place – but this is different, especially because Paul asks us not to discuss it with anybody outside our management team. That's why I decide to skip this week's dinner get-together with everyone at the restaurant down the street. I'm a dreadful liar. Seriously terrible. After being on the receiving end of deliberate manipulations by Jesse, all the kernels of false information caught up in a web of half-truths, I just can't do it. The idea of having to purposely mislead my coworkers is completely unappealing, so when Owen asks if I want to drive over together, I decline.

"I actually think I'm gonna go home," I say. "It's been a long day."

"That's the point of our dinners, though," he counters. "To relax and enjoy everyone's company without having to worry about anything else." He walks out from behind the front desk and waves to Shannon, who's taking over for him. "C'mon," he cajoles. "It'll be fun."

"I just don't think I'm up for it," I say, as we head down the steps and out into the muggy air. It's my favorite sort of evening on the island: sunny and warm, with fluffy cotton candy clouds up in the sky. Sometimes, even after living here so many years, I still think it looks like something right out of the pages of a storybook. The beauty is so vivid, it may as well have come from the tip of a writer's pen. I allow myself a couple moments to breathe it in before letting my attention fall back on Owen. He's already loosening the tie around his neck. The glare of the sun is dropping around him, and as he rolls up the sleeves of his shirt, his tattoo catches my eye.

I stare at it for a minute.

Thinking. Wondering. Imagining.

It's the same thing I've felt myself doing around him a lot lately, but this time it's also different.

Because I can feel Owen's eyes on me, too.

It makes me very aware, but in a good way. I think. Maybe. Possibly. It's tough to explain. All I know is that I can feel myself blush when I let my gaze rise up to meet his. There is something in his expression that makes it seem as though he's looking at me for the first time. A half-smile of sorts, an energy that reminds me of the one that crackled around us last month. So perhaps he *had* felt it then, too.

Or perhaps I'm being ridiculous.

There's only one way to find out.

I shuffle my feet a bit and replay Eliza's words in my mind for the umpteenth time. I wish Owen would say something. Then I could get my answer without being the one to ask the question. Being direct isn't normally an issue for me, but this . . . it reminds me of walking on the beach after a storm, trying to dodge the shells that have washed up onto the sand. You can't quite find the room to keep your footing steady.

This moment, it makes me feel off-balance.

"Owen," I say, at the same exact time he says my name. We both smile. He gives a laugh which is higher-pitched than usual, and I know, I just know, that the pink in my cheeks is deepening. This is awkward. But maybe also nice in its own way? I clear my throat and smooth a non-existent wrinkle in my skirt. "You go first," I tell him.

He shakes his head. "No, you."

Okay, then.

Here goes nothing.

Or not.

I don't even make it through a full sentence before a car door slams from a parking space a few feet away. Then a second. Then a third. A cacophony of voices sprout up around us, and out of the corner of my eye, I see a group of people start to head toward the hotel. I recognize the family from earlier in the day, when they knocked on the closed door of the restaurant at two-thirty, wanting to have lunch. If it had been up to me, I would have let them in even though we were finished serving at two o'clock, but the chef was already out of the building. The family was understanding enough, yet it still prickled at me to know I'd had to make things inconvenient for them.

They seem to have long since forgotten about it.

The father even says "Y'all have a terrific night" as they pass us by on their way inside. I used to marvel at that type of thing when I moved here. The strangers who smile at you, the ones who hold the door when walking into a store, the ones who strike up a conversation out of nowhere. People were friendly in the Poconos, but the South takes it to a whole new level.

Usually that's a good thing.

Tonight?

I'm not sure.

Because by the time the family's gone inside, whatever was happening between Owen and me – that spell, or moment, or bubble, I'm not too certain how to describe it – whatever it was, though, it isn't anymore. The spell is broken, the moment passed, the bubble popped. Owen is still looking at me and I'm still looking at him, but the nerve I'd gathered up before has disintegrated. All I feel is an overwhelming desire to smooth this over and pretend I hadn't just been about to broach a subject I never in a million years would've imagined bringing up to him.

Yes.

That interruption *was* a good thing.

If I had gone through with it, we might never have been able to come back from that. I breathe a sigh of relief when Owen averts his gaze. It seems like we're on the same page. Thank goodness. I never could've forgiven myself if I'd said something that would've ruined the decade of friendship we have built.

"So, umm . . . I think I'm going to stick with my original plan and head home," I tell him, unzipping my bag and fishing around for my keys. My hands seem to need something to do. "Do me a favor? Let everyone know I'll be there next week for sure. I just think I'd like a bit of downtime. Maybe I'll read a book or watch TV. Something quiet. You know." I am well aware that I'm starting to ramble, but I can't stop. It's like I suddenly have to fill up every inch of the space between us, because if we fall into silence I'm worried we'll find our way back to the conversation we abandoned. That'd be a mistake.

Wouldn't it?

It feels like it at the time. But later, as I curl up on the couch with a book in one hand and a glass of wine in the other . . . it's not that I'm having any regrets, it's just that I'm not getting much reading done, either. My thoughts keep bouncing back to what might have been, if that family had returned to the hotel a few minutes later. I wish I could talk to someone about it. Eliza's on vacation with her family, though, visiting Nathan's parents and sister in Tennessee. And who else could I call? In any other situation, it'd be Owen. He and Eliza are the ones I turn to in moments big and small. A wave of loneliness washes over me as I consider my other options. Everybody else at work is off limits. It would be too embarrassing to confide in them about this. I used to talk to my Grandmom Kathleen all the time – even after the divorce, my dad's parents kept in touch and called every week – but she passed away last winter, which left another heart-shaped hole inside me.

There's Grandma June, up in Pennsylvania. I know she'd love to hear from me. But suppose my mother is with her? I don't want to put her in the position of having to withhold information. She's always trying so hard to rebuild the bridge between her daughter and granddaughter. It isn't fair to ask her to keep this a secret. And the thought of my mother finding out and calling with relationship advice?

No. I'm not going there. Things have changed too much.

My mother was the one who stood at the front door and saw me off on my first date. The one I asked for advice when I wanted to invite a boy I liked to the prom. She was even the one I squealed to about my first kiss. Maybe some other parents would have been uncomfortable, talking to their kids about that, but not my mother. She made a bowl of popcorn, topped it with butter and brown sugar, and told me all about the time she and my dad shared their first kiss. "It was like fireworks," she said. "Like every piece of me went sky-high and exploded in a burst of happiness."

"Does it make you sad now, to think about it?" I asked.

She contemplated that. Then she shook her head. "No," she said, "because for all the problems your father and I had, our love was never one of them."

Sometimes I still think about what she said.

Sometimes I still wish that love *could* have been enough for them.

Enough for us.

What would it be like, to have the closeness and comfort to simply pick up the phone and talk to her the way I used to? I wonder what she would say about Owen. I could ask her. I know she'd be delighted, and part of me longs for that, to wrap myself up in her words like I always did before. So many times over the years, I've tried to figure out if there's some way to forgive the things she did. The things she didn't do. But I always come back to the same memory of that day in the church, the day I pleaded with her to choose me and she didn't. I don't know how to forgive that.

Wanting to isn't the same as being able to.

I reach over and pick up my phone from the coffee table, scrolling through its contacts until I get to my mother's home number. I remember being so happy when she bought that house. It was the fall before my thirteenth birthday, and she'd decided it was time to give my grandparents back their space, after we'd been living with them for more than four years. We had toured a bunch of houses together, and had fallen in love with the one that had blue siding, French doors in the kitchen, and a front porch with shiny white railings. There was even a skylight upstairs, so I could use my telescope whenever I wanted. That house was a fresh start for my mother and me. We had a picnic out in the yard the night we moved in, and I flopped down on the grass, spreading my arms wide as I looked up at the endless sky above.

"I love it here," I said.

My mother laid down beside me, folding her hands behind her head. "Me too, honey," she said.

For three and a half years, that house was ours.

Then Jesse and Brendan moved in.

That was the beginning of the end for my mother and me. Sometimes it makes me angry when I think about it. Tonight, it just makes me sad. I set my phone down and take a sip of my wine. Then I return my attention to my book. Maybe the way to forget about my life is to get lost in somebody else's, if only I can concentrate.

But I can't.

And then my phone pings with a text from my dad.

Check this out. Sounds like it'll be pretty close to you, it says, along with a link to an article about the upcoming total solar eclipse.

I have to hand it to him: this attempt is more subtle than the one back in May, when he flat-out suggested I apply for that astronomy job in New York. And if I'm being honest, I *am* more excited to see this eclipse than I'd like to admit. I might've stopped the stars from shining onto me a long time ago, but this is a big deal.

Which gives me an idea.

Quickly, I type out a response to my dad. *Can you take some time off from work? Come visit me that week and we can road-trip up to northern Georgia and watch the eclipse together. It will be like old times. I'll take the week off from work, too.*

His reply zings back a minute later. *I'd love that. Count me in.*

For the first time since I got home this evening, I feel a smile grab hold of me.

Right then, there's a knock on my door.

Phone still in hand, I stand up and walk over to it. I don't know who I am expecting to be there, but it's certainly not the face I see staring back at me as I look through the peep hole. Owen. What is he doing here?

"Hey," I say, opening the door. "Is everything okay?"

"No," he says. "But it will be."

Then he steps forward, winds an arm around my waist, and kisses me.

KALEIDOSCOPE OF STARS

19

Hillary

September 25, 1992

There were so many things I knew I would never forget from my pregnancy with Noelle: the first time I looked in the mirror and saw the curve of a bump smiling back, the first time I felt that fluttery movement deep inside, the first time Carter and I discussed possible names for our little one. All of those firsts, and more, would always be embroidered on the fabric of my heart. I was excited to add new rows of stitches for this baby, even though, from the start, my second pregnancy felt different. The waves of nausea that had persisted into the afternoon the first time around dissipated earlier in the day, which was a welcome change, but at the same time, I felt so much more exhausted. Never before had I been the type of person who took naps, and yet now I often found my eyelids growing so heavy it was like I had no choice.

"Mommy, do you wanna borrow Floppity?" Noelle asked me one evening, when I was sitting on the porch steps, stifling my yawns as I blew bubbles for her to pop. My heart felt like it might burst wide open in that moment. Oh, my sweet girl. At first, I hadn't thought it was even possible to love her any more than I did on the day she was born, the day she made me a mom and turned my entire life as I knew it upside-down in the best way, but

I'd been wrong. The thing about parenthood was that its bonds grew deeper with every passing day. When Noelle ran over and sat next to me on the steps, holding out her favorite stuffed animal for me to take, it was another reminder that she was a treasure whose value would forever increase. The sweetness of her offer made me melt. Normally she didn't part with that rabbit for anyone.

"That's okay, Sweetpea," I said, running a hand through her silky curls. "Floppity's yours. I know how much you love him."

She spread her arms wide. "I love him *this* much," she proclaimed. "But you're tired, Mommy. I can tell 'cause you keep yawning. Floppity helps me fall asleep. He'll help you, too."

"You're such a generous girl." I wound my arm around her slender shoulders and pulled her to me in a hug. The fruity smell of her strawberry-scented shampoo tickled my nose as I kissed the top of her head. "It's so thoughtful of you to share Floppity," I told her. "He belongs with you, though. I'll be able to fall asleep without him."

"How do you know?"

I wanted to tell her about the reason I was so tired, about her baby brother or sister who was on the way, but I kept the words locked safely inside the walls of my heart. Except for our parents and Meredith, Carter and I were waiting until I reached the second trimester to tell everyone about the baby. Although we'd discussed sharing the news with Noelle sooner, it just didn't seem possible to ask her to keep the secret. She was at the age where there was no filter whatsoever, and we figured she would be so excited about being a big sister that she wouldn't make it even a day before letting it slip. Besides, we thought it'd be easier for her to envision the baby once I started to show. Since that was still awhile off, it meant staying quiet for the time being.

"I have your daddy," I told her instead. "He helps me fall asleep the same way Floppity does for you."

"Because you love Daddy a lot."

"Exactly," I said. "You're a very smart girl."

"I know." She giggled, then hopped up from the step and took the bubble wand from my hand. I could have watched her for hours, chasing after those bubbles in the light of the setting sun. It was funny. Before I became a mother, I'd assumed it would be the milestone moments I cherished most of all, but honestly, times like this were what left the strongest impact. Watching as Noelle skipped around the backyard . . . listening in as she set her stuffed animals up in a circle and told them a story . . . seeing the smile on her face when she brought home a worksheet from school with a gold star on top . . . it was all priceless.

Sometimes the quieter moments spoke to the soul as deeply as the louder ones did.

I was reminded of that again when Carter unearthed the old, dusty telescope my parents had in their basement and set it up so Noelle could see the stars in a whole new light. "Oh my goodness!" she exclaimed, as he picked her up to look through its lens. It was a clear and chilly evening in mid-October, and I had a blanket draped around me as we stood by the pond on my parents' farm. I had brought a thermos of hot cocoa, and my mom had whipped up a batch of grape thumbprint cookies, but Noelle was too enthralled to pry herself away, even for a special treat. "It's like magic!" she said breathlessly.

"Does that mean you're having fun?" Carter teased.

Her laughter filled the air. "The funnest time ever!" she declared.

The joy and wonder in her voice made something leap inside me. What a gift it was, witnessing your child experience something that captivated her. "This was a fantastic idea," I told Carter. "I'm glad you thought of it. I'd forgotten my parents even owned a telescope."

"I remembered coming across it when we were packing up some of your stuff to move into our house," he said. He moved the telescope so Noelle could see a different part of the sky, but instead of peering into it, she twisted around to face me.

"Come look with us, Mommy," she implored.

I loved that she wanted to share her excitement with me.

I hoped she always would.

I knew, of course, that someday she and the baby blossoming inside me wouldn't be so quick to share every detail with their mom, but when I gazed up through the telescope, I made a wish on the glittery points of light: that no matter where life took us, we'd be able to create memories as special as the ones we did that night. It had been an arduous year in many ways, with Carter's schedule and all the demands it'd placed onto our family, and sometimes I had wondered how – or if – we'd make it through unscathed. Right then and there, though, standing beneath that wide, open sky with the loves of my life, the struggles seemed to fade away.

That night was about seeing our daughter's enchantment light up in technicolor. It was about a picnic by the water, accompanied by the hoot of an owl, the smell of burning leaves, and the sight of Noelle's smile as she drank the hot cocoa. "I love you, Mommy," she said. "I love you, Daddy. And I love the kaleidoscope of stars."

Kaleidoscope of stars.

We could've corrected her and explained it was actually a telescope, but neither of us did. It felt better to let her be a little girl. Besides, I liked her description. Kaleidoscopes made the world burst with color, and that was what she did for us. She painted life's canvases in the boldest, most vibrant shades.

Oh, if only things could have stayed that way.

* * *

With this pregnancy, it turned out there was something else I would never forget: the song that was on the radio at exactly eleven-thirty-three on the morning of Monday, November ninth. It was called "End of the Road," and it'd been playing on the local station fairly regularly for the last several weeks. I hummed along to it as I ducked into the bathroom at Home Grown. I had been feeling a bit off that morning, and now that the flow of customers had slowed, I needed a break. Or, at least, I'd thought that was what I needed. In a heartbeat, it became something different.

The blood was spotty at first.

I tried not to panic when I saw it, but it was absolutely no use. My heart instantly started to race dangerously ahead of itself, and so did my head. For someone who didn't generally get caught up in what-ifs and hypotheticals, that all vanished as I sat there in the bathroom. Dread dropped over me like a heavy cape, the lyrics from that song infiltrating my thoughts and inserting themselves into my mind. I was powerless to stop them, to stop any of it. I knew there was a possibility this *wasn't* the end of the road – I'd read in a pregnancy book that light bleeding could happen early on – and I tried to remind myself about that, tried to quiet the fear screaming inside my brain long enough to think straight.

I would close the store and go right to the doctor. I didn't want to upset Carter unnecessarily, so I'd hold off on calling his office until I had a better idea of what was going on. Having a plan helped me feel just the slightest bit calmer. I might not have been able to control what was happening, but I could take charge of how I handled it. I hurried back out to the store, scribbled a note about being closed, and taped it on the door before practically running to my car.

The drive to the doctor's office felt interminable. With each mile I went, my stomach seemed to churn more and more. Was that from my own nerves, or from something else? *Please,* I prayed, as I pulled into the parking lot, *please let our baby be okay.* It was the same thing I'd prayed for nearly six years earlier, when Noelle's birth had turned into an emergency and we'd been so terrified. That time, Carter and I got our miracle. Could we possibly be that lucky again?

I was hopeful, as the doctor spoke to me in a soft voice.

"One out of four women have light bleeding early in the pregnancy," she told me. "That doesn't necessarily signify a miscarriage. I know it's easier said than done, but please try to relax. Tell me: is this the first time you've noticed the bleeding?"

I nodded.

My vocal chords didn't quite feel capable of cooperating.

"And have you had any cramps?" the doctor asked. "Pain in your abdomen or back?"

This made me freeze. I *had* felt a little achy when I'd woken up that morning, but I'd attributed it to the fact that I was sleeping on my side, rather than my stomach or back. That position seemed to be the most comfortable for me during pregnancy, but sometimes it caused an old riding injury to flare up in the small of my back. My stomach had felt queasy earlier, too, but I'd brushed it aside as typical morning sickness. My voice shook as I relayed that information to the doctor. Had I missed a sign that something was wrong? The idea filled me with horror. If this was my fault . . . it was such a sickening thought, it made me burst into tears.

"Hillary," my doctor said, resting her hand on my arm. "Please take a breath. Getting so worked up isn't good for you. We'll run some tests and do an ultrasound." She paused, concern in her eyes as I tried to dry my tears. "Is there anyone I can call?" she asked. "Carter, maybe?"

That only made me start to cry all over again.

Carter was two hours away. Every day, he was two hours away.

I'd thought I had gotten used to that, but in that moment, it was like the doctor had pulled off a bandage and revealed a wound that was still more raw and gaping than I had known. It was the last thing I wanted to acknowledge, so I simply shook my head. "My mom," I said. "Can you call her?"

"Of course."

A half hour later, my mom came flying into the exam room. She was still dressed in her farming clothes – an old, faded sweatshirt and jeans which had green smudges on the knees – and there was something peculiarly comforting about it, seeing her the way she had always been. It made me feel like maybe things could still be alright, like maybe the bottom wasn't about to just drop out from my world. "I'm here," my mom said, pressing a kiss on top of my head, the way I so frequently did with Noelle. "Don't worry, sweetheart. We'll get through this."

It helped, having her there.

As she sat with me, holding my hand, it reminded me of something I had said to Noelle recently, about how she'd always be my baby, no matter how grown-up she became. I understood then that it went both ways. I was thirty-three years old, but I still needed my mom. She was truly one of the best people I had ever known. Hardworking . . . loyal . . . dedicated . . . intuitive . . . those were just some of the ways people around town described her. To me, she was all that and more. She was the one who'd taught me to get back up on the horse when I fell down, the one who'd let me eat ice cream for breakfast when I was sick and who'd always kept me home from school on the first day of spring so we could choose flower seeds for that year's garden. She had shown me how to plant herbs and when to harvest them, and whenever I'd had a nightmare as a child, she'd stayed with me until I fell back to sleep.

If only the nightmares of adulthood could have been as easily quieted.

My abdominal pains got worse, and so did the bleeding.

I felt it before I saw it, the river of red soaking into the gown the doctor had given me to change into for the tests. It was warm, like it still had life inside it, like my very heart was not being crushed right in that breath of time. I couldn't bring myself to look at the doctor, because I knew the expression on her face would only validate my devastation. The same went for my mom. Her hand was still creating a shell around my own, but it was in the words she didn't say that I heard the brutal truth.

There were no more reassurances.

There was only a deep exhale of sadness when the doctor tried to find the baby's heartbeat on the ultrasound. There was a wail, too, a high-pitched wail that seemed like it was crying out straight from the center of someone's soul. It took a second to realize it was *my* soul, my wail, my voice that held such anguish. I didn't understand, couldn't understand. How could the baby have been there one minute and not the next? Literally, everything had changed in a heartbeat.

"I'm so very sorry, Hillary," the doctor said.

Out of the corner of my eye, I saw her switch off the ultrasound machine. Its screen went black: a shadowy abyss, just like the one opening up inside of me. There would be no chance for Noelle to feel the baby kick, no nursery to decorate and no list of names to debate. That little angel had been a whim at first, but oh, how I'd fallen in love over the past eleven weeks. Now, where was that love going to go?

I didn't know.

I cried until my chest hurt and my eyes stung.

My mom left my side only once, to call Carter and Meredith. "She wanted to come right over," my mom told me, as she sat back down beside me. "I asked if she could pick up Noelle from school for me instead, because I don't want to leave you here alone."

I didn't want her to leave me there alone, either.

"Thank you." I reached for her hand, clinging to her like she was my lifeline.

She squeezed back. "Carter is on his way," she said.

That made me feel better for a few minutes, but then I thought about how excruciating it would be to look into his eyes and see the same pain reflected back. That morning, we had woken up with all of our hopes and dreams for the baby who was growing inside me. Now that life was gone. That breath was extinguished. It was impossible to wrap my head around. I was shocked. I was stricken. I was numb.

I was broken.

20

NOELLE

July 7, 2017

The phone slips out of my hand.

I hear it hit the floor with a thud, but it's odd, because the noise seems muted somehow. Like it is far off in the distance, or maybe like I am far off in the distance. An island in a sea that sweeps me up and carries me away with no warning. That's how Owen's kiss makes me feel. His mouth is soft on mine, and I think I will remember it forever. All of it. The scent of his cologne, the warmth of his breath as it meets my own, and the intensity that fills his sky-blue eyes when he pulls back ever-so-slightly.

He looks at me steadily, silently. Waiting for me to say something.

But I can't.

My thoughts are misty. Messy. This is so far from what I know my connection with Owen to be, yet so close, too. Because he's always been there for me. Even when I was only a stranger who had been having a tough day, he was the one who made me feel better. But does that explain this? Can *anything* explain it? I have no idea.

It is Owen, finally, who fills the space between us. "I'm sorry," he says.

"Sorry?" I echo. "You are?"

"Yes. No. Maybe. Should I be?" He shrugs a little, and it's an instantaneous relief to realize this has thrown him as much as it has me. The lines between us have always been so clear. Now they're blurred, with no way to tell where one ends and the next begins. And so there's really no answer to his question. I can't say *I* am sorry about the kiss, not when it set off tiny electric charges below my skin, but that doesn't mean it wasn't a mistake.

"I don't know," I admit, as I shut the door behind him. I bend down to retrieve my phone, then gesture for him to follow me to the living room.

"We should talk," he says, as he sits on the sofa.

"Yes," I agree. "I guess we should. Just . . . hang on a minute." I hold up a finger before hurrying out of the room so quickly I nearly trip over my own feet. Once I make it to the kitchen, I grab onto the counter and take a breath, trying to calm the frenzy of thoughts bouncing inside my head.

This wasn't supposed to happen.

Even when I was going to bring it up in the parking lot earlier, I never imagined the conversation would lead to this. Owen is my friend, one of the few people I can count on to be a constant. There is no running with him. No hiding, and no leaving. He's a reminder that sometimes people *do* stay. Why would I risk screwing that up? I'd decided against it. But that was before he showed up at my condo. Before the kiss. Friends don't kiss each other like that. Also, friends don't want to kiss each other like that again, and I kind of do.

Holy crap.

Holy crap.

I sneak a glance into the living room, watching as Owen stands up from the couch and meanders over to the wicker table that holds my plants. Then, before he can turn around and see me staring, I spin toward the refrigerator and pull out a pitcher of water. I think we can both use something cold right now. I pour two glasses and carry them to the living room. Owen's now looking at the trinkets on my desk – a framed picture of Eliza and me at our eighth grade graduation, a glass figurine of the Empire State Building from a trip to Manhattan to visit my dad, a bottle that I filled with sand on my first day living here on Tybee Island. There's also a stack of papers, research I've been doing on how to entice guests to eat at the hotel's restaurant, and hanging from the knob on one of the drawers is a keychain with a rabbit jumping over the moon. It is the only thing from my mother I've displayed in my condo. She gave me that keychain the day I got my driver's license.

"To watch over you when I can't," she said, with a smile.

It's bizarre, the way I feel compelled to keep it out when everything else from that period in my life is boxed away. I suppose, on some level, I still like the idea of her watching over me. Even when she can't.

"My mother bought that for me years ago," I tell Owen, as I notice him looking at the keychain.

"It's really nice," he says. "I'm glad you have it out. I thought you kept all the memories of your time with her hidden."

"Yeah, well, people can surprise you sometimes." I offer him one of the water glasses as we sit down on the sofa. "Speaking of . . . " I clear my throat, wrapping my hands around my own glass and holding tight. Truth be told, I'd rather swap it out for my half-empty glass of wine still sitting on the coffee table. A little bit of liquid courage sounds good right about now.

Owen gives me a smile that's almost shy. "The kiss," he says.

"What *was* that?" I ask.

"Honestly? It's what I hoped would happen earlier." He sets his glass on the table without even taking a sip, and I feel my heart start to practice its two-step as he inches closer to me on the couch. "When we were in the parking lot, and you were looking at me, and I was looking at you . . . it's hard to describe. I guess it felt like something shifted?"

I nod. "Was that . . . was it the first time you felt that shift?"

"Not really. There have been a few times over the years . . . I would catch a glimpse of you in the restaurant, or you'd give me a high-five during one of the employee softball games, or I'd be sitting with you on the beach and the sun would light up your face . . . " He begins to avert his eyes, to look beyond me and out the window instead, but stops himself. "I've wondered at times," he confesses, "if we could ever possibly be more than friends. There'd be these fleeting moments, you know?"

What?

No, I didn't know. I am stunned. Completely and utterly shocked.

"Why . . . why didn't you say anything?" I stammer.

"Because I didn't think you felt the same way. I wasn't going to chance it unless you gave me a reason to. You're too important to me." His words are flowing faster now, as though they've been waiting all this time for an opportunity to be heard. "I've seen you break it off with every guy you've ever dated," he says. "I've listened when you say relationships aren't worth it, and I've felt the pain that seems tangible when you talk about your mom. It never felt like you were in a place where we could be anything other than friends. And that's fine," he adds quickly. "If that's what you want, we can continue on that way. But that night at the restaurant last month . . . "

So he *had* noticed it then.

"That night at the restaurant," I say. "That was a fleeting moment for me. I'll be honest, it was the first one I've had. I don't know if that's because of what you said, how I wiped love off my radar, or because you've always simply been Owen, the guy who's there to pick me up when I fall – "

I break off abruptly as something occurs to me.

"What?" Owen asks. "What are you thinking?"

I'm thinking of Memorial Day weekend, when we were on the beach and the feel of his hand on my shoulder pulled me out of our conversation. Maybe that night at the restaurant wasn't the first time things had shifted, after all. Maybe I'd been having these little flashes and hadn't even realized it.

But how do I tell Owen that?

How do I explain something I don't even understand myself?

"I'm thinking that I'm completely confused," I say to him. "You're right. Something did change that night. I didn't know it at the time. But then I was telling Eliza about it, because I couldn't shake the feeling that something was different, and she said she'd always believed we would make a great couple. I thought she'd lost it." I laugh a little.

So does Owen. "Is it really that hard to envision?" he asks.

"Then? Yes. I told her she was being ridiculous. But then I started to think about it, more than I wanted to. I'd see you at work, and notice something I never had before, even after all the years we have known each other. And I couldn't figure it out, if it was only because Eliza had planted the idea in my head, or if maybe it'd been there all along and I hadn't known it."

"And?"

"And . . . I don't know." I set my glass of water next to his and turn to face him, curling my legs at my side. "I don't know how to feel about any of this. But in the parking lot tonight . . . like you were saying, there was something between us that felt new. If that family hadn't interrupted, I was going to put it out there and see if you had any of the same thoughts I did."

"I kind of figured."

This makes me smile.

He always *has* been able to read me like a book.

"I've been thinking about it all evening," he says. "I did end up going to dinner with everybody, but I couldn't concentrate because I kept coming back to what might have been." His eyes lock with mine. "Finally, I decided to just come over to talk to you about it. I didn't plan to kiss you like that. When you opened the door, though, and I saw you . . . I really *am* sorry for being so forward. I know this is a complicated situation."

"It is," I agree. "I couldn't stand losing you, Owen. If we were to give this a go and explore what it could be, and then it doesn't work out . . . I don't want to imagine a life that doesn't have you in it. And truly, even if it would work, I don't know if I could give you everything you deserve. My heart's not built the same way as other people's, not anymore, and I can't do to you what I did to the other guys I've dated. When they got too close, I stepped back. I don't want to step back from you."

"So don't."

"I don't intend to. But I'm not sure yet what that means."

He reaches over, letting his fingertips brush against my wrist.

It feels unfamiliar. Unusual. Unexpected.

But also good. Also, like I'm okay to stay inside this moment, not knowing what comes next and not necessarily needing to. We will figure this out. There's plenty of time for that. Right now, I just want to kiss him again. So I do. It seems different than the first time, our confessions inside it now, an action instead of a reaction. I rest my hand on his knee as his fingers play lightly in my hair. This territory we're diving into is uncharted, but there's a naturalness to it, like something has aligned. It is scary, exhilarating, and mystifying, all at the same time.

Owen.

Steady, loyal, dependable Owen.

Who would have imagined he'd be the one to tilt the earth onto a different axis?

Not me.

It's tough to think of anything else all weekend long. The memories replay in my mind, a movie reel on constant repeat, but by the time Monday morning rolls around, I'm still not too sure where I stand. The only thing I'm certain of is that my friendship with Owen fits like a glove. Snug, solid, and secure. With him, I'm free to be exactly who I am, who I want to be, and know it's accepted without condition.

That goes both ways. I could never do some of the things Owen does: parasailing high up in the sky, surfing on waves that often send him hurtling off his board, and water skiing behind a boat that turns the calm ocean choppy. For all his dependability, Owen also knows how to live on the edge. It is so different from the rest of his family. His father is a principal and his mother a school counselor. One of his older sisters is an IT specialist for an environmental firm, the other is an anesthesiologist, and his younger brother is in college to study finance. I've met his family before – they come to stay at the hotel the same week in June every year – and they are lovely people. But I think it's tough for them to understand Owen sometimes: moving four hours away because he was drawn to living near the ocean, leaving the quieter life and embracing the rush of those watersports, that isn't who they are. A lot of it's also not who I am. Despite the way I left the Poconos and refused to look back – or perhaps because of it – security is something I crave. And yet, it's never occurred to me to question Owen's choices.

He is who he is.

I am who I am.

Now I can't help wondering: who could we be together?

So many times since Friday, I've been tempted to text Eliza about what happened. I know she'll be excited. That's exactly why I *don't* say anything, though, not to her or anyone else. Not yet. This is such a fragile possibility I'm holding in my grasp. Right now it seems like I need to shelter it, wrap my hands around it and keep it close so it doesn't shatter. Is Owen doing the same thing? As I walk into the hotel and my eyes instinctively flick toward the front desk to check for him, I realize that, as deep as our discussion went on Friday, we never said anything about work.

Will it be awkward now?

Will he be looking out for me, like I just did for him?

Will he hold my gaze for a beat longer than usual?

And will people notice?

I don't want everybody's eyes on us, not until we figure out what it is they're seeing, so I simply smile at Owen when he waves hello, then duck back to the employee lounge and sit on the sofa for a minute, trying to decide how to proceed. I think it's best to play it cool, so no one will know things have changed. Except that's easier said than done.

Because Owen is everywhere today.

Seriously.

Everywhere.

When I walk into the restaurant, he's standing next to Joan and handing her a cell phone that a guest accidentally left at the front desk before coming in to eat. When I take my lunch break out on the sundeck, he's in the pool, using his own break to swim laps. How can I *not* take note of the way the water droplets bead against his skin, catching the light of the afternoon sun? Before, I wouldn't have thought twice about that. Now I can't seem to stop myself from sneaking a glance when Sierra and Diego are looking in a different direction. I'm going to have to be much more disciplined during our afternoon management meeting.

Owen is already seated at the table when I walk in, and it makes me stop in my tracks.

Do I sit next to him?

Across from him?

Nowhere near him?

We usually sit together, so it'd seem odd for me to do anything else. But what if somebody can sense the secret guarded between us? I feel like it's got to be glaringly obvious. Yet no one appears to have caught on. It's business as usual. Gail is telling a story about a boy who drew on the walls of a guestroom with crayons and marker, how upset his parents were when they reported it to one of the housekeeping staff and, in turn, how impressed they were when Gail used one of her foolproof cleaning tricks to take care of it.

"I thought the mother was going to hug me," she laughs. "I

told her, 'Honey, when you get to be my age and you've worked in this field for thirty years, you know how to get a mess off of anything.'" This makes everyone else chuckle, too, including Owen as I decide to sit next to him so as not to draw any attention our way.

It works.

Gail moves on to another story about a girl who got into her mom's makeup and spilled an open bottle of nail polish onto the guestroom carpet, and then Joan jumps in, talking about the kid who pushed back her chair in the restaurant at the exact moment a waitress was bringing over a full tray of food. I still remember the way the restaurant went completely silent as the plates clattered onto the floor. Food splattered everywhere and drinks spilled like rivers. At the time, it seemed like such a disaster. Now, it's funny. And it hits me again as I sit here with everybody, these people who are maybe more like family than friends, how sincerely sad I would be if this faded away.

But perhaps it won't have to.

Because when Tim joins us, his walkie-talkie clipped to his belt and grease still dotting his hands from the maintenance job he was just finishing, there's a grin on his face. He doesn't even sit down before the words pop out of his mouth. "Alright," he says. "I was able to work it out. Count me in. Let's save this hotel."

KALEIDOSCOPE OF STARS

21

Hillary

November 9, 1992

It turned out we were both broken.

The look on Carter's face when he saw me for the first time after the miscarriage made the ache in my chest deepen. His eyes were filled with agony, his mouth quivering as he rushed to my side. I tried to tell him it was okay to cry, that he didn't have to stay strong for me, but the words seemed to get lost on their way to being spoken. The sob that came out instead was low and strangled, and Carter took my hand in both of his, leaning down as he rested his forehead to mine.

His skin felt warm against the ice of my own.

How long did we sit there together in silence, listening to the ticking of the clock on the wall as it counted us forward into a new chapter of our lives we'd never wanted to write? A few minutes? An hour? I had no idea. Time seemed warped. I knew my mom left to pick up Noelle from Meredith's house, I felt her kiss my cheek and heard her say how much she loved me, but not much else broke through the fog. Even as I dug deep for the courage to fill Carter in on the awful details, everything still felt hazy. It was like I was watching my own life from an outside perspective. This couldn't have been happening to me.

It was, though.

The emptiness inside, the despair, the grief, the guilt . . . it all clung to me.

"I'm so sorry," I whispered to Carter. "Do you hate me?"

"What?" His eyes widened. "Of course not. Why would you say that?"

"Because . . . " The walls of my throat constricted. "Because it's . . . " I tried a second time to relay what the doctor had said, her questions about the cramping and pain, and to tell him how terrified I was that it was my fault we'd lost the baby. I couldn't do it, though. My emotions squeezed me so tightly there was no room left to breathe. Not until Carter handed me a cup of water could I funnel the air back in. "It was my job to protect the baby," I said, once I'd sipped enough water to open up my voice again. "But I failed."

"Hillary, no." Carter rubbed his thumb in small circles on my wrist. It was comforting in a way I felt I didn't deserve. "You are *not* to blame," he said. "This happens sometimes. It isn't because of anything you did or didn't do."

That was also what the doctor had told me. She'd talked about chromosomes and implantation, and had provided me with statistics, but it was still difficult to believe. Logically, I knew this loss was a senseless one, with a reason we might never fully understand, yet I couldn't find a shred of solace in that.

If only I hadn't brushed aside that ache in my back.

If only I'd taken it easier at work.

If only.

They seemed like the two longest words in the English language right about then.

They did in the weeks to come, too.

It was jarring to see life around me go on as usual. I would take Noelle to school and hear other mothers talking about the upcoming holidays, or what plans they had for the weekend, and I'd stand there, a bit stupefied. It felt even stranger not to be at work. Both my parents and Carter suggested I take some time off, and I agreed, so I spent three long weeks at home. I watched far too much TV, read the entire pile of books on my nightstand, and tested out a good amount of the unused recipes I had saved through the years. I knitted two afghans, made several trips to the library so I could lose myself in the place that had written its story on my heart when I'd worked there, and spent a lot of time with Meredith. Sometimes she brought a meal, sometimes she convinced me to get out of the house and go for a walk, and sometimes she simply sat with me, listening when I needed her to and kindly obliging when I asked her to talk about her own life rather than concentrating on mine.

"Tell me about work," I said. "You mentioned you're going to be teaching snowboarding classes this year, too?"

"Yes, but don't worry," she said, with a grin. "I'm not going to make you be my test student like I did with skiing." That actually made me smile, too. For all of her athletic prowess, Meredith hadn't had much experience teaching when she was first hired at the ski resort, so she'd asked if she could practice on me. We'd had fun with it, and truth be told, I wouldn't have minded if she had asked me to do it again. Honestly, it might have been a good distraction.

Oh, how I needed one.

Carrying the grief around with me all the time was exhausting. There were only so many ways I could sidetrack my thoughts, which is why, after those three weeks at home, I was itching to go back to work. At least at the store I'd be able to focus on other things. When I was there, I could pretend – that I hadn't lost a piece of my heart, that the red of blood didn't stain my dreams sometimes, that everything was fine. Even when I talked to customers and had to hide behind the facade of a smile, it was still preferable to being home.

When I sat in our living room now, I saw the pictures on the mantel and couldn't help but mourn the new little face that would never smile at me. When I walked by Noelle's room, I thought of the 'Big Sister' shirt I'd bought her shortly after finding out I was pregnant. I had been planning to put it in her closet one day, when we were ready to share the news, so she could find it and feel like she'd made the discovery. Now it was hidden away in the closet in our bedroom. Out of the whole house, that room was the hardest for me to be in, because when I lied down in bed, my thoughts drifted to the night Carter and I had decided to have another baby. We had been so full of optimism then, this hope that the baby would be exactly what we needed to reconnect the threads of our lives.

Now that was gone, too.

In a way, so was Carter.

He'd been wonderful in the days following the miscarriage. He had taken a week off from work and spent all his time trying to make me feel better. "Tell me what you need," he'd said. "What can I do?" He was determined to help, and I understood, because that guilt I felt, that crushing regret? It wasn't only my burden. It weighed heavily on him, too. "I hate that I wasn't there for you," he'd said, the day after the miscarriage. We were home then, sitting on the back porch as Noelle played on her tire swing. My parents had offered for her to stay with them for a couple days, but I'd opted against it.

I needed my girl.

I needed her sunshine.

It was the only thing that could break through the storm rumbling inside me.

How grateful I was, how grateful we both were, that we hadn't told her about the baby. Having to explain the loss . . . how could we have handled that? It was tough enough at that point to handle each other. I told Carter not to blame himself for being in New York, reminded him that he couldn't have known anything would go wrong, and I meant it. "I'm sorry I didn't call you right away," I said. "I didn't want to worry you unnecessarily. But when you heard from my mom . . . you were there as quickly as possible. This was beyond your control, too."

It was so much like what he'd said to me the day before.

Yet, we couldn't listen to our own advice.

We couldn't banish the remorse and sorrow.

As the weeks went on, I found myself waking up early to go out and watch as the sun peeked up over the mountains in the distance, and after Carter came home from work, he'd frequently pick up his guitar. The songs he played sounded so sad, I wanted to go over and wrap my arms around him to let him know it was okay. It wasn't okay, though, not yet. Where was the peace we desperately craved?

The first hint of it crept in on Noelle's sixth birthday. Her party would be the following weekend, but we didn't want to wait to give her the present we'd carefully picked out: a shiny new telescope. As we had suspected, she was delighted with it. "Thank you!" she squealed, launching herself at us with a hug. "This is the best day ever!"

It *was* a good day.

We were determined to make it special, to give her a birthday free from all the despair that had snaked itself around our little family and refused to let go. Noelle might not have known about the miscarriage, but more than once, she'd caught Carter and me inside a difficult moment. There was the time I opened a kitchen cabinet and the bottle of my prenatal vitamins fell out, rolling across the counter until I snatched it up and flung it into the trash. There was the time a package arrived from an upscale shop in Manhattan, and I'd gasped from the jolt of it as I opened the box to reveal a crib mobile that Carter had ordered as a surprise and then forgotten to cancel. Also, there was the time we had the news on one weekend and Carter had said "Shut that off," when a story about newborn quintuplets flashed on the screen. I hated that Noelle had to witness those scenes. Little ears heard things in a big way.

She questioned us sometimes. She'd cuddle up next to me on the couch, or motion for Carter to bend down until he was eye-to-eye with her, and ask why we were upset. "Your smiles got erased," she said to me once, and it felt as though my heart was splintering. For as hard as we were working to keep Noelle's world as even and innocent as possible, sometimes we slipped up. Sometimes life slipped us up.

Noelle's birthday was different, though, and so was her party. That day was about laughter and love, about balloons and pony rides and chocolate fudge cake homemade by my mom. It was chilly outside that afternoon, the winter wind sneaking down from the mountaintops, but it felt good, the literal breath of fresh air we needed. Watching as Noelle and her friends had potato sack races, and tossed bean bags, and played Pin the Tail on the Bunny using the backdrop Meredith had painted, it was like a sense of calm settled itself around me.

"Maybe this is the turning point," I told Carter. "Maybe things will get better from here on out."

"Maybe we *make* them better from here on out."

"We can do that," I said.

We couldn't, though, not really – not when our ideas of how to move forward took us in totally opposite directions. Carter wanted to try for a baby again, and I did not. The first time he brought it up, I changed the subject before it grew into something I wasn't ready to face yet. The second time, a few weeks later, I told him I'd think about it. It was the first lie I had ever told him, and it upset me to do it, but how could I be honest? How could I confess that I wasn't sure I'd be ready to try again *ever*? Carter was looking at things through a very different perspective than me.

He wasn't the one who'd lied there helplessly as a life bled out of him.

He wasn't the one who'd spend the next nine months fearing every ache, or twinge, or pain.

He wasn't the one. I was.

So, the third time he asked, I forced myself to give him the answer he deserved, even if it wasn't the one he wanted. "No," I said. "Not now. Truly, I don't know if I'll ever be ready to give it another try. I think of the possibility of having a miscarriage again, of going through that torture for a second time, and I just . . . can't."

He rested his hand atop mine, the gold of his wedding band cool against my skin. "I understand why you feel that way," he said. "And I respect where you're coming from. Do we really want to let fear paralyze us, though? Do we want to let it win?"

"This isn't about winning or losing," I said. "It isn't about gathering up strength and overcoming the odds, because we have no way, *absolutely* no way, of being sure that will happen. I think that's what it would take for me." I could feel the sting of tears behind my eyelids and tried to blink them away. "If I knew this next pregnancy would be viable, I'd do it in a heartbeat. I would take all of the worrying and anxiety, and say to hell with fear. There isn't a guarantee, though. You can't promise me it'll be alright."

"No." His voice was quieter than perhaps I'd ever heard it. "No, I can't."

"I'm sorry, Carter." My tears slipped out then, despite my best efforts to contain them. "I know you want this, and I wish I could say yes, I wish I could say I'm brave enough to face it again without knowing how it will turn out, but . . . " I stared down at my hands, because it seemed too hard to look at him.

"Hey." I felt his warmth as he wound an arm around my shoulders, pulling me close as he kissed me on the temple. "You *are* brave," he said. "You're brave, and you're strong, and you're insightful enough to know your own heart and listen to it. That's a good thing."

"Even if you don't agree with what my heart's saying?"

"Even then."

"So what do we do now?" I asked. "Are you okay with the possibility of not having more kids?"

His sigh was heavy. "I love you enough not to just pretend

I'm fine with it," he told me. "I want Noelle to grow up with a sibling to love, and look out for, and play with, the same as I did. I have so many great memories with my brother, and it saddens me to think of Noelle not having a chance to experience that."

His words shot an arrow straight into my soul.

I wanted that for Noelle, too.

I wanted her to have a confidante and companion, a brother or sister who'd be a forever friend. I had missed out on that. Being an only child meant I never had the chance to whisper secrets with someone long after the bedroom light had been turned out, or to sit next to anybody in the back of my dad's tractor as he drove it around the farm. It hit me then, that if I held firm to my feelings, and if that night was the end of a discussion rather than the beginning, that Noelle wouldn't have those things, either. I hadn't really allowed myself to think about that previously. Maybe it was a defense mechanism, or the sort of tunnel vision that grief could impose. Either way, it really gave me a lot to consider.

"Let's take more time," I suggested. "Let's give ourselves the room to heal, and then revisit it."

As it turned out, time was exactly what we needed.

The grief changed with each day. The pain stopped throbbing so badly and settled into more of a dull ache instead, and I no longer lived each moment through a veil of loss. Outside, the snow and ice started to melt, dripping from the roof and tap-dancing against the siding, and the first sprigs of green appeared in the garden. I let myself appreciate all the beauty. I let myself soak in the sight of the cottontails hopping about, the sound of the sparrows chirping in the trees, and the smell of the freshly cut lawns that seemed all-encompassing up in the mountains where the fields stretched for miles. I spent a lot of time riding Twinkle again, volunteering in Noelle's classroom, and working on ideas for the store. I even let myself consider how it'd feel to hold another baby in my arms.

Perhaps Carter had been right, and I *could* do it.

We hadn't discussed it since that night when I was finally honest about my feelings, and I loved him for giving me the space I needed. He knew me well enough to know I would come to him when I was ready to continue the conversation. I thought maybe I was now . . . at least, until I checked the calendar to see when Noelle's next Girl Scout meeting was. Of all the possible days, it just had to be that one: May thirty-first, what would have been my due date.

I'd been doing so much better lately, but this knocked the breath out of me. I placed a hand to my heart, feeling the beats pound against it. How close we were now to the time which should have been one of the best of our lives, but also, how very far away. I knew then that I wasn't quite ready . . . not yet.

22

NOELLE

August 10, 2017

I have never worked so hard in my life.

For a month straight, the management team pulls double duty at the hotel, giving our all to both our regular positions and our salvage efforts. I can't lie, it's challenging. The process is much more complicated than I imagined. Everything has to be considered from multiple angles. Adding in new nighttime swim hours? We need to determine whether the pool area has enough lighting. Offering refreshments in the lobby each afternoon? We need to write down lists of the ingredients to order. Purchasing umbrellas and chairs for our guests to use on the beach? We need to figure out a place we can store them when they're not set up.

And the list goes on.

A lot of the initial ideas the team brainstormed are too complex to tackle immediately. It takes time to establish a babysitting service, remodel the dining room, and convert the conference rooms to banquet halls. We're all in agreement that we have to start implementing the changes as quickly as possible, so we hold off on the more extensive choices in favor of those we can put into practice now. We print coupons for twenty-percent off at the restaurant. Reach out to ocean conservation groups to discuss ways we can partner with them. Research different green options for the hotel to go along with that. Update our website and social media to reflect the changes in our check-in and check-out times – an hour earlier for arrival and an hour later for departure, plus extended benefits for returning guests. We even begin to plan a scavenger hunt for Labor Day weekend so people can win prizes.

Then there's the survey. Owen volunteers to compile its results with me and suggests we work on it at his house. The thought makes me a little nervous. What will happen when it's just the two of us? I have been trying to avoid that until we can figure out what's going on between us. With the other guys I dated, it was clear-cut. I was happy when they asked me out, and relieved when I broke it off. But there isn't any clarity with Owen. There is only this back-and-forth, this game that neither one of us really knows how to play.

Sometimes I'll catch him looking at me when he thinks I won't notice.

Sometimes I'll catch myself doing the same with him.

It's easier to dance around it at the hotel, to redirect my attention to something else, but at his house? That's another story entirely, and I almost say no. I have been to his house many times over the years, but I'm worried it will feel awkward now, given this limbo we're in. Still, I want to go. The idea of spending an evening with him – talking, working, eating dinner outside on the upstairs deck where you can just make out a faint hint of the ocean in the distance – puts an involuntary smile on my face. It's completely out of my control.

So I go with it.

I go with him.

Any reservations I had fade away the instant he unlocks the front door and holds it open for me. I don't feel uncomfortable here. Quite the opposite. Everything is familiar, welcoming. There's the surfboard propped up against the wall, the framed photos of the Atlanta skyline that hang above the denim-colored sofa, and the models of ships that line a shelf along the far wall. It's all so classically Owen that it puts me right at ease.

"I'm just gonna change out of these work clothes," he says. "Then we can order dinner and get to work. I have take-out menus in the drawer by the phone in the kitchen. Pick whatever place you want. I'm cool with anything."

"Okay, sounds good." I wait until he disappears up the stairs, then head into the small kitchen. I pause for a minute by the refrigerator, looking at the photos he has tacked up. There's one with his whole family on the beach, taken when they came to visit this June. One of our staff's holiday party last year, everyone dressed up and posing in front of the Christmas tree in the lobby. One of Owen with Sandy, his family's golden retriever, and one with no people, just the cotton candy sunset that's turned the ocean pink in the twilight.

You can tell a lot about people by the pictures they choose to display.

Also by the way they keep their drawers.

Owen's is neat. Tidy. A place for everything and everything in its place. The menus are stacked into a pile, and I take them out, flipping through the many options. "Do you *ever* cook?" I joke, as he walks into the kitchen, clad in jeans and a t-shirt that makes the blue in his eyes pop. "Or is it a goal to single-handedly keep every restaurant on the island in business?"

He laughs. "Let's just say the smoke alarm gets a workout if I try to cook anything besides pizza or macaroni and cheese." He leans back against the counter, folding his arms across his chest, and I feel a heat flush inside my cheeks as I notice the way it makes his muscles strain a little bit under his shirt.

Stop it, Noelle.

My brain pipes up with a cautionary reminder, and I try to listen, but it's really tough to yank my attention away from what's right in front of me. I could make this easy. I could take a step forward, close the distance between us, and see if our third kiss would be as incredible as the first two were. How would Owen react? I bite my lip as I study him, trying to read his body language. His shoulders are relaxed, his smile warm.

But he doesn't make any kind of move.

He doesn't graze his fingers against mine when I hand him the menu.

He doesn't take the chair next to me, but rather across, when we eat our dinner on the deck.

He doesn't even sit too close to me on the sofa when we go back inside and start to work.

But he does order a chocolate banana milkshake with dinner because he knows I love them.

He does lean over to brush away the bug that lands on my shoulder as we're eating.

And he does drape his arm across the back of the couch as I'm pulling up the survey, almost like he wants to put it around me but isn't quite sure if he should.

So which is it?

God, this is confusing. It reminds me why I decided that relationships aren't worth all the risk . . . but, also, it reminds me why they *are*. Because I like that he remembers what my favorite foods are. I like that he looks out for me. I like that he wants to be close to me, even though he doesn't know yet where we stand. I even like the way he debates me about the survey. Whereas I'd much prefer to highlight the open-ended responses, Owen points out all the reasons why we should focus on the rating scale instead. I think it says a great deal, when somebody can both respect and challenge you at the same time.

Whoever would've thought Owen might turn out to be my greatest challenger yet?

Eliza, that's who.

"I told you so," she'd said in an airy voice, when I filled her in on what happened with him at my condo. "There's something so real between you guys. I hope you don't throw it away just because you're afraid." She'd paused for a second. "I don't think you're going to like what I have to say, but maybe you should call your mom. Visit her, even. Hear her side of the story again, now that you've both had all this time to distance yourselves from the emotion. You just might find that her choices don't have to drive yours anymore."

"They don't."

"Yes," she said. "They do. You may have started over here, and sure, you're obviously your own person, but I think your mom is still more a part of you than you would care to admit. The only way to change that – or not change it, if it turns out you don't want to – is to talk it out."

"I can't."

"Yes, you can. Can't and won't are very different things. Promise me you'll at least think about it?"

I'd sighed. "Okay."

And I have thought about it. So many times since then, I've let my mind travel to the mountains. To the memories. To my mother. Every time, I've come to the same conclusion: that even after all these years, that part of my heart is too fragile to offer it to her again. Not when she has the power to take the cracks I've patched up and split them wide open once more.

Tonight, though, as Owen walks me out to my car, leaning in like he wants to kiss me but settling for a hug instead, I consider that maybe we have to let the cracks open up again. Maybe we have to break our hearts apart before we can piece them together in a new way. I thought I had done that a long time ago, but if I had, if I'd really found peace with the past, then I wouldn't be questioning the present so much.

Eliza was right.

I have to talk to my mother.

But first, there's someone else I need to speak with: my dad.

He'll be here for the eclipse in just over a week, so I decide to wait until then to discuss things. I think this is something best done in person. When his plane touches down the following Friday, I'm there to meet him. I see him before he sees me, and for a second, it makes me feel like a kid again, when I stood at the window and watched for his car to pull into the driveway. I did that a lot when I was younger. Dad worked long hours, especially in the years leading up to the divorce, and I missed having him home. I didn't understand why he couldn't be there to help me with my homework or to cheer me on during my soccer games. But perhaps I should have. Because sometimes, late at night, when I'd wake up and tiptoe to the bathroom to get a drink of water, I'd hear the voices behind my parents' closed bedroom door. I knew something was wrong. They didn't sound happy any longer. When you're a child, though, I suppose you're still naive enough to fool yourself into thinking it'll all work out.

Ha.

Lesson learned.

As my dad makes his way over, I can't help thinking of what Eliza said that day we took her kids to the beach. She was right: I *am* much harder on my mother than my dad. Maybe that's because I was only a child when he left. I had many extra years with her, and she was more than my mother. She was also my friend, my guide, my mentor. She was the one I looked up to, and the one I trusted above everyone else. I think that's why forgiveness hasn't felt like an option. Not forgiving my dad hadn't even been a choice. I missed him so dearly that there wasn't any time for anger whenever we were reunited. Our visits were about catching up, not doubling down.

They still are.

Two or three times a year, I fly to Manhattan, but never once have I told my dad how hurt I was when he left. When he hid behind the words of a note, instead of saying goodbye in person. When he made me afraid to close my eyes at night, when he shattered my mother's heart, when he ripped our family portrait in half. So long, too long, I've spent avoiding that. I can't anymore.

If I have any hope of letting Owen in – *really* letting him in, the way I'd need to for us to give a relationship a fair chance – then it's time to stop hiding behind my own insecurities. For the past twelve years here in Georgia, I've been able to tuck them away. I've been able to build a life, a good one, and to know it would always be there for me.

But maybe there's no such thing as always.

Who knows if our plans to save the hotel will work?

Who knows if Owen and I can make the leap to something more?

I could lose so much, so quickly.

The thought is terrifying. Because that's what happened before. My life as I knew it was stolen away. But here's the thing: I'm still standing. I made it to the other side then, and I'll do that again now, if I have to. This time, though, I want it to be on my terms. Instead of watching powerlessly as my safety zone disappears, I'm going to have to take the first step. As my dad walks over to me and opens his arms for a hug, I feel certain that the journey begins with him.

But not yet. He'll be here for a week, and I don't want to do anything that will ruin the time we have together. I was able to take off from work, and I have lots of activities planned. On Saturday, we go out to lunch at a new restaurant that opened in the spring and stop for dessert at one of the many creameries dotting the island. On Sunday, I take him to see Tybee Island Light and the Marine Science Center before we pack up my car and drive to the northern corner of the state to experience the sun's total eclipse the following day.

"Excited?" he asks on Monday morning, as we walk down to the lobby of the hotel where we're staying, so we can have the complimentary breakfast they offer.

"Definitely," I say. "How about you?"

"I can't wait." He grins. "Thanks for suggesting this. I'm really glad you did."

"Me, too."

"Other than the best part – spending time with you, of course – it's nice to have a bit of a break from work," he says. "Things have been even busier than usual. It's so late by the time I get home, I just have dinner in front of the television and go right to bed. Before I know it, it's time to wake up and do it all over again."

"That doesn't sound especially fun," I say.

"I've had a lot of tough cases recently," he says. "Not that I haven't had other difficult ones over the years, but . . . " He shrugs. "I guess after all this time, it gets tiring now and then."

Tiring? Practicing law?

Did he seriously just say that?

"Do you ever regret it?" The words fall out of my mouth before I can stop them. Shit. *Shit.* I'd been planning to wait until later in the week to bring this up. Today is not the time, so I instantly try to backpedal. "I mean, do you ever think you should have rented an apartment closer to the office? Then you wouldn't have such a long subway ride home after an exhausting day."

He shoots me a bemused glance as we take our plates and survey the choices for breakfast. "It's still better than driving," he says. "It's funny: for all the complaints I used to have about the roads in the Poconos, how narrow and windy they are, and how you need to be on constant alert for animals darting out . . . I suppose I got used to them. It felt weird, at first, going back to the traffic and all the pedestrians crossing the street. The subway is just easier." He chuckles. "I can't believe I'm saying this, but sometimes I actually still miss those country roads."

"Is that all you miss?"

Again, the question comes involuntarily.

But it's a good thing, actually. Because as we sit down to eat our breakfast, my dad answers in a way I never expected. "I miss a lot," he tells me. "I miss the fireflies that lit up the yard on summer nights. I miss the feeling I got when your mom convinced me to go hiking with her and it looked like we were standing on top of the world. I miss getting to see stars at night, because that's impossible in the city, with all the lights. I miss you." He smiles, but it doesn't quite reach his eyes. "And I miss your mom."

"Sometimes I miss all of that, too," I confess.

He nods, his eyes filling up with nostalgia. "Sometimes I wonder what would've happened if I'd never lost my job," he says, "and if your mom hadn't lost the baby, if we hadn't lost track of who we were to each other. Where would we all be right now?"

It is the perfect opening.

So I take it.

"It broke us, you know. The way you just . . . left." He gives a little start, and the fork he's holding clatters onto his plate. The noise seems to reverberate in my ears much louder than it should. But I don't let that stop me. "I understand it was easier for you that way," I say. "Maybe you didn't think you'd be able to go through with it otherwise . . . or maybe you were trying to protect yourself . . . but Dad, it was so much worse for us. Do you know how often we cried? I used to sit up in bed at night, because I was afraid to go to sleep in case that meant I would wake up to a house without a mother, too."

"Oh, Noelle." His face crumples like *he* is the one about to cry.

"Wait," I say, as he begins to apologize. "Please, let me finish. We pushed through, clearly. We leaned on Meredith, Grandma June, and Grandpa Travis. But mostly on one another. And we were stronger for it. That doesn't mean it didn't hurt, though." My voice catches. "I always did what you said in the note you left for me. I looked up at the stars at night and knew they were shining on you, too, even if you couldn't see them in Manhattan. It helped, but . . . " I force myself to keep my gaze steady, not to turn away from his eyes as they well up with tears. "Honestly, what would've helped most is if you'd given us the respect we deserved. Even if you felt like there wasn't any other way to make things right besides a divorce, even if the love stopped being enough for you both . . . it wasn't fair, what you did."

He is quiet for a long time.

A very long time.

I feel bad, watching as a tear slips out of his eye. I never meant to cause him any anguish. I just wanted to be truthful, to say the things I should have said many years ago. Even if it means we have to cut this trip short, if we don't get to see the eclipse and if Dad gets on the first plane back to New York, I can't regret opening myself up and confronting him. Only if I clear out the baggage I've been carrying all this time, will there be room to let something else in. Owen, maybe. But it's about more than him.

It's about me.

It's about the road that led me to where I am now and the paths that stretch forward from here.

Forward.

Not backward.

Except sometimes you have to go back before you can move ahead.

Dad takes a long breath. "I'm sorry," he says finally. "So, so sorry. The thing is . . . Noelle, honey, it was you and your mom who I wanted to protect. Not myself. It was hard enough, knowing I'd be leaving you, that I wouldn't get to hear you play the flute, or sing you a song before bed every night, or see the way your nose crinkled up every time you laughed, just like your mom's does. One of my greatest pleasures in life was making you both laugh, knowing I was responsible for that moment of joy. I thought if I ducked out during the night, if you didn't have to say goodbye, if your mom could explain why our marriage wasn't working anymore . . . " He reaches across the table to take my hand. "I thought it was the best choice. I was trying to do right by you both."

Wow.

That is not what I'd expected him to say.

It makes me wish I had done this before. Because I should've realized then when I do now: that nothing would drive my dad away. He will be there for me when I need him, and even when I don't. The divorce changed many things, but not that. He is still my dad, the man who painstakingly strung purple and green streamers through the handlebars of my bike, who made sock puppets to stop me from scratching when I had the chicken pox in first grade, and who let me stand on his feet to dance to the songs on the record player. Above all else, he's still the man who would've given my mother and me the world, if only life hadn't interfered.

"I love you," I tell him. "And I accept your apology."

"I wish you would've come to me with this a long time ago," he says. "I wish we had discussed it sooner."

Me, too.

But better late than never.

And maybe, also, better now than then, because this is when I finally feel ready to own my past.

This is when I'm truly ready to step outside it.

23

Hillary

July 3, 1993

It took until summer before I reached a place where I felt like I could handle the roller-coaster of emotion that would come with being pregnant again – and it was strange, because after all the back and forth, all the time I spent questioning if the walls of my heart were built strong enough to keep on standing through another loss, it was like clarity just found me one Saturday morning. Carter was still sleeping when I woke up, his dark curls mussed against the pillow, and I could hear Noelle out in the hallway, the floorboards creaking beneath her feet. It made me smile. Saturday mornings were my favorite time, because we had the whole weekend ahead of us. There was no listening to Carter getting dressed for work in the dark, no hurrying to take Noelle to camp, and no stocking shelf after shelf at the store. Weekends were a time for us.

"Mommy," Noelle whispered, as she poked her head into the room, holding her new plush troll doll that seemed to go everywhere with her. "Can we have chocolate chip pancakes today?"

I nodded, and she pumped her fist in the air, doing a little happy dance before she crept over to the bed and climbed in next to me. It was her routine most weekends, but as she nestled close, this time felt different. She no longer fit quite so neatly in the space below my arm. My girl was growing up. Soon she'd be losing her first tooth, and reading chapter books, and entering the science fair at school. In that moment, as Carter's eyes opened and Noelle scrambled over me to settle in between us, I realized that I didn't only want another baby because of her, or because of them. I wanted this for myself, too. I wanted a chance to once again experience the magic that came from adding a new life to the family.

It would be difficult. It would be painful.

It would be one of the highest mountains I'd ever had to scale.

Weren't those the ones, though, that offered the most breathtaking views?

I thought of the time when Meredith and I had climbed a particularly steep and rocky mountain trail, the summer after college. Even with our most padded and broken-in hiking boots, we'd had to stop every mile or so to take a break. The cold water in the thermoses we carried wasn't enough to extinguish the flames in our cheeks, and my muscles hurt so badly by the time we finally reached the summit that I didn't think I'd be able to make it back down.

"But you have to admit, this is worth it," Meredith had said, as we sat on the ground and looked at the Delaware Water Gap down below, a sea of green with a ribbon of blue curling through it. She was right. My hair was practically stuck to my neck from sweat, and I knew I would have blisters on my feet for weeks, but that view *was* worth it.

This would be, too.

"Let's go for it," I said to Carter, the minute Noelle left the room to brush her teeth and the two of us were alone. "Let's have another baby."

He stared at me, trying, I supposed, to make sense of the

sudden enthusiasm behind my words after so many months of using them as a shield. "Are you sure?" he asked, as he propped himself up on his elbow and locked his eyes on me. "Don't get me wrong," he said, "I'm elated. What changed, though?"

"Nothing," I said. "But also everything." I inched closer, tracing the line of his jaw with my nail. "I'm learning to live with the grief of the miscarriage, to live *through* it. If I give in to fear forever, it wouldn't be honoring the baby we lost. Then there's Noelle. Seeing her this morning, it just hit me, how time stops for no one. You're right. She should have a sibling to grow up with, and I don't want to wait any longer to give her that gift."

As it turned out, I did have to wait . . . and wait . . . and wait.

Carter and I started trying to get pregnant that very same night, but it just wasn't happening for us. It was an exhausting cycle. Over and over again, I let my hopes buoy themselves up every single month, only for them to come crashing back down. We tried not to get too upset – after all, it'd also taken longer to get pregnant the second time around, so maybe this was the norm for us now – but as the months slipped by, it began to feel like the universe was playing a cruel joke. I'd finally gotten to a place where I was ready to have another baby, and yet, we couldn't.

"I don't understand," I said, as I pitched a pregnancy test into the trashcan for what felt like the thousandth time. "The doctor said there wasn't any damage from the miscarriage, so why is this so impossible?" I spun on my heel and marched out of the bathroom. Carter followed, sitting with me on our bed and resting his hand on my leg.

"Maybe we should talk to the doctor," he suggested.

"Maybe we should," I agreed.

Even that wasn't enough, though. We followed the doctor's recommendations to the letter – all the charting and medical testing and scheduling – but none of it made a difference. It was the same sad story, month after month after month. The ending never gave us our happily-ever-after. Finally, one long year after that morning when I'd been filled with such faith about giving it another try, I let go instead.

"I can't keep doing this," I told Carter, as yet another pregnancy test mocked us. "It's too hard."

"But – "

"I hate that word," I said. "But maybe next time will be different . . . how often have we said that, and how much longer are we going to fool ourselves into thinking it's true?" I slunk down onto the side of the tub in the bathroom and buried my head in my hands.

"I don't think we're fooling ourselves," Carter said, as he put his palm on my back. "We're being optimistic. There isn't anything wrong with that."

"Yes, there is." I lifted my face from my hands and stared at him. "Don't you see? This is killing me. I can't do it anymore. My heart breaks all over again every time it's a 'no.' I want to stop."

"Alright." He kept his hand on my back, but it made me feel uncomfortable instead of at ease. I wanted to stand up and walk away, to scream into my pillow or to climb onto a saddle and go riding until it seemed like I'd left my heartache behind. I didn't, though. I stayed where I was, listening as Carter said all the right things. He talked about not wanting me to hurt anymore and said if it was so painful for him to go through this, he couldn't imagine how it was for me. "It's been a lot," he said. "And it's been nonstop. You're right: we *do* need a breather."

"No, not a breather." I curled my fingers around the edge of the tub, bracing myself against the cool porcelain. "I don't want to take a break. I want to stop for good." My heart picked up its pace, and my cheeks suddenly felt tingly, like my body knew the magnitude of what I was saying and was responding accordingly. "We have Noelle. She's more than enough." I took a long, shaky breath. "I don't want to try for a baby anymore. This is the end. It has to be."

The color blanched from his face. "Suppose I don't want that?" he asked.

I knew he didn't want it.

I knew I wasn't being fair to him.

I knew it was a decision we should have come to together.

I also knew that the hole I'd thought was finally patched up after the miscarriage was being torn open fresh and raw with each month. I was tired of that, tired of the prayers that went unanswered and the hope that went unfulfilled. I simply couldn't keep daydreaming of a future that wasn't ours to have.

"I'm sorry," I said quietly.

"I am, too," Carter said, and then he stood up and walked out of the bathroom.

* * *

For so many years, Carter had been the one I turned to first when I was upset. When our family farm was struggling, due to a terrible weather pattern that destroyed all the crops . . . when one of my favorite customers at the store passed away a week after his hundredth birthday . . . when I took Noelle to a friend's house shortly after the miscarriage and saw the baby that family had welcomed home a few months earlier . . . whatever flipped my emotions upside-down, he was there to help me right them. I tried to do the same for him. I was his sounding board, and he was mine.

This time was different.

How were we supposed to comfort each other when *we* were the problem?

"Can't we at least discuss this?" Carter asked. He wanted us to meet with a fertility specialist in Manhattan, and even went so far as to contact the doctor one of his work colleagues had used when she and her husband had had trouble conceiving. "It can't hurt to talk to him, right?" he said, when he came home from work one night with the phone number and address of the office on the Upper East Side.

That was where he was wrong.

It *could* hurt.

What if we talked to this doctor and still nothing changed? I couldn't handle that. It already felt like I had been slogging through quicksand on this journey to get pregnant. I needed to free myself from it. "Look," I said, "I understand why you want to do this. I just hope you can understand why I don't. We have no guarantee that doctor can help, and even if he can, there's also no guarantee the pregnancy would last. Please." I interlaced my fingers with his, holding on tight, holding on for dear life. "We've been going through this for too long. Can't we let it go and focus on everything we *are* lucky enough to have?"

Carter closed his eyes, and I could feel his sigh before I heard it. "I'll try," he said.

Sometimes trying wasn't enough, though.

It was like we couldn't stop ourselves from getting pulled into the same conversations. Around and around we went, talking in circles. The thing about circles? They led you right back where you started from – and the longer our discussions dragged on, the more tense they became. "I wish you would stop with these stories," I told Carter one night. It was late, and we should've been sleeping, but he had insisted on telling me about his best friend Finn's sister, who'd given birth that day after wrestling with infertility for years. I knew he meant it to be encouraging, but it felt like the opposite. It felt like pressure. "I've told you already," I said. "My heart can't take any more of this."

He leaned back against the headboard of our bed, folding his arms across his chest. "I guess I'm still struggling," he admitted. "With how you can give up on it."

"Give up?" My hands balled into fists. How could he say that to me after all I had been through, after all *we* had been through? "That's not how I see it," I said. "You make it sound like I don't care enough to try. Do you know how much of myself I've put into this? How much of myself I've *lost* in this? I don't want to do that anymore. I don't want to dread the day when I can take the pregnancy test each month, I don't want Noelle to catch me wiping away tears, and I don't want to look at our girl and feel despair for what we can't give her, instead of joy for what we can. And let me just put it out there, because I know you and I know this is something you've probably considered, but I don't think I can steel myself against the whole long, difficult process that'd come with adoption, either. It seems best to forget about it all."

Carter's silence was deafening.

Finally, he nodded. "Fine," he said, and reached over to shut off the lamp.

That was that.

He didn't bring it up again. I should have been relieved, but the issue was, once that circle we'd been traveling tore apart, it left a distance between us that seemed too far to bridge. Carter started working even later, and though I hated myself for it, I'd sometimes pretend to be asleep by the time he got home, lying there with my eyes closed as he climbed into bed beside me. There was an ache inside our words when we spoke, a disappointment that latched onto our conversations even when we didn't want it to, so it felt easier at times not to talk at all. Even when I was tempted to settle in his arms and let him hold me there the way he'd used to, I was too worried it wouldn't be the same anymore.

Too much had changed, and we had changed too much.

I missed the people we used to be: the couple who danced beneath the stars, and ate ice cream from the carton while watching old movies on television, and left little notes for one another on the bathroom mirror. How could we get back to that? Even when we did try – when I got up extra early to make Carter's favorite breakfast, and when he came home from work with tickets to a Broadway show I'd been dying to see, and when we drove to the beach for a weekend so Noelle could see the ocean and build sandcastles – there was still something missing. For as hard as we tried to pretend things were okay, they clearly weren't.

"Do you resent me?" I asked Carter one afternoon in early

November. He'd actually taken a day off, because we had a parent-teacher conference at Noelle's school, and as we drove home from it, listening in silence to the radio, I just couldn't stand it for another minute. How many times had we sat in the car together, talking and laughing, and, in the early days when we were only beginning to explore a relationship, wishing the red lights would last longer so we wouldn't have to say goodbye to each other yet? This silence was brutal.

As was Carter's response.

"No," he said, but it was too quick and too firm.

Who was he trying to convince, me or himself?

"I love you," he said. "And I really do see where you're coming from. Maybe I'll get there, too. Maybe one day soon, everything will stop being difficult. I want that, you know." He glanced in the rearview mirror, then pulled over to the shoulder of the road. It was just like our first date, when I'd shown him that field of dandelions. Oh, how I wished everything could be like it was then, shiny and new and filled with possibility. How could we get that luster back? How could we polish away what had tarnished?

Carter held my hand, and I told him how desperately I wanted things to be better, as well. I told him I loved him, I missed him, and I wasn't ready to give up on us, not by a long shot. We were truly worth fighting for with all we had left. "Perhaps it would help us out to see a marriage counselor," I suggested.

A shot of pain flashed in his eyes. "God, how did we get here?" he said. "How are we at a place where we need counseling?" He leaned forward, grazing his thumb over my cheek. "I'll go," he said softly. "We need to try."

The day we first walked into the therapist's office, it almost felt as though I was living someone else's life. I introduced myself, sat next to Carter on the overstuffed gray sofa, and listened as Tracy, the therapist, shared some statistics with us and explained the ways that we could help to make the counseling successful. She talked about honesty, and vulnerability, and a process she called "setting emotions free." It made sense when she explained it, that the more willing Carter and I were to put it all out there, to put *ourselves* all out there, the better a chance we had at being able to pick up the pieces of our marriage and fit them together in a new way. I just still couldn't believe we had to do it. I thought back to the day Carter proposed – that crystal clear spring day, with the birds chirping, the sun shining, and the wildflowers on the mountain smelling impossibly sweet. He had taken me back to the place where we'd met, and I could still remember his beautiful smile when he got down on one knee.

"This is where I fell for you," he said. "Literally." A sparkle danced in his eyes. "The concussion I ended up with was worth it. I love you, Hillary, more than I knew it was possible to love somebody, and I want nothing more than to spend every day of my life making you as happy as you make me." He reached into his pocket and pulled out a small velvet box. "Will you marry me?"

"Yes!" The word was out of my mouth before he could even open the box. I cried when he did, when he slipped the glittery diamond onto my finger and took me in his arms, spinning me around. I had never been so deliriously happy.

Now, sitting here in the counselor's office, listening as she asked if we could each identify where we thought our marriage had gone off-track, I couldn't help crying because I was so very sad – and, it turned out, so entirely out of sync with Carter. He told Tracy that our trouble had begun when he first brought up the idea of having another baby after the miscarriage, but I knew it was before then. Letting my thoughts meander backward, thinking of the path that had led us here, I was certain we hadn't traversed the whole distance in that time. "Honestly," I said, dabbing my eyes with the tissue Tracy offered me, "I think it started when Carter went back to work in New York."

"What?" His eyes went wide, filled with hurt, as he looked at me.

It was awful.

I tried to hold his gaze, but it was hard. I hated seeing that pain and knowing I was the one who was causing it. "Or maybe it was even before that," I said quietly, forcing myself to speak my truth, though I didn't want to. This could only work if we held nothing back. "Remember when you asked if I ever felt like I was suffocating here?" I said to Carter. "When you said something was missing for you? It crushed me to think that our life together wasn't enough." I nodded, maybe more to myself than to him. "*That's* where it began. A baby was supposed to fix the problems that we were already having, but instead things broke even more. The miscarriage, the infertility, the arguments . . . " My shoulders started to shake as my tears turned to sobs.

"Don't cry," Carter said, but Tracy shook her head.

"Let her," she said. "You can't move forward if you get in your own way."

What happened, though, when you couldn't move forward even when you *did* try not to be your own worst obstacle? Carter and I did everything Tracy suggested. We went to our weekly sessions. We talked about the way it had left me reeling when Carter returned to work in Manhattan, the way he had felt so conflicted between his happiness at being back in the city he loved, doing the work he loved, and his guilt over not being home more for Noelle and me. We said maybe it hadn't been the best decision to try to have another baby when we did, that it'd been the wrong idea for all the right reasons. We took action, too. We made a conscious effort to rekindle the romance in our marriage, to take Noelle to my parents' house two weekends a month and spend that time concentrating only on the two of us. Sometimes, when Carter played his guitar for me or when we went to chop down our Christmas tree together, it seemed like it was helping. Other times, it reminded us things were so different now – but we kept on trying, however and whenever we could.

We shifted our focus to Noelle. We talked to each other every night before bed, rather than let the silence take over. We followed the ideas Tracy laid out for us, and we even brainstormed some of our own. In the end, though, none of it changed the fact that Carter and I simply didn't want the same things out of life anymore. I needed him to be back in the Poconos full-time, and he still could not let go of having another baby. All the effort in the world couldn't reconcile our divergent paths. Sometimes fighting too hard just took the fight out of you instead.

Perhaps I shouldn't have been so shocked, then, when I woke up one morning, a couple months after Noelle's eighth birthday, to an envelope on Carter's pillow, addressed to me. Tears swelled up behind my eyelids as I opened it and read the letter he'd written. No. This couldn't be. What I was reading, it had to be wrong. My brain began to scream wildly, desperately. How could he do this to me? How could he do this to us? My hands clutched the letter, unable to let go, as I read his words again.

My dear Hillary,

As I write this, I can't help thinking of our wedding day. It was one of the best and happiest days of my life. Knowing the future was ours . . . I can't explain how excited that made me. Maybe I don't have to explain, because you understand. You know my heart, and I know yours. That's why I can't do this face-to-face. I can't look into those pretty green eyes of yours, knowing I'm about to change the way they look at the world forever. It'd break me, and I think it might break you, too.

I'd never forgive myself if I did that to you.

In the eleven years since we met, I've always tried to do right by you. Our marriage isn't working anymore, though. I don't see how we can save it, and I hate that. It tears me up inside when I think about it, and I can tell it's been doing the same thing to you. We have to stop. I know we could still continue the counseling, but I truly believe it wouldn't do any good. We've gotten to the point where I think staying together hurts more than being apart, and I love you enough to put an end to that. I'll always love you: for better or worse, just like we promised. Walking away is the best way I know to honor that.

I hope you can forgive me. I hope we can both heal now.

And more than anything else, I hope you can find happiness again.

Love,

Carter

Just like that, he was gone.

24

NOELLE

August 21, 2017

The eclipse is out of this world.

For all the articles I've read about total eclipses and all the pictures I've looked at online, nothing could've really prepared me for how majestic it would be to see it in person. The articles described it as captivating, an astronomical phenomenon. And it is. Watching the sky grow darker, the moon seemingly slipping down from the heavens above, it gives me goosebumps, and not just because the temperature drops more and more with each ray of light that disappears.

"This is amazing," I say to my dad.

"Mesmerizing," he agrees.

We're sitting together by the lake, our eyes laser-focused on the sky. We opted against joining the big crowds of people gathered together to watch the eclipse. Sure, it might've been fun, but this is something we wanted to do just the two of us. Dad and daughter, the same as when I was young. We sit quietly, looking through the protective glasses that my dad ordered. The moon keeps sinking lower, the sun bowing in reverence, until there's a black circle which appears to be suspended in the sky. We take off our glasses, and my breath catches in my throat. A total eclipse.

It's extraordinary. The fuzzy halo around the moon, the burst of glowing white light . . . getting to see the corona of the sun is beyond words.

It is a wonder. It is a spectacle.

It is awe-inspiring.

And it is also a reminder.

Experiencing this with my dad takes me right back to all the times when we used to look through the lens of a telescope and study the stars. It's been so long since I let the sky teach me a lesson. It feels right, doing that today. Like the sun starting to shine again as the moon continues its journey. Even after my dad and I put the glasses back on, after the cloak of darkness begins to lighten, I can't shake the feeling of enchantment at it all.

"So?" my dad asks. "What do you think?"

"I think that was incredible." I watch as the crescent of sunlight grows into a disc. "I remember something Owen told me on the day we met. He was talking about why he's so drawn to the ocean, and he said it makes him feel big and small at the same time. That's exactly what this does for me." I smile at him. "I'm so glad we get to share this. That makes it even more special."

"For me, too," he says.

We sit there awhile longer, and I expect him to bring it up again, the way I can still dust off those old dreams of mine and see if there's anything left to make of them, but he doesn't. He just asks me how the *Anchor Stop* is doing and offers up a few pieces of news from his own life. I learn about the guitar lessons he's been giving to a colleague's son, helping him master the chords so he can try out for the school band, and also that he broke things off with Marie, the woman he had been seeing for the past couple months.

"It didn't feel right," he says. "She's a great woman, but we weren't clicking."

"How do you know that wouldn't change in the future?" I ask.

He glances off in the distance for a minute, watching as a bird swoops down and perches in one of the trees. Then he turns back to me. "Because once you've experienced true love, you can't ever forget how it makes you feel," he says. "Everything else gets measured up against it. It isn't fair, but that's how it goes. Your mom . . . she made everything bigger . . . brighter . . . better. When something good happened, she was the person I wanted to share it with, and when something bad happened, she was the one I turned to to help me through it. The connection we had was so strong. It wasn't like that with Marie. Honestly, it wasn't like that with any of the women I've dated since your mom and I got divorced."

There's something in his voice that gives me pause.

It's more than nostalgia. Regret, maybe?

"Do you ever second-guess your choice to leave?" I ask.

"I used to," he says. "Even though I knew getting divorced was what we needed, I still hated it. Sometimes the best decisions are also the worst ones." He sighs, then shakes his head slightly, like he's trying to snap himself out of his thoughts. "Hey, do you want to go for a drive?" he asks. "We can see some of the sights before we head back to Tybee Island."

"Sure," I say. "Sounds good."

The area of Georgia where we traveled to see the eclipse is all the way up by the Carolinas, and it feels so different than the coast. Looking out the window as my dad drives, it's tough to believe I'm even in the same state anymore. There are fields that stretch far and wide, rocks that lead down to hidden swimming holes below the trees, and waterfalls that splash with such intensity you can often hear them before they come into view. The scent of pine needles drifts toward us when I lower the window. It's immediately familiar. It's strange, how you can leave a place behind, but it never fully leaves you. The Poconos. That's what it reminds me of here.

The memories hit me at full force.

The time we went on a family hike and Dad got his shoelace stuck under a rock.

The time I was looking through my telescope and caught a shooting star racing across the sky.

The time my mother and I camped out and toasted s'mores for breakfast.

The time my grandparents taught me how to harvest the lettuce they grew.

The time I walked in on Jesse's phone call that I was never meant to hear.

So many memories.

Too many.

"Are you okay?" my dad asks, as I turn my attention away from the window.

Suddenly, I don't want to sightsee anymore. I just want to go home.

"I'm fine," I say.

"Are you really?"

I could maintain the facade. I could change the subject back to the eclipse, or the rest of his visit to Georgia, or . . . anything, really, because there is nothing I would rather talk about less than Jesse, the man who so cavalierly shook up my life without any regard as to how it might settle. But then I think about Owen. Owen, who sent me a picture of the eclipse over the ocean, so I could see how it looked there, too. Owen, who made me smile even from afar. What Dad was saying before, about experiencing true love, I don't know what that's like, but maybe Owen could be the one to show me. Or maybe not. I have no idea. But what I do know is this: I owe it to him, and to myself, to find out. That can't happen if I continue to sidestep these conversations about Jesse. It's not just my mother I need to talk about Jesse with, but also my dad.

So I drop the act.

"No," I say. "I'm not fine. This place is so much like the

Poconos. It brought up some memories I'd rather not think about again."

"Jesse," he says, and I nod.

"He saw me, you know. On the day of the wedding. He was in the lobby of the church with his parents and Brendan, and he looked up as I ran out. The way his eyes narrowed, maybe he thought the wedding was off. I *hope* he thought that, even if only for a short while." My voice twists around itself. "I despise him," I say. "I'm not proud of that, and I wish I could let go of the bitterness, I wish I could forget about him – "

"You can't," my dad says. "Maybe what you can do, though, is forgive."

I stare at him, baffled. "Forgive?" I echo.

"Okay, so perhaps not Jesse," he concedes. "But your mom. Yourself."

"Myself?"

What does he mean?

"Noelle, sweetheart, you couldn't have stopped him." His voice is soft. "You didn't have all the facts. You did what you could, and that was enough."

"Except it wasn't," I point out. "She still married him."

"That was her decision to make," he says. "And you've gotta remember, she didn't have all the facts, either. All of us, we can only go by what we know and how we feel. Look, I surely don't agree with what she did, and I know it's far easier said than done, but try not to let one bad choice destroy all the good ones."

One bad choice.

It was so much more than that.

Is my dad right, though? Could I possibly forgive it?

I'd like to.

I think again of the eclipse, of the way it brushed the sky into total blackness, only to brighten it back up. It was like witnessing magic, and it had stirred something deep inside of me. Something I'd thought was long gone, something I'd convinced myself I no longer wanted . . . and something I didn't even realize I missed until it was right there in front of me again. And it makes me see: perhaps we really *do* need a shadow sometimes. After all, when the sky is darkest, that's when we can best view the stars.

* * *

I have a lot of thinking to do.

My mind is all aflutter on the drive to Tybee Island, constantly flitting back to the things my dad said, trying to make sense of them. Not once, in all the years since my relationship with my mother splintered into a shell of its former self, did I stop to consider that perhaps she and Jesse weren't the only ones I was furious with. I couldn't see it then. When I'd left, I was too blinded by my tears, my fears. I was so desperate to get away, I hadn't even changed out of my maid-of-honor's dress. I still remember the look I got when I burst into the small tattoo shop by the Pennsylvania-Maryland state line. The guy working there was probably only a few years older than I was, and his eyebrows went sky-high when I pushed through the door. I knew I must've looked like a mess, my face splotchy and mascara-stained, my carefully-styled curls flopping down my back after I'd driven with the windows open for the past two and a half hours.

"Can I help you?" the guy asked. "Is everything alright?"

I'd been worried that I would lose it again when I answered, that those simple words of kindness from a stranger would be all it took to unravel my emotions which were hanging on by a thread. But I surprised myself. My voice was steady, filled with the sort of clarity that can maybe only be found in the midst of chaos. "It hasn't been the greatest day," I told him. "I know what can make it better, though."

An hour later, the stars were forever inked into my skin.

And it *had* made things better, at least for a little while, until I stopped at a nearby hotel for the night. I could feel the anger pushing back then, straining against the walls of my chest. I was mad at Jesse for taking my mother away from me. I was mad at her for letting herself get so manipulated. I was mad at Meredith and my grandparents for supporting a wedding that shouldn't have happened. I didn't sleep much that night. I just stared at the water-stained ceiling of my hotel room, bouncing back and forth between pulsing fury and, still, the tiniest sliver of hope that my mother would come get me.

She didn't, of course.

I hadn't been surprised.

I was used to her letting me down by then.

I guess maybe that's why it was so easy to pile all the anger on her instead of directing any of it toward myself. Tonight, though, I find myself staring at a ceiling once again. I keep hearing the echo of my dad's words in my head: *you did what you could, and that was enough*. All of this time, is that what it's really been about? Because my mother did eventually reach out. She begged me to come home, and she drove straight to see me after Jesse's ugly deception was fully revealed, and she has apologized over and over. But maybe it's not her betrayal I can't shake. Maybe it's the quieter truth that rests inside it: that I hadn't been enough. Enough for her to believe me instead of him. Enough for her to back me up, no questions asked, because I am her daughter and mothers are supposed to be there for their children unconditionally. All those years together, just the two of us, feel like they were a lie. No, I hadn't been able to stop my mother from falling into Jesse's trap, but there's more to it than that, too.

I get out of bed, flip on the light, and walk over to my closet.

There it is, nestled into the furthest corner, my box of memories.

I carry it into the middle of my bedroom, sit down cross-legged on the carpet, and slip off the lid. The letters are at the bottom, tucked beneath my high school diploma, the mosaic fox that Eliza and I created for art class in fifth grade, and the first afghan my mother knitted for me after I was born. I don't know what made me take it as I was packing my things, but I unfold it now and graze my hand over the soft pink and yellow yarn. Then I unearth the letters. All three of them.

I take a deep breath, pick up the first one, and begin to read.

Dear Noelle,

My sweet daughter, I hope you know how much I adore you. Life took on a new meaning when you were born. Your mom and I were forever changed. How I've loved watching you grow up these past eight years. You're smart, fearless, and inquisitive – the brightest star in my sky. Do me a favor, okay? Keep asking those questions, and chasing those fireflies, and turning those cartwheels across the yard. Also, don't give up on that flute. Don't give up on anything you want, ever. I know things are going to be confusing for awhile, and that you'll be sad not to see me. I'm going to be very sad, too, but I'll always love you. Here's what I want you to do: each night, as you look at the stars, know that they're shining down on me, the same way they are on you. Even though we will be in different places, the stars will connect us still.

I want you to know, this isn't about you. I'm not leaving because of something you did or didn't do. Sometimes marriages just don't work out, no matter how hard people try or how much they love each other. That's what happened here. Your mom will need you now, more than ever. Give her so many hugs, let her do the same for you, and don't forget, I'm just a phone call away. We'll see each other soon, honey, I promise.

Lots of love,

Daddy

I've read that letter so often over the years, I practically have it memorized. My mother read it with me the first time. I didn't understand then, of course. Even after I did, I still often returned to my dad's words. They made me feel close to him when he was far away. The next letter in the pile, though, the one that had caught me so off-guard when I got it in the mail eleven years ago . . . that's a different story. I've only read it once. Maybe there was something I missed, in all of my anguish. I hope so. I take another breath and steel myself against the words.

Noelle,

It's hard to believe it's been a year. How shocking to think I've gone three hundred and sixty five days without my girl, but at the same time, it feels like much longer since you left. Your absence still fills everything I do. I still add extra garlic to the rolls I make, because that's how you like them, I still go into your room to get the lilac lotion you always borrowed from me, and I still reach for the phone after every episode of American Idol, ready to hand it to you so you can vote.

Still . . . that's the word which seems to characterize all I do.

I hope you know how much I love you, sweetheart, how much I forever will. No one can change that, including Jesse. I'll always regret the way things unfolded with him, but I want you to know, he is still here. He hasn't abandoned me, and he hasn't ruined my life, like you were worried he would. I hope you can make peace with that. We'd love for you to come home, so we can all be a family. It may not be easy, but we want to try. It would make me so happy if you would, too. Please give me the chance to make things right.

I miss you, and I love you with all my heart.

Mom

I remember the way my breath had come in quick rasps as I read her letter the first time. It got to me in the beginning, her mention of the rolls, the lotion, and the show we had watched together religiously, ever since it premiered. She tugged on all the right heartstrings. Then I kept reading. Hearing about her life with Jesse made me bristle. I knew she was trying to smooth things over and assure me that my suspicion was misplaced, but it did the opposite. Because she was wrong about him. I was even more certain then than I'd been on the day they got married.

Now she's certain, too.

I think, again, of the morning I opened the door and found her on the other side, after she had driven all night to Georgia to apologize. I wanted to forgive her then, to put my arm around her the way she'd done so often for me, but when I looked at her, all I could see was the image of her in the bridal suite, just standing there as I ran out. She didn't come after me. She let me go, and she chose to stay. I couldn't get past that.

Can I now?

Can I do what my dad said, and give myself the freedom that comes with forgiveness?

I don't know.

I lie back right in the middle of my bedroom, holding the letters from my parents to my chest. I don't think I have it in me to read the third one. The one from the college I'd wanted to go to more than anyplace else, the college where I wasn't only accepted to the physics and astronomy program, but was also granted enough scholarship money to make the tuition manageable. I'd been beyond excited to go to school there. I had my classes all picked out. But then life got in the way.

Then *I* got in my way.

The question is: can I get out of it now?

25

Hillary

March 30, 1995

It was like someone had ripped my heart out of my chest.

Carter was gone.

His clothes were still in the closet, hanging in rows above his neatly lined up loafers, but all over our bedroom, the little things were missing. His electric razor no longer sat in its charger, the books he kept on his nightstand had been removed, and his terrycloth robe wasn't hanging from the hook on the bathroom door anymore. It was all such a terrible nightmare . . . except it wasn't. As I stood in the bathroom, unable to look away from the place where that robe had been every single day since we'd moved into the house, the realization was so visceral, a literal slap in the face would have hurt less.

How was this happening?

My eyes flicked toward the window, where bright sunshine was filtering in through the blinds. I knew it meant I had to get moving, that I couldn't just stand there, staring at a room which suddenly felt foreign. Noelle had to get ready for school. Noelle. What was I going to tell her? She wouldn't know anything was amiss, not yet, because Carter always left for work before I woke her up. Could I pull myself together and fake normalcy for her sake?

It was doubtful, but I had to try.

If I could just somehow hold it together until I dropped her off at school, then I could talk to my parents, and Meredith, and maybe even Carter, if I was able to find him. Perhaps he was headed to his brother's place in New York, or to Finn's. Really, though, what would happen if we discussed it? He'd come home? We'd discover a way to work it out? Even as I wandered out of the bedroom, his letter still clutched in my hand, I knew I was being naive. I also knew Carter was right. What he had written, how our marriage wasn't the same anymore, how it was breaking us down in ways we could never have imagined, was true. It'd been such a slow fall that I didn't know if either of us had even realized the depth of the drop until it left us unable to climb back up.

God, we'd been so euphoric on our wedding day. We'd gotten married outside by the pond on my parents' farm, and I'd worn an off-the-shoulder gown, all lace and beadwork. I'd never been one for fairytales, but in that dress, I felt like a princess. The smile on Carter's face when he saw me for the first time would stay with me for as long as I lived. It was as though his soul was full of sunshine. Mine had been, too. As I stood there holding his hands, promising to love him forever, it felt like my heart would burst with happiness. After we were declared husband and wife, we had our reception right there by the pond. The dancing, the speeches, the cutting of the cake . . . I loved it all, but there was one special moment in particular, as I was preparing to toss my bouquet. It was all wildflowers, and so was the boutonniere attached to the lapel of Carter's navy suit jacket.

"These were the perfect choice," he'd said. "I think they mean our marriage will bloom in ways we can't even know right now. I'm glad we didn't opt for something traditional, like roses or tulips. This feels more fitting." He was right, because we were untraditional, too. I was the country girl, he was the city boy, and together we were magic. At least, that was what it felt like that evening, as he twirled me around to dance and we toasted each other with the fancy champagne flutes his parents had gotten engraved with our initials.

The thing about magic, though, is that it can't last forever.

Nothing ever truly disappears behind the curtain.

Carter and I tried. Through the job struggles, the miscarriage, the infertility . . . we kept doing our best to show up for one another. He was right, though: when being there made it worse, not better, why keep doing that to ourselves? For as much as I wanted to tear his letter into pieces, I couldn't. I couldn't lie to Noelle, either. I stood outside her room for . . . honestly, I lost track of how long. Time slipped away from me as I thought about how I could ever make this okay for her.

Her father had left without saying goodbye.

She knew how much he loved her, how Carter and I both felt the sun rose and set by her smile, but still, she was just eight-years-old. There was no way she'd be able to understand the complexity of the situation. As I eased open her door, watching as she slept, curled up on her side with Floppity settled in her arms, I was reminded of when she was a baby. Everybody told me then to sleep while she slept, and they were right, but sometimes I only wanted to sit and watch her, to memorize every little thing about her as she found her own dreamland. It was the same now. She looked peaceful, innocent.

I couldn't bring myself to take that away from her, not yet. She could miss school for one day, I decided. If I kept her home, it would give me awhile longer to figure out how to handle things, how to protect her to the best of my ability.

As it turned out, though, I couldn't do that at all.

I went downstairs, sinking into the sofa and reading Carter's letter over and over, and I must've gotten so lost in my thoughts that I didn't even hear Noelle come down the steps. It wasn't until she was standing right in front of me that I realized she was there – and that she was holding something. It was an envelope similar to the one with my name on it. Carter had written her a letter, too.

I felt my chest begin to ache as I looked at it.

"I found this on my desk when I got up," Noelle said. "It's from Daddy. He always puts a smiley face inside the 'o' of my name." She sat beside me. "How come you look so sad?" she asked. "And why didn't you wake me up? I don't have school today?"

"Honey, I . . . " Those two words were all it took for my voice to crack.

"Mommy?" Noelle tilted her head to the side, looking at me with worry.

I took a deep breath so I could try to reassure her it was all going to be okay, that *we* were going to be okay, but I knew there wasn't any point. There was a bond between Noelle and me, a mother-daughter connection my own mom had talked about, but that I hadn't been able to fully understand until I, too, was a parent. No matter how my girl was feeling, I could tell just by looking at her, and it went both ways. Noelle was very smart. She was reading at a grade level above her classmates, she knew more about the stars and the solar system than I could ever hope to learn, and she got straight As on her report cards. Beyond that, she had terrific intuition. She'd know if I wasn't being honest, and it wasn't fair to burden her like that.

I owed her the truth, but where did I even begin?

I glanced over at the mantel.

In the center was a framed picture from our wedding. We'd taken the classic shots – the two of us by the pond, both of us with our families, the bridal party in front of the barn – but I'd requested quirky ones, too. There was a photo on horseback, Twinkle with wildflowers woven into her mane, and another in the field where we had made wishes on those dandelions on our first date. This one was my favorite, though. Carter had lifted me up, and I had one arm around his shoulder, the other holding my bouquet high in the air. Both of us were positively beaming.

I'd looked at that picture so many times over the years.

That day, though, I didn't see it the same way. *I am so furious with you*, I thought, as I stared at Carter's image. *No matter what pain you were trying to spare us, leaving like this actually made it a million times worse. Now I have to explain this all on my own.*

His choice, helpful as he might have intended it to be, felt like the opposite, but what could I do about it?

Nothing.

He'd robbed me of taking part in the decision. I could only work with what I had.

I pulled Noelle onto my lap and wrapped my arms around her, resting my chin on her shoulder. "I think we should read that letter from your dad, sweetie," I told her. "That'll answer some of your questions, and then I can try to help you sort through the rest. Okay?" When she nodded, her silky curls tickled my cheek.

"Okay," she said.

It was so much worse than I could have imagined. Carter had written all the right things to her, but pretty words couldn't disguise an ugly reality. Of course Noelle didn't understand. We had tried to keep our problems from her, and although I knew we hadn't always been successful, I also knew the idea of her parents not being together wasn't even on her radar. The look on her face when she turned to me to help her make sense of it, this combination of distress, fear, and incomprehension, squeezed unbearably at my heart.

"Daddy doesn't want to live with us anymore?" she asked.

"Oh, baby." I tucked her hair behind her ear, the same way I had done so many times when she was little and her curls had escaped the barrettes that tried to hold them in place. "He thinks it's for the best that he lives someplace else right now, but I want you to always remember how very much he loves you," I said.

"But he doesn't love you? Did you have a fight?"

"Not exactly," I said. "Your daddy still loves me, and I love him – "

"Then why did he go away?"

"It's a grown-up thing." I struggled to find the words to

explain. None of them felt adequate for the situation. "It's just, sometimes love isn't enough. When your dad and I got married, we had the same ideas of what we wanted in our lives, but that's changed over time. It's like . . . remember how you used to love playing with your Cabbage Patch dolls? You dressed them up, took them for walks in the stroller, and set them up on the porch swing so you could give them a lesson about the stars. They aren't your favorite anymore, though. Now you'd rather play with pogs, or your Skip-It, or our board games. That's what happened to Dad and me. The things we want have changed."

"But can't you meet in the middle? That's what my teacher always says. Like the last time when we had indoor recess. Half of us voted to play Seven-Up and the other half wanted to do Hangman. Mrs. Hutchinson said we could do each one for part of the time. If you and Daddy share your ideas, too, then you can both be happy and he'll come home." She looked at me so eagerly, I was tempted to tell her what she wanted to hear, just so I wouldn't have to be the one to take away her hope.

This agony was Carter's fault.

Anger thrummed at my temples as I saw the way Noelle was still clutching his letter. How dare he think that was enough. I wanted to storm out of the house, drive to wherever it was he'd fled to, and drag him back to be part of this conversation. I had no doubt that Noelle would've had trouble accepting a separation between us no matter what, but at least if we had been able to talk through it together, then maybe we could've helped make it a bit easier for her.

Instead, I was left alone with this impossible task.

"I'm sorry, sweetheart," I said. I felt crestfallen as her face fell. There was nothing worse in the world than knowing you were the person responsible for your own child's unhappiness. "I'm afraid this is more complicated than your recess games," I tried to explain. "Sometimes it isn't possible to compromise, even if you want to more than anything."

"Why?" she asked.

I had that very same question. *Why?*

"I don't know," I said. "I wish I could answer that, but I can't."

Tears started to roll down her cheeks and drip onto her pajamas. I didn't know what to do – not for her, and not for myself, either. There was no bandage to put on a wound that cut this deep. All I could do was hold her, brush away her tears, and promise that somehow everything would be fine, even if it didn't feel like it at the time. I couldn't tell whether she believed me. Honestly, I couldn't tell whether I believed myself.

That was how it went for so many weeks and months ahead.

Noelle and I leaned on my parents a lot, and Meredith, too. My mom insisted on bringing meals so I wouldn't have to worry about cooking, and my dad's clunky station wagon showed up in front of the house every morning. He could have just called, but it was like he needed to see for himself that I was still standing. It was the same with Meredith. She was back in school, working at the ski resort by day and attending classes to get her masters' degree in sports medicine at night, but even with all that, she still found time to be there for us.

"I don't know how to thank you," I told her one evening. It'd been an especially brutal day. My divorce papers had arrived in the mail, and holding them in my hands, seeing the dissolution of our marriage written in such formal terms, had literally brought me to my knees. Thankfully Noelle had been at her new friend Eliza's house, because if she had witnessed my reaction I wouldn't have ever forgiven myself. Holding the papers to my chest, I had let myself sink down onto the floor, sobbing until my eyes stung. I had wanted to call Carter and ask him how in the world our happily-ever-after could've turned into this, maybe even plead with him to rip up his set of papers before the vows we had taken were broken for good. I'd come close to doing it, but before I could dial the number to his new apartment in Manhattan, I thought about the days when he'd worked for twelve hours straight, the nights when I had yearned to kiss him but ended up turning the other way instead. Falling back into a marriage that had failed us wasn't fair to anyone, most of all Noelle.

I'd called Meredith instead, and there she was. There she always was.

"You never have to thank me," she said. "You are my best friend, and you've always been there for me. You come to every art show and have smiled through all the concerts I've ever dragged you to, because it was no fun to go alone. Remember the time my car broke down and you had to come pick me up from Philadelphia at one in the morning? You never hesitated. So yes, damn straight I'm here when you need me." I was sitting in the family room, watching some game show but not really seeing it, and she dropped down beside me, holding a carton of fudge brownie ice cream. "You can do it," she promised. "You can figure out how to live without him. You already are."

"It doesn't feel like it sometimes."

"I know." She handed me a bowl and kept the second one for herself. I appreciated her candor, how she didn't try to gloss things over. Sometimes that was exactly what I needed, but other times it was just about having someone sit there next to me. Meredith was my person for that, and for so much more. She was there when I signed the divorce papers, when I took off my wedding ring and locked it away in the jewelry box, and, when all of the memories became too much, when I could no longer stand to spend another day in the house that'd been my home with Carter, I decided to move in with my parents. She even helped me pack things up.

Noelle did, too, although she had mixed feelings about selling the house. "I really love Grandma and Grandpa," she said, as we sat on her bed and boxed up the books from her shelves. "And I think it will be fun to live in their farmhouse and be around the animals. But I'll miss it here."

"Come here." I set down a stack of books and held out my arms. She settled into them. "This is hard," I told her. "All of this has been so very, very hard, and I want you to know how proud I am of you for showing such grace through everything."

"Grace?" She looked up at me. "What do you mean?"

"I mean . . . this." I reached over to pick up the notepad on her nightstand. "The letters you have been writing to your dad, the pictures you've been drawing of the stars you see in your telescope, so he can look at them, too, the phone calls you have with him, and your visits to New York every month . . . it'd be easy to be upset with your dad, but instead you're putting on a brave face."

"Not always. Sometimes I get super sad," she said. "Like when he couldn't come to my science fair and it made me feel left out 'cause my friends had both parents there. Or when I can't sleep at night and go into your room to be sure you're still there. I don't feel brave then."

"Oh, my girl, but you are. Sometimes being brave means letting yourself feel all that sadness in here." I put a hand to my chest. "It's tough to let ourselves hurt," I said. "But when we do that, and we stand tall anyway, that's what courage is."

"Like you?" she asked. "Standing tall all by yourself?"

I kissed the top of her head. "I'm not all by myself," I told her. "I've got Grandma and Grandpa, Meredith, and most especially you. We'll keep on getting through this, Noelle. I promise. We'll do it together."

"Together," she repeated. "Okay, Mommy. We can do that."

In that moment, sitting there with her in my arms, surrounded by cartons and packing tape and the whispers of a fresh start that came from leaving this ending behind . . . in that moment I believed, for the first time, that maybe we actually could.

26

NOELLE

August 25, 2017

$\mathcal{T}$he rest of my dad's visit goes by far too fast. Wednesday is spent on a dolphin watching cruise, and on Thursday we relax on the beach and by the pool at the *Anchor Stop*. When we first discussed his trip, I'd offered for him to stay with me at my condo, but he had been firm about not wanting to inconvenience me. "I'll book a room at your hotel," he said. "I have it on good authority that it's the best one on Tybee Island."

"If only everyone else agreed," I said.

It's been over a month and a half now since I had that conversation with him, but I can't tell yet if other vacationers have that same opinion. The incentives we've been offering seem to be helping. The restaurant's seen an uptick in business since we added the twenty-percent off coupons to every guest's welcome packet, and Owen says people have been commenting on the revised check-in and check-out times. "The extra hour really appears to be a big deal," he says on Friday morning, when I stop by the front desk to say hi before meeting my dad for breakfast in the restaurant.

"It was a good idea to change it," I say. "The person who suggested it must be incredibly smart."

This makes him grin, which makes *me* grin, too. Instinctively. Widely.

So of course that's the moment the elevator doors open and my dad walks out into the lobby.

Of course.

"Good morning," he says, as he joins us. I hear the inflection in his voice, that what-is-going-on-here tone, and I see the way he raises his eyebrows as his gaze passes from me to Owen, then back again. "How are you both today?"

"Doing well, thanks," Owen says. "How about you?"

He shoots me a look before turning to my dad, and a flush sneaks into my cheeks. It's like we're sharing a secret, just the two of us, and I love that. And as I stand there, listening as Owen talks with my dad, I realize how different life is when I'm around him now. Its volume is turned up. Even right at this moment, knowing I'm going to get an inquisition from my dad as soon as we're alone, I'm still okay with it.

Which is a good thing, because sure enough, once Dad and I are seated at a window table in the restaurant, he jumps right in. "So . . . Owen," he says. Tell me about him."

I give my most nonchalant shrug as I open my menu and glance inside. "There's not much to tell that you don't already know. We've been working together even more than usual recently, trying to keep the *Anchor Stop* afloat. He's had some fantastic thoughts."

"I'm sure he has," my dad says. "But there's only one I'm interested in right now, and that's the one which pertains to you."

I look up from the menu and meet his eyes. "What do you mean?"

"I mean," he says, "that it's obvious something is going on between you two. I saw the way you were looking at him, and I saw the way he was looking at you, like you're the sunshine."

My smile is involuntary. I try to fight it back at first, but I can't.

And why should I, really?

Owen makes me happy. There's no point in denying that. So I don't.

"Nothing is going on," I say to my dad. "At least, not yet, anyway." I pause as Kerry comes over to take our order. It feels odd, being on the other side of things, ordering the Dolphin's Tail combo-breakfast instead of checking on guests to see if they're enjoying it. But nothing could feel stranger than the conversation with my dad that picks up again after Kerry's gone back to the kitchen. Telling Eliza how I feel about Owen is one thing. Opening up to my dad is another. It seems cruel to say the truth, that the divorce is part of what has made me hesitant. We've come too far, especially on this trip, to take a step backward.

Luckily, my dad has it covered.

"Owen is a good guy," he says. "And more importantly, he's a good guy for you."

"How do you know that?" I ask.

"Because I'm a lawyer," he says. "Which means I'm trained to notice every detail, big and small. When I walked out of the elevator before, I saw how Owen was standing. He was leaning in to your conversation, like he couldn't get close enough. And when I checked-in last week, he recognized me from your pictures and immediately started talking about how you've been trying to save the hotel. It wasn't so much what he said, as how he said it. He had the same smile you have whenever you're talking about him."

Almost as if on cue, the corners of my mouth curl up again.

"See?" My dad gives a quick wink. "The prosecution rests. Case closed."

What about the defense, though?

What about *my* defenses?

"Knock them down," my dad advises, after I confide in him how nervous I still am about messing with the decade of friendship Owen and I have built. "Maybe it'll work, or maybe it won't, but you'll never know unless you try."

"Do you regret doing that?" I ask. "Trying for so long to save your marriage?"

"No," he says. "Not at all."

"Even with the way things ended up?"

"Especially because of that." He glances down at the place where his wedding ring used to live. "I'm proud of the way your mom and I fought for our marriage. Even if we eventually lost the battle, that doesn't mean it wasn't worth the fight. I actually think the divorce is a testament to how much we cared. Does that sound weird?" He chuckles a bit, but it seems more sad than anything. "It got to a point where we loved each other enough to recognize it was time to give in," he explains. "We didn't give up, though, and I think that's an important distinction. We just did what was best. Now it's time for you to do the same. Forget about your mom and me. Think about yourself, and Owen, and how you'd feel if you opt not to pursue this and he shows up at work one day and tells you he's met someone else."

His words set off an alarm in my head. I've never thought about it that way.

All this time, I have been going over the situation again and again, trying to decide if the reward would outweigh the risk. But suppose that risk actually comes not from taking a chance, but instead from letting it pass me by? Owen's had two girlfriends in the years since we've known one another. Rachel and Lindsay. I never particularly cared for either of them, though I couldn't pinpoint exactly why. They were perfectly nice, but it was like my dad had described things with Marie: I didn't think they were right for him.

If Owen were to find someone else, someone who isn't me, and it *did* seem right?

I feel like my heart might not be able to recover from that.

I've been so cautious about putting our friendship on the line, so firm in my belief that I'd never forgive myself if I did anything to destroy it. But maybe *this* is where I'd never forgive myself: if I let him slip away without seeing where this could go. I look across the table at my dad. A touch of gray is starting to creep into his dark hair these days, and the tortoiseshell glasses he always used to wear have been replaced by rimless ones. He's changed a lot since I was a child. The twinkle in his eyes is no longer quite as bright. I think of what he said the other day, how he has never been able to find anyone else he loves like he did my mother, how sometimes he still misses her, even after all these years. I don't want to be like that.

And so, after I drive my dad to the airport that evening, hugging him goodbye and promising to come to New York to visit him again soon, I know what I have to do. I head straight home, sit down on the sofa, and pick up my phone. I have a call to make.

* * *

My mother answers almost immediately. "Noelle!" she exclaims. Her voice pitches up with joy, then tempers itself with caution. "Is everything alright?" she asks.

How sad is that, for a parent to automatically assume something is wrong because her daughter is calling? But I understand why she'd leap to that conclusion. When was the last time I was the one to reach out first? Other than her birthday, I don't know. So her wariness makes sense, even after I reassure her that everything's fine. Perhaps *especially* then, because we both know I wouldn't have called if that were the case.

"I'm good, honest," I say. "There's just something I'd like to talk to you about, if you have a few minutes?"

"Of course. I'll always have time for you."

Like a reflex, a reminder jumps into my brain: that perhaps her words are true now, but always? No. My instinct is to tell her that, but I suppress it. That's not what this conversation is supposed to be about. I'll never get to a different place with her if I keep taking the same road. What Eliza said, about not letting my choices be dictated by my mother's, this is a small step toward achieving that, but still, it *is* a step.

It is a start.

Now I have to keep going.

"There's something that's bothered me all these years," I say. "I mean, there have been a lot of things, but this in particular . . . " I trail off, looking at the keychain hanging from my desk drawer, the one she had waiting for me after I took my driver's test. I remember asking how she knew I'd pass. She had smiled and said she had faith, that she believed in me. She was always telling me things like that. I think that's what makes it so tough to ask her this question now. How can I listen to her talk about the moment it all stopped?

"Noelle?" she prompts gently. "Are you certain everything's okay?"

No. Maybe I'm not so certain, after all.

"Why didn't you come after me?" I blurt out. No finesse. No easing into it. Just . . . putting it out there. Putting myself out there. "After I ran out of the church . . . how could you still walk down the aisle, and stand next to Jesse, and promise to love him forever? Didn't it upset you that I left? That you hurt me so badly I couldn't be in the same room with you?" I feel a vein in my forehead start to throb. "You let me go," I say. "Do you know how often I checked my phone that night? All you did was ask if I was okay. I kept waiting for you to offer to come get me."

"Would you have let me?" she asks softly. "If I'd followed you out of the church, or called later and said I'd meet you wherever you were to bring you home . . . would you have agreed? That wasn't the impression I got. You were livid," she continues. "Of course my instinct was to go after you. No mother ever wants her child to hurt so deeply. Here's the thing, though: I knew I was the reason for that pain. The way you looked at me when you dropped your bouquet, it shattered me. That's why I chose to keep my distance – not because I didn't care, or because I loved Jesse more, but because I loved you most. I didn't want to make things worse for you, so I thought it was best to give you the space you seemed to need."

"Seemed to need," I repeat. "But things aren't always what they seem, are they?"

She sighs. "Should I have postponed the wedding?" she says. "In hindsight, yes, but I didn't feel that way then. In that moment, stepping back and giving you the time to work through it all in your own way felt like the right choice. You clearly never would have supported the wedding, so it made sense to do it while you weren't there. I felt like it'd be less upsetting for you. Never did I think you had no intention of coming back."

"Even after you got home and saw that I'd packed my suitcases?"

Another sigh. "That's when I should've done something more," she admits. "Asking if you were okay wasn't enough. Neither were the calls and texts as time passed. I told myself I was respecting your wishes, but I think maybe I was afraid." Her voice grows thick. "If I didn't go after you, then it didn't give you a chance to push me away again, to shut me out for good. The thought of losing you was more than I could handle, so I kept on convincing myself that if I only gave it enough time, you'd come home to me." She clears her throat, but it does nothing to still her wobbling voice. "For that, I'm truly sorry. You deserved so much better."

This is the apology I've waited twelve years for.

Not the letter where she tried to rationalize things.

Not the flood of tears when she showed up at my front door that time.

But this. Open, honest, raw.

This is what I've needed from her all along.

"You were my safe place," I say. "The person who protected me, and loved me, and taught me I could do anything I wanted, if I believed in myself enough." I think of the conversation my dad and I had earlier in the week, all that talk about forgiveness. "I realized something," I say. "Well, actually, Dad helped me realize it, that this has never been just about being furious with you and

Jesse. I was angry at myself, too, for not being able to stop it. Being able to stop you. But there's even more to it than that."

"What?" my mother asks, almost inaudibly, like she's afraid of hearing what comes next.

"When Jesse accused me . . ."

I hear her sniffle, and it reminds me of the morning after Dad left, when she read his letter with me. She tried so hard to be strong, to keep it together for my sake. She's doing that again now, and maybe it should make me feel good, that even after everything we've been through, her inclination is still to shelter me. But I'd actually prefer the opposite. We're never going to claw our way out of this if we're anything less than entirely honest.

Which is why I have to finish my thought, even if it hurts.

"When Jesse accused me," I say again. "And when you questioned me because of that . . . do you have any idea how that broke me inside? My whole life, you'd stood up for me and showed me how to stand up for myself. But not when it mattered most. Not when he told you something you knew could never be true. And that's the worst part, knowing I wasn't enough for you to put me first. For you to know my heart."

She gasps. "Oh, Noelle, it was *never* like that."

"It was, though," I say. "Maybe not for you, but for me."

"I'm sorry," she says again. "So very, very sorry, if I ever made you feel that way. God, I . . . " She stumbles over her words. "This isn't . . . I never meant to . . . no apology is ever going to be sufficient. You're right: a mother is supposed to be her child's safe place. Always, I tried to be that for you, and you were for me, too, do you know that? You've always been the light of my life. I loathe myself for letting Jesse come between us."

"Then why did you?" I ask. "How *could* you?"

"You saw how I was after the divorce," she says. "We made our way through it, you and I, but I never truly stopped missing your dad. Losing him left a hole that didn't fully close. I was vulnerable. When Jesse came along, he was everything your father wasn't, and that appealed to me. I thought maybe it was finally my chance at finding another man I could love. I wanted that so badly, to be in a relationship which was easy, where I didn't have to think about any of the previous pain. I fell too fast, and I regret it now. I regret so many things now."

She clears her throat again, and I imagine her sitting outside on the front porch of the home we used to call our own. I can see the sprinkling of stars in the sky, the moonlight casting its glow down on the evergreens, and an afghan draped around her shoulders, since sometimes summer evenings can get a bit cool up in the mountains. And suddenly, I have this urge to be there. To be having this conversation in person, instead of from hundreds of miles away.

It catches me off-guard.

But in a good way.

My mother's questions, though?

Not so much.

"Do you mind if I ask where all this is coming from?" she says. "Don't get me wrong, I'm so glad, and grateful, to finally have a chance to talk about this with you, but . . . what prompted this, Noelle? What aren't you telling me?"

27

$\mathcal{H}illary$

March 30, 1996

People often said the first year following a loss was the most difficult.

That was true.

Going through a divorce really was like grieving. I missed the small things, like the musky scent of Carter's cologne, and also the larger ones, like celebrating holidays together as a family. I missed the feeling of his arms around me, the sound of his gentle breathing as he slept, and the taste of his kiss on my lips. The sweetness of him teaching Noelle to play chess, the familiarity of hearing guitar chords fill the house with music, the security of knowing I had found my partner in life . . . all of it was gone.

Things did brighten a bit after Noelle and I moved in with my parents. It was a relief, having the freedom to walk around a house without fearing what memories would pop up around the corners. Sure, there were still some that hit with a one-two punch, but they felt easier to deal with now that I was back in the home where I'd grown up. It was comforting to know my mom and dad were under the same roof. I supposed a girl just needed her parents sometimes, even when she was a thirty-six-year-old woman with a child of her own.

"I'm glad you took us up on our offer," my mom said, on the day Noelle and I moved in. "I think it'll be good for you both." My dad was busy hauling in cartons of our belongings – I had tried to join him, but he had shooed me away and told me that was what fathers were for, to help whenever and however they could – and as he passed by with a big box of Noelle's board games, he nodded to us in agreement.

"Sometimes you've gotta get a different perspective to see what's right in front of you," he said. "And you know, I've always said tending to this farm is therapeutic. You just let me know when you want to jump in with your mom and me. The lettuce and herbs are ripe for the picking." He winked. "Literally." He chuckled at his own joke, and I laughed a little, too. My mom was right. It *would* be good for all of us, living together.

It was an adjustment, though.

My parents had a very set schedule. They were awake by six o'clock every morning, coffee and breakfast was on the kitchen table half an hour later, and then it was off to the fields. Dinner was at the same time each night, and they sat down to watch their favorite shows, *Jeopardy* and *Wheel of Fortune*, like clockwork. It all took some getting used to for Noelle and me. Our evening schedule . . . well, we hadn't really had one since Carter left. Sometimes I had dinner ready at seven, other times I brought home a pie from work as a treat and we ate it with vanilla ice cream until we were too full for anything else. Noelle didn't have a regular bedtime anymore, either. I was just so relieved when she fell asleep without fretting. Living with my parents helped with that, and a few months after we moved in, her sleep troubles faded away.

"I feel safe here," she told me one day, as we were walking out to the pasture where the horses were grazing. I'd promised to take her for her first riding lesson, and she skipped ahead, stopping to pick a handful of buttercups. "It doesn't feel like something bad will happen anymore," she said, as she presented me with the tiny yellow bouquet.

Her words were the greatest gift she could've given me.

For as much as it did my heart good to see her on a horse that day, her grin stretched wide and proud, nothing could've compared to the moment she uttered those words. One of the worst parts about the divorce was knowing what it'd done to Noelle. The innocence had faded from her eyes in the months since Carter had left, and it killed me, not being able to fix it. I felt like I was failing her. I could listen when she told me how much she missed her father, and reassure her that she was doing a great job being strong. I could even feign a smile each month, when Carter picked her up for their weekend together, pretending it didn't hurt me at my very core to see him again and to say goodbye to her. In the end, though, none of it felt like enough, and I worried that Noelle might never be the same again.

The truth was, she wouldn't be.

No one who lived through a divorce came out unscathed.

We just had to try our best to pick up the pieces and fit them together a new way.

As time rolled on, that was precisely what we did. We went for hikes in the mountains, camped out under the stars, and drove into town every Sunday for some type of special treat. Sometimes it was a sno-cone and soft pretzel, sometimes it was one of the invisible ink coloring books she loved, and sometimes it was a Beanie Baby, these toys that seemed to be all the craze, even up in our little slice of the country. I made a mental note to see if I could order them for the country store. I knew Noelle would like that, and her happiness was my priority above all else.

"It's important to take some time for yourself, too," my mom advised. "Sometimes the best way to be there for your child is to also be there for yourself."

"I know," I said.

"Then do something about it."

I could tell she was concerned about me, and I couldn't blame her, especially since I had asked if she and my dad could hire someone to split the work with me at Home Grown. It was just too hard to be there so frequently. The divorce had stirred up all the awful memories of the miscarriage, and although customers meant well when they asked how I was, it made things worse, having to answer the questions I wished they'd have left unspoken.

I needed something else in my life, something, like my mom said, that was just for me.

I found that in Twinkle, my trusty old friend who I knew I could count on to never let me down. That was one of the things I'd always loved about horseback riding: the bond, the respect, the faith that went into the partnership. When I felt the familiar curve of the reins in my hands, when there was nothing but the sound of Twinkle's hooves trotting across the ground and the feel of the breeze ruffling my hair, it was as if I had no worries anymore, as if an inner peace rose up inside with a firm reminder that everything would be okay. "You are *my* therapy," I told Twinkle, as I climbed onto the saddle and gave her a gentle rub behind her ears. "My mom and dad have their work on this farm, and I have you. Thank you for being my escape." I grinned as she let out a low whinny. Sometimes I swore she actually understood what I was saying.

Twinkle was comfort, and freedom, and familiarity.

So was something else, something that popped up rather unexpectedly.

I didn't know what made me go into the library one day. I was early for my lunch with Meredith – we were celebrating her graduation from her masters' program – and it was strange, this pull I felt to stop in to the library on my way. It'd been so long since the last time I had walked through those doors. Carter and I had taken Noelle frequently when she was younger, but now she had her school library. She would come home with a backpack full of books, and after she finished her homework, she'd curl up on the couch beneath the bay window or in the bean bag chair my parents bought for her room at their house.

Sometimes I even found her by the pasture, her voice brimming with enthusiasm as she read to the horses. It turned out she didn't love riding like my mom and I did – she was too afraid of falling to really let go – so I'd stopped giving her lessons, but still, she liked to be around the animals in her own way. I found her there when I returned that afternoon, after I'd gotten a volunteer application at the library – because being there again had sparked this hope, this inspiration, in me I hadn't felt in so long – and after I'd toasted to Meredith's graduation with a glass of wine and a delicious lunch. It had been such a nice day. I was learning to enjoy those again, to take the moments for what they were, instead of what they could've been.

It seemed like Noelle was doing the same thing.

"Hi," she said, as I sat down beside her.

"Hi." I smiled. "How was your day at school? How did it go with the spelling bee your grandpa was helping you practice for?"

She smiled, too. "I got second place," she said. "That means I get to be in the next round. The top five from each class are in it. Then the winners from that go to the finals." She looked up at me. "If I'm in the finals, will you come to the assembly at school to watch?"

"Of course, sweetheart."

"How about Dad? I know he's in New York, but . . ."

"But nothing," I said. "He loves you. I'm sure he'll find a way to be there." Perhaps I shouldn't have said that without speaking to Carter first, but I felt confident about him following through. He really was making such an effort. When Noelle wrote him a letter, a response arrived within a week, and when she called him, he always called back, even if he was at work. That helped her a lot. She still missed him, but she was learning to be alright with things.

We both were.

Day by day, month by month, year by year, we found our footing again.

Sometimes the tug at our heartstrings was stronger, harder, than others – on anniversaries, and birthdays, and holidays. The first Christmas that Noelle spent with Carter instead of me nearly broke my heart all over again. I sat in front of the sparkly tree at my parents' house for what felt like hours on end, my hands wrapped around a mug of hot cocoa that turned cold long before I finished it. The ache that'd filled the corners of my soul after Carter left snuck its way back in. What I'd have given to go back in time and just have one more happy day together. Those were gone, though. I knew it when I finally stopped staring at the tree and joined my parents for Christmas dinner, I knew it when Noelle made the school soccer team and I was the only parent who could be there to cheer her on, and I knew it when there was a father-daughter dance at her school and Carter came to pick her up. He was dressed in a suit and tie, and it made tears spring to my eyes, watching him slide the corsage of wildflowers onto Noelle's wrist. They were the very same flowers that had once meant so much to us, but not anymore.

Some days that hurt.

Mostly, though, I was learning to blossom in a new way.

Volunteering at the library made more of a difference than I could've imagined. Not until I was surrounded by books again did I realize how much I had missed it. Reading to kids during storytime, helping a student find resources for a paper, talking to the couple who stopped by each week to pick out a new book for one another to read . . . there was something refreshing about it. It filled me up in ways I couldn't have anticipated. That was why, one day just over a year after I began volunteering, I sat down with my parents and told them that the children's librarian was leaving and that I planned to apply for the job. "I've loved managing Home Grown," I said, "but I hope you'll understand why I want to do something different now, why I need a change. I have to get back to *me*, and I think the library will help with that."

I saw the disappointment in their eyes, but also the relief that I'd found some joy again.

"Of course," my mom said. "You should do what's best for you, always."

"We can find someone else for the store," my dad added. "All we want is for you to be happy."

I was getting there.

More than the library, though, or the rides I went on with Twinkle, or even the new house that I eventually moved into with Noelle, it was just . . . time. The saying about it healing all wounds didn't hold true, but at least they stopped feeling raw. There were memories of my time with Carter that couldn't and wouldn't fade, and yet, the stitches that composed the fabric of everyday life began to weave together more easily. I no longer sat, staring at the phone in my hand, when I had to call him to discuss something about Noelle, and the sound of his voice stopped twisting my chest into knots. Carter was living his life, and I was living mine. Sometimes I still missed him so much it actually hurt, but I was learning to accept that.

"I'm proud of you," my mom said.

"You're doing terrific," my dad said.

"Noelle has a kickass role model," Meredith said.

It didn't always feel that way, but I was trying. More than anything, I wanted to do right by her. Sometimes a wave of guilt would crash over me – when her class went on a field trip that I couldn't chaperone since I had to work, or when I heard her practicing the flute, the notes tentative without Carter there to lend his expertise. That was the tricky thing about guilt: it never fully disappeared. It fooled you into thinking it was gone, but sometimes it returned with a vengeance and latched on to your vulnerabilities.

That was how it was on the morning I met Jesse.

It was a cool, damp Saturday in mid-October, just about seven and a half years after Carter left. Noelle was visiting him in New York, which should've made me happy, since their last two scheduled weekends had to be cancelled due to his working overtime on a tough case and her taking the PSATs at school. Yet, instead of the normal joy I got from knowing she was spending time with her father, I felt uneasy. It was just a little over a year since the Twin Towers had fallen. I knew that the city was probably safer than it had ever been before the attack, and truly, I'd been in awe of the unwavering resilience of New Yorkers in the face of incomprehensible tragedy. Still, every time Noelle had been there since, I couldn't help feeling an ache in my chest.

I had been at home on that crystal-clear September day the year before, pouring myself a cup of tea from the kettle on the stove. The television was on, but I wasn't really paying attention, focused instead on the fall reading program I was planning for the library – until the words of a news anchor caught my ear and made my entire world screech to a halt. The mug I was holding dropped from my hand. I heard the ceramic shatter as it slammed onto the floor and saw the dozens of jagged pieces scatter, yet I was too paralyzed by panic to do a thing about it. Was Carter safe? How close was he to that part of the city? Suppose this was just the start, and all of Manhattan would soon be under siege?

The six hours it took to reach Carter were petrifying, and desperate, and filled with an absolutely excruciating horror. I'd cried when I finally heard his voice, and now I teared up when Noelle left for the city. I felt foolish for it, but it was a mother's instinct to always want to protect her child. Noelle was my heartbeat in life, after all. As I sat in the kitchen that day, though, waiting for the carpenter who was coming to give me an estimate on replacing our cabinets, I felt guilty about my discomfort. Noelle didn't get to see Carter often enough, and she'd been so excited when he arrived to pick her up the night before. It seemed wrong not to share in that.

"Snap out of it," I told myself, as three knocks sounded on the front door, quick and purposeful. When I pulled the door open, the man on the other side was tall, the sleeves of his plaid shirt cuffed around his forearms and a tool belt slung around his waist.

"Hi," he said, in a voice that was gruff around the edges. "I'm Jesse. The carpenter."

I nodded, taking a step back and motioning him in. "I'm Hillary. Thanks for coming," I said, as I shut the door behind him and led the way back toward the kitchen. "Someone at the library where I work highly recommended you," I explained. "She told me you did an amazing job on her bathroom remodel."

He grinned. "Amazing is the name of my game."

"Well, that's good to hear." I gestured at the cherry wood cabinets. "These were here when my daughter and I moved in. I've never been a fan. The wood is so dark."

"Definitely," he agreed. "You want a lighter shade for a room like this, especially because of all the sunlight that must come in through those French doors." He crossed his arms as he studied the room. "It should be a fairly straightforward job," he said. "My schedule is booked for the next two weeks, but I'll pencil you in for the following one. A job like this will take two days. Three max." As he looked at me expectantly, I couldn't decide whether I was impressed that he was so self-assured or irritated that he'd already given himself the job without even telling me how much it'd cost.

Perhaps both?

"I'm not quite ready to commit yet," I told him, and he chuckled.

"The good women never are," he said. I raised my eyebrows, surprised by his candor. I knew he noticed, I saw the way he kept his attention focused on me, but he didn't explain or apologize. "Tell you what," he said. "I'll write up your estimate and block off time in my schedule, just in case. Feel free to shop around, but I guarantee you won't find better work for a cheaper price. You'll be in the best hands with me."

"If you do say so yourself."

He laughed out loud. "I promise you'll be pleased," he said.

When he met my eyes that time, I could see a challenge playing within his.

When he handed me the written estimate, he didn't let go for a beat too long.

When he walked out the door, he smiled and said he'd see me soon.

Forget about self-assured, this man was overconfident. Also, though, he was kind of handsome. Platinum hair, eyes the color of cocoa beans, muscles that flexed as he raised an arm to wave before sliding into his work van . . . there was something about him that made me sit up and take notice in a way I hadn't in a long time.

What was that about?

I had no idea. All I knew was that it shocked me.

As it turned out, though, Jesse was right. I had three other carpenters come to the house. They were all nice enough and clearly knew their way around a toolbox, but none could beat Jesse's price. In the end, that was what I had to go for. In fact, that was why it had taken so long to replace those cabinets in the first place, because my paychecks went toward the mortgage and other necessities. Money *was* an object when you didn't have a lot of it.

That was how it came to be that Jesse knocked on my door again, bright and early on the same morning he had penciled me in for originally. It was how we got to talking while he hammered and drilled, how I learned that his wife had left him thirteen years earlier, just over a year after their son Brendan was born, and how I actually began to feel sorry for the man. Perhaps I'd been too quick to judge, and his arrogance was nothing more than a mask. What else could he be hiding behind it?

It surprised me to realize I wanted to find out.

It also scared me.

I hadn't felt that way about anyone in so long. Meredith had raised the idea of me dating more than once, and I'd considered it, but it seemed like it would be too painful. I had already found the love of my life, and if it hadn't worked out with him, I saw zero point in trying with someone else. I was better off concentrating on Noelle and myself. I had sincerely believed that, but I couldn't deny that I liked talking with Jesse or that I was disappointed as I watched him finish sanding the very last cabinet. I wasn't quite ready for the job to be over, even though the kitchen looked marvelous. The whitewash was much nicer than the original cherry wood. It was rustic and quaint, and it made the whole room look airy and light.

"I love it," I said to Jesse. "You did a phenomenal job."

His grin wasn't flashy that time. It simply tugged at the corners of his mouth oh-so-slightly. "I'm glad you like it," he said.

He stole a glance at me, and I thought he was going to say something more, but then he busied himself with gathering his tools. As he cleaned up, I found myself thinking of ways to stall. I offered him a glass of lemonade, I promised to recommend him when anyone I knew needed work done in their house, and I took my time going to get my checkbook. When I came back, I found him looking at the refrigerator door. Mine wasn't cluttered with photos like my parents' was, but along with my work schedule and the calendar from Noelle's school, there were also a few pictures. Jesse gestured to one of them.

"Your daughter looks a lot like you," he said.

That made me so happy to hear. Typically people said the opposite, that with Noelle's dark hair and milky complexion, she resembled Carter most. She had my eyes, and I had always seen my own smile inside of hers, but still, it was nice to know somebody else noticed it, too. "You made my day," I told Jesse. "Thank you."

He tipped an imaginary hat to me. "Quite welcome."

We fell into silence then, each of us looking at the other and not really knowing what came next. "I'll just write this out," I told him, as the pause stretched into awkwardness. I could feel his eyes on me as I signed the check. "Here you go," I said, handing it to him. "Thanks again for all of your hard work."

"It was a pleasure." He reached out to shake my hand, then hooked his thumbs around the belt loops of his jeans. "Hey, would you want to go out for coffee sometime?" he asked. "I never do this – mix my personal life with my professional one – but I think it would be nice. You understand what it's like to raise a teenager mostly on your own. Not many people do. Maybe we could trade stories about it."

My heartbeat began to pick up a little. Could I do that? Could I put myself out there again?

I supposed I wouldn't know unless I tried.

I smiled. "You're right," I said. "That would be nice."

We made plans for the following Saturday, but the closer it got to our date, the more I started to question if I'd made the right choice. What if there wasn't enough to talk about, or if we didn't click at all . . . or, on the flip side, what if we *did*? That thought was more unnerving still. Suppose he tried to kiss me? It had been so long since the last time I went out with somebody new. The dating world was obviously different now, and I felt unprepared to tackle it. What had I been thinking, accepting Jesse's offer?

It was Noelle who answered that question for me.

"Mom, chill out," she said on Saturday, as I stood in front of the mirror in my bedroom, holding a green cardigan in one hand and a cream-colored one in the other. I glanced at Noelle's reflection as she sat cross-legged on the bed behind me. "Seriously, stop worrying," she said. "Both sweaters are pretty. Whatever you pick will be fine."

I turned around to face her. "It's not that – "

"I know," she said. "It's the dating in general."

I sat down next to her. "Are you truly okay with this?" I asked. "I know you said you were, but if you're second-guessing that, if you don't want me to go, I don't have to. I can say something came up."

"Don't. Honestly, I'm cool with it. You and Dad have been divorced for a long time. I don't have any illusions about you getting back together. If you want to go with Jesse, you should." She tilted her head as she looked at me. "But if you don't want to, then you shouldn't. It's like you always tell me: you've gotta listen to your heart *and* your head. Together, they know what's best."

"I do give good advice, don't I?" I joked.

Her laughter warmed my soul, just like it had from the first time I heard it. "Yes. Now you have to follow it," she said. "So which is it: are you going, or staying home?"

I considered my options.

I could cancel the date and spend the day with Noelle instead. If I did that, though, if I bailed on Jesse, then how could I find the next part of myself? I was never going to move forward if I allowed myself to stay stationary. Meredith's words came to mind: *Noelle has a kickass role model.* I hoped to always be that for her. If she were in my shoes, if she came to me confused, what would I say? I looked at her sitting next to me, this baby girl of mine who seemed so grown-up now. I would want her to take a chance, to open up whatever had been closed off inside her.

That was why I opted to do the same.

I settled on the green sweater, took the beaded necklace of Noelle's that she offered for me to wear, and marched myself out the door. "Good luck," Noelle called after me, and that gave me the last little boost I needed. I loved that she was looking out for me now, the same as I'd always done for her.

I was going to make her proud.

I was going to make myself proud.

I took a deep breath before pulling open the door to the coffee shop, and let it out slowly when I saw Jesse already sitting at one of the small tables. I could do this. I *would* do this. If all else failed, we'd just do what he'd suggested and swap stories about our kids.

We did talk about them a lot. He told me that Brendan loved to play soccer and swim, that he'd struggled in school but had worked hard to raise his grades, and that he still asked about his mother sometimes, even though he hadn't seen her in more than thirteen years. "It sucks, I can't lie," Jesse said, breaking off a piece of the crumb cake he'd ordered with his coffee. "Tanya – my ex-wife – was never one for settling down. We only got married because she was pregnant. Talk about a gigantic mistake."

I didn't really know what to say to that. I wasn't ready to share anything about my marriage yet. My years with Carter felt too precious to put on display for somebody I was just beginning to get to know. "I'm sorry," I said instead. "That must've been so difficult. Is Tanya nearby? Maybe she'd be open to the idea of seeing Brendan?"

He shook his head. "She made it clear she wanted me to have sole custody. It wouldn't matter anyway, because no, she's not in the area. She moved out west after the divorce. She was never a big fan of the Poconos, which I couldn't understand, but hey, I guess we have all gotta do what feels right."

"We do," I agreed. I wrapped my hands around my coffee mug, just so I'd have something to do with them. "I can't imagine not liking it here," I said. "To me, it's the perfect place."

"Finally, someone who gets it!" He tossed a grin at me. "I was born here. Wouldn't want to live anywhere else. It's just different in the Poconos, you know? One of my all-time favorite things is to take my motorcycle out at night and breathe in the fresh air."

"A motorcycle," I said.

There was that wide, impish smile again. "Maybe I'll take you out for a ride sometime."

It was bold and brazen of him to say.

He was bold and brazen.

I was shocked at how much I liked that. This man was so different from Carter, his antithesis not only in looks, but also personality. Perhaps that was why I felt drawn to him, because it was like he and Carter existed in different worlds. I wouldn't have to compare them, and I thought maybe that had been my biggest fear of all, one I hadn't even realized until right then. I'd been afraid to go out with Jesse because I hadn't wanted to measure him against Carter.

It wasn't like that, though. I was intrigued by Jesse not only for who he wasn't, but also for who he was, and so, when we lingered outside the coffee shop and he asked if I'd like to see him again? I didn't hesitate that time.

My answer was yes.

28

NOELLE

August 25, 2017

When I was younger, I used to tell my mother everything.

The day I snuck into her closet to play dress-up and accidentally uncovered the stack of birthday presents stashed behind her shoeboxes? I confessed within hours. The time Eliza and I had to stay in during recess because we'd been whispering to each other during class? Our teacher didn't send a note home, but I'd still let my mother know. And that was always how it went. When a boy asked me out on my first date, when I struggled to wrap my head around trigonometry and failed a test for the only time in my life . . . my mother was there. Sometimes she'd offered advice. Sometimes we'd talked it through and she'd let me draw my own conclusions. And sometimes she'd declared a time-out and made us ice cream sundaes that we ate while watching old *I Love Lucy* reruns.

It was so easy to talk to her then. Now, it seems much harder.

But I knew that going in to this conversation. So I could just call it quits and be thankful that we managed to discuss things which had felt impossible to talk about before. I'd gotten an explanation and an apology. Why not leave it at that? Answering my mother's questions about what prompted the call would mean telling her about Owen. I'm not sure if I want to do that. It's personal, and she and I don't do personal anymore.

But we could. I could.

Just this once, I could take a chance on her again.

"Noelle?" she asks. "Are you still there?"

"Yes," I say. "Sorry."

"So am I," she says. "Look, forget I asked. It isn't my place anymore." She changes the subject quickly, telling me about the ballroom dance class my grandparents signed up for to celebrate their sixtieth-fifth wedding anniversary. "They're amazing," she says. "We should all be so lucky."

And that's when it hits me: how lonely must my mother feel sometimes? After her marriage to Jesse went up in flames and left so much scorched ground in its wake, she had vowed to give up on love for good. She told me that when she came to see me here on Tybee Island. Most of her tearful confessions had been focused on how horrible she felt for what she had done to me, but there was a moment toward the end when she swore that was it, that she was finished with relationships since they only caused anguish in the long run.

I consider this. Is it hard for her to leave work each night, knowing an empty house is waiting for her? It's different for her than it is for me. I started new with this condo. From the plants sprouting beneath the windows, to the collage of seaside photos hanging up on the wall, this place is what I've made from a blank canvas. But my mother still lives in the house we moved into when I was twelve. I've often wondered why she didn't sell it and go elsewhere, like she did with our other house after things crumbled with my dad, but I've never asked. Suddenly, I want to.

So I do.

"I know it seems strange," she says. "This house is obviously filled with memories, too. I think it has a lot to do with how things ended, though. When your dad and I split up, I was distraught. With Jesse, I was the one to kick him out and file for divorce. I despised him for what he had stolen from me, what he'd stolen from *us*. There was no way I was going to let him take anything else. You and I had such special times in that house before he came into the picture, and I refused to throw away the place that'd been so good to us simply because he had brought so much bad into it." She laughs a little. "You'd better believe I had those cabinets redone a second time, though. I couldn't look at them without feeling ill. Everything else . . . I suppose I'm still not willing to let go of it."

"And that's good," I say, and I mean it sincerely. Not everybody would have the courage to stay in the place where things fell apart, but then again, my mother has always had unwavering strength. She taught me to have it, also. She showed me by example. But I think every now and then I can be a bit too strong-willed. Too stubborn. Like now. Maybe letting my mother in again, even if it's only a little, doesn't have to be about what happened all those years ago. Maybe it can be about what's happening now. She apologized, and laid her heart on the line, even though she had to have known I could have walked all over it like she did mine. If she took those steps, then perhaps I can meet her halfway.

"Owen," I say.

"Excuse me?" she says.

"The reason I called. My friend Owen, the front desk manager at the hotel . . . we've been trying to figure out if there's something more between us. He thinks there is, and so do I, but I've been so hesitant. Honestly, Owen's changed my life. I have no idea where I'd be now if not for him. Surely not at the *Anchor Stop*. He's been such a constant for me here, and I was afraid to do anything that might jeopardize it. But then I talked to Dad. He came to visit, and we had a couple discussions that made me look at things differently. I needed to hear it from you too, though."

"Hear what from me?"

"Why you made the decisions you did," I explain. "I needed to understand where your thoughts were. You know what surprised me?" I say. "When I asked Dad whether he regrets trying so hard to save your marriage, he immediately said no, that it was worth it."

"He's right."

"So you don't regret it, either?" I ask.

"Not in the slightest," she says. "It *was* worth fighting for. The years I had with your father and you were the happiest of my life. The sadness of it ending can never take that away."

"And Jesse?" I ask.

"Jesse was a mistake I didn't even realize I was making until it was too late," she tells me. "Now, of course I don't know this Owen of yours, but he sounds wonderful. If he's stood up for you, stood by you . . . it's your decision, obviously, but if you'll indulge me for a minute and let me be the mom I used to be . . . well, I would say it's worth pursuing. Let me ask you a question," she says. "Is your life better with Owen in it?"

"Absolutely."

"That's all you need to know, then."

"But suppose it doesn't work out?" I ask. "Suppose I lose him for good, like – "

"Like I did with your father," she says.

"Yes. I'd opted to stop looking for love," I say. "I saw what you went through and figured, why set myself up for that? It was easier to block off that part of my life. And I've been fine with it. But now I keep coming back to Owen, even when I try not to."

"There's something your grandma told me shortly after I started dating your dad," she says. "If you want to know where your heart is, it's your mind that will take you there. That's stuck with me, because she's right. Our minds wander to the things we wish for most. Sometimes I still find myself thinking about your dad," she admits. "I wonder what could've been, what *would* have been, if only things had played out differently. Don't do that with Owen. Please, don't dwell on what happened to me. Concentrate on what could happen for you. Don't let my past change your future."

I can't help smiling.

She *does* sound like the mother she used to be.

"And Noelle?" she adds. "Thank you – for calling, for trusting me, and for opening up like this. It means more than you know."

"Thank you, too," I say. "I really appreciate the honesty and the advice." I gaze at the keychain hanging from my desk drawer. Maybe, after all this time, my mother *is* still able to look out for me. It's a strange feeling.

But a good one.

A wave of calm washes over me.

Finally, I understand what went wrong before.

And I also know, without a shadow of a doubt, what's right for me now.

* * *

The sun has just started to tuck itself away for the evening when Owen arrives at the beach the following day. My heart gives a little pitter-patter when I see him. This is it. This is when everything I thought I knew gets turned inside-out. And maybe I should be afraid of that, maybe I *am* still a bit afraid, but what I realize now is that fear can't be my excuse anymore. For years, I've let myself hide out amongst the waves. Now it's time to create some of my own.

I smile as Owen walks over and sits beside me.

How many times have we done this before? How many times have we played Frisbee, or looked for dolphins, or just sat and talked? Too many to count. But today is different. The beach is mostly empty at this hour, which makes it feel like the whole lovely place belongs only to us. The soft sand, the ocean brushing the shoreline, the sanderlings that dip into the water and skitter back out, I wish there was a way to bottle it all up and save it forever.

Maybe there is.

"Thanks for meeting me," I say, as I turn to look at Owen.

"Of course," he says. "So what's up? Why'd you want to see me?"

I inch a bit closer to him, so our knees are almost touching, but not quite. It's funny – I spent so much time last night going over this conversation in my head. Now, though, sitting next to him and watching as two boats go by in the water, the words that come to me are completely different than the ones I'd planned. "See those?" I ask, gesturing to the ocean. "Ever since I moved here to Tybee Island, I have been more like that sailboat. Slow and steady. It takes its time, but it still gets where it wants to go."

As we look on, the other boat, a speedboat, reaches the one with yellow and orange sails, then zooms by. The two boats are spaced widely apart, distance-wise – the sailboat overlaps the horizon and the speedboat kicks up the water closer to shore – yet it's still striking. The differences between them, and the similarities, too. They each have their own kind of strength. One just displays it in a more dramatic fashion.

"I don't know if I'll ever be a true speedboat," I confess. "But I've realized something recently: it doesn't have to be one or the other. I can take my time if I need to, let the current lead the way. Or I can try to create a current of my own. That's why I wanted to see you."

"I'm listening," he says. "Talk to me."

I tell him about the conversations I had with my parents. How they surprised me with their love for a marriage that'd fallen apart, how they both offered the same advice about not allowing my life to be dictated by theirs. "But it was more than that," I say. "Talking to them made me see that the two parts of my life don't have to be completely separate. It's always been a before and after, you know? I drew this invisible line. Pennsylvania and Georgia. The mountains and the beach. The past and the present." As I glance at Owen, he smiles with such tenderness it takes my breath away. Ten years we have known each other. Ten years of phone calls, and softball games, and drives along the coast. Part of me is sad it's taken so long to realize what he could be to me, but another part is glad. Because I wouldn't trade our friendship for anything.

Slow and steady. Like the sailboat. But now, also, so much more.

"I'm happy you finally had that talk with your mom," Owen says. "You needed it."

"I did." I reach over, letting my hand drape across his just a bit. "I think we should give it a try," I say. "You and me. I'd already come to that conclusion on my own, and then talking to my parents, knowing it would've been worse for them to have never loved one another at all . . . I don't want that. I don't want to wake up one day twenty years from now and realize I missed out on the best thing to ever happen to me, just because I was too afraid of getting hurt. I'm starting to understand that it's better to take action . . . to take a chance."

Owen doesn't answer me right away.

In face, he's quiet for what seems like an eternity.

Usually I'm really good at knowing what he's thinking, but this time I can't quite get a grip on it. And so I measure my breath against the crash of the waves, watching and waiting, hoping I haven't already lost out on something I've only just found. We *are* worth the risk. I know that now.

But does he?

My heart is running two beats ahead of itself as I wait for him to say something. Every moment of silence feels magnified. And then, suddenly, he kisses me. He rests a hand on my face, his thumb grazing my cheek ever-so-gently as he dips his head down and brushes his mouth to mine. It's a bit breathless, like he's been waiting too long to do it, like the both of us were nearly running out of air until right at this moment. I don't ever want it to end. The feeling of the breeze ruffling my hair, the smell of the salty sea air that's never seemed quite so intoxicating . . . I memorize it all. But mostly, I memorize Owen. I drink him in. The way his second kiss is deeper than the first, the way his fingers feel so soft as he traces them down my arm, the way he smiles almost shyly as we pull apart.

"So, is that a yes?" I tease.

He laughs as he interlaces his fingers with mine. "That is definitely a yes," he says. "I know how much it took for you to tell me those things. It means the world that you did. Even with all we have shared over the years, this seems different. I like that. I like that we still have things to learn about each other."

His words remind me of the night we met.

The night we sat outside of that diner, when something made me let my guard down with Owen even though he was a stranger. A penny for your thoughts. Trusting him that night was one of the best choices I've ever made, and sitting with him now, watching as the sun's rays put on a show for us before slipping away, I'm just so grateful. Even if the *Anchor Stop* doesn't make it, I know I will. I even have an idea of what could come next. But right now, I simply want to be in this moment with Owen. We walk down to the water's edge, our eyes on the horizon as it disappears into the sky and the sea. Then a sprinkling of stars appears. I don't think they've ever looked quite so enchanting as they do tonight.

How long has it been since I've let myself appreciate their splendor?

Too long.

It feels fitting to let their beauty back in now. Ten years ago, Owen told me this was his favorite time of day, when the stars come out over the ocean. "There's something so peaceful about it," he said. He was right. I glance at his hand, wrapped around mine like that's exactly where it's meant to be, and catch sight of his tattoo. It warms my heart. Because I get it now. That night we shared our first kiss, I remember thinking there was a naturalness to it. Even as that whirlwind of emotion had dropped on me all at once, it felt like something had aligned.

Now I know what it was. The stars.

Tonight, they are sparkling extra brightly.

Tonight, for the first time in so very long, they make me feel limitless again.

29

Hillary

January 18, 2003

Jesse was an adventure.

We took things slowly at first, seeing each other for an occasional dinner or movie, and I liked it that way, I liked that he was giving me space to ease into the dating life at my own pace. For awhile, it still felt odd, seeing someone else's smile greet me when I opened the door and settling my hand into one that didn't fit mine like a glove. Jesse's fingers were calloused and rough from his work in a way Carter's never were. It took some getting used to . . . honestly, all of it did. For so long, it'd been just Noelle and me. I couldn't deny it made me feel guilty sometimes, going out with Jesse while she was at home, working on a report for science class or watching television. She always waved off my concern, but still, it was tough. The two of us had been a team for so many years, and it wasn't that we weren't anymore, it was just different.

"Do you ever feel that way with Brendan?" I asked Jesse one afternoon. It was a Saturday in the middle of January, and we were sitting on a bench at the outdoor skating rink, tying the laces on our ice skates. "When you first started dating again, did it seem weird?"

He shook his head. "Truthfully, no. Brendan was a baby when

Tanya left. He has no memories of her. For him, it's normal for me to be dating. It's all he's ever known." He stood up and held out his hand, steadying me as I wobbled on the skinny blades. It had been forever since the last time I'd skated. Meredith and I had taken Noelle for her tenth birthday, and I remembered how nervous she'd been at first, clasping our hands so tightly.

She'd done it, though. She circled around slowly in the beginning, holding on to us for dear life, but after a handful of revolutions she'd gotten brave and loosened her grip. By the time my parents met us so we could go to lunch, Noelle was gliding across the ice on her own. "I'm proud of you," I'd told her, as she skated over to hug me.

"I'm proud, too," she'd said. "I was afraid, but I did it anyhow. I think that's the best way."

Sometimes it was the parents who learned a lot from their children.

I thought of Noelle's words as Jesse and I stepped onto the rink, and I realized: I was doing what she'd said all those years ago. I was scared of this – opening my heart to somebody again, changing up the status quo – but I was doing it anyway. Noelle was right. It *was* the best way.

That was why I didn't flinch when Jesse brought up the one topic I'd been hiding from ever since he and I decided to keep seeing one another. We were sitting on the bench again after we finished skating, sipping hot chocolate, when he reached over and rested his hand on mine. "It'd be nice to do this with the kids sometime," he said.

"The kids?" I echoed.

He nodded. "We've been dating for almost three months. I think it's time everyone meets each other, don't you?" He grinned. "I know Brendan would like that. I'm always telling him how terrific you are."

My cheeks were cold from the icy winter air, but hearing that made the warmth seep back into them. Jesse thought I was terrific. He had talked about me with his son. That was a huge deal, and I didn't know why it came as such a surprise. After all, I sometimes told Noelle about him. I usually waited for her to bring up the subject, because I didn't want to be insensitive to the love she had for her dad, but still, she knew enough about Jesse that it should've occurred to me that Brendan would know about me, too. It was just . . . the thought of involving the kids in this made it feel so real. Right now, Jesse and I were taking things date by date. If we brought Brendan and Noelle into the mix, it would become something else entirely. It would be serious.

Was I ready for that?

I looked at Jesse, with his hat pulled down over his ears and the stubble on his face. He was not Carter. Maybe Noelle could find room for him in her life, though, and Brendan, too. I had to admit, the idea made me go fuzzy somewhere around the corners of my heart. "Okay," I said. "Sure. Let's do it."

"Really?" Jesse asked, sounding like a child on Christmas morning.

"Really," I said. "But only if Noelle and Brendan are alright with it. Their feelings come first."

"Agreed." He leaned over to kiss my cheek. "You'll see," he said. "This will be a good thing."

I hoped so.

I wasn't quite sure how to broach the topic with Noelle, so I waited until dinnertime that night. My mom had brought over her homemade vegetable soup earlier in the day, and Noelle was happy as could be, breaking off chunks of French bread and dipping them into her bowl. "I'm telling you," she said, "Grandma should do something with the recipe for this. It's so good."

"It is," I agreed, taking a spoonful of the soup. If home had a taste, that'd be it. I thought about how frequently my mom had made that soup in the days after my divorce, when my stomach had a perpetual ache and most food tasted like sawdust. It hadn't mattered that she was so busy with the farm, she still found time to be there for me. She *made* the time. That was what I tried to stress to Noelle, as I told her about the conversation I'd had with Jesse. "You can say no," I assured her, "and I'll drop it. If you'd like to give it a try, though, I promise: even if the four of us hit it off, nothing will take me away from you. You're my priority."

"I know. It's been that way for as long as I can remember." She smiled. "Thanks for that, Mom. I probably don't say that enough. Thanks for always being here for me. I really do appreciate it, and I love you."

"I love you too, honey," I said. "So very, very much."

That was when I knew it would be okay, that letting Noelle get to know Jesse and Brendan *was* a good thing. I found myself surprisingly calm in the days leading up to it, and I actually felt excited as I pulled my car into the parking lot of the restaurant that we'd decided upon. It was a place none of us had ever been to before, free of any old memories that would hold us back from making our new ones.

"Ready?" I asked Noelle, as we got out of the car.

"Ready," she said.

I could see Jesse and Brendan as we approached. Sitting in a booth by the front windows, they looked so much alike. Brendan had the same blonde hair as his dad, the same squared jawline and easy smile. Seeing them together gave me a little pang, especially as Noelle and I joined them. It hit me, in that moment, what we must've looked like to the other diners: a family. The idea brought a smile to my face, particularly because Noelle was the one to kick-start the conversation.

"Hey," she said to Brendan. "I recognize you from school. You're on the soccer team, right?

"Yep." He grinned proudly. "I'm one of the starters."

"Cool," she said. "I used to play soccer, too. I was the goalie. What position are you?"

"It depends," he said. "Sometimes a forward, sometimes a winger."

The conversation took off from there, and I could not have been happier. I loved that they had something in common, and hoped it'd set them up to become friends. In order for anything to work between Jesse and me, our kids had to be on board. It seemed like they were. They chatted during dinner, comparing notes on teachers, the school cafeteria, and what extracurriculars they'd joined. At one point, Noelle even asked Brendan if he'd be interested in being part of an astronomy club she was trying to start.

"Told you so," Jesse mouthed to me.

"You were right," I mouthed back.

I felt so relieved in that moment, so hopeful – and perhaps a bit surprised, too, because I hadn't realized how much I'd been yearning for a second chance until I was living inside it. That continued as the months went on. Being with Jesse awakened something in me that'd been sleeping for a long time. Although it still felt different at times – when I first let him reach for the buttons on my shirt, when he and Brendan joined us for Easter brunch, when the four of us went hiking on the same trail I'd once showed Carter – it was a good type of different, filled with the possibility I had given up on until Jesse came along.

"He's amazing," I told Meredith one day, when she stopped into the library to check out books. How I loved working there again. After a few years in the children's department, I'd been promoted to head librarian, and I looked forward to going to work every single day. Sometimes I still thought about Home Grown, but I had no regrets. It was doing well without me. I'd spent so long inside the walls of that store. It was refreshing now to walk outside them. Refreshing was the way to describe Jesse, too. "You won't believe what he did yesterday," I said to Meredith, as we sat in the armchairs by the wall of windows. It was hard to choose a favorite spot in the library – the cozy tree-house in the kids' section, the circulation desk that looked out over all the shelves – but there was something so peaceful about this area, with the sunbeams streaming in, casting a warm glow on the stories just waiting to be discovered. I couldn't wait to share one of my own with my best friend. "My doorbell rang at seven in the morning," I said.

"That's inhumane," she said. "Who's voluntarily out at that hour, especially in the rain?"

I laughed. "Jesse, evidently. He loves the rain and said he wanted to take full advantage before it stopped. You know, I think that's one of my favorite parts of being in a relationship again, getting to learn all about somebody. With Carter, it got to the point where we knew each other inside and out. I loved that, but it's nice to have this now."

"So what'd Jesse do?" she asked. "You're killing me with the suspense, girlfriend."

I smiled. "He asked me to go for a walk in the rain before we had to leave for work. I wasn't too enthusiastic, but he swore I wouldn't regret it, and he was right. I saw things I never would've if I'd stayed home . . . raindrops clinging to the corn husks in the field, and the cardinal that looked so red against the clouds, and this brief peek of sun that made the puddles seem like they were sparkling. I ended up having an incredible time."

"I'm glad," she said. "You deserve it."

"As do you." I raised my eyebrows. "Speaking of which, I still have a little time left on my break, so tell me . . . how's Ari?" My question made her blush, which amused me. Meredith never blushed. She also never really dated anybody. She was all about her independence. Art and adventure were her passions, and she didn't want anything to get in their way. When she'd met Ari a couple months ago, though, at a physical therapy conference, something had changed. I recognized the light in her eyes, because it was the same as the one that illuminated my own.

How wonderful it was to see her that way.

How wonderful it was to let myself feel that way, too.

How wonderful it was to kiss Jesse until I was breathless,

to have movie nights with the kids, and to watch as Brendan and Noelle became the brother and sister the other had never had. For all the reasons I was grateful to have Jesse in my life, that was the greatest one. What a gift he'd given me. This family we were becoming, it was what Carter and I had wanted so desperately, maybe even too desperately. I'd forever be sorry for the way it drove us apart in the end, but, with Jesse, everything seemed to be coming back together. I didn't think twice before giving him the key to my house, and when he reciprocated, I got goosebumps. We were really doing this. We were really committing to each other.

"This feels right," Jesse said.

It did. It felt like love.

The way my heart leaped inside my chest when I saw his car parked in my driveway . . . the way I instinctively reached for the phone to call him when I got a raise at work and couldn't wait to share the news . . . the way I felt so content when I woke up in the morning with his arm draped around me . . . maybe these things should've frightened me, but they didn't. I was over-the-moon to have found this again.

"You know what I'm thankful for?" Jesse asked one morning, just over a year after we'd started dating. We were lying in his bed, and he traced his finger teasingly along the edge of the red blanket I had wrapped around me. Noelle was in Manhattan that weekend to visit Carter and Brendan had slept over at a friend's house, which meant we had the whole place to ourselves. That was rare for us, and I was savoring it.

"What?" I asked.

He looked at me for a long time, and he suddenly seemed so serious that my curiosity went into overdrive. What was he about to say? I inched a bit closer and he leaned over, pressing his mouth to mine in a lingering kiss before pulling back slightly and winking. "Ugly kitchen cabinets," he said, completely deadpan.

I laughed out loud, sat up, and whacked him with my pillow.

He didn't hesitate to toss his back at me.

"Seriously," he said, "I really am thankful for those cabinets. When I knocked on your door that day, I never could have imagined it would lead to this." He kissed me again, and pulled me on top of him, and I let myself get lost in this man who'd given me all the things I hadn't even dared to expect anymore. In the months after Carter left – when up was down and in was out – something like this had been so far off my radar. It was probably better that it was, though. Sometimes the best things in life came when we didn't expect them.

Unfortunately, sometimes the worst ones did, too.

That was how it happened for Jesse.

When a group of men who worked for his contracting business just up and left at the same time, switching to another company that was bigger and able to pay more than he did, it was a slap in the face. "I thought of those guys as brothers," he said, shaking his head as he told me about it. "One of them worked for me for ten years."

"I'm so sorry," I said. "It's not fair."

"I get that I can't offer a huge salary," he said. "I try to keep the prices down for the customers, and that rolls over. But it isn't like they're making peanuts, either. Even if one of them turned down the other company's offer . . . " When he looked at me, worry clouded his eyes. "I have jobs lined up for the next two months," he said. "I can't do them all myself."

"You'll hire new people," I said, trying my best to sound optimistic. "It'll work out."

It didn't, though.

Jesse's business took a real hit. Hiring qualified new workers was a longer and more involved process than I'd realized, and he ended up having to back out of half the jobs he'd booked. It meant half the income and less to offer future employees, not to mention the onslaught of negative word-of-mouth. It just snowballed from there. By the time spring started to blossom, he was dangerously close to losing the business he'd painstakingly built.

"I can't afford it," he told me. "I'm gonna have to find another way before I can't pay any more of my bills."

Another way . . . maybe I had one.

"I have an idea," I told him. "It won't solve everything, but I think it could help. Why don't you and Brendan move in? Come live with Noelle and me."

* * *

It seemed like such a good idea. By selling his house and moving into mine, Jesse wouldn't have to worry about mortgage payments or utility bills. He could take the money he made from the sale and funnel it into his business instead. Truly, though, even if his company hadn't been on the line, I still would've wanted him to move in. The past year and a half together had been so marvelous, and I loved the thought of spending every day with him. It would be the little things: hearing the sports radio station he liked to listen to, seeing his toothbrush next to mine, feeling the wind tousle my hair when he took me for a spur-of-the-moment ride on his motorcycle.

"I can't believe you don't hate that thing," Noelle had said, the first time I got back from riding it with him. "It's so loud. And are you sure it's safe?"

"I'll always wear a helmet," I'd promised. "In a way, it actually reminds me of horseback riding. There's something freeing about it." She'd shrugged her shoulders and joked that it was such a role reversal, for the teenager to be questioning the parent about safety, and we'd both laughed it off. I knew she still wasn't happy about it, though. She'd had to grow up so fast after Carter left, too fast. She'd seen how upset I was and had felt like she needed to protect me, to take care of me the way I did her. We had each other's back, and that inclination didn't change, even if things were different now.

I loved how deeply Jesse understood that. He knew exactly where I was coming from, because he'd been there, too. That was why I was filled with such optimism the day he and Brendan moved in. They arrived in a big white truck Jesse had rented to transport their things, and as they got out, I saw he was holding a bouquet of roses. "For you," he told me. "I can't thank you enough for letting us do this. It's gonna be great."

It was, in many ways.

Getting used to living in a four-person household took time, to be sure. Noelle and I had grown accustomed to our routine – lunch with my parents on Sunday, watching *American Idol* together on Tuesday and Wednesday, making a pizza for dinner on Friday – and of course Jesse and Brendan had routines of their own. I learned that they often ate their meals in front of the TV, that they woke up at the crack of dawn many Saturdays to go fishing, and that Brendan didn't have a curfew like Noelle did. Still, we all made an effort to combine our lifestyles. When I cooked dinner, Jesse and Brendan sat at the table to eat with us and even cleaned up afterward. They joined us at my parents' house, and sometimes Noelle and I tagged along on their fishing trips, although we always released the fish back into the lake.

"Who knew this could be fun?" Noelle quipped, as we sat on the dock with our feet dangling in the water.

"It's pretty cool, right?" Jesse asked.

As she nodded, I felt a spark of joy. I was proud of her for welcoming him and Brendan into our lives.

I made certain it wasn't only about them, though. It was important to me that Noelle and I still had our time together. She had gotten her driver's license the year before, and I tossed her the car keys every now and then, telling her to choose somewhere for us to go. Sometimes it was a tourist resort, sometimes it was the movie theater in town, sometimes it was simply a drive with no actual destination in mind. We'd also done that a lot in the months following the divorce. I'd packed lunch and handed Noelle a map. "Let's see where our journey takes us," I would tell her.

Now she said the same thing to me.

Sometimes I could barely believe it, that she was old enough to get behind the wheel of a car. It seemed like only yesterday that she'd been born, and I had stared into those beautiful eyes, feeling my heart double in size. Time passed much too quickly, and in the months after Jesse and Brendan moved in, I often found myself wishing I could freeze it . . . well, some of it, at least, because it wasn't all sunshine and roses. Jesse was still having trouble getting his business to rebound. He depended on referrals from former customers, but after he'd had to cancel those jobs a few months back, the recommendations were fewer and farther between.

"It's so frustrating," he said one evening. He'd been sitting in the kitchen when I got home from work, a beer in his hand and a frown on his face. "I'm good at what I do. Maybe it sounds conceited to say that, but look." He gestured to the cabinets. "I do quality work at a fair price. Yeah, I backed out of jobs at the last minute, but it isn't like I wanted to."

"Give it time," I said. "All you need is one satisfied customer to get the ball rolling again. Maybe you can print up some flyers to put in mailboxes. You need to grab people's attention."

He sighed. "You make it sound so easy."

"That's because I have faith in you. Your work speaks for itself, Jesse. You *are* good at what you do. You just have to hang in there a bit longer."

"I hope you're right," he said.

I wasn't, though. Jesse did everything he should have. He printed those flyers, talked to people around town, and even placed an ad in the local newspaper. That did drum up some new business, but by that point his prices were no longer the ones to beat. He simply couldn't afford it, not when his income had dropped off so much. Even living with me, there were still other expenses to worry about. The kids were only a year apart from each other in school, which meant overlapping college tuitions were in the future. Noelle was already talking about attending a university with a top-notch astronomy program, and though

Brendan wasn't sure yet what he was interested in pursuing, he did want to choose a school with a competitive swim team. All of that would come at a price.

"Maybe it's time to give up and go work for someone else instead," Jesse finally said.

"Is that really what you want?" I asked.

"Obviously not." He crossed his arms over his chest. "I'm proud of the business I built. Seeing it fail is killing me. But I've gotta be realistic. At some point, I have to cut my losses." He walked over to the window and looked outside as the raindrops dripped in spurts, like the sky had a leaky faucet that needed to be fixed.

I joined him, pressing a kiss to his cheek. "Whatever you decide, I'm with you," I said. "We're in this together."

Were we, really?

As the months passed by, the honeysuckle sweet summer cooling into the crisp, goldenrod days of autumn, I began to feel a bit uncertain. Jesse did indeed say goodbye to his business and went to work for another contractor instead. "It's for the best," he told me. "Now I can focus on doing what I love without having to worry about the business side of it." The way he said that, I really did think he genuinely believed it. Perhaps he did or perhaps not, but whatever the case, his positive attitude faded fast. I started to lose count of the nights he'd come through the door long after dinner was on the table, a scowl etched onto his handsome face.

"Is everything okay?" I asked.

"Fine," he said. "I got held up at work, that's all."

That wasn't all, and I knew it, but each time I brought it up he found some way to skip out of the conversation. He asked how my day was, or what the kids were up to, or how my parents' farm was doing. Sometimes I tried to curve the discussion back to his day, but mostly I didn't. His evasiveness reminded me of the way Carter had acted when he hadn't wanted me to know about how much he was struggling, and the thought of going through that again, of losing Jesse like I'd lost my husband . . . I just couldn't. It felt safer to follow Jesse's lead, and to hope that in time he would share with me whatever he was burying inside. "I love you," I said one night, after he'd gotten home especially late and kept checking his phone all through the rest of the evening. "I'm here for you. I hope you know that."

"I do," he said. "Honest. Thanks, babe."

Things improved after that. He started to tell me about work again, talking about cabinets that clashed with backsplashes and front doors that didn't fit within their frames. I was so glad the cloud that had been following him around was dissipating. He still came home late sometimes, but he no longer seemed agitated, or restless, or whatever it was that'd stolen his spark of adventure. In fact, he even surprised us with a getaway to Florida for Christmas. The airline tickets were fanned out on the kitchen table when we came downstairs one morning in mid-December.

"This is awesome!" Noelle exclaimed. "Thanks, Jesse."

"Yeah, thanks, Dad," Brendon said. "This is super cool."

"It is," I agreed, pulling Jesse into a hug. "What an amazing thing to do. But . . . can we afford it?"

He winked. "Just wait," he said. "You ain't seen nothin' yet."

"That sounds rather mysterious. Care to give me a hint?"

"No." There it was, his grin that could melt the polar ice caps. "You'll find out soon."

Sure enough, I did.

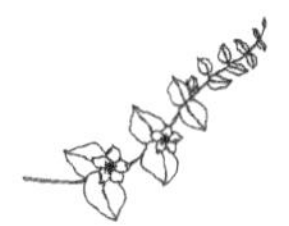

30

NOELLE

September 4, 2017

*L*abor Day.

Normally I can't help feeling a bit sad when the last of the three big holiday weekends sneaks up on us. The *Anchor Stop* is a fantastic place to be any time, but there's something extra special about the summer months. Light and laughter fill the hallways of the hotel. Kids' excited voices boom out from behind guestroom doors, the ocean air filters in each time the lobby door opens, and the scent of sunscreen is omnipresent. It's the purest sort of happiness. And so it's a letdown to see it come to a close. But not this year. This year, as I stand in the lobby with a group of coworkers and watch Paul greet the people joining us for the scavenger hunt we'd planned for today, I feel nothing except hope.

The crowd is a decent-sized one, and our occupancy numbers this weekend are on the rise from both Memorial Day and July Fourth. We even have some first-time vacationers, including the author Remi Parker, who's here with her husband and their two children. The sweetest newlyweds, Grace and Jonathan, have also checked in. I'm thrilled that people are starting to choose the *Anchor Stop* for their getaways again. Laughter is bouncing off the walls, in a way it hasn't been all summer.

Maybe Labor Day isn't an end this year.

Maybe it's only the beginning.

There's still a long way to go, but what a relief it is to watch the sea of people disperse after Paul finishes explaining the scavenger hunt that'll take them all over the common areas of the hotel. The excitement is exactly the kind of energy we'd been missing around here. "You know," I say to Owen, as he snaps pictures to post on our social media, "I think we needed this wake-up call. In a way, I'm actually grateful to *Sea Glass*, because it was the catalyst for the changes we should have made long ago. A place like this has to keep evolving."

He nods. "But I like that we've also stayed true to the heart of the hotel. It reminds me of that saying: the more things change, the more they stay the same."

I look at him. My dear friend Owen, who taught me how to fly a kite and who bought the cutest green teddy bear for me after he pulled my name for the *Anchor Stop*'s annual holiday gift exchange one year. Owen, who teared up a bit when I offered to accompany him to his granddad's funeral for moral support, and who wiped away my own tears the day I lost the bracelet my dad had given me for my twenty-first birthday. I hadn't realized the clasp was broken until it was too late. I remember the way he helped me retrace my steps, searching the hotel for it. He'd listened as I told him about the weekend I'd gotten the bracelet. I had visited my dad in Manhattan, and we'd seen a Broadway show, toured the wax museum, and taken the subway to Madison Avenue so I could choose any gift I wanted.

"Anything that calls out to you, just let me know," my dad had said.

He'd also done that often when I visited him in the first couple years after the divorce. I think it made him feel better, being able to treat me to something special, but the truth is, all I ever wanted was to spend time with him. Eating breakfast at a bagel shop, going to the Central Park zoo, playing my flute in tune with his guitar . . . I enjoyed all of it, because the two of us got to do it together. Our visits may have become fewer and farther between the older I got, but it didn't make them any less meaningful. Maybe more, honestly. So I hated that I'd lost the bracelet he'd bought me.

Owen was there for me then.

And he's here now, stealing a quick kiss when no one is looking.

He's right: sometimes the more things change, the more they do indeed stay the same.

But not always.

Because that evening, after I get home from the Labor Day festivities at the hotel, I sit down on the sofa, my laptop in one hand and the old letters I've saved in the other. I take a deep breath as I look at them. One from my dad, one from my mother, and one from the college I'd been so excited to attend. Slowly, I unfold the acceptance letter.

Dear Ms. Martin,

Congratulations! It's my pleasure to offer you admission into the Class of 2009. Your application was very impressive, and your commitment to excellence is something we share. It distinguished you in one of the most qualified, creative, and diverse applicant pools we've ever had. Ours is a campus of scholars, builders, and learners: those who seek to use their talents in a way that's uniquely theirs. We look forward to seeing where that takes you, and believe we are best-suited to assist in achieving the goals you so passionately and eloquently wrote about in your application.

I stop reading there, before I get to the paragraph on the college itself and exactly *how* it could help me turn my dreams into reality. That didn't happen, clearly. It was never my intention to skip college for good, to throw away the scholarship, the ambitions, and the stars that had once seemed within my reach. I'd thought I would take a year off – to stay away from Pennsylvania and let myself recover from the wound my mother inflicted – and then, when I felt steadier, I would pick up my life where I'd left off. The thing about distance, though, is that it becomes a safety net. I thought about going home when the following June came around. I imagined driving in the opposite direction and releasing the pause button that'd been saving my place for the last twelve months. I even called the college to see if I would still have a spot there.

But in the end, I couldn't do it.

I had an apartment in Georgia. I had two jobs. I had Eliza, who was home for summer break.

Also, I wouldn't have to face my mother or Jesse if I stayed.

I wasn't ready to leave yet. Maybe the next year, I told myself. But it was that next June when I met Owen, and he gave me another reason to stay. Two reasons, really. The *Anchor Stop* and him. And now another ten years have gone by. There wasn't any specific moment when I decided Tybee Island was my home. Somewhere along the line this just became who I am. I've never regretted it. I don't regret it now. But watching the eclipse with my dad, and standing below that sky full of stars with Owen . . . I see now how deeply I've missed that original dream.

I let my gaze fall back on the letter I had been so excited to find in the mailbox when I got home from school one day in March of my senior year. I'd opened the envelope right away, and then I ran into the house so fast I nearly tripped. "Mom!" I yelled, and she came out of the kitchen, her hands covered in flour from whatever she was baking on her day off. I held up the letter, and a grin swept across her face.

"Yes!" she exclaimed, grabbing me into a hug. "I knew it!"

Things had already grown strained between us by then, but in that moment, none of the tension mattered. I didn't care about Jesse or his not-so-thinly-veiled accusations. He was at work, Brendan was at swim practice, and it was just my mother and me for the first time in too long. She'd insisted on going out to celebrate, and as we sat in the ice cream shop she'd taken me to so many times as a child, sipping the largest milkshakes on the menu, I'd genuinely thought everything was going to be okay.

"I'm so proud of you," my mother had said.

Would she be proud of me now, too, if she knew what I was planning?

Probably, but I've learned that I only need to be proud of myself.

So I decide to go for it. I turn on the laptop and begin researching colleges down here that have astronomy programs. I hope what we've done at the *Anchor Stop* is enough. I hope it's able to keep its place along the coastline for so many years to come. And I hope I can still be a part of it in some way. But I think there's something else out there for me, too. A new path.

Or maybe an old one.

* * *

What a difference thirteen years can make. When I applied to colleges the first time around, it was such a complicated process. I met with my guidance counselor at school. Drafted four different essays. Toured the campuses. Sent my applications by mail. Now, I can apply online. It seems easy enough. It's too late for the fall semester, but there's always the spring. I try to picture what it'd be like: sitting in classrooms, taking tests, and doing practicums at night, when the darkness of the sky offers up so much light to be seen. Would I feel out of place? Perhaps. It's been a long time since I was in school. Plus, I'd be older than the other students. But it isn't like I haven't been the odd one out before. I knew next to nothing about Georgia when I moved here. The roads led to places I had never seen, and phrases I hadn't ever heard before peppered many conversations. And then there was the food. Sweet tea and grits? The first time I saw that on a menu, I wrinkled my nose.

Now I love sweet tea.

I eat grits with sliced banana and maple syrup mixed in.

I know where the roads will take me, and which restaurants are the best, and what to do when a storm threatens the coast, like there's a chance Hurricane Irma may do. Twelve years ago, all these things were foreign to me. Now they're a part of who I am. So maybe it'd be like that with college. I think about what my dad said months ago, when he was trying to convince me to inquire about the astronomy job at Columbia University.

"It's not too late," he told me. "It's *never* too late to reclaim a dream."

I'd scoffed at it then.

Now it inspires me: to bookmark the college websites, write a new essay, and research which of the programs would be the best fit. I don't tell anybody what I am doing. Not yet. This whole thing feels like going out on a limb even though I'm not sure it's strong enough to support my weight, and I need to be certain I won't fall first. If I share this with Owen, Eliza, and my dad, and then I *don't* get accepted? It'd seem like a betrayal of their belief in me. And so it stays my secret, from the night I begin my research until the day, two months later, when I open my email to see a message from the admissions staff at my top choice of schools. Tears blur my vision as I read it.

Congratulations, it begins.

It doesn't seem real, but there it is: an invitation to reach out and take what I once let slip away. I stare at the email, these words that are my gateway, but my mind is seeing something else instead: the last time my parents and I looked up at the stars together. It was the November before my dad left, and it'd been his idea to go camping one night, even though the chill of autumn enveloped the mountains. I remember my mother raising her eyebrows and asking if he was feeling okay, because he didn't even like camping on the most beautiful summer night, but he'd laughed and said it would be fun.

And it had been. We'd driven to one of the prettiest overlooks in the Poconos, tent, telescope, and sleeping bags in tow. An owl hooted long into the night, we had to keep ourselves warm by the fire, and my dad twisted his ankle when he tripped over a pinecone the next morning. Still, though, I am so glad we went. Collecting twigs to build the fire, sitting between my parents with a big flannel blanket draped over us, looking through the telescope and pointing out constellations . . . it was such a happy time. I forgot about the arguments I'd overheard between them, about the long hours my dad worked and the strain in my mother's eyes. I think that was the point. It was a chance for all of us to forget. But now, over twenty years later, it also gives me something great to remember.

The stars seemed closer, up there in the mountains.

The moon looked like I could reach out and touch it.

I can now.

I can reach out and grab the dream that maybe never really faded away, after all.

I blink back my tears, pick up the phone, and call my dad. He answers after the first ring. "Dad," I say. "You're never going to believe this." The words practically bubble out of me as I fill him in. "I wanted you to be the first person to know," I tell him. "Because you never stopped reminding me I could do this, even though I kept insisting I couldn't. So thank you. Thank you for not ever giving up on me."

"Never," he says. "All I want is for you to be happy. I really admire you, do you know that? It's tough to break out of the status quo, even when you know it's the right choice." He sounds wistful, but before I can question it, the excitement bounces back into his voice. "Congratulations, honey," he says. "I'm thrilled for you, and you have my full support, always."

The same is true with Eliza, who lets out a scream when I share my news. "This is fantastic," she declares. "*You* are fantastic."

Then there's Owen. My sweet Owen.

He isn't behind the desk when I get to work that day. But

there are people lined up in front of it. We've actually had a boost in business the past couple weeks. I think people really want to support Tybee Island in the aftermath of Hurricane Irma. It took awhile to clean up the hotel – we had water in the lobby and wind damage to the outer areas – but ever since we opened back up, we have had a decent amount of guests. Shannon's the one helping them as I walk in, though, not Owen. "Check the fourth floor," she tells me when I ask if she's seen him. "The vending machine is eating people's money again, and he's the only one who can knock some sense into it. Literally." She laughs, and so do I.

These are the things I'll miss come January, when I'll have to scale back my hours at the hotel so I can focus on school. The friendships I've formed with my coworkers. The way I know every inch of this place like it's my own home. I can recognize the hum the elevator makes before its doors open, remember the exact spot by the third floor stairwell where a boy drew on the wall with permanent marker, and smell the lemony scent of cleaning fluid even after the housekeeping staff has finished tidying the rooms. And it makes sense, because in a way, this place *is* my home.

Never have I felt that more than when I find Owen.

He's exactly where Shannon said he would be, pounding on the fourth floor's vending machine in the precise spot that'll release the bag stuck in the metal holder. I give a round of applause when he manages to free it and hand it over to the woman who's waiting. She joins in, which makes him grin.

"Thank you, thank you," he says, taking a bow.

"Thank *you*," the woman says. "I appreciate the help."

"Glad to do it."

She nods slightly, then turns to head back to her room.

"Hey, do you have a few minutes?" I ask Owen. "There's something big I want to tell you."

"Consider my curiosity piqued." He pulls out the master key card from his pocket and gestures for me to follow him. "This sounds like something we should talk about in private." He walks down the hall to the front corner room, the one with the seashell-printed couch, the double balcony, and the ocean view that takes my breath away every time I see it. I love that room. It's my favorite of all the ones we offer. Owen slips his key card into the slot and holds the door open for me. "Okay," he says, once we're inside. "What's going on?"

"A lot," I say.

I tell him about the acceptance email, and his reaction makes my heart burst. He says he'll miss having me at the hotel full-time, that it'll "lose some sunshine" without me, yet he doesn't hesitate to congratulate me. To pick me up, twirl me around, and tell me he's so happy I decided to do this. "I'll be with you every step of the way," he promises.

I know he will.

I've spent so long worrying about people leaving. Worrying I wasn't enough for them to stay.

But Owen isn't going anywhere, and neither am I.

In fact, as he pulls me into a kiss, I know that this is it for me. Owen is my meant-to-be. My own Northern Star. And I want to do something about it. I want to show him how glad I am that we took a chance on this. "Wait," I whisper, as he steps back slightly. He looks at me, and I look at him, and the answers are just like the question: the kind we can speak without ever saying a word.

Owen's hands find their way under my shirt, and I reach for his belt, my pulse thrumming. "Are you sure?" he asks, his voice husky. The heat of his fingertips on my skin is making it tough to think, tough to breathe, tough to do anything except melt into him. We've really been good about taking things slowly, about exploring our uncharted waters with the care they deserve, but I don't want to do that anymore.

I'm ready to dive in, whole heart.

"I'm sure," I say.

An impish gleam creeps into his eyes. "But . . . here?"

I toss my head back and laugh. "If these walls could talk,

right?" I ask.

"What a story they'd have to tell," he says.

"So let's add our story to it," I say. "It's fitting. The *Anchor Stop* is what brought us together, in a way." I drop a kiss onto his nose, then another on his mouth, and his chin, and the hollow of his throat. I can hear his breathing grow raspier, and I gaze at him. Taking him in. Taking this whole amazing surprise in and holding it close. And then he's kissing me again. He has his lips on my neck, my shirt on the floor, and my heart in his hands. It's as though a thousand tiny sparks are being set off along my nerve endings. It's an explosion of sensation unlike anything I have ever felt, and when we tumble onto the bed, when he pauses to brush the hair from my face and smile at me before we lose ourselves in one another again, it's simply . . . perfect. It's kisses showered onto my collarbone, and figure-eights traced atop his chest, and our bodies fitting together like the missing piece of each other's puzzle.

It's more than I could've imagined.

Better than I could've dreamed.

Which is why, when my phone rings afterward, I make no move to get it. I'm nestled in Owen's embrace, his arm circling my waist and my head on his chest, and I don't want anything to take away from our moment. But the phone persists.

"Go on, answer it," Owen says.

I sigh, kissing him before I reach down to grab the phone from where it had fallen out of my skirt pocket. The name on its screen is one I haven't seen in such a long time: Meredith. How odd. What could she want?

"Hello?" I say, holding the phone to my ear.

"Oh Noelle, thank God," she blurts out. "You need to come here. It's your mom. There's been an accident."

31

Hillary

December 23, 2004

The first evening we were in Florida, Jesse revealed the surprise he'd been planning. The four of us were at a lovely outdoor restaurant by the beach, complete with glimmering fairy lights and palm trees rustling in the breeze, when he reached into his pocket and pulled out a velvety ring box. Time stood still in that moment. The splash of the ocean softened into silence, and my eyes went wide as Jesse slid the box over to me. Had Noelle and Brendan known about this? I looked at them, and the way they beamed back answered that question right away. They definitely had. I loved that he had made them a part of it, because the ring nestled inside that box wasn't only about joining two lives. It was about bringing the four of us together. We were already a family in the ways which mattered, but I had to admit, I adored the thought of making it official.

"Go on," Jesse said, as my fingers brushed the lid of the box. "Open it."

A gasp escaped from my mouth when I did. The diamond sparkling up at me was breathtaking. It was cushion cut and set into a double band, catching the light from every direction. "Oh my God," I whispered. "Jesse, this is beautiful."

"I'm so glad you like it," he said. "You deserve something special. I love you, Hillary. No matter what else is happening, knowing I have you in my life is a reminder of everything good. So what do you say? Can we keep the good times rolling? Will you marry me?"

I was positively caught up in the wonder of it all. "Yes!" I exclaimed. "Of course." I held out my hand. "Will you do the honors?" As he slid the ring onto my finger, I got misty-eyed. For so long, I'd never let myself consider this as a possibility, not anymore, but here was the proof that sometimes life could rise up to meet your hopes in the most unexpected ways.

I practically floated with happiness that night. Our waitress brought over a bottle of champagne for Jesse and me, we splurged on a decadent dessert for the kids, and long after the moon turned on a light in the sky, Jesse and I sat out on the balcony, discussing wedding dates. I felt like the heroine of one of the romance novels people borrowed from the library. "Hey," I said, resting my hand atop Jesse's. "Thanks for including Noelle and Brendan in this."

"I wouldn't have had it any other way," he said. "This marriage will be about all of us. I thought it was only fair to be sure they were on board. They couldn't have been more excited, by the way." He flipped his hand over so his palm was against mine. "Noelle helped me pick out the ring. She has great taste."

I smiled as I looked at the glittery diamond on my finger. "She does," I agreed. "I never want to take this off."

"Then it's a good thing you don't have to."

When he leaned over to kiss me, something settled in my soul. I was truly, delightfully, perfectly content. I felt that way the entire trip. I'd never been to Florida before, so it was all new to me: the white sandy beaches, the towering palm trees, the exquisite turquoise water. I loved it. Even as we boarded the plane to fly home, I was already thinking about when we could come back. Maybe for our honeymoon? Jesse and I were hoping to get everything in place for a June wedding. It would be a challenge, but with Noelle graduating and heading to college at the end of the summer, we really wanted to get married sooner rather than later.

I kicked things into high gear when we got back home. There were people to call, lists to make, and vendors to book. Jesse accompanied me to some of the appointments, but he wasn't especially a details kind of man, so other than getting things for our engagement party, I mostly brought along my mom, Meredith, or Noelle. The day I went to look at wedding gowns, they all joined me. I must have tried on ten dresses that afternoon, until I found one that felt unlike anything else. It was off-white with a bateau neckline, a sheer back, and satin fabric, both elegant and simple – and, perhaps most important, completely different from the dress I'd worn when I married Carter.

"This is it," I said, looking in the mirror and smiling.

"It's gorgeous," my mom said.

"You're rockin' it," Meredith said.

"It's like it was made for you," Noelle said. She wrapped her arms around me in a hug, and as I held her close, I couldn't help thinking of how far the two of us had come since the day Carter and I brought her home from the hospital. She was more than my daughter. She was my friend, my confidante, my heart.

That was what made it so very difficult when the accusations began to fly. It was February when Noelle first came to me. I was in the living room, flipping through a bridal magazine for centerpiece ideas, when she walked up and stood there, staring at me. As I glanced up to meet her eyes, it took all of two seconds to realize something was wrong. "Sweetheart?" I said. "What's going on?" I slid over on the sofa and patted the cushion beside me, but she didn't say anything when she sat down, only gnawed on her bottom lip. "You know you can tell me anything, right?" I asked. "I always want you to feel comfortable coming to me with whatever's bothering you."

"You might change your mind when you hear what I have to

say."

"No." I put the magazine on the coffee table and turned to face Noelle. "I will never change my mind about that," I told her. "You are my best girl, and I'm your mom. That means I'm here for you, no matter what." I hoped that'd make her feel better, but it just seemed to do the opposite. As she took a long, deep breath, my stomach started to turn somersaults. What could be so bad that it was making her react this way? I had no idea.

"Something weird happened the other day," she finally said. "Jesse was here when I got home from school. He told me they finished up early at the house they were renovating and his boss gave the crew the rest of the day off."

"That does happen every now and then," I said.

"Right," she said. "Except it did again yesterday."

"What?" I thought back to the day before, baffled by what she was saying. Jesse hadn't gotten home early. In fact, he'd been late. The dinner plates were already stacked in the dishwasher, and I was settled on the couch with a pen and a pile of our homemade Save the Date cards when he had come in with a bouquet of tulips.

"For you," he'd said, holding it out to me. "Sorry I missed dinner. We had a flooring problem at a house we're working on. It took forever to fix. Any chance I can make it up to you?"

"I think that can be arranged," I responded. I'd put the flowers in water, and he'd joined me on the sofa, offering to help address the Save the Dates. None of that computed with what Noelle was telling me now.

"He was on the phone when I got home," she said. "He hung up really fast when he saw me, but before that, I heard him say that he'd find a way to make it happen, whatever that was supposed to mean. He sounded mad. Or insulted, maybe. I don't know. It was strange, though, especially since he told me he was working on something for the wedding and that he had to run. He asked me not to tell you. I went along with it at first, because I didn't want to mess up a surprise or anything, but it's been bugging me all day."

She peered at me from beneath her long eyelashes. "Something felt off, and I wanted you to know."

"Thank you," I said, reaching over to squeeze her hand. "I'm glad you came to me with this."

The relief on her face was palpable. I, on the other hand, could feel tension straining inside my chest. What was going on? Was it actually about the wedding, or was Jesse in some sort of trouble? Maybe things weren't going well at the new job and he was embarrassed to tell me. When I asked him about it that evening, he shook his head and waved his hand dismissively.

"No, no, nothing like that," he said hurriedly. "It was just, uh, something with a friend. I've told you about Grady, right? The guy I used to run track with in high school? Well, he was let go from his job a couple weeks ago, and he's been asking if there are any openings where I work." The corners of his mouth turned up in a smile. "Now, you'll meet Grady at the wedding, but let me tell you, he's not the carpentry type. His last job was in IT for a software firm. But he has three kids, and his wife doesn't make enough to support them on only her paychecks alone. So far he's had no luck finding anything in his own field, and I feel for the guy, so I told him I'd put in a good word. I must have said something about trying to find a way to make it happen. That's what Noelle overheard." He gave a shrug. "And I was home because yesterday's job finished early, but then there was that problem at the other house, so I got called back in. No big deal."

I looked at him for a long moment, trying to decide whether to push the issue or drop it.

It was like Noelle had said: something did seem off.

I really *wanted* to believe him. It was just . . . why tell Noelle that he was planning something for the wedding? Was that the truth, and this thing with Grady was only a cover? If so, I didn't want to ruin it. Jesse wasn't exactly a grand gesture type of man, so if he was working on something special, I found that sweet. Plus, he was already moving on, talking about a fundraiser the kids' school was having the following week, so it was just easier to go along with it. I didn't want to make waves, not when I was right on the verge of filling the empty space Carter had left behind. If Jesse said this was no big deal, then I'd choose to trust that, to trust him.

The thing was, though, these oddities kept happening.

There were mornings Jesse slipped out of bed when he thought I was still asleep, nights his key didn't fit into the lock until I was dozing on the sofa, trying to wait up for him. He was always ready with an explanation. There was the time one of his coworkers fell off a ladder and the rest of them pitched in to take his shifts, the time they found rotted wood in a basement that had to be replaced before it crumbled, and the time his truck broke down on a road in the middle of nowhere. I didn't know what to make of any of it, because honestly, all those things easily could've happened. It just felt like more than that. Jesse's mood seemed to follow the ups and downs of his schedule. Some days he came home with a hearty laugh and gifts he'd bought for us all, and some nights he walked in with his eyebrows pinched together and a grimace holding his smile hostage.

"What's up with you?" I asked him one night a couple of weeks later, when it finally became too difficult not to say anything. I couldn't worry about upsetting the status quo anymore, not when its baseline had shifted so very much. "Please talk to me," I said, as he turned to look out the window. Flurries were floating around outside, a reminder that winter wasn't quite over, and for a second, as I watched them fall, I couldn't help thinking about the time I had been in the middle of a snow globe with Carter. That day in Central Park, when I had asked him if he'd consider moving to the Poconos and he'd said yes, oh, how invincible I'd felt. It was like the world was in the palm of my hand. Now, as Jesse let out a sigh and told me I worried too much, it made me nostalgic for the times when life had seemed easy.

"Hillary, it's fine," he promised. His voice was firm, but as he turned back to me, softness filled his eyes. "I love you, and I swear, everything I'm doing is for you and our family."

"Everything you're doing?" I echoed.

"Look, weddings are expensive," he said. "If I pick up some additional shifts at work, that means we have extra cash for the organ player you want for the ceremony, or whatever else you can think of. I believe you mentioned a videographer?" He flashed a small, apologetic smile. "I'm sorry," he said. "I know I've been all over the place. Work has obviously been nuts, and I've been letting it get to me. I hope you can forgive me," he added, as he came over and skated his mouth atop mine.

I could feel my concerns retreat.

When he kissed me that way, like I was the only other person in the universe . . . how could I *not* forgive him? I loved that he wanted our wedding day to be perfect. I wanted that, too, which is why I had also started working extra hours at the library, so I could afford the gift I hoped to give him on our big day. He had been talking about a new motorcycle for awhile, and although I knew I couldn't set aside enough money to buy one, I'd spent hours researching accessories and upgrades to make his look like it was right out of a showroom.

Each time I got my paycheck, I skimmed a little off and hid the cash at the bottom of my knitting box. It was a secret I couldn't wait to share . . . until the day I opened up the box to add in the latest installment and saw that the money was gone. What? How could that be? I turned the box upside-down, sifting through the bundles of yarn that unspooled across the carpet, my heart beating louder and louder in my ears. It made no sense. Money couldn't just disappear. I leapt to my feet. Maybe Jesse had accidentally knocked the box off the edge of the dresser and tossed the yarn back inside, not realizing any money was there? I looked everywhere: beneath the dresser, behind it, beside it. No such luck . . . the money was gone.

"Hillary?" I was searching for a second time when Jesse's

voice came from behind and made me jump. "What are you doing?" he asked.

"Nothing," I said quickly, straightening up and whirling around to face him. "Hey, by any chance did you knock my knitting box off the dresser recently?"

He gave me an odd look. "No. Why?"

I tried not to let on how frantic I was feeling. "I had something in there that I seem to have lost, that's all."

He took a step back and nearly bumped into the wall. "Don't worry," he said. "It'll turn up once you stop looking for it. That's always how it goes." He glanced at the knitting box, then at me. "I'm gonna run out and get pizza for dinner," he said. "Do you want anything else?"

"Just pizza is fine," I said, eager for him to leave so I could keep looking.

He seemed eager, too. Not even a minute later, he was out the door.

The whole thing was bizarre.

The next day, it became even stranger.

Jesse was waiting for me when I got home from work, sitting outside on the front porch with his mouth flattened into a straight line and his fingers drumming against the arm of the chair in double time. "So I think we have a problem," he said, as soon as I walked up, and his face scrunched a little, like he was wincing against the words he'd yet to speak. "What I didn't tell you about all those extra hours I've been working . . . I was also saving for your wedding gift. There is a necklace that matches the bracelet I gave you at our engagement party, but it's out of my budget. I wanted you to have it, though, so I've been setting aside cash. I had it in my nightstand drawer. But it isn't there now."

What?

I stared at him, my mind reeling.

He'd been saving up, too, and his money was also missing?

"This is just . . . " I shook my head. "How is that possible?"

His sigh sounded like it had the weight of the world inside it. "I hate to be the one to have to tell you this, but you deserve to know . . ."

"Know what?" I asked, as he trailed off.

There it was again, his fingers tapping against the chair. "I saw Noelle leaving our room as I was going up the steps," he said. "She didn't say much when she noticed me, just smiled and hurried to her own room. Then when I went to add this week's cash to the envelope . . . nothing, nada. And you were missing something yesterday."

"Also money," I admitted. "For your wedding gift."

He nodded. "I figured as much. Now, I'm not accusing Noelle, but . . ."

A swell of intense irritation surged through my chest. "Are you certain?" I asked, flinching at the way my voice pitched up an octave higher than normal. "Because to me, it sounds like that's exactly what you're doing. You have to know she would never steal from us."

He reached over, resting his hand on my arm. "I love Noelle," he told me. "I think of her as my daughter. I know she has Carter, and I don't want to take away from that . . . but I hope I'll be a good stepfather. To me, that means doing what's best, even if it's tough. Hillary, I know what I saw. Just ask her about it, okay? I'll ask Brendan too, in case he knows something. It can't hurt."

That was where he was wrong. This hurt so much, it felt like I couldn't breathe.

There was absolutely no way Noelle would do what he was suggesting, so no, I was not going to question her about it. I refused to put my faith anywhere other than in her. Unless . . . if I didn't say something, would Jesse? That'd be even worse. It would destroy everything we'd built as a family. If the choice was between him or me, it had to be me. I would assure Noelle that I trusted her, that I was only telling her about it because we were trying to find answers. It would probably upset her as much as it did me, and I hated myself for that, but in the long run, it was the best way to handle the situation.

At least, that was what I told myself.

When I poked my head into her bedroom, though, and asked her to take a break from doing her homework so we could talk, it was like torture. The whole thing was, from the way I had to avert my gaze, too ashamed to look her in the eyes, to the way she yanked her hand out from under mine and jumped up from her bed. I felt sick as I watched her twist away from me, her back going rigid as she squared her shoulders.

"You think I did *what*?" she asked.

"I don't think you did anything," I rushed to say. "We're just trying to figure out what happened to the money. Jesse mentioned he saw you coming out of our room – "

"So that means I took it?" Her eyes flashed with pain, and it almost broke me, seeing her feel so betrayed. "I was in your room to return the earrings I borrowed for the school dance last week," she said. "Jesse rudely jumped to the wrong conclusion."

"See, I knew there was a logical explanation," I said.

"Yet you came to interrogate me anyway? Don't," she said, as I took a step toward her. "Please leave."

I cried a lot that day, and even more in the ones to come: when the money didn't turn up, when Jesse insinuated that perhaps Noelle wasn't being honest, and especially when I saw the pain in her eyes every time she looked at me. *I* did that. It was *my* fault. How had something wonderful turned into misery? I got my answer to that a few weeks later, when Jesse came home well after midnight one Friday night and crept into our room. The stench of alcohol on his breath was overpowering as he slipped into bed and leaned against the headboard.

"Where were you?" I asked, my voice clipped.

"A bar," he said, and then it all came out. In this long, rambling, clearly drunken speech, he told me that Noelle hadn't stolen any money and he'd known from the start. "She was in the right place at the wrong time," he said. "Or was it the wrong place at the right time?" He cocked his head, like he was trying to figure this out, then shrugged. "*I took the money.*" His confession stole the breath from my lungs, but he kept going, not even noticing my gasp. "I saw you one day, putting the cash in your knitting box. You didn't hear me walk into the room, so I left really quietly. And I never had any of my own money stashed. That just made the story believable. There was no necklace. There wasn't even any overtime at work." His face flushed crimson red. "But after you discovered that all your cash was gone . . . " He flopped his hand toward me, trying to reach out, but I recoiled. "I had to do something," he tried to explain. "So I made up the story. I never asked Brendan anything . . . and I knew you'd believe Noelle . . . but it bought me time."

He was making zero sense.

"Time for what?" I demanded. A vein throbbed in my forehead and I balled my hands into fists, trying to steady my breathing. He'd been lying all this time? I was so infuriated I couldn't even think straight. I wanted to jump out of bed, to get as far away from him as possible, but my legs wouldn't move. I was frozen in shock.

"I think . . . tonight . . . talk about rock bottom." Jesse's voice was barely a whisper. He closed his eyes briefly, and when he opened them again, I saw a flash of the man I'd fallen in love with, the one who'd made me so very happy. He was still in there somewhere. "I've got a gambling problem," he admitted. "Losing my business was more of a blow than I expected. Working for someone else was a big change, a tough one. I had to partner with contractors I didn't know and use blueprints I didn't always agree with. And I was making less than in the days when my business was doing well. So the first time some of the guys from work invited me to go to a racetrack with them, I figured, why not? It'd be a fun way to blow off steam. But then I won. And I kept winning. It made me feel important again. Like I mattered. Like I could provide for my family."

"So my engagement ring – " I said, as the light bulb went off inside my brain.

"Yeah." He hung his head. "That's how I could afford it. Can you forgive me?"

"I don't know."

"I'm really sorry," he said. "I should've been honest a long time ago. But my luck changed, and I ended up owing a lot. That's what Noelle heard me talking about on the phone that day. I thought if I borrowed your money, it could help pay off my debts and no one would have to know. Then I'd replace it and get out before I was in too deep. I finally earned enough back tonight, but then I went to the bar afterward, and all I could think about was placing another bet. Until I heard your voice in my head, telling me Noelle wouldn't ever steal from us. That's when I realized what I'd done. But I swear, I can change."

All I could do was sit there. Dumbfounded was an understatement.

"I'll go to counseling," he promised. "I'll get help. Just please, don't give up on me. I love you. I love our family. It's more important to me than anything."

"Right." An angry flush seeped into my skin as I stared at him. "That's why you accused Noelle, because our family's so important to you. You could've told me the truth then, or how many other times? Even if I find a way to forgive your lies, do you think I can get past you hurting my daughter? Not a chance."

Still, though, Jesse followed through with his promise and signed up for rehab the next morning. He opted for an inpatient one, because he thought being immersed in it would mean a greater shot at success, so he was gone for an entire month. It was really hard on Brendan – the shock of hearing what his dad had done, yes, but maybe even more so, not having him around for the first time in his life. I tried to fill in, to go on the weekend fishing trips and ask him every day how school had been, but it wasn't the same, of course, not for anybody. I spent the majority of my time dwelling on what would happen when Jesse returned. Some days I'd look at my engagement ring and wonder how it would feel to take it off. Other days I'd close my eyes and try to envision a future in which I found it in my heart to forgive Jesse. Aside from Brendan, no one wanted me to do that. Noelle begged me not to let him back into the house, Meredith told me I deserved somebody who'd never deceive me, and my parents kept dropping not-so-subtle reminders that Carter wouldn't ever have manipulated my trust the way Jesse did.

I was torn.

It wasn't that my fury faded during the time Jesse was away, but it did allow me to step back, to take the good into consideration along with the bad. There was more to him than his addiction, and if he was able to beat it, if he was coming home as the man he used to be instead of the one he'd let himself turn into, maybe he deserved another chance. Everyone made mistakes. Carter and I were never able to fix ours, and I loathed the thought of that happening again. Perhaps I wasn't ready to give up on Jesse, after all.

I still loved him.

That was how it came to be that I was standing in the bridal suite of a church on a beautiful June evening, my hair twisted into a chignon and a pair of pearl earrings in my hand. Jesse *had* returned a changed man, and I was willing to place my faith in him. Noelle was still having trouble with that, especially because Jesse had just pulled her aside a short while earlier to ask her to put my feelings ahead of her own. He'd meant well, but it had been the final straw for Noelle, being told what to do by a man she couldn't forgive.

"And let me guess, you'll let it slide. Again. How could you?" she screamed, then she repeated it more quietly. "How could you?"

I didn't know how to answer her. The right words eluded me. I both understood and respected her feelings, but at the same time, that didn't negate my own . . . and so I stalled a bit, slipping on my earrings as I tried to figure out how to make this okay for her. It was exactly the wrong thing to do. As I reached over to pick up the bracelet Jesse had given to me at our engagement party, she yanked it away. Her eyes zeroed in on me, pleading, but much as it broke my heart, I just couldn't give her what she wanted. "Noelle," I said softly. "Please, sweetheart, try to understand."

"I have tried. Over and over again. You know that."

"I'm sorry." I felt so sad as I met her gaze. "This has been difficult on all of us, and you certainly have every right to be upset, but this isn't the time or place for that. Jesse and I are getting married today, just as planned, and I so want you to know how much I appreciate that you're here." I grazed her cheek with my hand. "I love you more than anyone in this world. You're the light of my life." I smiled at her. "Nothing could ever change that."

"But don't you see?" she asked. "Something already has."

Her voice cracked, and I wanted to wipe away the tears that started to stream down her face. I just didn't think she'd want me to, and so we simply stared at one another for what seemed like an eternity. It wasn't until there was a knock on the door that our silence was broken.

It was Brendan. "Everyone is ready," he informed us. "The organ player is here, the guests are seated, and Dad's raring to go."

Noelle raised her eyebrows as she held my gaze. "It's up to you," she said.

My heart felt as if it was shattering. This wasn't what my wedding day was supposed to be, but I truly wanted to marry Jesse, so I eased the bracelet from Noelle's fingers and fastened it around my wrist. As I picked up my bouquet, she dropped hers.

"I hope he's worth it," she said, and then she just . . . left.

It was one of the worst moments of my life.

More than twelve years later, I get one of the best.

32

NOELLE

November 3, 2017

Twelve years, four months, and sixteen days.

That's how long it's been since the last time I breathed in the crisp mountain air of the Poconos.

How surreal it feels to be back.

I look out the window as Owen drives the rental car we picked up at the airport. The leaves are already off most of the trees, but the evergreens are still standing tall and proud. They blur through the window as we drive by, making our way to the hospital where my mother was taken after being thrown off her horse yesterday. My heart had dropped when Meredith told me about the accident. Concussion, bleeding, surgery. Her words ran into each other as I sat there, gripping my phone so tightly my fingers started to feel numb.

I had to go see her.

Owen and I were on the first flight up to Pennsylvania this morning. He had insisted on coming with me. I am immeasurably grateful for that, because honestly, I'm a jumble of emotions. All that time I spent away from my mother, all the moments together I made sure we missed by keeping my distance, I can never get those back. What if she had hit the ground at a different angle and injured her spinal cord instead of her ribs? What if her concussion had stolen all her memories? What if the doctors hadn't been able to stop the bleeding? Life could have completely changed in the breath of time it took for the horse to get spooked by a low-flying airplane and toss her to the ground. I could have lost my mother yesterday. She could've been taken from me before I ever had a chance to see her again. That realization had overwhelmed me after I got off the phone with Meredith, making it hard to breathe. And Owen had been at my side. He'd held my hand and put his arm around me for support as the room spun so dizzyingly.

"I have to be there for her," I told him.

"I'm coming with you," he said. "You need someone to be there for you, too."

Having him here helps, especially once we get to the hospital. My heart feels as though it might beat out of my chest as we walk down the hall to her room. This is it. It has been a decade since the last time I saw my mother, when she came to Georgia to apologize. The demons of Jesse's addiction had pulled him back into gambling, the work he had done in therapy falling prey to its pull, and that time it'd gotten so bad he had nearly cost our family the farm that had been its legacy. My mother's face had gone red with rage as she told me about the day two men showed up at my grandparents' front door, demanding access to the land that Jesse had promised them when he couldn't pay back his debts with cash. More lies. More manipulations. My mother took money from her own savings to repay what Jesse couldn't, and all of that had been enough to finally make her set their divorce in motion. From what I understand, Jesse's since gotten his act together, but that was it for them. For a long time, that was it for us, too. All of those years I spent stuck inside the walls of my own hurt. I can't change it, but I can be sure that things will be different from now on. The halls of the hospital, they smell of antiseptic, but also flowers. Pain, but also healing. Fear, but also hope.

Hope.

I see that in my mother's eyes when I walk into her room. She's propped up against pillows and her arm is in a sling, but as her eyes meet mine, none of that matters. The IV hanging from the pole by her bed, the gauze protecting the bruises on her face, the beeping of the monitors that measure her heart rate, I don't think she's cognizant of any of it. Because she can't stop staring at me. "You came," she whispers.

"Yes." My voice catches, so I try again. "Yes," I say. "I did."

She reaches out the arm that's not in a sling.

Offering me her hand. Offering me a chance.

And I take it.

I let her fingers close around mine, and somehow, even after all these years, it still feels natural. I think of all the times she's done this before, and a memory flashes through my mind: the day I first tried to ride my bicycle without training wheels. It was the spring after I turned seven, and I clearly remember how excited I was . . . until I made it all of fifteen feet before losing my balance and falling. I hadn't gotten hurt, but as my parents helped me up, I told them I was never riding a bicycle again. "Yes, you will," my mother said, giving my hand a gentle squeeze. "That's what we do when we fall down. We get back up, even if we're scared."

Can we do that now?

The two of us?

For the first time, I actually feel ready to try. I smile at Meredith, who's sitting in the chair by my mother's bed, and at Owen, who's standing just inside the door. I gesture for him to join us. "This is Owen," I say, and although my mother must be on some pretty heavy-duty pain medicine, I see the recognition that lights up her eyes.

"Owen," she repeats. "It's so nice to meet you. Thank you for coming, both of you. You didn't have to travel all this way."

"We wanted to," he says. "And it's nice to meet you, too. How are you feeling?"

Before she can answer, Meredith stands up. "I'm going to join

June and Travis in the cafeteria," she says. She heads for the door, but not before stopping to give me a hug. "I'm glad you're here," she says. "Your mom will downplay the accident, but I was here when they brought her in, and she was in pretty bad shape. She asked for you," she adds. "After she woke up from surgery, your name was the first word she spoke."

This is the stone which finally cracks the glass house of emotion I've built around me.

Tears well up in my eyes. I try to blink them away, but it's no use. Even after all the bridges that we both have burned, when she needed someone most, it was me she wanted. I think about what my dad said on the drive home from the eclipse: that maybe this isn't about forgetting, but forgiving instead.

I look at my mother.

My mom.

She seems so fragile, lying there in a hospital bed. This woman who raised me to follow the trail of my dreams, honor the strength of my convictions, and place the steadiest trust into my own self-worth . . . it stings to see her like this. And it makes me realize how deeply I have missed her. I don't know if we'll be able to get back to how we used to be. Too much has changed, and we've changed too much. But maybe we can start again. Maybe today can be the day I let the anger go and let the love back in.

Let her back in.

I know just the way to begin.

After asking about the accident and how she's doing, I take a steadying breath. "Mom, I applied to colleges back in September," I say. "I found out yesterday that I was accepted at my top choice. I start in January. I'll be studying astronomy."

She puts a hand to her heart, wincing a bit from moving. "You just made my day," she tells me. "It killed me, seeing you give up something you loved so much. Knowing I played a part in it . . ." She sighs. "Perhaps one day you will have a child of your own," she says, giving Owen a hopeful glance. "And if you do, I think you'll understand what I mean. I've only ever wanted the moon and stars for you. To know you're taking them back, literally and figuratively, is a gift."

There is so much I could say in response to that.

So many apologies I could offer. So many explanations I could give. So many stories I could tell.

But there will be time for that now. Because as I bend down to kiss her cheek, I can think of only one thing to say. "I love you," I tell her.

She inhales deeply, like she's breathing in my words. "I love you, too, my girl," she says. "I love you so much."

* * *

Some people say you can't go home again. That time and distance will change the feelings you once had for a place. And maybe that's true. Maybe it's not possible to recapture the past. But this is what I know now: home is more than just those memories. It's the people you are with, the ones who support and love you through it all. Home isn't a place you live. It's a place that lives inside of you.

And so, when I walk into the house that used to be mine, I don't feel the sadness I expected. A pop of nostalgia, maybe, when I first saw the faded blue siding, but nothing more. Now, that could be because Jesse's presence no longer fills the rooms like it did when I left. Or perhaps this is more about who is here, Owen, instead of who isn't.

"I'm glad your mom insisted we stay here instead of a hotel," he says, as he stands in the foyer, looking around. "I like it."

"Me too," I say, slipping off my jacket and hanging it up on one of the horse-shaped hooks next to the door. "It was hard to leave my grandparents after staying with them for four years, but this is what my mom and I needed." I gesture to the living room, with its sunny curtains and the matching couch. "That's where I used to sit and practice the flute. And that," I add, pointing down the hall to the kitchen, "is where my Grandma June taught my mom and me how to make her vegetable soup. My grandparents are all about carrying on family traditions."

"They seem like great people," Owen says. "It was nice meeting them and your mom today. I'd like to talk with them all more. It's good to get to know this part of your life better." He walks over, resting his hands on my shoulders and massaging them gently. "But for now, I think you should get some rest. It's been a long, emotional day."

"I'm not tired," I say.

At least, I didn't think I was.

But within ten minutes of settling onto the sofa with one of my mom's old photo albums, I can't help closing my eyes. Owen was right: it *has* been a long day, and sitting in my mom's hospital room for so many hours seems to have drained the energy straight out of me. She was still a little groggy, but in between catnaps she caught me up on her life and asked about everything going on in mine. I talked about Owen and the *Anchor Stop*, and she told me about her work at the library and how it's felt too quiet lately, like it's not quite as fulfilling anymore. And there was something else, too, this comment she made as she was drifting off, one I just haven't been able to stop thinking about ever since.

"I wish your father could be here with us."

"Do you think my mom meant what she said about my dad?" I ask Owen now, my eyes still shut. I feel the feathery touch of his fingertips grazing my hand.

"I don't know," he says. "She was half-asleep, and I guess the pain medicine could have affected her thoughts. But you know, I think it's when we're most free of our inhibitions that we can be our truest selves. Like the night I showed up at your condo," he adds, and this makes me sit up straight. I open my eyes, locking them on his as he continues. "Clearly it's a different situation," he says, "but once I kissed you, once it was out there how I felt, that's what really got us to talk about it. I wonder if it'd be the same for your parents."

"So do I."

I wonder about it all night long, in fact.

I lie there in my old queen-sized bed, staring up through the skylight at the stars twinkling above me. It is my favorite kind of sky tonight, one where it looks like a magician has waved a wand and a trail of stardust has spilled from its tip. How many times have I seen this before? It's different now, though. Because Owen is beside me. He's fast asleep, his chest rising and falling with the rhythm of his breathing, and it just feels right, having him here. I love him. I know this with as much certainty as I can point to every constellation in the sky. Still, I can do that. Some things we don't ever forget. As I look at Owen, I know this moment is one of them. It will stay with me forever.

But what about my parents?

I think of the conversations I've had with them both lately. The way my dad said he still misses my mom. The way she said her years with him, with us as a family, were the happiest of her life. It's more than that, though. It's the loneliness I saw in my dad's eyes when he told me he'd never found anyone else who could compare to my mom. The sadness I still remember seeing on her face when she said that for all the problems they'd had, loving each other wasn't one of them. And this is what I wonder most: could all the moments my parents shared stay with them forever, too? Is there still a thread that ties them to one another, even after all this time?

I don't know. But there's only one way to find out.

I call my dad in the morning to tell him about my mom's accident. "I thought maybe you'd want to call her," I say. "Don't feel obligated, though. It's just that when we were talking about her over the summer . . . " I trail off, suddenly uncertain if I'm doing the right thing. It's been so long since my parents' marriage fell apart. Why should I think anything can be salvaged now? "Never mind," I say hastily. "I shouldn't have called."

"Yes, you should have," my dad says. "I'm glad you did. Do

you think she'd mind if I visit her in the hospital? It's been such a long time, but I'd really like to see her."

An instant smile tugs at the corners of my mouth.

It's nothing, though, compared to the one that lights up my mom's face when my dad walks into her hospital room that afternoon. He's carrying a bouquet of wildflowers, and the moment she sees them, it's like the sun itself is illuminating her from within. "Carter?" she gasps. Her eyes go wide as she looks from him, to me, then back to him. "What are you doing here?" She sounds incredulous. But happy, too. "The flowers are beautiful," she says, as he walks over to hand them to her. "They remind me of – "

"Our wedding," he says, giving her a shy little grin. "That's why I chose them."

As I see the rosy flush creep into her cheeks, I know I *did* do the right thing. That even if nothing comes of this, if my parents still stay in the lives they've built without one another, at least they will have today. At least we all will. It feels odd, the three of us back together, but also wonderful. This is what I used to dream of after my dad left. I'd look up at the stars and wish on the brightest one I could find, that we'd all be a family again.

That's the beauty of wishes, I guess. The beauty of stars.

They're still there even when we don't see them.

I feel their beauty right there in my mom's hospital room. It's in the look she gives my dad as he sits in the chair next to her bed, and in the blush that colors his face when he reaches for her hand, as if by instinct, before quickly correcting himself and pulling away. "It's so good to see you again," he tells her.

"You, too," she says. "Kind of like slipping back into a comfortable old sweater."

"Better than an old bathrobe," he quips, and this makes them both laugh. "Your mother used to hate that old blue robe I kept on the back of our bathroom door," he explains to me, as I shoot them a quizzical glance.

"You know," she says, "I missed seeing it after you left. I missed a lot of things."

She's quiet for a minute, and so is he. But when they start talking again, it's like they can't stop. At one point, my dad tells us both that he's strongly considering leaving the law firm and becoming a music teacher instead. "You reclaiming your dream and going back to school is inspiring," he says to me. "Once upon a time, your mom suggested I do something with my love of music. Maybe now's the time. I've been practicing law for decades, and it just doesn't reach a place deep inside my soul anymore."

"It's funny you say that," my mom tells him. "Recently I've been feeling like maybe I want to do something different, too." She meets his eyes and doesn't let go. "All those things we thought were important, the choices we made . . . I guess they can change."

But sometimes change is a good thing.

Sometimes it brings us right where we're meant to be.

When my mom is released from the hospital the following week, my dad comes with me to pick her up. When she has to take the next month off from work, until her body heals and her strength is back, he visits on the weekends to keep her company. And when Owen and I fly up again to spend Christmas in the mountains, my dad is there, too, winding a string of lights around the tree. Just like he used to. Just like we used to. But it's different now, too. This family has lost a lot, and maybe it should make us weary, maybe it should make us cynical. In my case, it did do those things for a long time. Yet I also think that's what makes us grateful. Being here with my family again closes the hole that opened inside me all those years ago.

Home is where the heart is, that's how the saying goes.

It's the cherry pie my grandma bakes for our Christmas Eve dinner.

The cold air that sweeps into the house as Meredith and her husband Ari open the door to walk inside.

The mistletoe Owen keeps holding over my head.

The stories my grandpa tells about the farm back in its heyday. He and Grandma June live there still, but these days it is just their home, not a working farm. I think they miss it, and Home Grown, too, which they sold a few years ago, yet they also seem happy for a chance to simply enjoy the land they love so much.

Me too. Tybee Island is where I belong, but it's also really special to rediscover the magic of the Poconos. There's my old telescope that my mom gives me, so I can use it for my classes. The snow-capped mountains, which I see in the distance through the window. And, best of all, the bracelet my dad wraps up and hides under the twinkling Christmas tree for my mom to find: the very same one he surprised her with after I was born, the one she had put away after their divorce and that he had found stashed in her jewelry box. As he fastens it around her wrist, she murmurs something about finding a second chance at a once-in-a-lifetime love.

Then there's the job she tells me about while I help her pour the eggnog, an entry-level position with a publishing company in New York. "I think I'm going to apply," she says. "Even if I don't get it, it just feels like this is the time to try something new, somewhere new."

New York. Where my dad is.

I'm proud of them both for looking forward.

It's the only way to live, inside our own kaleidoscopes of wonder.

Our past is there for a reason, to help us grow, to help us learn, but only when we turn ourselves to the future do we find the path we are meant to follow. What I understand now is that where we belong isn't determined by the stars or the waves. It's up to us, because we must carve out our own place in the world. We must build it instead of letting it build us. And so, after everyone else is fast asleep that night, when Owen and I are sitting out on the porch, bundled in our coats and scarves as we gaze up at the sky, I don't hesitate even for a second when he asks if we should make a wish on a star.

"I don't have to," I say, resting my head on his shoulder. "Not anymore. Because I already have everything I wish for most."

Shari Cylinder believes in the importance of dreaming big, working hard, and embracing our own stories. She is a graduate of Arcadia University and lives in the suburbs of Philadelphia, where she spends her time as a writer, transcriptionist, and a member of the Board of Directors for Luv-N-Bunns Rabbit Rescue – and, thanks to her own rabbit, also a makeshift sprinter and gymnast who tries very hard to keep up with a bunny that runs much faster than she does. Sometimes she's even successful.

www.ingramcontent.com/pod-product-compliance
Lightning Source LLC
Chambersburg PA
CBHW060650190726
48289CB00002B/342